William Henry Giles Kingston

Paddy Finn

William Henry Giles Kingston

Paddy Finn

ISBN/EAN: 9783337418960

Printed in Europe, USA, Canada, Australia, Japan

Cover: Foto ©Andreas Hilbeck / pixelio.de

More available books at **www.hansebooks.com**

PADDY FINN

BY

W. H. G. KINGSTON

NEW EDITION

ILLUSTRATED IN COLOUR BY ARCHIBALD WEBB

LONDON
HENRY FROWDE
HODDER AND STOUGHTON

RICHARD CLAY & SONS, LIMITED,
BRUNSWICK STREET, STAMFORD STREET, S.E.,
AND BUNGAY, SUFFOLK.

CONTENTS

LIST OF ILLUSTRATIONS.

PADDY FINN.

CHAPTER I.

THE HOME OF MY ANCESTORS.

'THE top of the morning to you, Terence,' cried the major, looking down upon me from the window of his bedroom.

I was standing in front of the castle of Ballinahone—the seat of the O'Finnahans, my ancestors—on the banks of the beautiful Shannon, enjoying the fresh air of the early morning.

'Send Larry up, will you, with a jug of warm water for shaving; and, while I think of it, tell Biddy to brew me a cup of hot coffee. It will be some time before breakfast is ready, and my hand isn't as steady as it once was till I've put something into my inside.'

The old house had not been provided with bells for summoning the attendants; a loud shout, a clap of the hands, or the clatter of fire-irons, answering the purpose.

'Shure, Larry was sent to meet the postboy, uncle, and I'll be after taking you up the warm water; but Biddy maybe will not have come in from milking the cows, so if Dan Bourke is awake, and will give me the key of the cellar, mightn't I be bringing you up a glass of whisky?' I asked, knowing the taste of most of the guests at the castle.

I

'Arrah, boy, don't be tempting me!' cried the major in a half-angry tone; 'that morning nip is the bane of too many of us. Go and do as I bid you.'

I was about entering the house to perform the duty I had undertaken, when I caught sight of my foster-brother, Larry Harrigan, galloping up the avenue, mounted on the bare back of a shaggy little pony, its mane and tail streaming in the breeze.

'Hurrah! hurrah! yer honour; I've got it,' he cried, as he waved a letter above his carroty and hatless pate. 'I wouldn't have been after getting it at all, at all, for the spalpeen of a postboy wanted tinpence before he would give it me, but sorra a copper had I in my pocket, and I should have had to come away without it, if Mr. M'Carthy, the bailiff, hadn't been riding by, and paid the money for me.'

I took the letter; and telling Larry, after he had turned the pony into the yard, to bring up the warm water and the cup of hot coffee, I hurried, with the official-looking document in my hand, up to my uncle's room. He met me at the door, dressed in his trousers and shirt, his shirt-sleeves tucked up in order to perform his ablutions, exhibiting his brawny arms, scarred with many a wound,—his grizzled hair uncombed, his tall figure looking even more gaunt than usual without the military coat in which I was accustomed to see him. He eagerly took the letter.

'Come in, my boy, and sit down on the foot of the bed while I see what my friend Macnamara writes in answer to my request,' he said, as he broke the seal, and with a deliberation which didn't suit my eagerness, opened a large sheet of foolscap paper, which he held up to the light that he might read it more easily.

While he was thus engaged, Larry brought up the warm water and the cup of steaming coffee, and, with a look at the major's back which betokened anything but respect, because it was not a glass of whisky, placed the jug and cup on the table. Larry was, I must own, as odd-looking an individual as ever played the part of valet. His shock head of hair was unacquainted with comb or brush; his grey coat reached to his calves; his breeches were open at the knees; his green waistcoat, too short to reach the latter garment, was buttoned awry; huge brogues encased his feet, and a red handkerchief, big enough to serve as the royal of a frigate, was tied loosely round his neck. He stood waiting for further orders, when the major, turning round to take a sip of coffee, by a sign bade him begone, and he vanished.

Major M'Mahon, my mother's uncle, was an old officer, who, having seen much service for the better part of half a century,—his sword being his only patrimony,—on retiring from the army had come to live with us at Castle Ballinahone when I was a mere slip of a boy. Knowing the world well,—having been taught prudence by experience, though he had never managed to save any of his pay or prize-money, and was as poor as when he first carried the colours,—he was of the greatest service to my father, who, like many another Irish gentleman of those days, knew nothing of the world, and possessed but a small modicum of the quality I have mentioned. The major, seeing the way matters were going at Castle Ballinahone, endeavoured to set an example of sobriety to the rest of the establishment by abstaining altogether from his once favourite beverage of rum shrub and whisky punch, although he had a head which the strongest liquor would have failed to affect, and he was therefore well able to manage everything on the estate with prudence, and as much economy as the honour of the family would allow. My father was an Irish gentleman, every inch of him. He delighted to keep up the habits and customs of the country, which, to say the best of them, were not calculated to serve his own interests or those of his family. He was kind-hearted and generous; and if it had not been for the rum shrub, and whisky toddy, and the hogsheads of claret which found their way into his cellar, and thence into his own and his guests' insides, he would have been happy and prosperous, with few cares to darken his doors. But the liquor, however good in itself, proved a treacherous friend, as it served him a scurvy trick in return for the affection he had shown to it, leaving him a martyr to the gout, which, while it held sway over him, soured his otherwise joyous and happy spirits. It made him occasionally seem harsh even to us, though he was in the main one of the kindest and most indulgent of fathers. He was proud of his family, of his estate,—or what remained of it,—of his children, and, more than all, of his wife; and just reason he had to be so of the latter, for she was as excellent a mother as ever breathed, with all the attractive qualities of an Irish lady. That means a mighty deal; for I have since roamed the world over, and never have I found any of their sex to surpass my fair countrywomen.

I must describe our family mansion. Enough of the old building remained to allow it still to be called a castle. A round tower or keep, with two of the ancient walls surmounted by battlements, stood as they had done for centuries, when the castle had often defied a hostile force; but the larger portion had been pulled down and replaced by a plain structure, more commodious, perhaps, but as ugly as could well be designed. Round it ran a moat, over which was a drawbridge, —no longer capable of being drawn up,—while a flight of stone steps led to the entrance door, ungraced by a porch. The large hall, the walls of which were merely whitewashed, with a roof of plain oak, had from its size an imposing appearance. The walls of the hall were decked with firearms, —muskets, pistols, arquebuses, blunderbusses, — pikes, and halberts, symmetrically arranged in stars or other devices; stags' horns, outstretched eagles' wings, extended skins of kites, owls, and king-fishers, together with foxes' brushes, powder-flasks, shot-pouches, fishing-rods, nets, and dogs' collars; while in the corners stood four figures, clothed in complete suits of armour, with lances in their hands, or arquebuses on their arms.

Over the front door were the skin and wings of an enormous eagle, holding a dagger in its mouth,—the device of our family. A similar device in red brickwork was to be seen on the wall above the entrance on the outside. Paint had been sparsely used,—paper not at all,—many of the rooms being merely whitewashed, though the more important were wainscotted with brown oak, and others with plain deal on which the scions of our race had for several generations exercised their artistic skill, either with knives, hot irons, or chalk. The breakfast and dining rooms, which opened from the great hall, were wainscotted, their chief embellishments being some old pictures in black frames, and a number of hunting, shooting, and racing prints, with red tape round them to serve the purpose of frames; while the library so-called was worthy of being the habitation of an ascetic monk, though two of the walls were covered with book-shelves which contained but few books, and they served chiefly to enable countless spiders to form their traps for unwary flies, while a table covered with green cloth and three wooden chairs formed its only furniture.

The bedrooms were numerous enough to accommodate the whole of our large family, and an almost unlimited number of guests, who, on grand occasions, were stowed away in them, crop and heels. The less said about the elegance of the furniture the better; or of the tea and breakfast services, which might once have been uniform, but, as most of the various pieces had gone the way of all crockery, others of every description of size and shape had taken their places, till scarcely two were alike; but that didn't detract from our happiness or the pleasure of our guests, who, probably from their own services being in the same condition, scarcely noticed this.

I had long had a desire to go to sea, partly from reading Captain Berkeley's *History of the Navy*, *Robinson Crusoe*, and the *Adventures of Peter Wilkins*, and partly from taking an occasional cruise on the Shannon,—that queen of rivers, which ran her course past the walls of Ballinahone, to mingle with the ocean, through the fair city of Limerick.

Often had I stood on the banks, watching the boats gliding down on the swift current, and listening to the songs of the fishermen, which came from far away up the stream !

I had, as most boys would have done, talked to my mother, and pestered my father and uncle, till the latter agreed to write to an old friend of his in the navy to consult him as to the best means of enabling me to gratify my wishes.

But I have been going ahead to talk of my family, forgetful of my honoured uncle, the major. He conned the letter, holding it in his two hands, now in one light, now in another, knitting his thick grey eyebrows to see the better, and compressing his lips. I watched him all the time, anxious to learn the contents, and yet knowing full well that it would not do to interrupt him. At last he came to the bottom of the page.

'It's just like him!' he exclaimed. 'Terence, my boy, you'll have the honour of wearing His Majesty's uniform, as I have done for many a long year, though yours will be blue and mine is red; and you'll bring no discredit on your cloth, I'll be your surety for it.'

'Thank you, uncle, for your good opinion of me,' I said. 'And am I really to become a midshipman, and wear a cockade in my hat, and a dirk by my side?'

'Within a few days you may be enjoying that happiness, my boy,' answered the major. 'My old friend, Captain Macnamara, writes me word that he'll receive you on board the *Liffy* frigate, which, by a combination of circumstances, is now lying in Cork Harbour,—fortunate for us, but which might have proved disastrous to her gallant officers and crew, for she was dismasted in a gale, and was within an ace of being driven on shore. But a miss is as good as a mile; and when under jury-masts she scraped clear of the rocks, and got into port in safety. Here my letter, after wandering about for many a day, found him, and he has lost no time in replying to it. One of his midshipmen having gone overboard in the gale, he can give you his berth; but mind you, Terence, don't go and be doing the same thing.'

'Not if I can help it, uncle,' I replied. 'And Larry? will he take Larry? The boy has set his heart upon going to sea, and it would be after breaking if he were parted from me. He has been talking about it every day since he knew that I thought of going; and I promised him I would beg hard that he might go with me.'

'As Captain Macnamara says that the *Liffy* has had several men killed in action, I have no doubt that a stout lad like Larry will not be refused; so you may tell him that when he volunteers, I'll answer for his being accepted,' was the answer.

'Thank you, uncle; it will make him sing at the top of his voice when he hears that,' I said. 'And when are we to be off?'

'To-morrow, or the day after, at the furthest,' answered the major. 'I intend to go with you to introduce you to your captain, and to have a talk with him over old times.'

'Then may I run and tell my father and mother, and Maurice, and Denis, and the girls?'

'To be sure, boy; but you mustn't be surprised if they are not as delighted to hear of your going, as you are to go,' he answered, as I bolted out of the room.

I found my brothers turning out of bed, and gave them a full account of the captain's letter. They took the matter coolly.

'I wish you joy,' said Maurice, who was expecting shortly to get his commission in our uncle's old regiment. I then went to the girls, who were by this time dressed. Kathleen and Nora congratulated me warmly.

'And shure are you going to be a real midshipman?' said Nora. 'I wish I was a boy myself, that I might go to sea, and pull, and haul, and dance a hornpipe.'

They, at all events, didn't seem so much cast down as my uncle supposed they would be. My father had just been wheeled out of his chamber into the breakfast room, for he was suffering from an attack of his sworn enemy.

'Keep up the honour of the O'Finnahans, my boy; and you'll only do that by performing your duty,' he said, patting me on the back,—for shaking hands was a ceremony he was unwilling to venture on with his gouty fingers.

My mother was later than usual. I hurried off to her

room. As she listened to my account her eyes were fixed on me till they became filled with tears.

'You have chosen a rough life, Terence; but may God protect you,' she said, throwing her arms round my neck, and kissing my brow. 'I could not prevent your going even if I would, as your uncle has accepted Captain Macnamara's offer; for a profession you must have, and it is a fine one, I've no doubt. But wherever you go, my dear boy, remember that the thoughts of those at home will be following you.'

More she said to the same effect. When she at length released me, I hurried out to tell Larry, Dan Bourke, and the rest of the domestics. At first Larry looked very downcast; but when he heard that he was to go too, he gave expression to his joy in a wild shout, which rang through the kitchen. Biddy, the cook, and the other females were not so heroic as my sisters, for they began to pipe their eyes in a way I couldn't stand, so I ran off to the breakfast room; whether it was at the thoughts of losing Larry or me, I didn't stop to consider. My speedy departure to become a son of Neptune was the only subject of conversation during the morning meal. It was agreed that to enable me to make a respectable appearance on board His Majesty's frigate, I ought to be provided with a uniform; and a message was despatched to Pat Cassidy, the family tailor, to appear forthwith, and exercise his skill in manufacturing the necessary costume. The major, who had frequently been at sea, believed that he could give directions for shaping the garments correctly; and as all were agreed that blue was the required colour, he presented me with a cloth cloak, which, though it had seen some service, was considered suitable for the purpose.

Pat Cassidy soon arrived with his shears and tape; and being installed in a little room, where he was sure of not being interrupted, took my measure, and set to work, under the major's directions, to cut out and stitch a coat and breeches in what was considered approved nautical fashion. The difficulty was the buttons; but my mother fortunately discovered a moth-eaten coat and waistcoat of a naval lieutenant, a relative, who had paid a visit to Castle Ballinahone many years before, and, having been killed in action shortly afterwards, had never returned to claim his garments. There being fewer buttons than the major considered necessary, Pat Cassidy proposed eking them out with a few military ones sewn on in the less conspicuous parts. Meantime, my mother and sisters and the maids were as busily engaged in preparing the rest of my kit, carrying off several of my brothers' shirts and stockings, which they faithfully promised in due time to replace. 'Where there's a will there's a way,' and before night, Pat Cassidy, aided by the busy maids, had performed his task, as had my mother and sisters theirs; and it was considered that I was fairly fitted out for my new career, the major promising to get for me at Cork such other things as I might require.

With intense satisfaction I put on my uniform, of which, though the gold lace was somewhat tarnished, and the buttons not over bright, I was mightily proud. My father presented me with a sword, which had been my grandfather's. It was of antique make, and, being somewhat rusty, was evidently unwilling to leave the scabbard. Nora, notwithstanding, proudly girded it on my side by a broad leathern belt with a huge silver clasp, which I thought had a very handsome appearance. I little dreamed that my costume was not altogether according to the rules and regulations of the naval service. The coat was long in the waist, and longer in the skirts, which were looped back with gold lace, Pat having also surrounded the cuffs with a band of the same material. The inside was lined with white silk, and there were patches of white cloth on the collar. The waistcoat, which came down to my hips, was of flowered silk, made out of one of my great-grandmother's petticoats, which had long been laid by, and was now by unanimous consent devoted to my use. The breeches were very full, Pat observing that I should be after growing rapidly on the salt sea, and would require room in them. White cotton stockings covered the lower part of my legs, and huge silver buckles adorned my shoes; a cockade,

manufactured by my uncle, was stuck in my hat; while a
frilled shirt and red silk handkerchief tied round my neck
completed my elegant costume.   Having once donned my
uniform,—if so it could be called,—I was unwilling to take it
off again ; and, highly delighted with my appearance, I paced
about the hall for some time.   My father watched me, while
he laughed till the tears streamed from his eyes to see me
draw my sword and make an onslaught on one of the mailed
warriors in the corner.

'Hurrah, Terence !   Bravo ! bravo !' cried Maurice.   'But
just be after remembering that a live enemy won't stand so
quiet as old Brian Boru there.'

The toils of the day over, my father, in spite of his gout,
was wheeled into the supper room, when he, in a glass of the
strongest whisky-toddy, and my uncle in one of old claret,
drank my health and success in the naval career I was about
to enter, my brothers joining them in other beverages ; and
I am very sure that my fond mother more effectually prayed
that I might be protected from the perils and dangers to
which I should be exposed.

CHAPTER II.

T was on a fine spring morning, the birds carolling sweetly in the trees, that I set forth, accompanied by my uncle and Larry Harrigan, to commence my career on the stormy ocean.

My father had been wheeled to the hall door, my mother stood by his side with her handkerchief to her eyes, my sisters grouped round her, my brothers outside tossing up their hats as they shouted their farewells,—their example being imitated by the domestics and other retainers of the house. The major rode a strong horse suitable to his weight. He was dressed in his red long-skirted, gold-laced coat, boots reaching above his knees, large silver spurs, three-cornered hat on the top of his wig, with a curl on each side, his natural hair being plaited into a queue behind. A brace of pistols was stuck in his leathern belt, while a sword, with the hilt richly ornamented, —the thing he prized most on earth, it having been presented to him for his gallantry at the capture of an enemy's fort, when he led the forlorn hope,—hung by his side. I was mounted on my own horse, my legs for the journey being encased in boots. A cloak was hung over my shoulders; I also had a brace of pistols—the gift of my brother Maurice—in my belt; while in my hand I carried a heavy riding-whip, as did my uncle, serving both to urge on our steeds, and to defend ourselves against the sudden attack of an unexpected foe. Larry followed on a pony, with uncombed mane and tail, its coat as shaggy as a bear's; his only weapon a shillelah; his dress such as he usually wore on Sundays and holidays. I need not describe the partings which had previously taken place. The major gave the word 'Forward!' and we trotted down the avenue at a rapid rate. I could not refrain from giving a lingering look behind. My sisters waved their handkerchiefs; my mother had too much use for hers to do so; my brothers cheered again and again; and I saw Larry half pulled from his pony, as his fellow-servants gripped him by the hands; and two or three damsels, more demonstrative than the rest, ran forward to receive his parting salutes. My chest, I should have said, was to come by the waggon, which would arrive at Cork long before the ship sailed. The more requisite articles, such as changes of linen and spare shoes, were packed in valises strapped to Larry's and my cruppers; while the major carried such things as he required in his saddle-bags. We soon lost sight of the Shannon, and the top of the castle tower appearing above the trees. For some time we rode on in silence, but as neither my respected relative nor I were accustomed to hold our tongues, we soon let them wag freely. He talked as we rode on in his usual hearty way, giving me accounts of his adventures in many lands. Larry kept behind us, not presuming to come up and join in the conversation. He was of too happy a spirit to mind riding alone, while he relieved himself by cracking jokes with the passers-by. I have spoken of his warm affection for me. He also—notwithstanding his rough outside—possessed a talent for music, and could not only sing a capital song, but had learned to play the violin from an old fiddler, Peter M'Leary, who had presented him with an instrument, which he valued like the apple of his eye. He now carried it in its case, strapped carefully on behind him. We rode on too fast to allow of his playing it, as I have seen him do on horseback many a time, when coming from marriages or wakes, where he was consequently in great request. We made a long day's journey, having rested a couple of hours to bait our horses; and not reaching the town of Kilmore till long after sundown.

The assizes were taking place. The judge and lawyers, soldiers, police, and witnesses, filled every house in the town. Consequently the only inn at which we could hope to obtain accommodation was crowded. All the guests had retired to their rooms; but the landlady, Mrs. M'Carthy, who knew my uncle, undertook to put us up. Larry took the horses round to the stables, where he would find his sleeping place, and we entered the common room. Mrs. M'Carthy was the only person in the establishment who seemed to have any of her wits about her. The rest of the inmates who were still on foot had evidently imbibed a larger amount of the potheen than their heads could stand, she herself being even more genial than usual.

'Shure, major dear, there are two gentlemen of the bar up-stairs who don't know their feet from their heads; and as your honour will be rising early to continue your journey, we'll just tumble them out on the floor, and you can take their bed. We'll put them back again before they wake in the morning; or if we're after forgetting it, they'll only think they have rolled out of their own accord, and nobody'll be blamed, or they be the worse for it; and they'll have reason to be thankful, seeing that if they had really tumbled on the floor, they might have broken their necks.'

My uncle, who would on no account agree to this hospitable proposal, insisted on sitting up in an arm-chair, with his legs on another, assuring Mrs. M'Carthy that he had passed many a night with worse accommodation.

'Shure, then, the young gentleman must go to bed,' observed the hostess. 'There's one I've got for him in the kitchen,— a little snug cupboard by the fireside; and shure he'll there be as warm and comfortable as a mouse in its hole.'

To this the major agreed, as the bed was not big enough for both of us, and indeed was too short for him.

Supper being ended, my uncle composed himself in the position he intended to occupy, with his cloak wrapped round him, and I accompanied Mrs. M'Carthy into the kitchen, which was in a delightful state of disorder. She here let down, from a little niche in which it was folded, a small cupboard-bed, on which, though the sheets and blankets were not very clean, I was not sorry to contemplate a night's rest. The landlady, wishing me good-night, withdrew to her own quarters. Molly, the maid-servant, I should have said, long before this, overcome by the sips she had taken at the invitation of the guests, was stowed away in a corner somewhere out of sight.

Pulling off my boots and laced coat and waistcoat, which I stowed for safe keeping under the pillow, I turned into bed by the light of the expiring embers of the fire, and in a few seconds afterwards was fast asleep. I was not conscious of waking for a single moment during the night; and had I been called, should have said that only a few minutes had passed since I had closed my eyes, when, to my horror, all at once I found myself in a state of suffocation, with my head downwards, pressed closely between the bolster and pillow, and my feet in the air. Every moment I thought would be my last. I struggled as violently as my confined position would allow, unable, in my confusion, to conceive where I was, or what had happened. I in vain tried to shout out; when I opened my mouth, the feather pillow filled it, and no sound escaped. I felt much as, I suppose, a person does drowning. Thoughts of all sorts rushed into my mind, and I believed that I was doomed to an ignominious exit from this sublunary scene, when suddenly there came a crash, and, shot out into the middle of the room, I lay sprawling on the floor, unable to rise or help myself, my head feeling as if all the blood in my body had rushed into it. The button which had kept the foot of the shut-up-bed in its place had given way.

'Murder! murder!' I shouted out, believing that some diabolical attempt had been made to take my life.

'Murther! murther!' echoed Molly, who, broom in hand, was engaged at the further end of the kitchen. 'Och, some-body has been kilt entirely.' And, frightened at the spectacle I exhibited, she rushed out of the room to obtain assistance.

My cries and hers had aroused Mrs. M'Carthy, who rushed in, followed by the waiting-man and my uncle, who, gazing at me as I lay on the floor, and seeing that I was almost black in the face, ordered one of the servants to run off for the apothecary, to bleed me. In the meantime, Mrs. M'Carthy had hurried out for a pitcher of cold water. Having dashed some over my face, she poured out several glasses, which I swallowed one after the other, and by the time the apothecary had arrived had so far recovered as to be able to dispense with his services. Molly confessed to having got up at daylight, and begun to set matters to rights in the kitchen; and, not observing me, supposing that her mistress—who usually occupied the bed—had risen, she had hoisted it up into its niche, and had turned the button at the top to keep it in its place. Had not the button given way, my adventures, I suspect, would have come to an untimely termination.

Having performed my ablutions, with the assistance of Mrs. M'Carthy, in a basin of cold water, I was perfectly ready for breakfast, and very little the worse for what had happened. Our meal was a hearty one, for my uncle, like an old soldier, made it a rule to stow away on such occasions a liberal supply of provisions, which might last him, if needs be, for the remainder of the day, or far into the next.

Breakfast over, he ordered round the horses, and we recommenced our journey. After riding some distance, on turning round, I perceived that Larry was not following us.

'He knows the road we're going, and will soon overtake us,' said my uncle.

We rode on and on, however, and yet Larry didn't appear. I began to feel uneasy, and at last proposed turning back to ascertain if any accident had happened to him. He would surely not have remained behind of his own free will. He had appeared perfectly sober when he brought me my horse to mount; besides which, I had never known Larry drunk in his life,—which was saying a great deal in his favour, considering the example he had had set him by high and low around.

'We'll ride on slowly, and if he doesn't catch us up we'll turn back to look for the spalpeen, though the delay will be provoking,' observed the major.

Still Larry did not heave in sight.

The country we were now traversing was as wild as any in Ireland. High hills on one side with tall trees, and more hills on the other, completely enclosed the road, so that it often appeared as if there was no outlet ahead. The road itself was rough in the extreme, scarcely allowing of the passage of a four-wheeled vehicle; indeed, our horses had in some places to pick their way, and rapid movement was impossible—unless at the risk of breaking the rider's neck, or his horse's knees. Those celebrated lines had not been written :—

> 'If you had seen but these roads before they were made,
> You'd have lift up your hands and blessed General Wade.'

I had, however, been used to ground of all sorts, and was not to be stopped by such trifling impediments as rocks, bushes, stone walls, or streams.

'Something must have delayed Larry,' I said at length. 'Let me go back, uncle, and find him, while you ride slowly on.'

'No, I'll go with you, Terence. We shall have to make a short journey instead of a long one, if the gossoon has been detained in Kilmore; and I haven't clapped eyes on him since we left the town.'

We were on the point of turning our horses' heads to go back, when suddenly, from behind the bushes and rocks on either side of the road, a score of ruffianly-looking fellows, dressed in the ordinary costume of Irish peasants, rushed out and sprang towards us, some threatening to seize our reins, and others pointing muskets, blunderbusses, and pistols at us. Those not possessing these weapons were armed with shillelahs. One of the fellows, with long black hair and bushy beard,—a hideous squint adding to the ferocity of his appearance,— advanced with a horse-pistol in one hand, the other outstretched as if to seize the major's rein. At the same time a short but strongly-built ruffian, with a humpback, sprang towards me, evidently intending to drag me off my horse, or to haul the animal away, so that I might be separated from my companion.

'Keep close to my side, Terence,' he said in a low voice 'Out with your pistol, and cover that villain approaching.'

At the moment, as he spoke, his sword flashed in the sunlight, and with the back of the blade he struck up the weapon of his assailant, which exploded in the air. He was about to bring down the sharp edge on the fellow's head, when a dozen others, with shrieks and shouts, rushed towards us, some forcing themselves in between our horses, while others, keeping on the other side of the major, seized his arms at the risk of being cut down. Several grasped his legs and stirrups. His horse plunged and reared, but they nimbly avoided the animal's heels. Two of the gang held the horse's head down by the reins, while an attempt was made to drag the rider from his seat. They doubtless thought if they could master him, that I should become an easy prey. Their object, I concluded, was to make us prisoners, rather than to take our lives, which they might have done at any moment by shooting us with their firearms. Still our position was very far from an agreeable one. My uncle, who had not spoken another word, firmly kept his seat, notwithstanding the efforts of the ruffian crew to pull him off his saddle. In the meantime, the hunchback, whose task, it seemed, was to secure me, came on, fixing his fierce little eyes on my pistol, which I fancied was pointed at his head.

'If you come an inch further, I'll fire,' I cried out.

He answered by a derisive laugh, followed by an unearthly shriek, given apparently to unnerve me; and then, as he saw my finger on the trigger, he ducked his head, as if about to spring into the water. The pistol went off, the bullet passing above him. The next instant, rising and springing forward, he clutched my throat, while another fellow caught hold of my rein.

CHAPTER III.

IN spite of my uncle's skill as a swordsman, and the pistols, on which I had placed so much reliance, we were overpowered before we could strike a blow in our own defence, and were completely at the mercy of our assailants. The major, however, all the time didn't lose his coolness and self-possession.

'What are you about to do, boys?' he asked. 'You have mistaken us for others. We are travellers bound to Cork, not wishing to interfere with you or any one else.'

'We know you well enough, Major M'Mahon,' answered the leader of the gang. 'If you're not the man we want, you'll serve our purpose. But understand, we'll have no nonsense. If you come peaceably we'll not harm you; we bear you no grudge. But if you make further resistance, or attempt to escape, you must take the consequences; we care no more for a man's life than we do for that of a calf.' The ruffian thundered out the last words at the top of his voice.

'Who are you, my friend, who talk so boldly?' asked the major.

'If you want to know, I'm Dan Hoolan himself, and you may have heard of my doings throughout the country.'

'I have heard of a scoundrel of that name, who has murdered a few helpless people, and who is the terror of old women; but whether or not you're the man, is more than I can say,' answered the major in a scornful tone.

'Blood and 'ounds, is that the way you speak to me? cried Hoolan, for there could be no doubt that he was the notorious outlaw. 'I'll soon be after showing you that it's not only women I frighten. Bring these fine-coated gentlemen along, boys, and we'll set them dangling to a branch of St. Bridget's oak, to teach their likes better manners. Och, boys, it'll be rare fun to see them kick their legs in the air, till their sowls have gone back to where they came from.'

I fully believed the outlaws were going to treat us as their leader proposed.

'You dare do nothing of the sort, boys,' said my uncle. 'You know well enough that if you ill-treat us there will be a hue and cry after you, and that before many weeks have passed by, one and all of you will be caught and gibbeted.'

'That's more aisy to say than to do,' answered Hoolan. 'Bring them along, boys; and mind you don't let them escape you.'

'Sorra's the chance of that,' cried the men, hanging on tighter to our legs. We were thus led forward, still being allowed to keep our seats in our saddles, but without a chance of effecting our escape, though I observed that my uncle's eye was ranging round to see what could be done. He looked down on me. I daresay I was paler than usual, though I did my best to imitate his coolness.

'Keep up your spirits, Terence,' he said. 'I don't believe that those fellows intend to carry out their threats. Though why they have made us prisoners is beyond my comprehension.'

Some of our captors growled out something, but what it was I could not understand, though I think it was a hint to the major and me to hold our tongues. The hunchback kept close to me, having released my throat, and merely held on to me by one of my legs. Hoolan himself stalked at our head, with the pistol, which he had reloaded, in his hand. The men talked among themselves in their native Irish, but didn't address another word to us. They seemed eager to push on, but the character of the road prevented our moving out of a foot's pace. On and on we went, till we saw a group of large trees ahead. Hoolan pointed to them with a significant gesture. His followers, with loud shouts, hurried us forward. I now observed that two of them had coils of rope under their arms. They were of no great strength, but sufficient to bear the weight of an ordinary man. We quickly reached the trees, when the outlaws made us dismount under one, which, I remarked, had a wide extending bough, about fifteen feet from the ground. My uncle now began to look more serious than before, as if, for the first time, he really believed that our captors would carry out their threats.

'Terence, we must try and free ourselves from these ruffians,' he said. 'I have no care for myself, but I don't want your young life to be taken from you. Keep your eyes about you, and if you can manage to spring into your saddle, don't pull rein until you have put a good distance between yourself and them.'

'I could not think of going, and leaving you in the hands of the ruffians, Uncle M'Mahon,' I answered. I'll beg them to spare your life, and will promise them any reward they may demand,—a hundred, or two hundred pounds. Surely they would rather have the money than take your life.'

'Don't promise them anything of the sort,' he said. 'If they were to obtain it, they would be seizing every gentleman they could get hold of. Their object is not money, or they would have robbed us before this. Do as I tell you, and be on the watch to escape while they are trying to hang me. I'll take care to give you a good chance.'

While he was speaking they were throwing the ropes over the bough, and ostentatiously making nooses at the end of each of them. They were not very expert, and failed several times in throwing the other end over the bough. The ends of each of the ropes were grasped by three men, who looked savagely at us, as if they were especially anxious to see our necks in the opposite nooses, and apparently only waiting the order from their chief.

'If you have prayers to say, you had better say them now,' cried the leader of the outlaws.

'It's time to speak to you now, Dan Hoolan,' said my uncle, as if he had not heard the last remark. 'Whether you really intend to hang us or not, I can't say; but if you do, vengeance is sure to overtake you. To kill an old man would be a dastardly deed, but doubly accursed would you be should you deprive a young lad like this of his life. If you have no pity on me, have regard to your own soul. There's not a priest in the land who would give you absolution.'

'Hould there, and don't speak another word,' shouted Hoolan. 'I have given you the chance of praying, and you wouldn't take it, so it's yourselves will have to answer for it. Quick, boys, bring them along.'

Our captors were leading us forward, and, as I had no wish to lose my life, I was looking out for an opportunity of obeying my uncle's instructions, when, with a strength which those who held him could not have supposed he possessed, knocking down one on either side, he threw himself upon Hoolan, who, not expecting such an attack, was brought to the ground. At the same moment the major, drawing a knife which the ruffian had in his belt, held it as if to strike him to the heart. The hunchback, seeing the danger of his leader, regardless of me, rushed forward to his assistance; when, finding myself at liberty, I darted towards my horse, which was held by one only of the men, who, eagerly watching the strife, did not observe me. Twisting his shillelah from his hands, and snatching the reins, I was in a moment in the saddle; but I had no intention of deserting my uncle. Firmly grasping the shillelah, I laid it about the heads of the men who were on the point of seizing the major. Hoolan, however, was completely at his mercy; and had they ventured to touch him, one blow of the knife would have ended the villain's life, though probably his companions would have revenged his death by shooting us the moment after. But just then loud shouts were heard in the distance, and a party of men on horseback, whom no one had observed, were seen galloping at a tearing rate towards us.

'Hoora! hoora! Tim Phelan's gained his cause!' shouted

a horseman. 'He's proved an alibi, and been set free by the judge.'

Our captors, on hearing the shouts, turned to greet the newcomers, forgetting for the moment their previous intention and their leader, who lay on the ground, the major still holding his knife at his throat. Presently, who should I see riding out from the crowd but Larry Harrigan himself.

'Thunder and 'ounds!' he exclaimed. 'What were they going to do to you? Shure I never thought they'd have ventured on that.'

He now came up to Hoolan with my uncle bending over him.

'Spare his life, major dear,' he exclaimed. 'He never intended to kill you; and if you'll let him go I'll tell your honour all about it by and by.'

'Is this the case, Dan Hoolan?' asked my uncle. 'On your soul, man, did you not intend to put your threat into execution?'

'No, I didn't, as I'm a living man,' said the outlaw, as, released by my uncle, he rose to his feet.

'I'll tell your honour. I wanted to see how you and your young nephew would face the death I threatened; and I intended at the last moment to release you both if you would promise to take a message to the judge who was trying Tim Phelan, swearing that he was free of the murder of Mick Purcell, and knows no more about it than a babe unborn; for there's one amongst us who did the deed, and they may catch him if they can.'

This announcement completely changed the aspect of affairs. The outlaws brought us our horses, and with many apologies for the trouble they had given us, assisted us to mount.

'I'm not the man to harbour ill-feeling against any one,' said the major, turning to the crowd of apparently humble-looking peasants. 'But, my boys, I'd advise you to follow a better calling without delay. And now I'll wish you good morning. If we ever meet again, may it be under pleasanter circumstances.'

Though the greater part of those present didn't understand what he said, the rest interpreted it in their own fashion: the outlaws and the new-comers raising a loud cheer, we rode off, followed by Larry, and continued our journey as if nothing particular had occurred.

'And what made you keep behind us, Larry?' asked my uncle, who summoned him up alongside.

'I'll tell your honour,' answered Larry.   'I was sleeping in the stables after I'd attended to the horses, when I heard three or four boys talking together; so I opened my eyes to listen, seeing it was something curious they were saying. I soon found that they were talking about Tim Phelan, who was to be tried in the morning. I thin recollected that Tim was my father's second cousin's nephew, and so of course I felt an interest in the fate of the boy.

'Says one to the other, "If the alibi isn't proved, shure we're bound in honour to try and rescue him."

'"There are a hundred at least of us bound to do the same," answered the other, "and of course we'll find many more to help if we once begin."

'"Thin I'll be one of them," I cried out, starting up without thinking that yer honour would be wanting me to continue the journey this morning. Blood is stronger than water, as yer know, major dear, and with the thought of rescuing Tim Phelan, I forgot everything else. When I joined the boys, I found a dozen or more met together, and they made me swear a mighty big oath that I would stick to them till Tim Phelan was acquitted or set free if condemned. So when the morning came, I knew that I could overtake yer honour and Maisther Terence by making my baste move along after the trial was over. As soon as yer honour had started, I went back to my friends, and after some time, while talking to them, I heard that Dan Hoolan was on the road to carry out another plan of his own, in case Tim should be condemned. What it was I didn't find out for some time, when one of the boys tauld me that Dan intended to get hold of one of the lawyers, or a magistrate, or a gintleman of consequence, and to threaten to hang him if Tim was not set free. I was almost shrinking in my brogues when I thought that Dan Hoolan might be after getting hold of yer honour, but my oath prevented me from setting off till the boys came rushing out of the court saying that Tim was acquitted. I thin tauld them about all I was afraid of, so they jumped on the backs of the horses without waiting to cheer Tim or carry him round the town. It was mighty convanient that we arrived in time; but, major dear, you will see clearly that if I hadn't stopped behind, there would have been three of us to be hung by Dan instead of two; so well pleased I am that I found out that it was Tim, my father's second cousin's nephew, who was going to be tried.'

'Well, master Larry, it's well for us all that you had your wits about you, so I'll say nothing more to you for neglecting your orders, which were to follow close at our heels,' observed the major.

'Thank yer honour; but you'll be after remembering that I didn't suppose that Dan Hoolan was really going to hang yer honour, or I'd have been in a much more mighty fright at hearing that he was going to have a hand in the matter.'

This little incident will afford some idea of the state of my native country at the time of which I write.

After Larry had given this explanation for his non-appearance, he dropped behind, and my uncle and I rode on side by side, talking of various matters, and whenever the road would permit, putting our horses into a trot or a canter to make up for lost time. Darkness overtook us before we reached the town at which my uncle proposed to stop for the night. I confess that I kept a look out now on one side, now on the other, lest any more of Dan Hoolan's gang might be abroad, and have a fancy to examine our valises and pockets. We rode on for nearly three hours in the dark, without meeting, however, with any further adventure. We reached Timahoe, where there being no event of importance taking place, we found sufficient accommodation and food both for man and beast, which was promised on the sign outside, though, to be sure, it could not be seen in the dark, but I observed it the next morning as we rode away.

I must pass over the remainder of the journey till we had

got over the greater part of our journey to the fair city of Cork. We had been riding on like peaceable travellers, as we were, when we reached a village, through the centre of which, having nothing to detain us there, we passed on at our usual pace. It appeared quiet enough. The children were tumbling about with the pigs in the mud, and the women peered out of the half-open doors, but seeing who we were, drew in their heads again without addressing us, or replying to any of Larry's most insinuating greetings.

'There's something going on, though what it may be is more than I can tell,' remarked my uncle.

Just as we got outside the village, though not a sound reached our ears, we caught sight, coming round a corner on the right, of a party of men, each armed with a shillelah, which he grasped tightly in his right hand, while he looked keenly ahead, as if expecting some one to appear. They had started forward apparently at the sound of our horses' feet, and stopped on seeing who we were.

'Good evening, boys,' said my uncle, as we rode on.

They made no reply.

We had got a little further on when I saw another party on the left coming across the country at a rapid rate. One of them, running forward, inquired if we had seen any of the boys of Pothrine, the name, I concluded, of the village we had just passed through.

'Not a few of them, who are on the look-out for you, boys, and if you're not wishing for broken heads, you'll go back the way you came,' answered my uncle.

'Thank yer honour, we'll chance that,' was the answer, and the man rejoining his party, they advanced towards the village. Scarcely a minute had passed before loud cries, whacks, and howls struck upon our ears.

'They're at it,' cried my uncle, and turning back we saw two parties hotly engaged in the middle of the road; shillelahs flourishing in the air, descending rapidly to crack crowns or meet opposing weapons. At the same time Larry was seen galloping in hot haste towards the combatants. My uncle

called him back, but the noise of the strife must have prevented
him from hearing the summons, for he continued his course.
I rode after him, being afraid that he was intending to join in
the scrimmage, but I was too late to stop him, for, throwing
his rein over the stump of a tree which stood convenient at
one side of the road, he jumped off, and in a second was in
the midst of the fray.

I had often seen faction fights on a small scale in our own
neighbourhood, but I had never witnessed such ferocity as was
displayed on the present occasion.

Conspicuous among the rest were two big fellows, who
carried shillelahs of unusually large proportions. They had
singled each other out, being evidently champions of their
respective parties, and it was wonderful to observe the dexterity
with which they assaulted each other, and defended their heads
from blows, which, if delivered as intended, would have crushed
their skulls or broken their arms or legs. In vain I shouted to
Larry to come out of it, and at last I got so excited myself,
that had I possessed a shillelah, I think that, notwithstanding
the folly of the action, I should have jumped off my horse and
joined in the battle. At length one of the champions was
struck to the ground, where three or four others on the same
side were already stretched. It was the one, as far as I could
make out, that Larry had espoused, and to which the men who
had spoken to us belonged. Presently I saw Larry spring out
from the crowd, his head bleeding and his coat torn.

On seeing me he shouted, ' Be off with yer, Maisther Terence,
for they'll be coming after us,' and running towards his pony,
which the tide of battle was approaching, he took the reins and
leaped on its back.

Knowing how annoyed my uncle would be if we got into
any trouble, I followed Larry's advice, but not a moment too
soon, for the defeated party came scampering along the road,
with the victors after them, shrieking and yelling like a party
of madmen let loose.

' On, on, Master Terence dear !' shouted Larry, and galloping forward, I soon overtook my uncle, who had turned back

on hearing the hubbub, to ascertain what had become of me. On seeing that I was safe, he again turned his horse's head, and as he had no wish to get involved in the quarrel, he rode forward, closely followed by Larry. The howls, and shouts, and shrieks grew fainter as we advanced.

'That boy will be brought into proper discipline before long if he gets on board the frigate,' said my uncle when I told him what had occurred, 'and that love of fighting any but his country's enemies knocked out of him, I've a notion.'

It was growing dusk when the lights of the town where we were to stop appeared ahead. Suddenly it struck me that I didn't hear the hoofs of Larry's steed. Turning round to speak to him, he was nowhere visible.

'Larry, come on, will you?' I shouted, but Larry didn't reply.

'The boy can't have had the folly to go back with his broken head to run the chance of another knock down,' observed my uncle. 'We must go and see what he has been after.'

We accordingly turned round and rode back, I galloping ahead and shouting his name. I hadn't gone far when I saw his pony standing by the side of the road. As I got up to the animal, there was Larry doubled up on the ground. I called to him, but he made no reply. Leaping from my horse, I tried to lift him up. Not a sound escaped his lips. I was horrified at finding that to all appearances he was dead.

My uncle's first exclamation on reaching me was, 'The lad has broken his neck, I'm afraid ; but, in case there may be life left in him, the sooner we carry him to a doctor the better. Help me to place him on my saddle, Terence.'

Stooping down, notwithstanding his weight, my uncle drew up his inanimate body, and placed it before him, whilst I led on his pony.

Fortunately, the inn was at the entrance of the town. My uncle, bearing Larry in his arms, entered it with me, and ordering a mattress to be brought, placed him on it, shouting out—

'Be quick, now ; fetch a doctor, some of you !'

My countrymen, though willing enough to crack each others'

pates, are quite as ready to help a fellow-creature in distress; and, as my uncle spoke, two, if not three, of the bystanders hurried off to obey his order.

Meanwhile, the stable-boy having taken our horses, my uncle and I did our best to resuscitate our unfortunate follower. His countenance was pale as a sheet, except where the streaks of blood had run down it; his hair was matted, and an ugly wound was visible on his head. On taking off his handkerchief, I discovered a black mark on his neck, which alarmed me more than the wound. I fully believed that my poor foster-brother was dead.

Scarcely a minute had elapsed before two persons rushed into the room; one short and pursy, the other tall and gaunt, both panting as if they had run a race.

'I have come at your summons, sir!' exclaimed the tall man.

'And shure, so have I! and was I not first in the room?' cried the second.

'In that, Doctor Murphy, you are mistaken!' exclaimed the tall man, 'for didn't I put my head over your shoulder as we came through the door?'

'But my body was in before yours, Mr. O'Shea; and I consider that you are bound to give place to a doctor of medicine!'

'But this appears to me to be a surgical case,' said the tall man; 'and as the head, as all will allow, is a more honourable part of the body than the paunch, I claim to be the first on the field; and, moreover, to have seen the patient before you could possibly have done so, Doctor Murphy. Sir,' he continued, stalking past his brother practitioner, and making a bow with a battered hat to the major, 'I come, I presume, on your summons, to attend to the injured boy; and such skill as I possess —and I flatter myself it's considerable—is at your service. May I ask what is the matter with him?'

'Here's a practitioner who doesn't know what his patient is suffering from by a glance of the eye!' cried the doctor of medicine. 'Give place, Mr. O'Shea, to a man of superior knowledge to yourself,' exclaimed Doctor Murphy. 'It's easy enough to see with half a glance that the boy has broken his

neck, and by this time, unless he possesses a couple of spines,
—and I never knew a man have more than one, though,—
he must be dead as a door nail !'

'Dead !' cried Mr. O'Shea; 'the doctor says his patient's
dead without feeling a pulse or lifting an eyelid.'

'You, at all events, ought to know a corpse from a live man,'
cried the fat medico, growing irate, 'when it's whispered that
you have made as many dead bodies in the town itself as would
serve for a couple of battles and a few scrimmages to boot.'

'And you, Doctor Murphy, have poisoned one-half of your
patients, and the others only survive because they throw the
physic you send them to the dogs.'

'Come, gentlemen,' exclaimed the major, 'while you are
squabbling, any spark of life the poor boy may contain will
be ebbing away. As I am not acquainted with the skill you
respectively possess, I beg that you, Doctor Murphy, as holding the higher grade in your profession, will examine the boy,
and express your opinion whether he is dead or alive, and state,
if there's life in him, which you consider the best way to bring
him round, and set him on his feet again.'

Mr. O'Shea, on hearing this, stepped back a few paces, and,
folding his arms, looked with supreme contempt on the little
doctor, who, stooping down over Larry with watch in hand, at
which he mechanically gazed with a serious countenance, felt
his pulse.

'His hand is cold and clammy, and there's not a single
thump in his arteries,' he said with solemn gravity ; and letting
fall Larry's hand he proceeded to examine his neck. 'The
vertebra broken, cracked, dislocated,' he continued, in the
same solemn tone. 'D'ye see this black mark down his throat?
it's amply sufficient to account for death. I hereby certify
that this is a corpse before me, and authorize that he may be
sent home to his friends for Christian burial.'

'Och ahone ! och ahone !' I cried out, throwing myself by
the side of the mattress. 'Is Larry really dead? Oh, doctors
dear, can't both of you put your heads together and try to
bring him to life again ?'

'When the breath is out of the body, 'tis more than all the skill of the most learned practitioners can accomplish,' exclaimed Doctor Murphy, rising from his knees. 'I pronounce the boy dead, and no power on earth can bring him round again.'

'I hold to the contrary opinion,' said Mr. O'Shea, advancing and drawing out of his pocket a case of instruments, from which he produced a large operation knife, and began to strop 't on the palm of his hand. 'It's fortunate for the boy that he didn't move, or Doctor Murphy would have been thrusting one of his big boluses down his throat and drenched him with black draughts. Stand aside, friends, and you shall see that a surgeon's skill is superior to a doctor's knowledge. I have your leave, sir, to proceed as I consider necessary?' he asked, turning to the major.

'Certainly,' answered my uncle; 'if Doctor Murphy considers him dead and you believe him to be alive, and act accordingly, I have more hopes in the results of your skill than in that of the other gentleman.'

'You'll remain in town some time, sir, I presume, and as you're a gentleman, I shall expect a visit from you,' exclaimed the fat doctor, as, nearing the door, he made a bow, and, gold cane in hand, waddled out of the room.

Mr. O'Shea cast a contemptuous glance at him, and then kneeling down, applied his knife to the nape of Larry's neck. Warm blood immediately spouted forth. 'I told you so,' he exclaimed; 'blood doesn't flow like this from a corpse. Bring hot water and cloths.' These he applied to Larry's neck, and continued to pour the water on them, 'to draw out the blood,' as he said, and relieve the patient's head. Then pressing his knees against Larry's shoulders, he gave a pull at his head which seemed likely to dislocate his neck, if it hadn't been broken already.

As he did this, he exclaimed, 'There now, I have taken the twists out, and the boy will be all to rights in the course of an hour.'

A groan and a heavy sigh proclaimed that there was still life in poor Larry. Presently he opened one eye and then the other, and some spoonfuls of whisky and water, which Surgeon O'Shea poured down his throat, contributed still further to revive him.

In the course of half-an-hour Larry asked in a low voice, 'Did yer beat back the O'Sullivans, yer honour? shure they were coming after us at a mighty great rate, and I fancy some one of them gave me a whack on the crown which brought me to the ground.'

'Keep quiet and don't be talking,' answered the surgeon, who, proud of his success, had been carefully watching his patient. 'He'll do now, gentlemen,' he added, looking up at my uncle and me. 'We'll put him to bed, and by to-morrow morning he'll be as blithe as a lark, barring a stiff neck.'

CHAPTER IV

MY FIRST DAY ON BOARD.

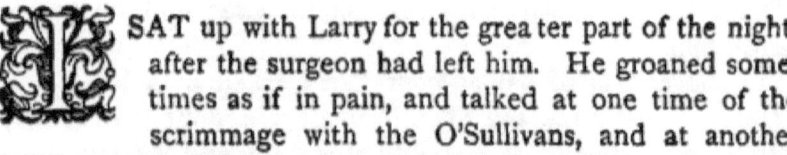

I SAT up with Larry for the greater part of the night, after the surgeon had left him. He groaned sometimes as if in pain, and talked at one time of the scrimmage with the O'Sullivans, and at another of his fiddle, which he feared had been broken. I accordingly, to pacify him, went down and got it, and managed to produce some few notes, which had the desired effect. The major after some time came in to relieve me, for we could not trust any of the people at the inn, who would to a certainty have been dosing our patient with whisky, under the belief that they were doing him a kindness, but at the risk of producing a fever.

In the morning Mr. O'Shea came in.

'I thought you said that the boy would be all to rights by this time,' I observed.

'Shure that was somewhat hyperbolical,' he answered, with a wink. 'You can't expect a man with a broken neck, and a gash as big as my thumb at the back of it, to come round in a few hours.'

We couldn't complain, for certainly the worthy surgeon had been the means of saving Larry's life; but the incident detained us three whole days, before he was fit to mount his pony and accompany us to Cork. Before leaving my uncle called on Doctor Murphy, who, to his great amusement, he found had no intention of calling him out, but merely expected to receive a fee for pronouncing a living man a dead one. Though my uncle might have declined to pay the amount demanded, he handed it to the doctor, and wished him good morning.

I afterwards heard that Doctor Murphy had challenged Mr. O'Shea. That gentleman, however, refused to go out on the plea that should he be wounded, and become a patient of his brother practitioner, he should certainly go the way of the rest of those under his medical care. For many a long day Doctor Murphy and Mr. O'Shea carried on a fierce warfare, till their patients agreed to fight it out and settle the matter, when the doctor's party being defeated, no inconsiderable number of broken heads being the result, he left the town to exercise his skill in some other locality, where, as Mr. O'Shea remarked, ' there was a superabundant population.'

We were too late on arriving at Cork to go on board the frigate that evening, and thus Larry got the advantage of another night's rest, and I had time to brush up my uniform, and, as I conceived, to make myself as smart as any officer in His Majesty's service. The next morning my uncle hired a boat to proceed down the fair river of Cork to the harbour where the frigate lay. As we approached her my heart thrilled with pleasure as I thought of the honour I was about to enjoy of becoming one of her officers.

'There's the *Liffy*, yer honour,' said the boatman, pointing her out as she lay some distance from the shore. Her masts had already been replaced, and her yards were across, though the sails were not as yet bent ; this, however, I did not observe.

'I hope I have not detained her, uncle,' I said ; 'I should be sorry to have done that.'

The major seldom indulged in a laugh, but he did so on this occasion till the tears rolled down his cheeks.

'Midshipmen are not of so much account as you suppose, Terence,' he said, still laughing. 'If you were to go on shore and not return on board in time, you would soon discover that the ship would not wait for you a single moment after the captain had resolved to put to sea.'

3

As we approached, the sentry hailed to know who we were. In my eagerness I replied, 'Major M'Mahon and the new midshipman, Mr. Terence O'Finnahan,' whereat a laugh came forth from one of the ports at which, as it appeared, some of my future messmates were standing.

'You'd have better have held your tongue,' said my uncle. 'And now, Terence, remember to salute the flag as you see me do,' he added, as he was about to mount the side of the ship. He went up, I followed, and next came Larry. On reaching the deck he took off his hat, and I doffed mine with all the grace I could muster, Larry at the same time making a profound bow and a scrape of his foot. The master's mate who received us, when my uncle inquired for Captain Macnamara, pointed to the after part of the deck, where my future commander, with several other well-dressed officers, was standing. My uncle at once moved towards him, and I and Larry followed in the same direction. The captain, a fine-looking man, seeing him approach came forward, and they exchanged cordial greetings.

'I have come expressly to introduce my nephew Terence to you, Macnamara,' said my uncle. 'You were good enough, in a letter I received from you a few days ago, to say that you would receive him as a midshipman on board your ship. He's a broth of a boy, and will be an ornament to the service, I hope.'

'Can't say that he is much of an ornament at present,' I heard one of the officers remark to another. 'Looks more like a mummer or stage player than a midshipman.'

Looking up, I observed a smile on their countenances, as they eyed me from head to foot.

'Wishing to present the boy in a respectable way to you on the quarter-deck of His Majesty's ship, we had a uniform made for him at Ballinahone, which is, I fancy, such as your officers are accustomed to wear on grand occasions,' said the major, taking me by the arm as if to exhibit me to more advantage.

'I thought rather that it was the fashionable dress worn by

young gentlemen in the west of Ireland at wakes or weddings,' remarked the captain ; 'but I confess, my dear M'Mahon, that I do not recognise it as a naval uniform, except in the matter of the buttons, which I see are according to the right pattern. The young gentleman will have to dress differently, except when he has a fancy to go to a masquerade on shore.'

The major stepped back with a look of astonishment ; then surveying the uniform of the officers standing around, and taking another look at my costume, he exclaimed, laughing, 'Faith, I see there is a difference, but as no regulations or patterns were procurable at Ballinahone, we did the best we could.'

'Of that I have no doubt about, M'Mahon ; you always did your best, and very well done it was,' said the captain ; 'but I would advise you to take your nephew on shore, and get him rigged out in a more proper costume as soon as possible.'

I was completely taken aback on hearing this, and finding that instead of making a favourable impression on the captain, my costume had produced a very contrary effect. In a short time, however, somewhat regaining my confidence and remembering Larry, I turned to my uncle and begged that, according to his promise, he would introduce him.

'To be shure I will,' he answered, and then addressing the captain, he said, 'My nephew has a foster-brother, the boy standing there, who has made up his mind to go to sea. Will you receive him on board your ship? I own, however, that he will require a good deal of licking into shape before he becomes a sailor.'

'He appears to be a stout lad, and I have no doubt but that in course of time we shall succeed in making him one,' answered the captain. 'Do you wish to go to sea, boy?'

Larry, who didn't quite understand, I suspect, what licking into shape meant, answered notwithstanding, 'Shure, yer honour, wherever Maisther Terence goes, I'm desirous of following, and as he's to become a midshipman, I'd wish to go wherever I can be with him.'

'That cannot be so exactly,' answered the captain, laughing;

'but if you become one of the crew, you'll not be far from him, and I hope I may see you some day following your leader on board an enemy's ship, and hauling down her flag.'

'Hurrah! shure that's what I'll be after doing, and anything else your honour plaises,' exclaimed Larry at the top of his voice, flourishing his hat at the same time above his head. 'I'll be after showing yer honour how the boys in Tipperary fight.'

That matter being settled much to my satisfaction, Larry was taken off to have his name entered on the ship's books, for in those days a fish having been once caught in the net, it was not thought advisable to let him go again. In the meantime, my uncle having gone into the captain's cabin to take luncheon, I was led by a person whom, though I thought he was an officer, I supposed, from his appearance, to be one of very subordinate rank, to be introduced to my new messmates, in the midship-men's berth.

'And so you think we wear silks and satins on board ship, I see, young gentleman, do you?' he said with a comical grin, eyeing my new coat and waistcoat. 'You'll have to send these back to your grandmother, or the old woman who made them for you.'

'Arrah, sir, d'ye intend to insult me?' I asked. 'Were they not put together by Pat Cassidy, the family tailor, under the direction of my uncle, Major M'Mahon, and he shure knows what a young gentleman should wear on board ship.'

'No, my lad, I only intended to laugh at you; but do you know who I am?'

'No, but I'll have you to understand that an O'Finnahan of Castle Ballinahone, County Tipperary, Ireland, is not to be insulted with impunity,' I answered, trying to look as dignified as I could.

'Then I'll give you to understand, young sir, that I'm the first lieutenant of this ship, and that lieutenants don't insult midshipmen, even if they think fit to send them to the mast-head. It will be your business to obey, and to ask no questions.'

As I knew no more, at the time, of the rank and position of

a first lieutenant on board ship than I did of the man in the moon, this announcement did not make much impression on my mind. I only thought that he was some old fellow who was fond of boasting, and had a fancy to try and make me believe that he was a personage of importance, or perhaps to frighten me. I soon discovered, however, that though he generally wore a shabby uniform, he was not a man to be trifled with. I may as well here say that his name was Saunders, that he was a thorough tar, who had come in at the hawse-hole, and had worked his way up to his present position. 'Old Rough and Ready' I found he was called. His hands were continually in the tar bucket, and he was never so happy as when, with a marlinespike hung round his neck by a rope-yarn, he was engaged in gammoning the bowsprit, or setting up the rigging. But that I found out afterwards.

'Now come along, youngster, for I don't wish to be hard on you; I'm only laughing at the ridiculous figure you cut,' he said, giving way to a burst of rough merriment. By the time it was over we reached the door of the berth, where the midshipmen were assembled for dinner.

'Young gentlemen,' said Mr. Saunders with perfect gravity, opening the door, 'I have to tell you that this is Mr. Terence O'Finnahan, of Castle Ballinahone, County Tipperary, Ireland, who is to become your messmate as soon as he is docked of his fine feathers; and you'll be pleased to receive him as such.'

Saying this he took his departure, and two of my new messmates seized me by the fists, which they gripped with a force intended perhaps to show the ardour of their regard, but which was excessively painful to my feelings. I restrained them, however, and stood looking round at the numerous strange faces turned towards me.

'Make room for Mr. Terence O'Finnahan, of Castle Ballinahone, County Tipperary, Ireland,' cried an old master's mate from the further end of the table; 'but let all understand that it's the last time such a designation is to be applied to him. It's much too long a name for any practical purpose, and from henceforth he's to be known on board this ship as Paddy Finn, the Irish midshipman; and so, Paddy Finn, old boy, I'll drink your health. Gentlemen, fill your glasses; here's to the health of Paddy Finn.'

Every one in the berth filled up their mugs and cups with rum and water, in which they pledged me with mock gravity. Having in the meantime taken my seat, I rose and begged to return my thanks to them for the honour they had done me, assuring them that I should be happy to be known by the new name they had given me, or by any other which might sound as sweet.

'Only, gentlemen, there's one point I must bargain for,' I added; 'let me be called Paddy, whatever other designation you may in your judgment think fit to bestow on me, for let me tell you that I consider it an honour to be an Irishman, and I am as proud of my native land as you can be of yours.'

'Bravo, Paddy!' cried several. 'You're a trump,' observed the president.

'The chiel' has got pluck in him,' said the Scotcn assistant surgeon, who sat opposite to the president, a man whose grizzled hair showed that he had been long in the service.

'Where did you get those clothes from?' asked a young gentleman, whom I afterwards found to be the purser's clerk.

' He picked them up at a theatrical property shop as he passed through Cork,' remarked another.

'Haul in the slack of your impudence,' cried the president, whose favour I had won. 'If his friends had never seen a naval uniform, how should they know how to rig him out?'

'I'm mightily obliged to you, sir,' I said, for I was by this time getting heartily ashamed of my gay feathers; 'and as the ship won't be sailing yet, I hope to get fitted out properly before I return on board.'

'All right, youngster,' said the president. 'Now, I will have the pleasure of helping you to a slice of mutton. Hand the greens and potatoes up to Paddy Finn.'

The plate was passed round to me, and I was allowed, without being further bantered, to discuss the viands placed under my nose, which I did with a good appetite. I was not silent, however, but introducing my journey to Cork, amused my messmates with an account of the various incidents which had occurred. When, at length, one of the midshipmen who had being doing duty on deck appeared at the door to say that Major M'Mahon was about to return on shore, and wanted his nephew, my new friends shook me warmly by the hand, and the president again proposed three hearty cheers for their new messmate, Paddy Finn.

CHAPTER V.

WAS in much better spirits when I rejoined my uncle than when I had been led below by Mr. Saunders. I found him standing with the captain on the main-deck, they having just come out of the cabin.

'I should like to take a turn round the ship before we leave her, in case I should be unable to pay you another visit,' said the major. 'I wish to brush up my recollections of what a frigate is like.'

'Come along then,' answered the captain, and he led the way along the deck.

As we got forward, we heard loud roars of laughter and clapping of hands. The cause was very evident, for there was Larry in the midst of a group of seamen, dancing an Irish jig to the tune of one of his most rollicksome songs.

'Stop a bit, my boys, and I'll show you what real music is like,' he exclaimed after he had finished the song. 'Wait till I get my fiddle among yer, and I'll make it squeak louder thin a score of peacocks or a dozen of sucking pigs;' and he then began again singing,—

> 'A broth of a boy was young Daniel O'Shane,
>   As he danced with the maidens of fair Derrynane.'

Then he went on jigging away, to the great delight of his audience,—no one observing the captain or us.

It was very evident that Larry had without loss of time made himself at home among his new shipmates. They treated him much as they would have treated a young bear, or any other pet animal they might have obtained. I had expected to find him looking somewhat forlorn and downcast among so many strangers; but in reality, I ought to have trusted an Irish boy of his degree to make friends wherever he goes.

'I think we may leave your follower where he is, as, should you not require his services, he is much more likely to be kept out of mischief here than he would be ashore,' said the captain to the major.

To this my uncle agreed. We had got some way along the deck when I felt a touch on my shoulder, and turning round, saw Larry's countenance grinning from ear to ear.

'Shure they're broths of boys these sailor fellows, and I'm mighty plaised to be among them; but, Maisther Terence dear, I have a favour to ask you. Would you tell the captain that I'd be mightily obliged to him if he would let me go back to Cork for my fiddle. I left it at the inn, and if I had it now I'd set all the boys on board a jigging, with the captain and officers into the bargain.'

I told him that as the captain thought it better he should remain on board, I could not ask leave for him to go on shore; but I promised that if I had an opportunity, I would send him his violin at once, or if not, would be careful to bring it myself.

'You'll not be long then, Maisther Terence; for the boys here are mighty eager to hear me play.'

Assuring him how glad I was to find that he was happy, I advised him to go back to his new friends again, promising not to forget his violin.

We had come on board on the larboard side; we now went to the starboard. On each side of the gangway stood several officers and midshipmen, while on the accommodation-ladder were arranged two lines of boys. The captain's own gig was waiting for us, manned by eight smart seamen, their oars in the air. The captain himself descended, returning the salutes of

the officers and men. I followed my uncle, who was treated
with a similar mark of respect; but as I thought a portion was
intended for me, and wishing to act in the politest way possible,
I took off my hat altogether, and made several most polite
bows. I had a suspicion, however, from the expression on the
countenances of the midshipmen, with the suppressed titter
among them, together with the grin on the faces of the men
and boys, that I was doing something not altogether according
to custom. Perhaps, I thought to myself, I hadn't bowed low
enough, so I turned, now to my right, now to my left, and, not
seeing where I was going to, should have pitched right down
the ladder had not one of the men standing there caught my
arm, bidding me as he did so to keep my hat on my head.

In my eagerness to get into the boat I made a spring, and
should have leapt right over into the water had not another
friendly hand caught me and forced me down by the side of
the major.

The captain, taking the white yoke-lines, gave the order to
shove off; the boat's head swung away from the side of the
frigate; the oars fell with their blades flat on the water; and we
began to glide rapidly up the harbour, propelled by the sturdy
arms of the crew. I felt very proud as I looked at the captain
in his cocked hat and laced coat, and at the midshipman who
accompanied him, in a bran new uniform, though, to be sure,
there wasn't much of him to look at, for he was a mere mite of
a fellow.

Had I not discovered that my own costume was not accord
ing to rule, I should have considered it a much more elegant
one than his. After some time, the captain observing, I fancy,
that I looked rather dull, having no one to talk to, said
something to the midshipman, who immediately came and sat
by me.

'Well, Paddy, how do you like coming to sea?' he asked in
a good-natured tone.

'I've not yet formed an opinion,' I answered.

'True, my boy; Cork harbour is not the Atlantic,' he remarked. 'We may chance to see the waves running mountains

high when we get there, and all the things tumbling about like shuttlecocks.'

'I'll be content to wait until I see that same to form an opinion,' I answered.   'As I've come to sea, I shall be glad to witness whatever takes place there.'

'You're not to be caught, I perceive,' he said.   'Well, Paddy, and how do you like your name?'

'Faith, I'm grateful to you and my other messmates for giving it,' I answered.   'I'm not ashamed of the name, and I hope to have the opportunity of making it known far and wide some day or other; and now may I ask you what's your name, for I haven't had the pleasure of hearing it.'

'Thomas Pim,' he answered.

'Come, that's short enough, anyhow,' I observed.

'Yes; but when I first came aboard, the mess declared it was too long, so they cut off the "h" and the "as" and "m" and called me Tom Pi; but even then they were not content, for they further docked it of its fair proportions, and decided that I was to be named Topi, though generally I'm called simply Pi.'

'Do you mind it?' I asked.

'Not a bit,' he answered.   'It suits my size, I confess; for, to tell you the truth, I'm older than I look, and have been three years at sea.'

'I thought you had only just joined,' I remarked, for my companion was, as I have just said, a very little fellow, scarcely reaching up to my shoulder.   On examining his countenance more minutely, I observed that it had a somewhat old look.

'Though I'm little I'm good, and not ashamed of my size or my name either,' he said.   'When bigger men are knocked over, I've a chance of escaping.   I can stow myself away where others can't get in their legs; and when I go aloft or take a run on shore, I've less weight to carry,—so has the steed I ride.   When I go with others to hire horses, I generally manage to get the best from the stable-keeper.'

'Yes, I see that you have many advantages over bigger fellows,' I said.

'I'm perfectly contented with myself now I've found that out, but I confess that at first I didn't like being laughed at and having remarks made about my name and my size. I have grown slightly since then, and no one observes now that I'm an especially little fellow.'

Tom spoke for some time on the same subject.

'I say, Paddy Finn, I hope you and I will be friends,' he continued. 'I've heard that you Irishmen are frequently quarrelsome, but I hope you won't quarrel with me, or, for your own sake, with any of the rest of the mess. You'll gain nothing by it, as they would all turn against you to put you down.'

'No fear of that,' I replied, 'always provided that they say nothing insulting of Ireland, or of my family or friends, or of the opinions I may hold, or take liberties which I don't like, or do anything which I consider unbecoming gentlemen.'

'You leave a pretty wide door open,' remarked Tom; 'but, as I said before, if you don't keep the peace it will be the worse for you.'

We were all this time proceeding at a rapid rate up the stream, between its wooded and picturesque banks. On arriving at Cork, the captain wished the major good-bye, saying that I must be on board again within three days, which would allow me ample time to get a proper uniform made.

I asked Tom Pim what he was going to do with himself, and proposed that, after I had been measured by the tailor, we should take a stroll together.

'Do you think the captain brought me up here for my pleasure?' he said. 'I have to stay by the boat while he's on shore, to see that the men don't run away. Why, if I didn't keep my eye on them, they'd be off like shots, and drunk as fiddlers by the time the captain came back.'

'I'm sorry you can't come,' I said. 'By the bye, talking of fiddlers, will you mind taking a fiddle on board to the boy who came with me,—Larry Harrigan? I promised to send it to him, though I didn't expect so soon to have the opportunity.'

'With the greatest pleasure in the world,' said Tom Pim.

'Perhaps I may take a scrape on it myself. When I was a little fellow, I learned to play it.'

'You must have been a very little fellow,' I couldn't help remarking, though Tom didn't mind it.

As our inn was not far off, I asked my uncle to let me run on and get the fiddle, and take it down to the boat. As I carried it along, I heard people making various remarks, evidently showing that they took me for a musician or stage-player, which made me more than ever anxious to get out of a costume which I had once been so proud of wearing. Having delivered the violin in its case to Tom Pim, who promised to convey it to Larry, I rejoined my uncle.

We proceeded at once to the tailor recommended by Captain Macnamara, who, having a pattern, promised to finish my uniform in time, and to supply all the other articles I required We spent the few days we were in Cork in visiting some old friends of the major's.

I was very anxious about the non-appearance of my chest, but the night before I was to go on board, to my great satisfaction, it arrived.

'It's a good big one, at all events,' I thought; 'it will hold all the things I want, and some curiosities I hope to bring back from foreign parts.'

It was capable of doing so, for although it might have been somewhat smaller than the one in which the bride who never got out again hid away, it was of magnificent proportions, solid as oak and iron clamps could make it; it was big enough to hold half-a-dozen of my smaller brothers and sisters, who used to stow themselves away in it when playing hide - and - seek about the house.

Soon after the chest arrived the tailor brought my uniform.

It certainly was a contrast to the comical suit I had hitherto been wearing. I put it on with infinite satisfaction, and girded to my side a new dirk, which my uncle had given me, instead of my grandfather's old sword. The latter, however, my uncle recommended me to take on board.

'You may want it, Terence, maybe on some cutting-out

expedition,' he said; 'and you'll remember that it belonged to your ancestors, and make it do its duty.'

As the chest was already full, I had a difficulty in stowing away the things the tailor had brought. I therefore began to unpack it while he was waiting, and I observed that he cast a look of supreme contempt on most of the articles it contained. He even ventured to suggest that he should be allowed to replace them with others which he could supply.

'The boy has enough and to spare, and I should like to know how many of them will find their way back to Cork,' said my uncle.

Some of them I found, on consideration, that I should be as well without. Among other things were a pair of thick brogues, which Molly the cook had put in to keep my feet from the wet deck, and a huge cake; this, though, I guessed would not be sneered at in the mess, and would travel just as well outside. At length I found room for everything I required, and the chest was once more locked and corded.

I don't believe I slept a wink that night with thinking of what I should do when I got on board the frigate. It was a satisfaction to remember that the ice had been broken, and that I should not appear as a perfect stranger amongst my messmates. I already knew Tom Pim, and he had told me the names of several others, among whom were those of Jack Nettleship the old mate and caterer of the mess, Dick Sinnet the senior midshipman, Sims the purser's clerk, and Donald M'Pherson the assistant-surgeon. The others I could not remember. The lieutenants, he said, were very nice fellows, though they had their peculiarities. None of the officers were Irishmen, consequently I had been dubbed Paddy.

CHAPTER VI.

THE morning came. My chest and my other strat things had been carried down in a cart to the river, where they were shipped on board a shore-boat.

As we walked along following it, my uncle, after being silent for a minute, as if considering how he should address me, said: 'You have got a new life before you, away from friends, among all sorts of characters,—some good, it may be, many bad or indifferent, but no one probably on whom you may rely. You will be placed in difficult, often in dangerous situations, when you'll have only yourself, or Him who orders all things, to trust to. Be self-reliant; ever strive to do your duty; and don't be after troubling yourself about the consequences. You will be engaged in scenes of warfare and bloodshed. I have taken part in many such, and I know their horrors. War is a stern necessity. May you never love it for itself; but when fighting, comport yourself like a man fearless of danger, while you avoid running your head needlessly into it. Be courteous and polite, slow to take offence,—especially when no offence is intended, as is the case in ninety-nine cases out of a hundred where quarrels occur. Remember that it always takes two to make a quarrel, and that the man who never gives offence will seldom get into one. Never grumble; be cheerful and obliging. Never insist on your own rights when those rights are not worth insisting on. Sacrifice your own feelings to those of others, and be ever ready to help a companion out of a difficulty. You may be surprised to hear me—an old soldier and an Irishman—talking in this way; but I give you the advice, because I have seen so many act differently, and, wrapped up in intense selfishness, become utterly regardless of others,— reaping the consequences by being disliked and neglected, and finally deserted by all who were their friends. There's another point I must speak to you about, and it's a matter which weighs greatly on my mind. Example, they say, is better than precept. Now your father has set you a mighty bad example, and so have many others who have come to the castle. Don't follow it. You see the effect which his potations of rum shrub and whisky toddy have produced on him. When I was on duty, or going on it, I never touched liquor; and no man ever lost his life from my carelessness, as I have seen the lives of many poor soldiers thrown away when their officers, being drunk, have led them into useless danger. So I say, Terence, keep clear of liquor. The habit of drinking grows on a man, and in my time I have seen it the ruin of many as fine young fellows as ever smelt powder.'

I thanked my uncle, and promised as far as I could to follow his excellent advice.

As we reached the water-side, my uncle stopped, and putting one hand on my shoulder and taking mine with the other, looked me kindly in the face.

'Fare thee well, Terence, my boy,' he said; 'we may not again meet on earth, but wherever you go, an old man's warmest affection follows you. Be afraid of nothing but doing wrong. If your life is spared, you'll rise in the profession you have chosen, second only in my opinion to that of the army.'

I stepped into the boat, and the men shoved off. My uncle stood watching me as we descended the stream. Again and again he waved his hand, and I returned his salute. He was still standing there when a bend of the river shut him out from my sight. I was too much engaged with my thoughts to listen to what the boatmen said, and I suspect they thought me either too dull or too proud to talk to them. As we pulled up on the larboard side, thinking that I was now somebody, I shouted to some men I saw looking through the ports to come down and lift my chest on board, though how that was to be done was more than I could tell. A chorus of laughs was the reply.

Presently I heard a gruff voice say, 'Send a whip down there, and have that big lumber chest, or whatever it is, up on deck.' My chest was quickly hauled up, and as quickly transferred by the orders of the lieutenant in charge of the watch below, before Mr. Saunders' eyes had fallen on it. I mounted the side in as dignified a way as I could, saluting the flag on reaching the deck, as my uncle had told me to do.

I had recognised Tom Pim, who was ready to receive me. 'You must go to the first lieutenant,—he's in the gun-room,— and say, "Come aboard, sir," and then when you're dismissed make your way into the berth,' he said.

'But how am I to be after finding the gun-room; is it where the guns are kept?' I asked.

Tom laughed at my simplicity. 'No; it's where the gun-room officers, the lieutenants and master, the doctor, and purser, and lieutenant of marines, mess. They all mess together, as do the mates, and we the midshipmen, the second master and master's assistant, the clerks and the assistant-surgeon.'

'And have you no ensign?' I asked.

'No; there are none in the marines, and so we have no soldiers in our berth,' he answered; 'but let's come along, I'll show you the way, and then you'll be in time for dinner.' We descended to the gun-room door, where Tom left me, bidding me go in and ask for the first lieutenant. I didn't see him, but one of the other officers, of whom I made inquiries, pointed me to the first lieutenant's cabin.

I knocked at the door. 'Come in,' answered a gruff voice. I found the lieutenant with his shirt-sleeves tucked up, he having just completed his morning ablutions, an old stocking on one fist and a needle and thread in the other, engaged in darning it.

'Come on board, sir,' I said.

4

'Very well, youngster,' he answered; 'I should scarcely have known you in your present proper uniform. There's nothing like being particular as to dress. I'll see about placing you in a watch. You'll understand that you're to try and do your duty to the best of your abilities.'

'Shure it's what I hope to do, sir,' I answered briskly; 'and I'm mighty glad you like my uniform.'

'I didn't say I liked it, youngster,—I said it was proper according to the regulations. Turn round, let me see. There is room for growing, which a midshipman's uniform should have. You'll remember always to be neat and clean, and follow the example I try to set you youngsters.'

'Yes, sir,' I answered, my eyes falling on a huge patch which the lieutenant had on one of the knees of his trousers.

'Now you may go!' he said. 'Understand that you're not to quit the ship without my leave, and that you must master the rules and regulations of the service as soon as possible, for I can receive no excuse if you infringe them.'

Altogether I was pretty well satisfied with my interview with old Rough-and-Ready, and hurrying out of the gun-room I directed my course for the young gentlemen's berth, as it was called, which was some way further forward on the starboard side. I intended, after making my appearance there, to go in search of Larry, but the mulatto steward and a boy came hurrying aft along the deck with steaming dishes, which they placed on the table, and I found that the dinner was about to commence.

'Glad to see you, Paddy,' said Jack Nettleship, who had already taken his place at the head of the table. 'You look less like a play-actor's apprentice and more like an embryo naval officer than you did when you first came on board. Now sit down and enjoy the good things of life while you can get them. Time will come when we shall have to luxuriate on salt junk as hard as a millstone and weevily biscuits.'

Plenty of joking took place, and everybody seemed in good humour, so that I soon found myself fairly at my ease, and all I wanted to be perfectly so was to know the ways of the ship. I succeeded in producing several roars of laughter by the stories I told, not attempting to overcome my brogue, but rather the contrary, as I found it amused my auditors. When the rum was passed round, of which each person had a certain quantum, the doctor sang out to the youngsters, including Tom Pim and me, 'Hold fast! it's a vara bad thing for you laddies, and I shall be having you all on the sick list before long if I allow you to take it. Pass the pernicious liquor along here.'

Tom obeyed, and so did I, willingly enough, for I had tasted the stuff and thought it abominably nasty, but two or three of the other midshipmen hesitated, and some seemed inclined to revolt.

'I call on you, Nettleship, as president of the mess, to interfere,' exclaimed the doctor. 'What do these youngsters suppose I'm sent here for, but to watch over their morals and their health; and as I find it difficult in the one case to do my duty with the exactitude I desire, I shall take care not to neglect it in the other. There's young Chaffey there, who has stowed away enough duff to kill a bull, and now he's going to increase the evil by pouring this burning fiery liquid down his throat. Do you want to be in your grave, Jack? if not, be wise, and let the grog alone.'

Chaffey, the fattest midshipman among us, looked somewhat alarmed, and quickly passed up the rum. I observed that the doctor kept it by his side, and having finished his own quantum, began to sip the portions he had forbidden the youngsters to drink. It was difficult to suppose that he was perfectly disinterested in his advice.

Being in harbour, we sat much longer than usual. At last I asked Tom if he thought I could venture to go and look out for Larry.

'Oh, yes; this is Liberty Hall,' he answered.

I was going forward, when I heard my name called, and going to the spot from whence the voice came, I saw the first lieutenant standing before my chest, at which he cast a look of mingled indignation and contempt. By his side was a warrant officer, whom I heard addressed as Mr. Bradawl, with a saw and chisel and hammer in hand.

'Does this huge chest belong to you?' asked old Rough-and-Ready, as I came up.

'Yes, sir,' I answered; 'I'm rather proud of it.'

'We shall see if you continue so,' he exclaimed. 'Do you think we have room to stow away such a lumbering thing as this? Where's the key?'

I produced it.

'Now tumble your things out.'

'But please, sir, I haven't room to pack them away. I have got this bundle, and that case, and those other things are all mine.'

'Tumble them out!' cried the lieutenant, without attending to my expostulations.

I obeyed. And the carpenter began sawing away at a line which old Rough-and-Ready had chalked out not far from the keyhole. Mr. Bradawl had a pretty tough job of it, for the oak was hard. The lieutenant stood by, watching the proceeding with evident satisfaction. He was showing me that a first lieutenant was all-powerful on board ship. I watched this cruel curtailment of my chest with feelings of dismay.

Having sawn it thus nearly in two, the carpenter knocked off the end of the part he had severed from the rest, and then hammered it on with several huge nails.

'Now, youngster, pick out the most requisite articles, and send the others ashore, or overboard, or anywhere, so that they're out of the ship,' exclaimed the first lieutenant; saying which he turned away to attend to some other duty, leaving me wondering how I should stow the things away. Tom Pim, who had seen what was going forward, came up to my assistance; and by putting the things in carefully, and stamping them down, layer after layer, we managed to stow away more than I had conceived possible.

'I think I could find room for some of them in my chest, as we have been to sea for some time, and a good many of my own have been expended; and, I daresay, the other fellows will be equally ready to oblige you,' said Tom.

I was delighted at the proposal, and hastened to accept it, —but I didn't find it quite so easy to get them back again! Tom, however, soon smelt out the cake. At first he suggested that it would be safe in his chest, but Chaffey coming by, also discovered it; and though he was most anxious to take charge of it for me, Tom, knowing very well what would be its fate, insisted on its being carried into the berth. I need hardly say that by the end of tea-time it had disappeared.

I had no difficulty in finding Larry, when I at length set forth in quest of him. The sound of his fiddle drew me to the spot, where, surrounded by a party of admiring shipmates, he was scraping away as happy as a prince. On catching sight of me, he sprang out of the circle.

' Och, Misther Terence, I'm mighty glad to see you; but shure I didn't know you at first in your new clothes. I hope you like coming to sea as much as myself. Shure it's rare fun we're having in this big ship; and is his honour the major gone home again?'

I told him that I concluded such was the case, and how pleased I was to find that he liked his life on board,—though it didn't occur to me at the time that not having as yet been put to perform any special duty, he fancied he was always to lead the idle life he had hitherto been enjoying. We were both of us doomed ere long to discover that things don't always run smoothly at sea.

CHAPTER VII

THE frigate was not yet ready for sea, and I had therefore time to pick up some scraps of nautical knowledge, to learn the ways of the ship, and to get a tolerable notion of my duties. I quickly mastered the rules and regulations of the service, a copy of which Jack Nettleship gave me.

'Stick by them, my lad, and you can't go wrong; if you do, it's their fault, not yours,' he observed.

'But suppose I don't understand them?' I asked.

'Then you can plead in justification that they are not sufficiently clear for an ordinary comprehension,' he answered. 'I do when I make a mistake, and old Rough-and-Ready is always willing to receive my excuses, as he can't spell them out very easily himself, though they are his constant study day and night. Indeed, I doubt if he reads anything else, except Norrie's *Navigation* and the *Nautical Almanack*.'

Nettleship showed me a copy of the former work, and kindly undertook to instruct me in the science of navigation, All day long, however, he was employed in the duties of the ship, and in the evening I was generally sleepy when it was our watch below, so that I didn't make much progress. Though I got on very well, I was guilty, I must own, of not a few blunders. I was continually going aft when I intended to be going forward, and *vice versa*.

The day after I came aboard I was skylarking with Tom

Pim, Chaffey, and other midshipmites (as the oldsters called us), when I told them that I would hide, and that they might find me if they could. I ran up the after-ladder, when seeing a door open, I was going to bolt through it. Just then a marine, who was standing there, placed his musket to bar my way. Not wishing to be stopped, I dodged under it, turning round and saying,—

'Arrah, boy ! don't be after telling where I'm gone to.'

The sentry, for such he was, not understanding me, seized hold of my collar.

'You mustn't be going in there, whoever you are,' he said in a gruff tone.

'I'm a midshipman of this ship, and have a right to go wherever I like, I'm after thinking,' I said, trying to shake myself clear of his grasp. 'Hush, now ; be pleasant, will ye, and do as I order you !'

'I shouldn't be finding it very pleasant if I was to break through the rules and regulations of the service,' he answered. 'Now go forward, young gentleman, and don't be attempting to playing any of your tricks on me.'

'I'm your officer, and I order you not to interfere with me, or say where I'm gone,' I exclaimed.

'I obey no orders except from my own lieutenant or the captain and the lieutenants of the ship,' answered the sturdy marine. 'You can't go into the captain's cabin while I'm standing here as sentry ;' and he proceeded to use more force than was agreeable to my dignity.

'Shure you're an impudent fellow to behave so to an officer,' I exclaimed ; at which the sentry laughed, and said,—

'Off with you, Master Jackanapes, and consider yourself fortunate that worse hasn't come of your larking.'

Trying to look dignified, I answered,—

'You're an impudent fellow, and I shall make known your conduct to your superiors. I know your name, my fine fellow, so you'll not get off.' I had observed his name, as I thought, on his musket.

Just then Tom Pim popped his head above the hatchway,

and I, finding that I was discovered, made chase after him. He quickly distanced me; and as I was rushing blindly along, I ran my head right into the stomach of old Rough-and-Ready, who, as ill luck would have it, was on his way round the lower deck. I nearly upset him, and completely upset myself.

'Shure, sir, I never intended to behave so rudely,' I said, as, picking myself up, I discovered whom I had encountered.

'Go to the masthead, and stay there till I call you down,' thundered the lieutenant, rubbing the part of his body I had assaulted.

'Please, sir, I had no intention in the world of running against you,' I said, trying to look humble, but feeling much inclined to laugh at the comical expression of his countenance.

'Look to the rules and regulations of the service, where all inferiors are ordered to pay implicit obedience to their superiors,' cried Mr. Saunders. 'To the masthead with you.'

'If you please, sir, I should be happy to do that same if I knew the way; but I haven't been up there yet, as the men have been painting the rigging with some black stuff, and I should be after spoiling my new uniform,' I answered.

'Go to the masthead,' again shouted the first lieutenant; 'and you, Pim, go and show him the way,' he exclaimed, catching sight of Tom Pim, who was grinning at me from the other side of the deck.

Tom well knew that it was against the rules and regulations of the service to expostulate; therefore, saying, 'Come along, Paddy,' he led the way on deck.

'Do as I do,' he said, as he began to mount the rigging. Just hold on with your hands and feet, and don't let the rest of your body touch the rattlings or shrouds, and don't be letting go with one hand till you have got fast hold with the other.'

Up he went, and I followed. He was nimble as a monkey, so I had difficulty in keeping pace with him. Looking up, I saw him with his back almost horizontal above me, going along the futtock shrouds to get into the top. These are the shrouds which run from the side of the mast to the outer side of the top, and consequently a person going along them has his face to the sky and his back to the deck. Tom was over them in a moment, and out of sight. I didn't like the look of things, but did my best; and though he stood ready to give me a helping hand into the top, I got round without assistance. We now had to ascend the topmost rigging to the cross-trees, where we were to stay till called down. This was a comparatively easy matter, and as I didn't once cast my eyes below I felt no giddiness. Tom seated himself as if perfectly at home, and bade me cross my legs on the other side of the mast.

'It's lucky for you, Paddy, that you are able to gain your experience while the ship is in harbour and as steady as a church steeple. It would be a different matter if she were rolling away across the Bay of Biscay with a strong breeze right aft; so you ought to be duly thankful to old Saunders for mastheading you without waiting till we get there. And now I'd advise you to have a look at the rules and regulations of the service. It will please old Rough-and-Ready if you can tell him you have employed your time up here studying them, but don't forget you are up here, and go tumbling down on deck.'

I was very well disposed to follow Tom's advice, and I held tight on with one hand while I pulled the paper out of my pocket and read a page or two relating to obedience to superiors. Having thus relieved my conscience, I took a look round at the beautiful panorama in the midst of which the ship floated: the wooded banks, the magnificent harbour dotted over with numerous vessels; ships of war and merchantmen,—the latter waiting for convoy,—while among the former was the admiral's flag-ship riding proudly, surrounded by the smaller fry. The pretty town of Cove, with neat houses and villas on the one side, and the mouth of the river Lee, running down from Cork, to the westward.

Sooner than we expected we heard old Rough-and-Ready's voice summoning us down. He was not an ill-natured man. He knew well that my fault had been unintentional, and that Tom had certainly not deserved any punishment at all, for grinning at a brother midshipman in his presence could scarcely be considered disrespectful.

'You may go through the lubber's hole,' said Tom, when we reached the top.

'No, no. If you go round, I'll go to,' I answered. For being thus put on my mettle, I determined to do whatevei he did. By holding fast with my feet and following him, I managed to put them on the rattlings underneath, and thus, though I didn't like it at all, got down on to the main rigging.

'Next time you run along the deck, youngster, you'll look where you're going,' said the first lieutenant, when I reached the deck.

'Aye, aye, sir,' I said, touching my hat.

'Did you read the rules and regulations?' he asked.

'Yes, sir,' I answered; 'though I hadn't time to get through them all.'

He was pleased with the respect I paid him.

'Well, you'll know them by heart soon; and to ensure that, remember to take them with you whenever you're mast-headed.'

'Of course, sir, if you wish it,' I answered.

He gave a comical look at me under his bushy eyebrows, and turned on his heel.

After this I accompanied Tom into the berth. Old Nettle-ship was there. I told him of the way the marine had behaved, and said that for the sake of keeping up the dignity of the midshipmen, I considered it necessary to make his conduct known, though I had no ill-feeling towards the man himself.

At this remark the old mate burst into a hearty fit of laughter.

'Midshipmen generally find it necessary to carry their dignity in their pockets; and I'd advise you, Paddy, to put yours there, though I approve of your spirit. The man will have been relieved some time ago, and you'll find it difficult to recognise him among others.'

'Oh! I know his name,—it was Tower,' I said in a tone of confidence.

At this there was a general roar of laughter.

'According to your notion all the jollies are Towers,' cried

Nettleship, when he regained his voice. 'Why, Paddy, the muskets are all marked with the name of the Tower of London, where the arms are stored before they are served out.'

'Shure how should I know anything about the Tower of London?' I asked. 'I'm after thinking it's a poor place compared with Castle Ballinahone.'

This remark produced another roar of laughter from my messmates.

'What are you after laughing at?' I exclaimed. 'If any of you will honour us with a visit at Castle Ballinahone, you'll be able to compare the two places, and my father and mother, and brothers and sisters, will be mighty plaised to see you.'

The invitation was at once accepted by all hands, though for the present my family were pretty safe from the chances of an inundation of nautical heroes.

'And what sort of girls are your sisters?' asked Sims, who, I had discovered, was always ready for some impudence.

'Shure they're Irish young ladies, and that's all I intend to say about them,' I answered, giving him a look which made him hold his tongue.

Still, in spite of the bantering I received, I got on wonderfully well with my new messmates; and though I had a fight now and then, I generally, being older than many of them, and stronger than others who had been some time at sea, came off victorious; and as I was always ready to befriend, and never bullied, my weaker messmates, I was on very good terms with all of them.

Tom Pim took a liking to me from the first, and though he didn't require my protection, I felt ready to afford it him on all occasions. He was sometimes quizzed by Sims and others for his small size. 'I don't mind it,' he answered. 'Though I'm little, I'm good. If I've a chance, I'll do something to show what's in me.' The chance came sooner than he expected. There were a good many raw hands lately entered, Larry among others. From the first he showed no fear of going aloft, looking upon the business much as he would have done climbing a high tree; but how the ropes were rove, and what

were their uses, he naturally had no conception. 'Is it to
the end of them long boughs there I've got to go, Misther
Terence?' he asked the first time he was ordered aloft, looking
up at the yards as he encountered me, I having been sent
forward with an order to the third lieutenant.

'There's no doubt about it, Larry,' I said; ' but take care
you catch hold of one rope before you let go of the other,' said
I, giving him the same advice which I had myself received.

'Shure I'll be after doing that same, Misther Terence,' he
answered, as, following the example of the other men, he
sprang into the rigging. I watched him going up as long as
I could, and he seemed to be getting on capitally, exactly
imitating the movements of the other men.

A day or two afterwards we were all on deck, the men
exercising in reefing and furling sails. The new hands were
ordered to lay out on the yards, and a few of the older ones to
show them what to do. Larry obeyed with alacrity; no one
would have supposed that he had been only a few times before
aloft. I had to return to the quarter-deck, where I was standing with Tom Pim, and we were remarking the activity displayed by the men. I saw Larry on the starboard fore-topsail
yard-arm, and had just left Tom, being sent with a message to
the gun-room, when, as my head was flush with the hatchway,
I saw an object drop from the yard-arm into the water. It
looked more like a large ball falling than a human being, and
it didn't occur to me that it was the latter until I heard the
cry of 'Man overboard!' Hastening up again, I sprang into
the mizzen rigging, from which, just before I got there, Tom
Pim had plunged off into the water. It was ebb tide, and a
strong current was running out of the river Lee past the ship.
The man who had fallen had not sunk, but was fast drifting
astern, and seemed unconscious, for he was not struggling,
lying like a log on the water. Tom Pim, with rapid strokes,
was swimming after him. I heard the order given to lower a
boat. Though not a great swimmer, I was about to follow
Tom to try and help him, when a strong arm held me
back.

'Are you a good swimmer, youngster?' asked the first lieutenant, the person who had seized hold of me.

'Not very,' I answered.

'Then stay aboard, or we shall be having to pick you up instead of saving the man who fell overboard. I know Pim well; he'll take care of himself.'

Saying this, the lieutenant stepped in on deck again, taking me with him. While he superintended the lowering of the boat, I ran aft, and watched Tom and the drowning man. Just then I caught sight of the countenance of the latter, and to my dismay, I saw that he was no other than Larry Harrigan. The boats usually employed were away, and the one now lowered was not in general use, and consequently had in her all sorts of things which should not have been there. It appeared a long time before she was in the water. I watched my poor foster-brother with intense anxiety, expecting to see him go down before Tom could reach him. He was on the point of sinking when my gallant little messmate got up to him, and throwing himself on his back, placed Larry's head on his own breast, so as completely to keep it out of the water. My fear was that Larry might come to himself and begin to struggle or get hold of Tom, which might be fatal to both. They were drifting farther and farther away from the ship. Tom had not uttered one cry for help, evidently being confident that the boat would be sent to pick them up. Every movement of his showed that he was calm, and knew perfectly what he was about. At length the boat was got into the water, the first lieutenant and four hands jumped into her, and away the men pulled as fast as they could lay their backs to the oars. It was blowing fresh, and there was a good deal of ripple in the harbour, so that the wavelets every now and then washed over Tom. Suddenly Larry, coming to himself, did what I feared; he seized hold of Tom, and in another instant would have dragged him down had not Tom dexterously got clear and held him up by the collar of his shirt. The boat was quickly up to them, and they were, to my intense satisfaction, safely hauled on board. She then rapidly pulled back to the ship, and both greatly exhausted, Larry being scarcely conscious, were lifted up on deck. M'Pherson, the assistant-surgeon, who had been summoned at once, ordered Tom to be taken below.

'Never mind me,' said Tom; 'I shall be all to rights presently, when I've changed and had a cup of grog. You'll let me have that, won't you, M'Pherson? And now you go and attend to the poor fellow who wants you more than I do.'

'Vara true; he ought, from the way he fell, to have broken every bone in his body; and it's wonderful he did not do it. He seems, indeed, not to be much the worse for his fall, except a slight paralysis,' he remarked when he had finished his examination. 'Take him down to the sick bay, and I'll treat him as he requires.'

I first went below to thank Tom Pim for saving my follower, and to express my admiration of his courage and resolution.

'Oh, it's nothing,' he answered; 'I can swim better than you, or you'd have done the same.'

I then went forward, where I found Larry—his wet clothes stripped off—between the blankets, in a hammock.

The doctor administered a stimulant, and directed that he should be rubbed on the side on which he had fallen.

'Shure that's a brave young gentleman to save me from going to the bottom, Misther Terence dear; and I'll be mighty grateful to him as long as I live,' he said to me.

Having spent some time with Larry, who was ordered to remain in his hammock, I returned to the midshipmen's berth.

All were loud in their praises of Tom. Tom received them very modestly, and said that though he felt very glad at being able to save the poor fellow, he didn't see anything to be especially proud of in what he had done.

By the next morning Larry was almost well, only complaining of a little stiffness in one side of the body.

'He may thank his stars for being an Irishman,' said M'Pherson; 'no ordinary mortal could have fallen from aloft as he did, into the water, without breaking his bones, or being stunned.'

Larry could scarcely believe that it was little Tom Pim who had saved him from drowning.

'Shure, young gintleman, I'll be after lovin' ye, and fightin' for ye, and seein' that no harm comes to ye, all the days of my life!' he exclaimed, the first time he met Tom afterwards on deck. 'I'm mighty grateful to ye, sir, that I am.'

I was very sure that Larry meant what he said, and, should opportunity offer, would carry out his intentions.

We were seated talking in the berth after tea, when old Nettleship was sent for into the cabin. There were many surmises as to what the captain wanted him for. After some time, to my surprise, I was summoned. I found it was only Nettleship that wanted to see me on deck.

'Paddy,' he said, 'we are to have an expedition on shore, and you are wanted to take part in it, and so is your country-man, Larry Harrigan. The captain, Mr. Saunders, and I have planned it. We want some more hands, and we hear that there are a goodish lot hiding away in the town. They are waiting till the men-of-war put to sea, when they think that they will be safe. They are in the hands of some cunning fellows, and it'll be no easy matter to trap them unless we can manage to play them a trick. I can't say that I like particu-larly doing what we propose, but we're bound to sacrifice our own feelings for the good of the service.'

'What is it?' I asked. 'Of course I should be proud to be employed in anything for the good of the service.'

'All right, Paddy; that's the spirit which should animate you. Now listen. Mr. Saunders and I are going on shore with a strong party of well-armed men, and we want you and the boy Harrigan—or rather, the captain wants you, for remember he gives the order—to go first and pretend that you have run away from a man-of-war, and want to be kept in hiding till she has sailed. You, of course, are to dress up as seamen in old clothes—the more disreputable and dirty you look the better. We know the houses where the men are stowed away, in the lowest slums of Cork, and we can direct you to them. You're to get into the confidence of the men, and learn what they intend doing; when you've gained that, you're to tell them that one of the lieutenants of your ship is going on shore with a small party of men, to try and press anybody he can find, and that you don't think he knows much about the business, as he is a stupid Englishman, and advise them to lie snug where they are. Then either you or Harrigan can offer to creep out and try and ascertain in what direction the press-gang is going. There are several houses together, with passages leading from one to the other, so that if we get into one, the men are sure to bolt off into another; and it must be your business to see where they go, and Harrigan must shut the door to prevent their escape, or open it to let us in. I now only describe the outlines of our plan. I'll give you more particulars as we pull up the river. We shall remain at Passage till after dark, and you and your companion in the meanwhile must make your way into the town.'

'But shure won't I be after telling a lie if I say that Larry and I are runaway ship-boys?' I asked.

'Hush, that's a strong expression. Remember that it's all for the good of the service,' said Nettleship.

Still I was not altogether satisfied that the part I was about to play was altogether an honourable one.

He, however, argued the point with me, acknowledging that he himself didn't think so, but that we were bound to put our private feelings into our pockets when the good of the service required it. He now told me to go and speak to Larry, but on no account to let any one hear me, lest the expedition might get wind among the bumboat women, who would be sure to convey it on shore.

To my surprise, Larry was perfectly prepared to undertake the duty imposed on him, feeling flattered at being employed, and taking rather a pleasure at the thoughts of having to entrap some of our countrymen.

'They may grumble a little at first, but they'll be a mighty deal better off on board ship than digging praties, or sailing in one of those little craft out there,' he said, with a look of contempt at the merchant vessels.

Mr. Saunders took me into his cabin, and made me rig out in a suit of clothes supplied by the purser. I had to rub my hair about till it was like a mop; then, with some charcoal and a mixture of some sort, he daubed my face over in such a way that I didn't know myself when I looked in his shaving-glass.

'You'll do, Paddy,' said Nettleship when he saw me. 'We must be giving a touch or two to Harrigan. He seems a sharp fellow, and will play his part well, I have no doubt.'

In a short time the boats were ready. We went with Mr. Saunders and Nettleship in the pinnace. She was accompanied by the jolly-boat, which it was intended should convey Larry and me into the neighbourhood of the town. We were, however, not to go on board her until we reached Passage. The crew gave way, and as the tide was in our favour we got along rapidly. I found that the expedition we were engaged in was a hazardous one, especially for Larry and me; for should the men we were in search of discover who we were, they might treat us as spies, and either knock our brains out, or stow us away in some place from which we should not be likely to make our escape. This, however, rather enhanced the interest I began to feel in it, and recompensed me for its doubtful character.

Neither Mr. Saunders nor Nettleship looked in the slightest degree like officers of the Royal Navy. They were dressed in Flushing coats; the lieutenant in a battered old sou'-wester, with a red woollen comforter round his throat; Nettleship had on an equally ancient-looking tarpaulin, and both wore high-boots, long unacquainted with blacking. They carried stout cudgels in their hands, their hangers and pistols being concealed under their coats. In about an hour and a half we reached Passage, when Nettleship and Larry and I got into the jolly-boat.

'I'm going with you,' said Nettleship, 'that I may direct you to the scene of operations, and am to wait for Mr.

5

Saunders at the "Fox and Goose,"—a small public-house, the master of which knows our object and can be trusted.'

Nettleship, as we pulled away, minutely described over and over again what Larry and I were to do, so that I thought there was no chance of our making any mistake, provided matters went as he expected. It was dark by the time we reached Cork. The boat pulled into the landing-place, and Larry and I, with two of the men, went ashore, and strolled lazily along a short distance, looking about us. This we did in case we should be observed; but on reaching the corner, Larry and I, as we had been directed, set off running, when the two men returned to the boat, which was to go to another landing-place a little way higher up, whence Nettleship and his party were to proceed to our rendezvous. When we had got a little distance we pulled up, and to be certain that we had made no mistake, we inquired the name of the street of a passer-by. We found that we were all right. We now proceeded stealthily along to the lane where Mother M'Cleary's whisky-shop was situated. I had no difficulty in recognising the old woman, as she had been well described to me. Her stout slatternly figure, her bleared eyes, her grog-blossomed nose,—anything but a beauty to look at. Her proceedings were not beautiful either. Going to the end of the counter where she was standing, I tipped her a wink.

'Hist, mither! Can yer be after taking care of two poor boys for a night or so?' I asked.

'Where do yer come from?' she inquired, eyeing us.

'Shure it's from the say,' answered Larry, who had undertaken to be chief spokesman. 'We've just run away from a thundering big king's ship, and don't want to go back again.'

'Why for?' asked the old woman.

'For fear of a big baste of a cat which may chance to score our backs, if she doesn't treat us worse than that.'

CHAPTER VIII.

'THAT'S a big thundering lie,' I heard Larry whisper.

'Come in,' said the old woman, lifting up the flap of the counter. 'I'll house yer if yer can pay for yer board and lodging.'

'No fear of that, ma'am,' I replied, showing some silver which I had ready in my pocket for the purpose.

'Come along, my boys,' she answered, her eyes twinkling at the thought of being able to fleece us, as she led us into a small room at the back of the shop.

There was no one else in the place at the time, except a boy attending to the counter, so that there was little chance of our being observed. Having lit a small lantern, the old woman drew aside a curtain at the further end of the room, which had served to conceal a strong-looking door; then taking a big key out of her pocket, she opened it, and told us to go through. Carefully closing the door behind her, she led the way along a narrow dark passage. It seemed of considerable length. At last we reached another door, and emerged into a court or alley, crossing which she opened a third door, and told us to pass through. We obeyed, and followed her past a couple of rooms, in one of which several men were sitting, drinking and smoking. Unlocking another door, she showed us into a much larger apartment than any we had as yet seen. Though low, it was spacious enough to be called a hall. I took in the appearance of the place at a glance. On one side was a recess with a counter before it, at which a couple of damsels were serving out liquors and various sorts of provisions. At the further end, four large casks supported some planks which served as a platform, and on this a chair was placed,—the seat being evidently for a musician. Three doors besides the one by which we had entered opened from the room, which was occupied by a dozen or more rough-looking men, mostly sailors. Some were standing at the counter, others lounging on benches round the walls, most of them having dhudeens in their mouths. The place was redolent with the fumes of whisky and tobacco. No one took notice of us as we entered, but, seeing Mother M'Cleary, seemed satisfied that all was right.

'You'll find a stair through that doorway,' she said, pointing to one near the orchestra, if so it could be called; 'it will lead you to the sleeping-room, where you'll be after finding some beds. You'll remember that first come first served, and if you don't be tumbling into one it will be your own fault, and you'll have to prick for the softest plank in the corner of the room. Now, boys, you'll be after handing me out a couple of shillings each. I don't give credit, except to those I happen to know better than I do you.'

I paid the money at once for Larry and myself. The old woman, bidding us make ourselves at home, returned by the way she had come, locking the door behind her. I soon found that we were among as ruffianly and disreputable a set of fellows as I had ever fallen in with, but none of them interfered with us, and I began to doubt whether we should obtain the information we were in search of. To try to get into conversation with some one, we walked up to the counter, took a pork pie apiece, and called for a glass of whisky, which we prudently mixed with plenty of water. 'Don't be drinking much of it,' I said to Larry, 'it's as hot as fire.'

Two seamen then came up, and I asked one of them when the fun was to begin. 'Arrah, then it'll be before long, when Tim Curtin, the fiddler, has come to himself; but he's been drunk all the blessed morning, since last night, and they're dousing him outside with cold water to bring him to.' My new acquaintance being evidently inclined to be communicative, I plied him with further questions, and I gained his confidence by calling for another glass of whisky, with which I insisted on treating him. I, however, let Larry carry on the chief part of the conversation.

'If you've run from a man-of-war, you'll have to lie snug as mice in their holes till she sails, or there's three dozen at least for each of you, if they don't run you up at the yard-arm, as they did at Portsmouth the other day to a poor boy, just because he wanted to go home to his wife and family,' said the man.

This, though a fact as far as the hanging was concerned, I hadn't heard of before. Larry didn't show that he doubted the truth of the story, but pretended to be very frightened.

'Thin what should we be after doing?' he asked.

'Why, as I tell yer,' he said, 'keep close; you'll be wise not to show your noses out of doors for a week or two to come, if you've got money enough to pay old Mother M'Cleary, for she doesn't keep us boys for nothing, you may stake yer davey.'

'What should we be after doing, then, supposing the press-gang were to come down upon us and find us out?' asked Larry.

'It will be at the end of a long day before the press-gang get in here; but see now, there's a room overhead where you can sleep secure, either in bed or out of it. Then there's that door in the middle of the room, that leads to a long passage, just like the one you passed through when you came in here. At the end of it there's a court, and on the opposite side you'll find a door. Go through that when it opens, which it will do when you have given three raps quick together, and you'll be in a house with well nigh as many rooms and cellars as there's days in the month. It will be a hard matter if you don't stow yourselves away out of sight in one of them. I'll be after showing you the way by and by, when the dancing is over, and we've had a few more glasses of Mother M'Cleary's whisky.'

While our friend, whose name we had not as yet learned, was speaking, I observed several more persons entering the room; and presently others came in, carrying among them a humpbacked little fellow, with a fiddle under his arm, who seemed scarcely able to walk by himself. They made their way to the platform I have described, and speedily lifted him into the chair.

'Strike up, Tim,' cried several voices. 'Give us a tune to set our feet agoing. Be alive, man, if you know now where you are.'

Tim, though apparently half-asleep, put his fiddle to his chin, and began scraping away, nodding his head and stamping with his foot in time to the tune he was eliciting from his instrument. The effect was magical. The whole party, men and women,—there were not a few of the latter, not among the most refined of their sex,—began dancing jigs. Tim next played slower, but his speed increased again as he saw the dancers warming to their work, till his bow moved so rapidly over the strings of his fiddle, and his arm and his head gave such eccentric jerks, that I half expected at any moment to see the one fly off at a tangent and the other come bounding into the middle of the room. Larry and I kept on one side, trying to look greatly interested with the performance, while we managed to have a few words now and then with some of the men, who were either seated on the benches or standing against the wall. Among them were several who had not the appearance of seamen, and who, I surmised, were highwaymen or housebreakers. Two of them were especially ruffianly looking. As I examined the countenance of one of these, I felt convinced that I had seen it before, and not long ago either. I was careful, however, that he should not discover that I was observing him. I took an opportunity of asking Larry if he knew who the man was.

'Shure it's no other than Dan Hoolan himself,' he answered.

I fancied that at length his keen eyes were directed on Larry, whom he was more likely to recognize than me, seeing that I was the most completely disguised of the two.

At length, having gained all the information we could, I determined to try and get out of the place, so that I might make my way to Nettleship, and show him the best situation for posting his men to capture any who might attempt to escape. It had been arranged that Nettleship's party was to enter the grog-shop one by one; then, at a signal, force their way along the passage through which Mother M'Cleary had led us.

'I'm mighty afraid the press-gang will be coming this way, and if this hullaballoo reaches their ears, they'll be after putting their noses in to see what the fun is about. If they're from our own ship, bedad, we shall be worse off than we would have been outside,' I said to our new acquaintance, who, by this time, was not quite steady on his pins. 'I'd just like to slip away, and try and find out if they're near this at all. My mate here is plaised to stay behind, as he's mighty eager to dance himself.'

After further pressing the point with all necessary caution, our new friend, Barney Reillagan, as he called himself, offered to show me the way out, and to let me in again when I wished to return.

'You're free of the place, I'm supposing; and shure I am that I may be after trusting you,' he observed as he accompanied me into the passage I spoke of.

I hoped that we were unobserved by Hoolan or any of the other men, who might have suspicions of my true character. Larry followed so noiselessly, that I do not think Barney was aware he was with us. Larry's object was to see that no harm came to me; and besides which, he wanted to learn how to let me in again on my return. Barney himself was apparently an open-hearted seaman, who preferred serving on board a peaceable trader to a man-of-war, and I had no fear of his playing me false.

We had to grope our way to the end of the passage, which was as long as he had described. Unbolting a door, Barney led me out into a narrow court. I could hear even there the strains of the fiddle, and the shouts and screams of the dancers. Barney told me that if I turned to the left I should come to a narrow archway, which led into the lane, and that by turning again to the left, I should come to the front of Mother M'Cleary's whisky-shop.

This information was sufficient to enable me to find my way without difficulty. I was somewhat surprised at the ease with which I had made my escape. I had little doubt of being able to bring Nettleship and his men up to the right place. My only anxiety was about Larry, who, if recognised by Dan Hoolan, might be severely handled, if not killed,— for so determined a ruffian was not likely to hesitate in committing any act, however atrocious, should he suspect Larry of treachery.

I slipped out into the court, and Barney closed the door after me. The night was very dark; but I could see two or three shadowy forms flitting by, though no one stopped me. Now and then a ruffian voice, a wild shriek, or a child's cry, came from the narrow windows looking into the court. I walked on as fast as I could venture to move, till I found the narrow archway which Barney had described, and emerged into a lane, which, however, was not much broader than the court. Here the sounds of wrangling voices, and shouts, and the drunkards' wild songs, broke the stillness of night. A few men rolled by, who had come out of Mother M'Cleary's whisky-shop, or other similar establishments; but I carefully kept out of their way till I arrived at the 'Fox and Goose,' where I expected to find Nettleship. It hadn't occurred to me, however, that I might have been followed, and our plan for trapping the seamen discovered. I at once entered, and found my messmate with his men ready to set out.

'You've been longer than I expected, Paddy; but I hope it's all right,' he said.

'If we are quick about it, I expect we shall catch a good number,' I answered. 'Where is Mr. Saunders? We shall require a strong party to overpower the fellows, especially as there are some desperate ruffians among them;' and I told him how I had discovered the outlaw, Dan Hoolan,

'Mr. Saunders is waiting just outside, round the corner,' he said. 'I'll go out and tell him that you have come back, and meanwhile you remain here.'

In a short time Nettleship returned.

'You are to accompany Mr. Saunders,' he said, 'and lead his party round to the court, while I and my men take charge of Mother M'Cleary, so that no one may escape on this side.'

Mr. Saunders welcomed me in a good-natured voice.

'You have done well thus far, my lad. I've no doubt that we shall trap some of them,' he said, when I had given a description of the place and the characters it contained. 'I have got hold of a man who knows the town, and will lead us round by a different way to the court to that by which you escaped, while Nettleship goes directly up the lane,' he added. 'Come along!'

We set out at a rapid rate; the men being charged to make as little noise with their feet as possible. We must have gone a considerable way round, for it seemed a long while before we reached the archway, which I at once recognised. The lieutenant led, with a pistol in one hand and his hanger in the other, knowing that he was likely to be treated with scant ceremony should he encounter any of the residents of that neighbourhood.

'Now,' he said to me, stopping, 'do you creep forward and learn if Harrigan is at the door ready to open it. If not, wait to get in yourself, and then take the first opportunity of admitting us. If you can't get in we must try and force the door open, but it would be a great matter to get along the passage, so as to rush in upon the fellows while they are at their revels, and before they expect our approach.'

As he spoke we could hear the sound of Tim Curtin's fiddle, and the hum of voices coming from the interior of the building. Our fear was that any of the inmates of the neighbouring dens might be awake, and, catching sight of us, might give the alarm, and allow the men time to escape. As far as I had learned, however, the door we were now watching and Mother

M'Cleary's whisky-shop were the only outlets, though there
might be underground passages and cellars and holes, where,
should they stow themselves away, we might find it difficult
to discover them.

As I crept forward, I felt my heart beating more than it
was wont to do,—not from fear, certainly, but from anxiety
to succeed.   I didn't like the business; I considered it a
dirty one; but I was acting according to my orders, and for
the good of the service.   I had been told to give three rapid
knocks, followed by others at short intervals, at the opposite
door, and I concluded that this would be opened should I
make the same signal.   Without loss of a moment I knocked,
and presently I heard a bolt withdrawn, then another and
another.

'Is that yourself?' asked a voice that I knew to be Larry's.

'Yes, to be shure, and no other,' I answered in the same
tone.

The door opened slightly.

'They're suspecting me,' said Larry.   'Be quick.

Mr. Saunders, who was on the watch, hearing this, dashed
forward, followed by his men.   They sprang, led by the
lieutenant, one after the other, into the passage, nearly
knocking Larry and me over.   There was not a moment to
be lost, we knew, for the door at the further end was closed
with a loud slam before we reached it, but not being as strong
as the one on the outside, it was quickly battered in, when
we caught sight of a dozen or more fellows, some trying
to escape up-stairs, others through the two passages I have
mentioned.   Three or four of the men, however, stood their
ground in front of the passage leading to the whisky-shop,
with hangers or pistols in their hands, which they apparently
had just taken up from the corner of the room where they had
deposited them.   Among these I recognized Dan Hoolan.
Bestowing a not very complimentary epithet on Larry and me,
he flourished his hanger and dared any one to come on and
touch him.

'I and my friends here are not seamen,' he exclaimed.

'You're after trying to press some of the poor fellows, I suppose; but if any man tries to lay hands on me, he'll be wise to say his prayers before he begins.'

'I intend to lay hands on you, and every fellow I find here,' said Mr. Saunders. 'Drop your hanger, or you'll have to repent the day you drew it.'

Hoolan answered with a scornful laugh, and made a blow at the lieutenant, who, however, parried it.

At that moment the door behind him was burst open, and in rushed Nettleship and his party, who threw themselves at once upon Hoolan. The outlaw fired his pistol at my head, but fortunately his arm was thrown up, and the ball struck the ceiling. His men, seeing their leader overpowered, made but little resistance. But we had not yet got the men whose capture was desired. Mr. Saunders, leaving Nettleship to secure those below, followed Larry and me up the stairs.

In the meantime the female part of the assemblage, some of whom had retired to different parts of the room, were saluting us with the most fearful cries and execrations. The lieutenant, however, took no more notice of them than if they had been so many lambs bleating, and at once hurried up the stairs to the room above, where we found well-nigh a score of men, some trying to make their way out of the window, but which, having been closed, they had only just then succeeded in opening; others hiding inside the beds or under them. Three or four got away, but the remainder were knocked over by our men, or captured without resistance, scarcely any attempting to defend themselves. Our success had been as complete as could have been hoped for. Our captives were quickly dragged down the stairs, when Mr. Saunders ordered the women to clear out of the house forthwith, and proceeded to lash the hands of the men behind their backs. It was very easy to give the order to the women, but not so easy to get it obeyed. They shrieked and abused us in a way in which few of the female sex can beat the lower orders of my countrywomen. At length, however, finding that their eloquence had no effect, they retreated through the door that we had left open. It turned out that the means of escape were not so elaborate as had been supposed, and, as far as we could learn, all the men in the neighbourhood had on this occasion collected at Mother M'Cleary's. Most of those we had captured behaved quietly enough, but Hoolan and two or three others made violent efforts to escape, till a prog or two from a cutlass compelled them to be quiet.

'And what are you going to do with me, a landsman who never was to sea in his life?' exclaimed Hoolan.

'We shall turn you into a sailor before long, my fine fellow,' answered Mr. Saunders. 'You'll be wiser to walk along, and quietly too, as we've no time for nonsense.'

Our prisoners were now marshalled, in most cases with a seaman to attend to each. Hoolan had two to look after him, though one guard sufficed for some of the more peaceably disposed. Nettleship led the way, and Mr. Saunders and I brought up the rear, Larry being employed in guarding a fellow twice his size, with orders to cut him down if he made any resistance.

'We must be out of this as fast as we can,' said Mr. Saunders to me, 'for very likely those fellows who made their escape will rouse their friends, and we may have a mob of all the ruffians in the town upon us before we can reach the boats.'

What had become of Mother M'Cleary and her assistants we could not tell. She probably thought it wise to keep out of the way, lest any of her late guests might suspect her of betraying them, as she probably had done. We had not got more than half-way towards the boats, when our ears were saluted by a chorus of yells and shrieks, and we could distinguish through the gloom on either side of us a mass of human beings, apparently intending to attempt the rescue of our prisoners.

'I warn you, good people, that if you come nearer, I'll give my men orders to fire on you,' shouted my lieutenant.

A volley of wild yells burst from the mob, sufficient to unnerve many who had not before heard such cries. Directly
afterwards a brickbat flew past my head, aimed, no doubt, at
the more prominent figure of the lieutenant. Fortunately, it
missed us both.

'Remember, if any of you are killed, you'll have brought the
punishment on yourselves,' again shouted the lieutenant.

Though the people yelled as before, the warning had its
effect, and we could see the dark moving mass retreating to
a more respectful distance. They, apparently, only wanted
a leader to make an onslaught. That leader, however, was
not to be found. Had Hoolan been at liberty, I have no
doubt but that we should have fared but ill. As it was,
missiles from a distance came flying by us, though the prisoners
suffered more than we did. Mr. Saunders was naturally
anxious to avoid bloodshed. At length the boats were
reached. Again Hoolan made a desperate effort to get free,
but he was hauled on board, and thrust down to the bottom
of the pinnace, the rest of the men being disposed of, some
in her, and others in the jolly-boat, of which Nettleship took
charge. As we shoved off the people collected on the quay,
saluting us with renewed yells and execrations, and brickbats,
stones, mud, and filth were hurled at us. We speedily, however,
got beyond their reach, no one receiving any serious damage.

'We've made a fine haul,' observed Mr. Saunders as we
pulled down the river. 'We shall soon turn these fellows into
good seamen, as obedient and quiet as lambs.'

'I'm thinking, sir, that you'll not find Dan Hoolan as quiet
as a lamb,' I observed; and I told him of the encounter my
uncle and I had had with the outlaw and his followers.

'That'll make no difference,' answered Mr. Saunders.
'When he finds that he can't escape, if he's got any sense in
his brains he'll bend to circumstances.'

I still, however, doubted whether my lieutenant's opinion
would prove right.

When the boats arrived alongside the frigate, our captives,
being unable to help themselves, were hoisted up like bales

of goods, and made to stand on the deck in a line. They all looked sulky enough as the lantern was held up to their faces; but Hoolan's countenance wore a ferocious aspect, which made me think that it would have been as well to have left him on shore to be hanged, which in all probability would ultimately have been his fate. Mr. Saunders had changed his rough dress for his proper uniform, and as he went round to inspect the prisoners Hoolan recognized him, and so savage did he look that I thought he would have sprung at his throat.

'Are you the captain of the ship?' he asked in a fierce tone.

'No, I'm not the captain, but an officer, who you'll be compelled to obey,' answered Mr. Saunders, interrupting him. 'Keep down what was rising to your tongue, or it'll be the worse for you.'

'I'm no seaman, and I don't want to be after going to sea; and I beg you to tell me for what reason you knocked me down against the law?'

'You were found among seamen, and if you're not one we'll make you one before long, my fine fellow,' said the lieutenant.

'Arrah, it'll be a hard matter to do that same,' cried Hoolan, but he spoke in a less savage tone than at first.

'We shall see to that,' said Mr. Saunders as he passed on to the other men, most of whom appeared quiet enough. Even Hoolan's followers didn't venture to say anything, having a just conception of the stern discipline on board a man-of-war. The execution of one or more seamen for frequent desertion, of which I have before spoken, showed them that they could not venture to play tricks with impunity.

Having had their names,—or such as they chose to give,— ages, and other particulars entered, they were sent down to the main-deck under a strong guard, with a hint that should they exhibit the slightest degree of insubordination it would be the worse for them.

The light of a lantern happened to fall on my face while I

was passing Hoolan, who, with the rest, were seated on the deck, where they were to pass the remainder of the night. He started up, and glaring savagely at me, with a fierce oath exclaimed, as he stretched out his arm,—

'There's one of the young traitors who brought us into this trouble. I wish we had strung you up to St. Bridget's oak when we had you and your uncle in our power.'

'Then, as I thought, you are Dan Hoolan,' I said. 'You have now a chance of leading an honest life, and I'd advise you to take advantage of it.'

Hoolan, without replying, sank back on the deck.

I was glad enough to turn in, and slept soundly till the hammocks were piped up next morning.

On coming on deck I saw Blue Peter flying at the masthead of our own ship, and at those of the two other men-of-war, a frigate and a corvette, and of all the merchantmen. The admiral fired a signal-gun. We repeated it, and before the smoke had cleared away the merchantmen let fall their topsails, we setting them the example; the anchor was hove up to the merry sound of the fife, and, taking the lead, we stood out of the Cove of Cork with a fair breeze, the other frigate and corvette acting as whippers-in.

The sky was clear and the sea smooth. We hove-to outside to wait for the vessels we were to convoy. In half an hour or so they were all out of the harbour. Besides the men-of-war there were fully sixty merchantmen; and a beautiful sight they presented, dotting the blue ocean with their white sails.

We were bound out to Jamaica, where we were to leave the larger number of vessels, and proceed with the others to their several destinations, having then to return to Port Royal. Two line-of-battle ships came out afterwards to convoy the fleet till we were well away from the coast, that, should we be seen by an enemy, it might be supposed that we were too strong a force to be attacked.

I should have said that when we were getting under weigh I saw Hoolan, and the other pressed men, dressed as man-of-war's men, working away at the capstan. He evidently didn't like his task, but could not help himself, as he had to go round with the others pressing against the capstan bars. He and the other landsmen were set to perform such work as they were capable of, of course being compelled to pull and haul when sail was made or shortened.

'I'm after thinking, Mr. Terence, that Dan Hoolan, though he's mighty quiet just now, will be playing us some prank or other before long, if he can find a chance,' observed Larry to me.

'Well, then, Larry, just keep an eye on him, and let me know what he's about. I don't want to make you an eaves-dropper, but for the man's own sake he must not be allowed to attempt any mischief. He'd be sure to have the worst of it.'

'Arrah now, of course he would, Mr. Terence. They're honest boys aboard here, and they'd soon clap him in limbo,' observed Larry as I passed on along the deck.

He had already become thoroughly imbued with the right spirit of a British seaman.

I gave myself, however, little concern about Hoolan after this.

For some time we had a favourable breeze; the sea was calm, and everything went smoothly. We had plenty of work keeping the squadron together, compelling the fast vessels to shorten sail, and the laggards to make it. Some ran on with only their topsails set. Others had studding-sails set on either side. We were all day long sending the bunting up and down, and firing guns as signals.

'Why are all those bits of coloured stuff hoisted to the masthead?' asked Larry. 'They tell me that the captain makes the young gentlemen run them up and down to keep their fingers warm.'

I explained to him that each flag represented a figure or number, and sometimes a word or a sentence, according to the distinguishing pennant hoisted over it. For which purpose every vessel was provided with a book of signals, and we could thus communicate with each other just as if we were speaking.

CHAPTER IX.

A FIGHT AT SEA.

THE ocean continued so calm, that Larry was quite cockahoop, thinking that he had become a perfect seaman. 'I have heard tell, Maisther Terence, that the say runs mountains high, for all the world like the hills of Connemara, but I'm after thinking that these are all landsmen's notions. We have been getting along for all the world like ducks in a pond.'

The very next day, Larry had a different tale to tell. In the morning the line-of-battle ships parted from us, and we, the *Amethyst* frigate, and the *Piper* corvette, had to continue our course alone, to protect our somewhat erratic convoy. Dark clouds were seen coming up from the northwest. The scud sped across the sky, the spon-drift flying over the fast rising seas. In a short time the ship began to pitch into them as if determined to hammer them down, but they, not inclined to receive such treatment patiently, sent masses of spray flying over our bows, as if to show what they were capable of doing, should she persevere in her attempt. The merchantmen on all sides were bobbing away, and kicking up their sterns in the same comical fashion; and even the other frigate and corvette were playing similar pranks. The tacks were got aboard, however, and on we all went together, now heeling over when a stronger blast than usual struck us, till the water came hissing in at our main-deck ports. Sail after sail was taken off the ship. Now she rose almost on an even

6

keel, and then again heeled over as before. The convoy
followed our example, though not with the same rapidity.
The sheets had been let go, and the sails of some were flying
wildly in the breeze. Three or four lost their loftier masts
and lighter spars, but they were still compelled to keep up by
the signals which we or the *Amethyst* threw out. At length
I had to go aloft. I could not say that I liked it. It seemed
to me that with the eccentric rolls the ship was making, I
might at any moment be jerked off into the seething ocean;
but I recollected Tom Pim's advice, and held on with teeth
and eyelids. I got on, however, very well while I was aloft,
and I managed somehow or other to reach the deck. Then—
oh! how truly miserable I began to feel. Every moment I
became worse and worse. As it happened, my watch was just
over, and I descended to the berth. When I got there my
head dropped on the table. I felt as I had never felt before;
as utterly unlike as could be the brave Tipperary boy I fancied
myself.

'Why, Paddy, what's come over you?' exclaimed Nettleship,
who had just then come below. 'Why, you look as if you had
heard the banshee howl, or dipped your face into a pot of
white paint.'

'Oh! oh!' I exclaimed, my lip curling, and feeling the
most miserable of human beings, so I fancied. I could utter
no other articulate sound.

'Get up, youngster, and dance a hornpipe,' cried Nettleship;
'or I'll just send to the galley for a lump of fat pork, and if
you'll swallow an ounce or so, it will do you all the good in
the world.'

The very mention of the fat pork finished me off. I bolted
out of the berth, which was to windward, and went staggering
away to the opposite side of the ship, having made a vain
attempt to get to the main-deck, upsetting Tom Pim in my
course, and not stopping till I pitched right against Doctor
M'Call, our surgeon, much after the manner that I had treated
old Rough-and-Ready. Our good medico, not being so secure
as the lieutenant on his pins, was unfortunately upset, and

together we rolled into his dispensary, out of which he was at that moment coming. There we lay, amidst a quantity of phials, jars, and gallipots, which, having been improperly secured, came crashing down upon us. The doctor kicked and struggled, and endeavoured to rise, but I was too far gone to make any effort of the sort. Had he been inclined, he might have pounded me to death before I should have cried out for mercy. I was unable even to say that I could not help it, though he must have known that well enough. I need not describe what happened. Fortunately he had got to his feet before the occurrence to which I wish only delicately to allude took place. I felt wonderfully better.

'Why, Paddy, is it you, my boy?' he exclaimed, not a bit angry; for being a good-natured man, he was ready to make every allowance for the occurrence.

'I believe it's myself, sir; though I'm not altogether clear about it,' I answered as I got up and tried to crawl out of the place.

'Stay, youngster, you shall have something before you go which will set you to rights,' he said in a kind tone.

As well as he could, with the ship pitching and rolling, he poured out a mixture, which he handed to me, and bade me drink off. It revived me considerably, though I still felt very shaky.

'If I should ever want to have a leg or an arm cut off, I hope, sir, that you'll do it for me,' I said, for I could think of nothing else at the moment to express my gratitude.

The doctor laughed. 'I wish you better luck than that, my boy,' he observed. 'What makes you say that?'

'Because, sir, you didn't find fault with me for tumbling you over; now, when I ran against Mr. Saunders, he sent me to the masthead for a couple of hours.'

'You were skylarking then, my lad, and the ship was not pitching and tumbling about as she now is,' he said. 'However, go and lie down in the berth, if you can find room there, and you'll soon be all to rights.'

I willingly obeyed his injunctions, while he sent to have his dispensary cleaned, and the phials and gallipots which had escaped fracture picked up. I believe a good many were saved by tumbling upon us instead of upon the deck.

As Nettleship and the other midshipmen were merciful, I managed to have a good caulk on the locker. When I awoke I felt almost like myself again. I dreaded, however, having to go on deck to keep watch, and was much inclined to ask the doctor to put me on the sick list.

In my sufferings I had not forgotten my follower, Larry. As soon as I could, I hastened forward to see how he was getting on, as I had ascertained that it was his watch below.

As I got forward, a scene of human misery and wretchedness presented itself, such as I had never before witnessed. Half the marines were lying about the deck, unable to lift up their heads, while most of the boys were in the same condition. Among them I found Larry. He gazed at me with lack-lustre eyes as I approached.

'Shure, the say's not at all at all the place I thought it was, Mr. Terence,' he groaned forth. 'I've been turned inside out entirely. I don't even know whether the inside of me isn't the outside.'

There was a general groan, as the ship at that moment pitched into a sea, and I had to hold on fast, or I should have been sent in among the mass of human misery. When she rose again and was steady for an instant, I was able to speak to Larry.

'I can't say I feel very comfortable myself,' I said; 'but rouse up and try to prevent your feelings from overcoming you.'

'Och, Master Terence, but my faylings are mighty powerful, and for the life of me I can't master them,' he groaned out.

This was very evident; and what with the smells and the closeness of the air,—not to speak of the pitching and rolling of the ship,—I was again almost overpowered, when there came a cry of 'All hands save ship!' and down sprang the boatswain's mates, and began kicking away at the hapless marines and green hands. Larry in a moment leaped to his feet. I heard a savage growl close to me, and just then caught sight of Dan Hoolan's countenance. Though he was kicked and cuffed, nothing would make him get up, and I saw him still lying prostrate when I hurried off to gain the deck.

The ship, struck by a heavy squall, was lying over almost on her beam-ends; the officers were shouting out their orders through their speaking trumpets; the men were hurrying here and there as directed, some going aloft, others letting fly tacks, and sheets clewing up and hauling down. Suddenly the buoyant frigate righted herself. It seemed a wonder that none of the men were jerked overboard. The canvas was further reduced, and on we went, pounding away into the seas.

Larry was as active as any one. He seemed to have forgotten all about his sickness. It was the last time, too, that I ever suffered from the malady, and from that day forward—blow high or blow low—I felt as easy in my inside as I should on shore. A few spars had been carried away on board the merchantmen, but, as far as we could see, no other damage had occurred.

In a couple of days more the gale had completely worn itself out, and everything went as smoothly as heretofore. We were then within about a week's sail of the West Indies. The weather was now warm and pleasant,—sometimes, during a calm, a little too hot.

One morning, just at daybreak, the look-out from the mast-head announced that he saw three sail to windward. The second lieutenant went aloft, and looked at them with his glass. When he came down he pronounced two of them to be frigates, and the other a smaller vessel. We threw out signals to the convoy to keep together, while we and the other two men-of-war, hauling our wind, stood closer to the strangers. At first it was supposed that they were English, but their manœuvres made us doubt this, and at length they were pronounced decidedly French. That they intended to pick off some of the merchantmen there could be no doubt; and this it was our object to prevent.

'Paddy, my boy,' said Tom Pim, coming up to me as I stood looking at the enemy from the quarter-deck, 'we shall have some fighting before long, no doubt about that. How do you feel?'

'Mighty pleased, and very ready for it,' I answered.

'We're fairly matched, I should think,' remarked Tom. 'If we could count the guns of the enemy, I suspect there would not be found the difference of half a dozen between us. All depends on the way our ships are manœuvred, and how we fight our guns,—though I've no fear on that score.'

It was soon evident that Captain Macnamara intended to fight, and the order was given to clear the ship for action. The drum beat to quarters. All hands went about their duties with alacrity. I was sent down into the cockpit with a message. There I found the surgeons making their preparations; with their tourniquets, saws, knives, and other instruments, arranged ready for the expected operations; and there were buckets, and bowls of water, and sponges, and various other things likely to be required. In the centre was the amputating table, on which, before long, some poor fellow would probably be stretched, to be deprived of a leg or an arm; while an odour of vinegar pervaded the place.

The powder magazine had been opened. The gunner and his mates were engaged in serving out the ammunition, which the powder-monkeys were carrying up on deck in their tubs. Cutlasses were girded on, and pistols stuck in belts. Boarding pikes were arranged so as to be easily seized if wanted. The men, hurrying to their respective guns, loaded and ran them out; and as I passed along the decks I remarked their countenances all exhibiting their eagerness for the fight.

Among them I observed Hoolan, who had been stationed at a gun. He was apparently as ready to fight as any one on board. His features were as stern and morose as ever, but there was a fire in his eye, which showed that he contemplated the approaching battle with more pleasure than fear. Judging from the look of the men captured with him, I couldn't say the same of them. The crew generally were full of life and spirits, laughing and joking, as if they had forgotten altogether that in a short time they would be engaged in a fierce fight. I found Larry at his gun, looking as pleased as if he were at a wake or a wedding.

'Shure we'll be after making this fellow bark, Maisther Terence,' he said, slapping the breach. 'If the old chap doesn't drill a hole in the side of one of those ships out there, or knock away one of their masts, say I'm not a Tipperary boy.'

His remark produced a laugh among the seamen within hearing,—indeed they evidently thought that whatever Larry said ought to be considered as a good joke. Larry seemed to have a notion that his especial gun was to win the battle. As a similar feeling seemed to animate the rest of the crew, it was likely to contribute to our success.

We were still some distance from the enemy, when Tom Pim, Chaffey, and I were summoned to the quarter-deck, to act as the captain's aides-de-camp, so that I was enabled to see all that was going forward. The rest of the midshipmen were stationed mostly on the main-deck, each in command of a certain number of guns.

The *Liffy* leading, we were now standing close hauled towards the enemy, who approached us almost before the wind.

The *Amethyst* came next to us, and the corvette followed. We hoped that within another ten minutes we should get within range of the others' guns, when suddenly the enemy's leading frigate hauled her wind. Her consorts immediately afterwards followed her example. On seeing this, our captain ordered every stitch of canvas the *Liffy* could carry to be set, when, the breeze freshening, we rapidly came up with the enemy. I heard some of the officers say that they intended to make off. The men at the gun near which I was standing swore at their cowardice, and I began to think that there would be no fight after all.

Presently the French ships were seen to shorten sail, when our captain sent the hands again aloft to do the same. They had barely time to come down and return to their quarters, when a shot, fired by the leading French frigate, came flying across our deck. No one was hit, but a hammock and part of the hammock-nettings were knocked away. It showed what we had to expect.

I expected that the captain would return the compliment, but he waited calmly till we got nearer. We were to leeward, it must be understood; but although that would have been a disadvantage had there been any sea running, as the ocean was calm it didn't make much difference, while we were thus better able to protect our convoy, and prevent the enemy from running among them and committing mischief.

Again the breeze freshened, and standing on, we passed the corvette, which fired a few shots at us without doing any damage. We then received a similar compliment from the second French frigate, several of her shots striking the *Liffy*. In a few minutes we were up to our largest antagonist. As our bow gun came abreast of her quarter, our captain shouted, 'Fire!' and gun after gun was discharged in rapid succession, the enemy blazing away at us in return.

The *Amethyst* was meantime engaged with the second frigate, and the corvette with the French ship of the same size as herself.

Shot after shot came on board. First one man was struck down, then another and another, and several were carried below to be placed under the hands of the surgeons. Some were drawn aside, their fighting days over. What damage we were producing among the enemy could not at first be ascertained, for all the ships, from our rapid firing, were enveloped in clouds of smoke. Looking up, I could see that our sails were pierced in several places. Crash succeeded crash, as the enemy's shot struck our sides or bulwarks, and sent the splinters flying about in all directions.

It was somewhat trying work for us, who had nothing to do except to keep our eyes upon the captain, in case he should have any orders to give us.

We had made sure of capturing one of the French ships, if not all.

Presently, looking astern, I saw the fore-yard of the

Amethyst come down on deck, and shortly afterwards our fore-top mast was carried away. Our captain, hitherto so calm, stamped his foot on the deck with vexation. Our men, to make amends, tossed their guns in and out as if they had been playthings, firing away with wonderful rapidity; and I believe the gun at which Larry was stationed fully carried out his promise of drilling more than one hole in the side of our opponent. Her masts and spars were entire, as were those of the other frigate, but their bulwarks were shattered in several places, which was evident by the white streaks their sides exhibited.

'Blaze away, my lads,' cried the captain. 'We'll still have one of them, at least, for they'll not long stand the pounding you're giving them.'

Our crew cheered in reply; but just as we had delivered another broadside, signals having been made on board the leading French frigate, her crew were seen going aloft, and presently the courses, top-gallant sails, and royals were set, and she stood away close hauled, the other frigate and corvette doing the same.

Neither the *Amethyst* nor we were in a condition to follow, and to our vexation, we saw the enemy escaping from us. That we had given them a good pounding was very evident; but whether or not after repairing damages they would renew the contest was doubtful.

The little *Piper*, being uninjured aloft, gallantly followed, and kept blazing away at the enemy, till the captain made a signal to her to return, fearing that she might be overpowered and cut off before we could sufficiently repair damages to go to her assistance. She obeyed the order, and the Frenchmen didn't follow her. She had received less damage aloft than we had, though, as we afterwards found, she had lost several men killed and wounded. As she came within hail, she reported that the largest of the French frigates was pumping hard, and had evidently received much damage, while the second was not in a much better condition.

This accounted for their not wishing to continue the combat, and standing away, while it seemed doubtful whether they would venture to renew it.

We had plenty of work in repairing damages, clearing away the wreck of the fore-top mast, and getting a new one ready to send aloft. We could distinguish the convoy hull down to leeward, waiting the result of the fight.

I asked Nettleship whether he thought, as soon as we had got to rights, that we should follow the enemy.

'If our captain were to act as his feelings prompt him, I should have no doubt about it,' he answered. 'Fighting Macnamara, as he is known in the service, would not let an enemy escape if he could help it; but duty before all other things, and our duty is to protect the convoy under our charge. If we were to go in chase of the enemy, we might lose sight of the merchantmen, and any rascally privateers might pounce down and carry off the whole lot of them. My belief therefore is, that we shall bear up and let the Frenchmen go their way. It is not likely, after the taste they have had of our quality, that they'll again molest us.'

Nettleship was right. The captain ordered the corvette to run down to the convoy to direct them to stand on under easy sail till we should join them. The captain and Mr. Saunders, and the other officers, were exerting themselves to the utmost to get the ships to rights. The former sent me down into the cockpit, to learn from the doctor how the wounded men were getting on, and how many had been killed. I turned almost sick as I entered the place. There was anything but a fresh smell there now. I can't properly describe it,—perhaps it was more like the odour of a butcher's shop in the dog days, when the blue-bottles are revelling in the abundance hung up for their inspection. One poor fellow lay stretched on the table. The doctor was just then too busy to speak to me. I saw a foot sticking out of a bucket. It belonged to a leg which had just been taken off the man, who was in a dead faint. The assistant-surgeon was endeavouring to restore him to consciousness, while the surgeon was engaged in taking up the arteries. Another, who had lost an arm, was lying on a locker, waiting to be carried to the sick bay; and several others sat round with their heads and shoulders bandaged up. At last the doctor looked up, and I then delivered my message. 'Five killed and nine wounded, and I'm afraid one or two of the latter may slip through my fingers,' he said. I was thankful when I was able to hurry back on deck with my report. The captain was not addicted to the sentimental, but I heard him sigh, or rather groan, after I had delivered it. As soon as any of the men could be spared, the bodies of the killed were sewn up in canvas, with shot at their feet. As we had no chaplain on board, the captain read a portion of the burial service, and the sound of quick successive plunges told that they had sunk into their ocean grave. We and the *Amethyst* then stood away after the convoy.

'Our first action has not been a very glorious one,' I observed, when most of the mess was once more assembled in the berth. 'I made sure we should have captured one of those frigates.'

'It has been a successful one, Paddy, and we should be content with that,' said Nettleship. 'If we had taken one of the enemy, we should be probably more knocked about than we are, and should have delayed the merchantmen, or allowed them to run the risk of being captured. Depend upon it, our captain will get credit for what he has done, and the credit he gets will be reflected on us.'

The wind fortunately continued fair, the sea smooth, and by the time we sighted Jamaica we were again all ataunto. Having seen the greater part of our charge into Port Royal, and sent the wounded ashore to the hospital, we stood on with the remainder of the merchantmen to Barbadoes and other islands, where we left them in safety, and then made our way back to Port Royal. We saluted the forts, and the forts saluted us; flags were flying, the sea glittering, and everything looked gay and bright as we entered that magnificent harbour.

'Shure it's a beautiful place this, Misther Terence,' said Larry to me, as, the anchor being dropped, and the sails furled, we lay floating calmly on the placid waters. 'There's only one place to my mind that beats this, and that's Cork harbour, though, to be sure, the mountains there are not so high, or the sky so blue as out here.'

'Or the sun so hot, Larry,' I remarked, 'or the people so black. Did you ever see Irishmen like that?' and I pointed to a boat manned by negroes just coming alongside. Larry had never before seen a blackamoor, for, as may be supposed, Africans seldom found their way into Tipperary.

'Shure, your honour, is them Irishmen?' he asked.

'Speak to them, and you'll soon find out, and they'll tell you how long it has taken the sun to blacken their faces.'

'Then, Misther Terence, shall we be after getting our faces painted of that colour if we stay out here?' he inquired with some trouble in the tone of his voice.

'Depend upon it, Larry, we shall if we stay long enough,' I answered. I left Larry to reflect on the matter. I remembered a story I had heard of an Irishman who had gone out intending to settle in Demerara, where a large proportion of the white population have come from the Emerald Isle. As soon as the ship had dropped her anchor a number of blacks came off to her. The first he spoke to answered in a rich Irish brogue. The new-comer looked at the negro with astonishment.

'What's your name, my man?' he asked.

'Pat Casey,' was the answer.

'And, Pat, say as you love me, how long have you been out here?'

'Little better than six years, your honour,' was the reply, such being the time that had elapsed since the negro had been imported, having in the meantime had an Irish name given him, and learned to speak Irish.

'Six years, and you have turned from a white-skinned Irishman into a blackamoor!' exclaimed the new-comer; and not waiting for an answer, he rushed down into the cabin, which he could not be induced to quit until the ship sailed again, and he returned home, satisfied that the West Indies was not a country in which he could wish to take up his abode.

Not long after the conversation I have mentioned, Larry came up to me.

'I've been after talking, Misther Terence, with some of those black gentlemen, and shure if they're from the old country they've forgotten all about it, which no raal Irishman would ever do, I'll stake my davey!' he exclaimed. 'They've never heard of Limerick, or Cork, or Waterford, or the Shannon, or Ballinahone, and that proves to me that they couldn't have been in the old country since they were born. And now, Misther Terence dear, you were joking shure,' he added, giving me one of his comical looks.

'Well, Larry,' I said, 'it's a satisfaction to know that it will take us a long time to turn into niggers, or to forget old Ireland.'

As no one was near, I asked him how Dan Hoolan and the other pressed men were behaving.

'That's just what I wanted to be speaking to you about, Misther Terence,' he answered. 'I'm after thinking that they'll not be on board many days if they get a chance of slipping on shore. I heard them one day talking about it in Irish, forgetting that I understood what they were saying; and as we had a hand in the taking of them, says I to myself, we'll not let you go so aisy, my boys, and I'll be after telling Misther Terence about it.'

'You have acted rightly, Larry,' I answered. 'It's the duty of every seaman to prevent mutiny or desertion, and if you hadn't told me the fellows might have got off, though, to be sure, the best of them are king's hard bargains.'

I took an early opportunity of telling Mr. Saunders.

'Thank you, my lad,' he answered; 'I'll take care that an eye is kept upon them.'

Soon afterwards, while looking over the side, I saw a dark, triangular object gliding by at no great distance from the ship. It went about when it got under the stern, and appeared again on the other side. Mr. Saunders saw it also.

'Lads,' he said, 'do you know what that is? You may have heard of Port Royal Jack. That's him. He's especially fond of seamen's legs, and if any of you were to go overboard, he'd snap you up in a minute.'

The word was passed along the deck. Half the crew were now in the rigging, taking a look at their enemy, and among them were Dan Hoolan and his companions. I observed a flesh-coloured mass floating a short distance off. Presently the black fin sank; a white object appeared for a moment close to the surface, and a huge mouth gulped down the mass, and disappeared with it beneath the water. It was a lesson to any one who might have attempted taking a swim to the shore.

CHAPTER X.

I HAVE not attempted to describe Port Royal Harbour. It is large enough to hold 1000 sail. The entrance is on the left side. A strip of sand, known as the Palisades, runs east and west with the town of Port Royal, surrounded with heavy batteries at the further end. Here are the dockyard and naval arsenal, and forts with heavy guns completely commanding the entrance.

At the eastern end stands Kingston, the commercial town, before which the merchantmen bring up, while the men-of-war ride at anchor nearer the mouth. A lofty range of hills, with valleys between them, rise beyond the northern shore. Altogether, it is a grand place, and especially grand it looked just now, filled with a fleet of ships and smaller men-of-war.

Our captain, with the second lieutenant, the captain of the *Amethyst*, and the commander of the corvette, went on shore, and were warmly welcomed by the merchants, who said that they had rendered them signal service in so gallantly protecting the convoy. They presented each of the commanders with a piece of plate and a sum of money, to show their gratitude.

'I told you so,' said Nettleship when we heard of it; 'we did our duty on that occasion, though it was a hard trial to have to let the enemy escape.' As we were likely to be detained a week to replace our fore-top mast, to repair other damages, and to get stores and fresh provisions on board, most of our mess by turns got leave to go on shore, where, down to Tom Pim, we were all made a great deal of by the planters and merchants. We were invited to breakfasts, luncheons, dinners, and dances every night. Most of our fellows lost their hearts to the dark-eyed creoles, and Tom Pim confided to me that a lovely little damsel of fifteen had captured his.

'I didn't intend to strike to her, but I couldn't help it, for she blazed away at me with her smiles, and glances of her dark eyes, and her musical laughter, till I could stand them no longer, and I promised that when I become a commander I will return and marry her forthwith, if she will remain faithful to me.'

'And what did she say?' I asked.

'She laughed more than ever, and inquired how long it was likely to be before I could get my promotion. When I said that it might be in five or six, or perhaps eight years, she remarked that that was a terrible long time to wait, and that though constancy was a very fine thing, it didn't do to try it too much.'

Irishmen have susceptible hearts, I've heard, but I can't say that I lost mine to any one in particular.

We had altogether a very jolly time of it, which we enjoyed all the more because we knew that it must soon come to an end.

Tom Pim and I, who were inseparable, were at a party one evening, when a good-natured looking gentleman came up to us. 'I see that you have been dancing with my little daughter Lucy,' he said, addressing Tom. 'May I ask your names, and the ship to which you belong?' We told him.

'She's not likely, I understand, to sail for some days, and if you can obtain leave I shall be very happy to see you at my country house, some few miles away from this,' he said. 'My name is Talboys, and as I'm well known to Captain Macnamara I'll write a note, which you can take on board, asking him or his first lieutenant to give you leave for a couple or three days,—the longer the better,—and to allow any other midshipmen who can be spared to accompany you.'

'Thank you very much, sir,' I answered; 'but we have to return on board to-morrow morning by daylight, and I'm afraid that Mr. Saunders won't be inclined to let us go ashore again.'

'There's nothing like asking,' he observed; 'and I think that he'll not refuse my request, so you had better try.'

Taking us into an ante-room, he wrote the promised note, of which Tom Pim took charge. He told us, if we could obtain leave, to meet him at Mammy Custard's boarding-house, an establishment much frequented by midshipmen and other junior officers of the service. We had hitherto not slept on shore, but we knew the house well.

The ball was kept up to a late hour. As soon as it was over we repaired to the quay, where several boats were waiting to take off those who had to return to their ships.

Tom and I agreed that we had very little chance of getting leave, but that we should not refuse it if we did. The sky was clear as Nora Creina's eye; every star was reflected on the calm surface of the water in the harbour. We were all inclined to be jolly—officers and men. Our tongues went rattling merrily on. Now and then there came a peal of laughter, now snatches of songs. We had got more than halfway down the harbour when the officer in command sang out, 'Mind your helm. Where are you coming to?'

At that instant we ran slap into a shore-boat pulled by negroes, and stove in her bows. Loud shrieks and cries arose from the black crew, who began to scramble into our boat,— the wisest thing they could do, considering that their own was sinking.

'Oh, we all drown! we all drown!' they cried in loud tones. 'Jack shark catch me!'

The four blacks had saved themselves, but there were two passengers in the stern sheets who appeared to be less in a hurry to get on board. Presently, however, finding the boat settling down, one of them made a spring and tumbled on board.

'Why, Tim Connor, where did you come from?' asked one

7

of our men.   At that moment the other man, instead of trying
to save himself, plunged into the water, and began swimming
towards the southern shore.   Perhaps he thought that he
might escape in the confusion unperceived, but our lieutenant
caught sight of him.

'Never mind the boat,' he exclaimed.   'Out oars.   We
must get hold of that fellow, whoever he is.'

We were not long in coming up with the bold swimmer,
who, speedily caught by the hair of his head, was hauled on
board, in spite of his struggles to get free.   As he was
hauled aft by the orders of the lieutenant, I recognized Dan
Hoolan.

'Who gave you leave to go on shore, my men?' asked
the lieutenant.

'Plaise yer honour,' answered Tim Connor, 'we were only
going for a spree, and intended being off again in the mornin'.'

Dan Hoolan sat sulkily, with his hands between his knees,
not deigning to reply.

'You'll find that you'll have to pay somewhat heavily for
your spree,' remarked the lieutenant.

'Seeing as we've not had it,' I heard Tim mutter.

By the time we had got back to the boat she had almost
disappeared, and we could only pick up a few of the remaining articles she had contained.

A sharp look-out was kept on the two men, who had
evidently intended to desert.   No further words were exchanged with them.   Both sat with downcast looks, probably
well aware of the punishment they had brought on themselves.

On reaching the ship they were handcuffed, and placed
under charge of a sentry.   Tom and I had to keep our watch,
and got but little sleep that night.

As soon as we could we presented our note to Mr. Saunders.

'Why, you lads are always wanting to go on shore,' he
observed dryly; 'one would suppose you were born on shore.
However, as you conduct yourselves well, you may have the
leave your friend asks for, and may return by the first boat to
Kingston.'

'Thank you, sir,' we answered, highly delighted. 'And may Sinnet and Chaffey go too?' I asked.

'Were they invited?' he inquired.

'We were desired to bring two more of our mess, and we thought that they could be best spared, sir.'

'Yes, they may go,' said Mr. Saunders.

Without delay we conveyed the pleasant intelligence to them. Before long we were again pulling up the harbour, and thus escaped seeing the punishment inflicted on my unfortunate countrymen. I knew that they deserved it, and therefore didn't trouble my head much about the matter. We repaired at once to Mammy Custard's, and had not been there long before Mr. Talboys made his appearance.

'Glad you have got leave, my young friends,' he said, shaking us all by the hands, as we introduced Sinnet and Chaffey. 'The carriages will soon be at the door; but you must take some refreshment before we start, to fortify the inner man for the fatigues of the journey.'

Having told Mammy Custard to place luncheon on the table, and desired us to commence operations without waiting for him, he went out, and left us to discuss the viands and refreshing beverages.

We had just finished when Mr. Talboys returned, with his daughter, in one buggy, into which he invited me to mount, while he told Tom, Sinnet, and Chaffey to get into the other, which was driven by a black boy. As soon as we had taken our seats, the carriages dashed off, and away we went in a fine style out of Kingston. I'm no hand at describing scenery, nor can I remember the names of the tropical trees which grew in rich profusion on both sides of the road, the climbing plants, the gaily-coloured flowers, and other vegetable wonders. Miss Lucy and I chatted away right merrily. I couldn't help thinking how jealous Tom would be, and I would very gladly for his sake have changed places with him.

'And what do you think of Jamaica?' asked her papa after we had gone some distance.

'It's a wonderfully fine country, sir,' I answered. 'And if it were not that I love Ballinahone more than any other place on earth, I shouldn't be sorry to take up my abode here when I become a post-captain or an admiral, and wish to settle down for life, should peace be established, and my country not be requiring my services.'

'We have our little drawbacks, however,' observed Mr. Talboys. 'You have not been here in the hot season yet. We now and then have an outbreak of the blacks, for the rascals—strange to say—are not contented with their lot. Occasionally too, we are attacked by foreign foes, but we Jamaica men are right loyal, and are prepared to defend our shores against all comers.'

'I thought that the blacks were merry peaceable fellows, who never think of rebellion,' I observed.

'Nor would they, if they were not put up to it by designing knaves. But in different parts of the island we have had half a dozen outbreaks within my recollection, and not a few before it. Some have been instigated by the enemies of our country; others by newly imported slaves, who have been chiefs, or kings, as they call themselves, in Africa; and on some occasions the Maroons have taken it into their foolish heads to rebel. They are, as you're doubtless aware, free blacks, who live an independent vagabond life on the mountains, and are too ignorant and savage to know that they have no chance of success.'

'But I hope, sir, that they're quiet now, or it can't be very pleasant for you to live so far away from the city.'

Mr. Talboys laughed. 'My negroes are quiet and obedient, and I should get information in good time were anything likely to happen,' he answered.

'No one would think of attacking our house,' put in Miss Lucy. 'We are well prepared, and they would gain nothing by the attempt.'

We drove on through fine and wild romantic scenery, each turn of the road bringing us to some new point of view. We passed a beautiful waterfall, the bottom and sides of which appeared as if composed of glass or porcelain; it consisted of a number of steps rising up the sides of the hill. These, my friend told me, were incrustations which had formed themselves over the roots of trees growing on either side. The water came flowing down over them, transparent as crystal, and as the rays of sunlight played between the waving branches of the trees, the water glittered with a thousand variegated tints. We descended from our carriages to enjoy a more perfect view. Tom and Chaffey took it into their heads to attempt walking across some of the steps. Tom ran lightly over them; but Chaffey, while following in his wake, being twice as heavy, broke through the incrustation, and in he soused. He quickly managed, however, to scramble out again, though not until he was wet through nearly up to his middle.

'Why, I thought it was all hard stone,' he exclaimed as he reached dry ground.

We all had a hearty laugh at his expense. In that climate a ducking doesn't much matter, and he was dry again before we had proceeded much further on our journey.

Late in the evening we caught sight of a long low building, with a broad verandah, surrounded with plantations, and a garden of fruit-trees on the gentle slope of a hill. As we got near, a shout from the master brought out several black boys, accompanied by a number of barking dogs, who welcomed us by leaping round the horses' heads, and yelping and frisking about with delight.

Mr. Talboys jumped out, and Lucy leapt into his arms, while I descended on the other side. A stout lady in a sky-blue dress, accompanied by three small damsels in low white frocks, and a little boy in scanty clothing, appeared at the top of the steps. Lucy, running up, kissed them all round, and then Mr. Talboys introduced us in due form to his wife and younger daughters.

After a little conversation Madam Talboys led us into a handsome hall, with a table in the centre, on which ample preparations for supper were spread, the light from a dozen wax candles falling on the cut glass, the silver forks and glittering steel, and an épergne filled with fragrant flowers, surrounded by dishes containing salads, fruits of every description, and other cold viands.

'The young gentlemen would like to wash their hands before they commence operations,' said Mr. Talboys ; and he ushered us into a room off the great hall, in which were four snow-white beds, with muslin curtains closely drawn round them, and wash-hand basins filled with deliciously cool water.

We lost no time in plunging our faces into them, arranging our hair, and making ourselves neat and comfortable.

'I say, we have fallen into pleasant quarters,' exclaimed Chaffey. 'We owe it all to you, Tom. If you hadn't paid attention to Miss Lucy, we should not have been here.'

'Belay the slack of that,' cried Tom. 'Our host might overhear you, and he wouldn't be pleased ; nor would Miss Lucy herself.'

We were quickly ready ; and just as we returned to the hall several black boys entered, each carrying a steaming dish, on which we fell to, when helped, with keen appetites. Two other gentlemen came in,—an overseer and a head clerk on the estate. We all laughed and talked at a great rate. The overseer, Mr. Rabbitts, at the request of our host, sang a good song. The clerk followed with another. Then Miss Lucy got her guitar, and warbled very sweetly. Altogether we were merry as crickets.

At length our host remarked that we must be tired, and led us to our sleeping-room. We soon had our heads upon the pillows, with the mosquito curtains drawn close around us.

Though midshipmen are rightly supposed to sleep soundly, I was awakened by fancying that the doctor was running his lancet into me, and was about to assure him that he was operating by mistake on me instead of on some other patient, when I heard a loud whizzing, buzzing sound. I hadn't been careful enough in closing the curtains, and a big mosquito had got in, and was revelling in my fresh blood. I tried in vain to catch the active creature, who was soon joined by others of his abominable race. The humming concert was increased by

countless other sounds, which came through the open window,
—the croaking of frogs and tree-toads, the chirping and
whistling of insects and reptiles, while I could see a party of
fireflies glistening among the curtains of the bed. Now and
then a huge beetle would make its way into the room, and go
buzzing about round and round, till to my infinite relief it darted
out of the window ! But the noises and the stings of the mos-
quitoes drove sleep from my eyelids. Presently I heard some
one talking outside ; it was a nigger's voice, deep and husky.

'If de picaroons cum, den dey cum soon, and cut all our
troats.'

'Garramarcy, you don't say so !' exclaimed another. 'Better
tell massa; he know what do.'

'Me tink better run away and hide,' said the first speaker.
'Massa want to stop and fight, and den we hab to fight too,
and get killed.'

'But if we run away and don't tell massa, he get killed,
and Missy Lucy, and missus, and de piccaninies. Me tink
tell massa fust and den run away.'

'But if um tell massa, he make um stop and fight. No,
no, Cato; you one fool. Wiser to run away, and not say
where um go.'

The arguments of the first speaker appeared to prevail with
his companion. They probably were not aware that any one
was sleeping in the room overhead.

As far as I could judge, the matter appeared serious. I
recollected the conversation I had had in the morning about
the Maroons and the rebel blacks.

Without further thought I jumped from my bed, and rushing
to the window, sang out, 'Stop, you cowardly rascals. If
you move I'll fire at you. Tell your master what you have
heard, and he'll act as he considers necessary.'

The sound of my voice awakened my companions, who
fancied that the house was attacked by thieves.

As the blacks, notwithstanding my threats, seemed inclined
to be off, I jumped out of the window, which was of no great
height from the ground, followed by Sinnet and Tom. The

niggers fancied, I believe, that we were spirits of another world, as we appeared in our night-shirts, which were fluttering in the breeze, and came back trembling and humble enough. We made them show us the window of Mr. Talboys' room, as we could not get into the house. Shouting loudly, we awoke him, and I then told him what I had heard.

'You have acted judiciously, young gentleman, whether there is anything in it or not; but I'll be dressed directly, and come out to hear what account the black boys have to give. Take care they don't run off in the meantime.'

Presently I heard a bolt withdraw; the door opened, and Mr. Talboys made his appearance, a red night-cap on his head and wrapped in a flowered dressing-gown, a candle in one hand, and a thick whip in the other.

'I must examine these fellows,' he said as he came out. 'They're less liable to prevaricate if they see the whip. Come, now, young gentlemen, you may wish to put on your garments, and while you do so I'll hear what my negroes have to say.'

As he was speaking, however, Chaffey came out of our room, bringing our breeches, having first got into his own, lest, as he said, the ladies might inconveniently make their appearance.

'What's this you were talking about, Cato?' asked Mr. Talboys, looking sternly at the blacks, who stood trembling before him.

'Cæsar cum just now, and say dat Cudjoe, with great number ob niggers, just come down from de mountains, and dey march dis way with muskets, and bagonets, and big swords, and spears, and swear dey kill all de whites dey cum across.'

I saw Mr. Talboys start.

How did you hear this, Cæsar?' he asked.

'Please, massa, I out last night, to help bury Mammy Quacca, who die in de morning, when my brother Sambo cum in and say he almost caught by Cudjoe's fellows, and hear dem swear dat dey cum to kill all de white people, and before long he tink dey cum dis way to Belmont.' (That was the name of Mr. Talboys' place.)

'Cudjoe! Who are you talking about? The fellow has been dead these thirty years or more,' said our host.

'Dey say him Cudjoe. Perhaps him come to life again,' answered Cæsar, as if he fully believed such an event probable. 'Or maybe him 'Tree Fingered Jack.'

'Three Fingered Jack' was a negro leader who about that time made himself notorious.

'Possibly some fellow has assumed the name of the old Maroon leader,' I observed.

Mr. Talboys, after further questioning the blacks, again turned to us, and remarked, 'I'm afraid there's some truth in what these negroes say. At all events, it would be wise to be prepared.' He spoke in a cool tone, not a bit flustered.

'I'm very sorry to have brought you into a position which may not prove to be very agreeable,' he continued; 'but I know, young gentlemen, that I can rely on your assistance.'

Of course we could give but one answer.

'The first thing to be done is to barricade the house, and I'll get you to do that, with Cæsar to assist you,' he said. 'Keep an eye on the boy, lest he should run away, while I send off Cato to give notice to my neighbours, who will probably assemble here, as this house can be more easily defended than theirs. I will myself summon my overseer and clerks. I, of course, shall also despatch messengers to Kingston for assistance, and we may hope to hold out till the troops arrive. The rebels expect to take us by surprise, and to murder us without resistance, as they have the whites in other districts. I must, however, tell my wife and daughters, or they may be alarmed should they suddenly discover what is going on.'

We heard a good deal of talking in Mrs. Talboys' room, and then the master of the house came out, with a brace of pistols in his belt, and a sword in his hand.

'The ladies are quite prepared, and will give you all the help they can,' he said. 'They'll show you where the arms and ammunition are kept.'

Having finished dressing, we set to work, under Cæsar's directions, to put up shutters, and to strengthen the doors with planks and stout pieces of timber, which we found in a yard, apparently prepared for the purpose. We were soon joined by Mrs. Talboys and Miss Lucy, who both appeared equal to the emergency. Having shown us where the arms and ammunition were kept, they assisted to carry planks and to hold the boards up while we nailed them on. Miss Lucy had a hearty laugh at the grimaces made by Chaffey when he happened to hit his finger instead of the nail he was driving in. We worked away as busily as bees, and before Mr. Talboys returned had already secured most of the doors and the lower windows. They were all loopholed, so that on whatever side our enemies might assault the house, a warm reception would be given them. We were still working away when Mr. Talboys appeared.

'Our friends will soon be here,' he said. 'We shall muster nearly a dozen muskets, and I hope that with them we may be able to keep the rebels at bay; though, if they're disposed for mischief, they may ravage our plantations with impunity.'

The overseer and clerks, each armed to the teeth, soon afterwards came in, and our preparations for defence went on still more rapidly. It was now midnight, but as yet none of the neighbours had arrived; and we formed but a small garrison to defend so small a building from the host of foes who might attack it.

'Me go out and see whether niggers come?' said Cæsar.

'No, no; you stay in the house, and help fight,' answered his master, who hadn't forgot the black's purpose of running away and leaving us to our fate.

'Cato, you go out towards Silver Springs, and learn, if you can, the whereabouts of the rebels. Call at Edghill on your way, and tell Mr. Marchant and his family to hurry on here, and that we'll do our best to protect them.'

'Yes, massa,' answered Cato, who, for a black, was a man of few words, and was evidently a trustworthy fellow.

Cæsar looked somewhat disappointed. I suspect that if he had found the rebels approaching, we should not have seen his face again. We were kept fully employed improving the fortifications. Mr. Talboys, who was full of resources, devised three platforms, which were run from the upper windows above the doorway, with holes in them through which hot water or stones, or other missiles, could be dropped on the heads of the assailants. We had also means of access to the roof, so that if it were set on fire, we might extinguish the flames.

Still the enemy didn't appear, nor did Cato return to bring us information. Had we been idle, the suspense might have been more trying; but as we were actively engaged, we scarcely thought of what might possibly happen. At last Cato's voice was heard shouting,—

'Massa Marchant and de piccaninies come, but de rebels cum too, and dis nigger not know which get in first.'

'We must go and help our friends then. Who'll accompany me?' asked Mr. Talboys.

'I will, sir,' said I.

'And I,' said Tom Pim. And our other two messmates said the same.

The overseer seemed inclined to stop and defend the house. We immediately set out, Mr. Talboys leading the way, and we keeping close to him. The night was dark, and we might easily have missed our road. After going some distance he stopped for a moment to listen. There came through the night air the tramp of feet, and the hum of voices, though apparently a long way off.

'What can have become of Marchant?' exclaimed Mr. Talboys, after we had gone some way further.

'Here I am,' said a person who stepped out into the middle of the road with a child in his arms. 'My wife was tired, and our children declared they could go no further without resting; and except our two nurse girls, all the slaves have run away.'

'They might have rested too long,' said Mr. Talboys. 'Come, Mrs. Marchant, I'll help you; and these young gentlemen will assist the children.'

We discovered the family group seated on a bank; and each of us taking charge of one of the children, we followed Mr. Talboys back towards Belmont as fast as our legs could move. He strode along at a great rate, for the sounds, which before had been indistinct, now grew louder and louder, and we knew that the enemy could not be far off. That they were marching towards Belmont there could be no doubt. Mrs. Marchant gave a shriek of alarm every now and then, and the children cried with terror. We tried to soothe them, but it was no easy matter to do so as we ran along.

'Try and keep the children quiet,' said Mr. Talboys in a suppressed tone, 'or the blacks will hear us. Push on, young gentlemen; I'll bring up the rear and defend you.'

'I'll stay with you,' I said; for it struck me that Chaffey might easily carry the child I had charge of, and so I handed it to him.

'And I'll stay also,' said Tom, giving his charge to Sinnet, who, with one of the black girls, was dragging another along. Mr. Marchant had enough to do to support his wife and carry another of their progeny. The house was already in sight, but we could hear the tramp of the insurgents' feet coming nearer and nearer, though we could not tell whether we ourselves were yet seen. Mr. Marchant and his family hurried on, probably sorry that they had not made more speed at first. We had our pistols ready, a brace each, in our belts, and our swords by our sides, should we come to a close encounter; but the blacks had, we concluded, firearms, and might shoot us down, should they see us, at a distance. I could not but admire the cool gallantry of Mr. Talboys, with so much at stake, yet willing to risk his own life in the defence of those he had promised to protect. He stood for nearly a minute to enable his friend's family to get ahead. The ground rose gradually towards the house, and we could now distinguish a dark mass coming across the open space in the plain below.

'Now we'll move on,' said Mr. Talboys; and we proceeded deliberately towards the house.

'They must have got in now,' he added shortly afterwards, speaking as before in a suppressed tone.

It was time indeed for us to be hurrying on, for as we looked round, a party of blacks, forming the advance guard, and whom we had not previously seen, suddenly appeared, not fifty paces off. They saw us at the same time, and with loud yells came rushing up the slope.

'On, lads, as fast as your legs can carry you,' cried Mr. Talboys, and, facing round, he fired his musket into the middle of them. Whether any one fell we did not stop to see, but ran towards the house. The blacks followed, hoping to overtake us, and fortunately not stopping to fire. Mr. Marchant and his family were only just then entering the house. They had got safe in, and we were about to follow when a shower of bullets came whistling round our heads and rattling against the walls. We sprang in, Mr. Talboys following. No time was lost in closing the door and putting up the barricades. We had scarcely finished when a second volley was fired, showing that the rebels were in earnest, and meant, if they could do so, to destroy the inmates of the house. Still, finding that we had escaped them, instead of dashing on, they kept at a respectful distance, under such cover as the hedges and palings afforded them. As the bullets pinged against the shutters and walls the children began to cry, and Mrs. Marchant and her black damsels to shriek out. Mrs. Talboys and Lucy remained perfectly quiet, doing their best to calm the fears of their guests.

'We have a strong house and brave defenders, and we need not be afraid of the rebels,' said the former in a quiet tone.

Meantime Mr. Talboys, leaving us to defend the lower storey, mounted to the top of the house, where, keeping under shelter, he could take a look out at whatever was going on below.

Presently we heard him shout, 'Who are you, and what is it you want?'

'We free and independent people,' answered a voice from the crowd; 'we want our rights. We no get dem, den we kill all de whites.'

'Much obliged for your kind intentions,' answered Mr. Talboys. 'There are two sides to that question, and you must look out not to be killed yourselves, which you will be, I promise you, if you attack us.'

'We see about dat,' one of the blacks shouted out.

Mr. Talboys replied, and made what sounded to me so long a speech that I wondered the insurgents had patience to listen to it, till I discovered that his object was to prevent them as long as possible from recommencing hostilities. Like other brave men, being unwilling to shed blood, he would not allow any of us to fire until it should become absolutely necessary. He again asked the rebels what they wanted.

'We want our rights, dat's what we want,' they shouted.

'That's what all your friends in the island wish you to have, but you won't get them by murdering the few white people in your power,' answered our host.

'Dat you say is true, Massa Talboys,' cried a black from the crowd.

'Hold your tongue, Quembo; take dat!' and the sound of a crushing blow, accompanied by a shriek, reached our ears, as if the last speaker had brained his wiser comrade.

'We no cum here to talk, we cum to fight,' shouted several together. There was a good deal of jabbering, and once more I saw, through a loophole out of which I was looking, the sable army approaching.

'Stand to your arms!' cried Mr. Talboys. 'We mustn't let these fellows get too confident. Shade all the lights, but don't fire until I give the word.'

It was pretty evident, from the bold way the blacks came on, that they supposed we were badly supplied with firearms, one shot only having been discharged. Mr. Talboys waited till they got within thirty paces, when, just as two or three of them had hurriedly discharged their pieces, he gave us the order to fire, and we sent a shower of bullets among the sable mass. Without stopping to see what effect it had produced, we all reloaded as rapidly as possible. A few bullets rattled against the house, but before we again fired the greater number of our assailants were scrambling off, in spite of the efforts of their leader to induce them to make a stand. As far as I could judge, looking through my loophole, none were killed, though several must have been wounded.

CHAPTER XI

A NARROW ESCAPE.

HE overseer proposed dashing out, with a whip in one hand and a sword in the other.

'The rascals won't stop running if they see us coming after them,' he said.

Mr. Talboys, however, wisely ordered all of us to remain inside the walls.

'There are brave fellows among them, notwithstanding the cowardice of some, and they are very likely to turn round and cut us to pieces,' he observed.

This would certainly have been the case, for we heard the blacks shouting and shrieking at no great distance off, though beyond the range of our muskets. They had evidently halted.

'We must be ready for another attack, my friends,' cried Mr. Talboys. 'Keep at your posts.'

Miss Lucy came up to where Tom and I were standing.

'We're so much obliged to you,' she said. 'If those dreadful blacks had got in, we knew that we should all be killed. You have defended us bravely, and we're so glad that no one has been hurt.'

'When we think that we have you to defend, we'll fight as long as we have a charge of powder and a ball remaining, and after that, too, ror we should make good use of our swords, depend on it,' answered Tom gallantly.

After this the blacks were quiet for some time, but we could not judge whether they intended again to come on. Mr. Talboys assured us that they were still in the neighbourhood, and that we must be prepared at any moment for an attack. The time went slowly by. I heard Cæsar and Cato talking; and as the danger appeared to lessen, the courage of the former increased.

'Dem niggers, how dey did run when we fired at dem! great cowards! Just dey cum on again, and see how we pepper der legs,' said Cæsar.

'Better dey not cum,' observed Cato, like a true philosopher, probably doubting his companion's resolution.

As there was no necessity to keep at our posts, I went up and asked Mr. Talboys if he would allow me to take his place, while he joined the ladies.

'Thank you,' he said; 'I was intending to summon you, for I wish to take a look round our fortifications, to be sure that we have no weak points, for I strongly suspect we have not done with those fellows yet.'

He was just about to descend, when I caught sight of a bright light away to the northward.

'What is that?' I asked, pointing it out to him.

'It comes from the direction of Marchant's house,' he answered. 'I very much fear the rebels have set fire to it. Yes, there is no doubt about it,' he added, as forked flames were observed to burst up round the first light, and to extend on either side. Presently another light was seen in the south-east.

'That must be from Peek's estate. I hope they had warning, and made their escape in time, or the villains will have murdered them, to a certainty. Fortunately there are no women or children there.'

We stood watching the progress of the flames.

'We'll not tell the Marchants of the disaster,' he continued. It might drive them out of their wits; but they may consider themselves fortunate in having escaped with their lives.'

Loud shouts rising from the spot where we supposed the blacks to be showed the pleasure they felt at seeing the houses burning.

8

'They would be still more delighted could they destroy Belmont,' observed Mr. Talboys. 'They will, I fear, soon again attempt to carry out their design.'

He now begged me to remain where I was, and to give him immediate information, should I observe anything suspicious, and went down to carry out his intention of examining every assailable point in the house. I kept my eyes turned, first to one side, then to the other, peering into the darkness, when I observed something moving, away to the right. It seemed like a black line; and after watching it for a few seconds, I felt sure that it was formed by a number of negroes creeping cautiously on to the right of the house, and endeavouring to conceal themselves. I was afraid that my voice might be heard should I shout out, so I went down the steps and soon found Mr. Talboys. The moment I told him what I had seen, he sprang up with me, but we could see nothing, though we watched for some minutes.

'If they were really blacks you saw, they intend to take us by surprise,' he said. 'We must keep a look-out, and be prepared for them.'

Just as he was speaking, there came a loud crashing sound, and the next instant cries and shouts rang through the house. Mr. Talboys sprang down the steps, and I followed him. There was no difficulty in ascertaining in what direction to go. A door had evidently been burst open in the southern wing of the house. A piercing shriek was heard as we hurried on. The rest of the party, deserting their posts, had already gone to drive back our assailants. The overseer and clerk, Sinnet and Chaffey, were encountering them bravely. Two had already paid dearly for their temerity, when Mr. Talboys, springing forward, attacked them furiously. I kept with him, and did my best with my hanger, cutting and slashing at the woolly pates of the fellows, who evidently were not prepared for so determined a resistance. Those in front gave way, and others who were about to enter hesitated to advance. Mrs. Talboys was rendering us good service by holding up a lantern, by which we could see our assailants, while the light, falling on their eyes, prevented them from seeing us. Though I observed my other two messmates, I could nowhere see Tom Pim. What could have become of him? I thought. I was, however, sure that he would not have held back, for though he was but a little fellow, he knew how to use his hanger as well as any of us. The fight didn't last long; another black was killed, two lay wounded on the ground, and the rest bolted out of the door, which, though shattered, was not off its hinges.

'Quick! Bring some planks,' cried Mr. Talboys.

There were some near at hand, with which we had intended to secure that particular door. We were not long in putting them up, and placing a heavy chest of drawers against them. Just as this was done, Mrs. Talboys exclaimed,—

'Where is Lucy?'

'And where is Tom Pim?' I cried out.

Neither of them answered. Before any search could be made, Mr. Marchant, who had been watching at the other side of the house, shouted out,—

'The enemy are upon us! the enemy are upon us! Quick! quick!'

We hurried to our posts, and before many seconds had elapsed, a shower of bullets came rattling against the walls.

'Fire away, my friends,' cried Mr. Talboys.

We obeyed the order with alacrity. I was thinking all the time, however, as to what could have become of Tom and Lucy. In vain I expected my messmate to hasten to his post. Again the blacks were checked. Had they been a minute sooner, the case would have been very different. They calculated, of course, on their friends getting in at the back of the house, and causing a diversion in their favour. For twenty minutes or more we kept loading and firing as fast as we could. Mr. Talboys was everywhere, now at one window, now at another, while the clerk and Cato were guarding the back and wings of the house. How the hours had passed by I could not tell, when at length I saw a faint light in the eastern sky. It gradually increased in brightness, and in a wonderfully short time daylight burst upon the world. As the blacks had failed to get into the house during the night, it was less likely that they would succeed during the day. They fired a parting volley, and then, to our great satisfaction, beat a rapid retreat. The search for Lucy and Tom was now renewed.

'Oh, my dear husband, what can have become of her?' cried Mrs. Talboy in accents of despair.

That they were not in the house was very certain. I proposed to sally forth and search for them.

'I'll go myself,' said Mr. Talboys. 'The rebels will be on the look-out, and you very probably will be captured if you go alone.'

He consented, however, to my accompanying him. We went out at the back door, which Mr. Talboys ordered to be closed after us. We had not gone far when we discovered a ribbon, which I knew Miss Lucy had worn on her shoulder.

'She must have been carried off by the blacks when they first burst into the house,' cried Mr. Talboys.

'The wretches cannot have had the barbarity to injure her,' I said.

'I don't know! I don't know!' answered her father in an agonized tone of voice.

We followed the track of the blacks, which was distinctly marked by the plants and canes being trampled down where they had gone across the garden and plantation, and continued on for some distance. No other trace of Tom or Lucy could we discover. We had to proceed cautiously, as at any time we might come suddenly upon a party of them, when we might find it very difficult to escape. We were, however, both well armed, with muskets in our hands, braces of pistols in our belts, and swords by our sides, so that we hoped, should we fall in with any enemies, to keep them at bay while we retreated. We looked round on either side, in the expectation of seeing something else that either Lucy or Tom might have dropped; but sometimes I could not help fearing that they might have been killed, and that we should come upon their dead bodies. Still I tried to put away the thought from me, as it was too dreadful. I suspect the same idea occurred to

Mr. Talboys, who looked stern and determined, and seldom spoke, while his eye was ranging round, far and near. We were going in the direction we fancied the blacks had taken. Mr. Talboys was of opinion that, finding they could not succeed in destroying Belmont, they had gone off to attack some other house and ravage the plantations. We were making our way across the country instead of along the high road, where the blacks might have discovered us at a distance; but sometimes the foliage was so thick that we could not see a dozen yards ahead. This had its advantages and its disadvantages. It was evidently the line which the party of blacks who had nearly surprised us had followed. Now and then we got close to the high road, and we were able, while still keeping under shelter ourselves, to look along it either way.

'The rebels have not, I suspect, gone off altogether, and we may not be far from them now,' whispered Mr. Talboys. 'Be very cautious; keep under cover as much as you can, and avoid making any rustling among the branches.'

We had moved on scarcely a dozen paces after this, when suddenly a number of black heads appeared above the bushes close in front of us. The white eyes of the negroes, as they caught sight of us, showed that they were more astonished than we were at the sudden encounter. Exclamations of surprise escaped from their lips.

'On, lads,' shouted Mr. Talboys at the top of his voice, as, drawing his sword, he sprang forward. 'Send those rascals to the right about.'

Uttering a shout, I imitated his example.

The blacks, evidently supposing that a strong body of whites was upon them, turned, and endeavoured to make their way through the brushwood, without looking back to see who was pursuing them. As they had no other encumbrances than their muskets, they soon distanced us. Not one of them fell, for Mr. Talboys refrained from firing, as did I, waiting until he told me to do so.

'Now, my young friend, it will be well to beat a retreat before these rascals discover that we are alone,' he said.

We were about to do as he proposed, when, unfortunately, one of the blacks, who was nearer to us than the rest, looked round, and seeing no one besides us, shouted to his companions. Now one stopped, now another, till the whole party came to a stand-still, turned round, and faced us.

'Spring back and try to get under cover,' said Mr. Talboys in a low voice. 'If the fellows advance, fire; but not till then. I'll speak to them.' He then shouted, 'You have carried off two young people from my house. Give them up at once unhurt, and we will not punish you as you deserve; but if they're injured, not one of you shall escape hanging.'

'We not got de young white folks here,' sang out a voice from among the negroes. 'You talk ob hanging, massa; take care we not hang you. What we stop here for?' continued the speaker to his companions; 'dere not many dere, or dey cum on.'

From the way the blacks were looking, I guessed that they were trying to discover how many persons were opposed to them; but as yet they fancied that there were others behind us.

'Do you quietly retreat, my young friend,' said Mr. Talboys in a low voice. 'Make your way back to the house as fast as you can, and tell them to be on their guard. I can manage these fellows as well alone, and your life would be needlessly risked by remaining.'

'I will do as you wish, sir; but if there's to be fighting, I should prefer to stay by you,' I answered.

'I'll try to avoid it, then,' said my friend, and once more he spoke to the blacks.

'If the young folks are not with you, tell me where they are.'

'We know nothin',' answered the black. 'Maybe by dis time dey hang from de branch ob one tree.'

'I don't believe that any of you would have had the cruelty to kill them,' he cried out. 'Do as I wish you,' he continued, in a low voice, to me.

Still I could not bring myself, for the sake of saving my own life, to leave him to be taken by the blacks; for it seemed to me that he would have but a small chance of escaping from them. I was hesitating, when I heard a shout from beyond where they were standing, and presently a number more rushed up, who by their furious gestures, as soon as they saw us, seemed to threaten our immediate destruction.

'I'll kill the first who comes on,' cried Mr. Talboys.

They answered with derisive cries, and several of them levelled their muskets. Mr. Talboys and I kept ours pointed at them, sheltering ourselves as we could behind the trunks of two trees which stood close together.

Our chance of escaping appeared very small.

While we thus kept the blacks in check, a sound in the rear struck my ears. It was the tramp of many feet. It became louder and louder. The blacks, jabbering away as they were to each other, did not apparently hear it. Mr. Talboys did, however, and he knew that it was more important than ever to refrain from firing. He again shouted to them,—

'Do any of you who have just come know where my daughter and young friend are gone to?'

They didn't reply, but we heard them talking to one another. This further put off the time. The sound of tramping feet grew louder.

'You make fool ob us, Massa Talboys,' at last said one of the blacks, who, probably from his understanding English, had been chosen as spokesman.

Gesticulating violently, the whole body now gave vent to loud shouts and cries, and dashed forward, with the intention of overwhelming us. We both fired, in the hopes of delaying their advance, and then sprang back to the shelter of some other trees we had noted behind us. The blacks, as they rushed on, fired, but their bullets passed high above our heads, stripping off the bark and branches, which came rattling down upon us.

We had but a small chance of again escaping, should we attempt the same proceeding; but, as the blacks were within twenty paces of us, a party of redcoats dashed through the brushwood, one of their leaders being a small naval officer whom, to my joy, I recognized as Tom Pim. The blacks saw the soldiers, and, without waiting to encounter the sharp points of their bayonets, turned, and scampered off as fast as they could manage to get through the bushes, the speed of most of them being increased by the bullets poured in on them, while several bit the ground.

The soldiers continued the pursuit till the blacks, scattering in all directions, got out of range of their muskets. Mr. Talboys and I accompanied them; but not till the halt was called had we an opportunity of speaking to Tom.

'And where is Lucy, my dear fellow?' asked Mr. Talboys, grasping Tom by the hand.

'All right, sir,' answered Tom. 'She's safe in the house. When the blacks broke in last night, she was close to the door, and a piece of wood striking her, she fell to the ground. The blacks, rushing in, seized her before I was able to lift her up, and while I was shouting out for assistance, and trying to defend her, they got hold of me, and carried us both off. It was only a short time ago that I knew you were safe; for I was dreadfully afraid that they had got into the house, and murdered you all. Fortunately, the blacks allowed Miss Lucy and me to remain together; so I told her to keep up her spirits, and that I would try and help her to run away. Most of the blacks who at first had charge of us hurried back, expecting to pillage the house, and only two remained. We heard the shots you fired, but I still did not know that you had driven them out. Meantime our two black guards were so occupied in trying to find out what was going on, that I took the opportunity of drawing my hanger, which had not been taken from me, and giving one a slash across the eyes, and another a blow which nearly cut off his arm. I seized Miss Lucy's hand, and we ran off as fast as we could. Neither of our guards were in a condition to follow us, and we ran and ran, scarcely knowing in what direction we were going. Miss Lucy said that she thought we were on the high road to Kingston; but she became at last so tired that she could go no further, and we had to rest. It soon became daylight; and just as we were going on again, we met with the soldiers, who were being brought up by Captain Ryan to your assistance.'

'You behaved most bravely, and I am deeply indebted to you, my young friend,' said Mr. Talboys, grasping Tom's hand. 'Had you not offered so determined a resistance, I believe that the blacks would have got into the house, and we should all have been destroyed.'

As the men had had a long and rapid march, their commander was glad to accept Mr. Talboys' invitation to return at once to Belmont, to partake of the refreshments they so much needed.

Miss Lucy on our arrival rushed into her father's arms, and was warm in her praises of the gallant way in which Tom had rescued her.

Everybody was engaged either in cooking or carrying provisions to the soldiers, who had assembled under the shade of the trees in front of the house. Sentries were of course placed, to give due notice should the blacks rally and attempt another attack, though Mr. Talboys considered it very improbable that such would be made.

As our leave was to expire the day after these events took place, having enjoyed a sound sleep, early in the morning we started in the carriages that had brought us, Cato driving Tom and me. We were glad to think that our kind friends were well protected, as Captain Ryan said that his orders were to remain there until reinforcements arrived.

I won't describe our parting, or what Tom said to Miss Lucy; if not affecting, it was cordial.

On our way we met more troops moving towards Belmont. We got back to Kingston, and thence on board the frigate, within the time Mr. Saunders had given us leave to be absent.

The account of our adventures created great interest on board. When I told Larry of our narrow escape with Mr. Talboys,—

'Thin, Maisther Terence dear, don't be after going on shore again without me,' he exclaimed. 'If you had been killed I'd never have lifted up my head, nor shown my face at Ballinahone again; for they would be saying that I ought to have been by your side, and died with you if I could not save you.'

I promised Larry not to go anywhere, if I could help it, without him. We expected soon to have sailed, but we were detained by Sir Peter Parker, then the admiral at Jamaica. There were also several other frigates and three line-of-battle ships in the harbour. Tom and I especially wanted to be off, as we could not expect to obtain leave again to go on shore, though we determined if the ship was detained to ask for it.

'Not much chance of that,' observed Nettleship, who had just come from the shore. 'The people are expecting an attack from the French and Spaniards, who have large fleets out here under the Count De Grasse, and the Governor has just got a letter, it is said, taken on board a prize, in which the whole plan for the capture of the island is detailed. The inhabitants are everywhere up in arms, and vow that they will fight to the last sooner than yield. More troops are expected, and every preparation is being made for the defence of the island.'

We had seen the *Triton* frigate go out that morning, though we were not aware of her destination. She carried despatches from Sir Peter Parker, giving Lord Howe the information which had been received, and requesting that reinforcements might immediately be sent to the island. The people on shore were actively engaged in strengthening Fort George, Fort Augusta, and the Apostles' Battery, and throwing up new forts in various directions. While the blacks were labouring at the fortifications, all the white men were being drilled to serve in the militia, which was numerous and enthusiastic; so we hoped that even should the French and Spaniards land, they would be soundly thrashed.

Some days passed before we received any news of our friends at Belmont. No leave was granted, as the captain could not tell at what moment we should be ordered to sea. Tom and I were therefore unable to go to Kingston to make inquiries about them. At length a shore-boat came off with letters, and one, which I knew by the superscription to be from Mr. Talboys, was handed to me. As I opened it, a small delicate note—addressed, Tom Pim, Esq., H.M.S. *Liffy* —fell out. As Tom was standing close to me at the time, he eagerly snatched it up. I was right in my surmises with regard to my letter. Mr. Talboys having again expressed his thanks for the services my messmates and I had rendered him, after saying that his family were all well, went on to inform me that the outbreak of the blacks had been quickly suppressed, the ringleaders having been caught and hanged. Mr. Marchant's house and three others had alone been destroyed, and with the exception of an overseer and two clerks, the remainder of the inhabitants had managed to escape. 'I hope,' he added, 'that we shall see you and your messmates again, and I shall be especially pleased to welcome that brave young fellow who so gallantly rescued my daughter.'

'What does your letter say, Tom?' I asked, when I had finished mine.

'Well, I shouldn't like to show it to any one else,' he said; 'but as you know how I regard Miss Lucy, I will to you. I can't say that I am quite satisfied with it. It's a little too patronizing, as if she thought herself a great deal older than I am. You shall have it,' and he handed me the note.

'MY DEAR TOM,'—it began,—'you are such a dear little fellow that I feel I must write to you to say how grateful I am to you for having saved me from those dreadful blacks. I should not have supposed that you would have been able to do it, but I shall never forget your bravery. I long to come back to Kingston, to see you again, and tell you so. But papa says that you are not likely to obtain leave, so I must wait patiently till we have beaten the French and Spaniards who threaten to invade our island, and peace is restored. I wish I could promise to do as you ask me, but mamma says I should be very foolish if I did. Do you know, I think so likewise; because it may be years and years before you are a commander, or even a lieutenant; but I want you to understand, notwithstanding, that I like you very much, and am very grateful, and shall always be so, as long as I live. So, my dear Tom, believe me, your sincere friend,—LUCY TALBOYS.'

'It's very clear, Tom, that Miss Lucy will not commit herself, and it's fortunate for you probably that she is so hard-
hearted,' I observed. 'I'd advise you not to be downcast
about the matter, and be content with the friendship and
gratitude of her family.'

Tom, however, looked very melancholy, and some time
afterwards Chaffey observed to me that he was sure something was amiss with Tom, as he was completely off his feed.

While we were allowed to go on shore our life was pleasant
enough, but when confined on board it was somewhat dreary
work, and we all longed for a change of some sort. A climate
with the thermometer at ninety doesn't conduce to high spirits.

We were aroused one evening as most of us were below,
by Sinnet rushing into the berth, and exclaiming,—

'The *Glasgow* is on fire, and the boats are ordered away
to her assistance.'

The *Glasgow* was a frigate, lying at no great distance from
us, and was to have sailed with the land breeze with a company of troops to the westward. We hurried on deck. Our
boats were being lowered, as were those of the other ships in
the harbour. Smoke in dense volumes was rising from the
hatchways of the *Glasgow*, and more was pouring out of her
ports. Her crew were at their stations, hauling up buckets
of water, and labouring like brave men to quench the rising
flames; but all their efforts, as far as I could see, were ineffectual. Nettleship and some of the older midshipmen
went off in the boats.

'I hope that they'll draw the charges of their guns, or we
shall have some of their shot rattling on board us,' said Tom.
'There are plenty of boats, so I don't suppose any of the crew
will be lost.'

'I should think not, unless the magazine catches fire,' I
answered.

'They'll drown that the first thing, if they can,' remarked
Tom. 'I wish we could have gone in one of the boats. I
don't like to see people in danger and be unable to try and
help them.'

CHAPTER XII.

THE HURRICANE.

IN spite of all the exertions being made on board, with the assistance of the men from the other ships who had now arrived alongside, the smoke increased in denseness, and presently burst up above the hatchway, while we could see the red glare through the ports. The ship having been in the West Indies for some time, her woodwork was like tinder, and the flames rapidly gained the mastery. Now forked tongues of fire burst out from the midship ports, gradually working their way forward and aft. At length all attempts to save the ship were abandoned. The crew were seen descending into the boats, some collected forward, others under the quarter. Down they came by ladders and ropes, the midshipmen and the boys first, the men following, looking like strings of sausages surrounding the ship. Rapidly as every one moved, there was no confusion. As the boats were loaded they pulled off, others taking their places. So quickly had the fire spread that it seemed as if the officers had scarcely space left them to stand on before descending. Shouts were raised when the glitter of the gold lace on their coats was seen as they came over the quarter. The last man to quit was the brave captain of the ship. Almost in an instant afterwards she was in a fierce blaze fore and aft, the flames rushing out of the cabin windows as well as through the bow ports.

We in the meantime had got springs on our cables, as had

all the other ships, in case she should drift from her moorings.

'I suspect the shot were withdrawn,' I observed to Tom Pim.

'I hope so,' he answered; but just then—crash! there came a couple of round shot against our side, while more guns were heard going off in the opposite direction.

We immediately hauled away on one of our springs, just in time to escape several more iron missiles, which went bounding across the harbour. Three or four other ships were struck, but no one on board ours was hurt. Presently there came a loud roar, the mizen-mast shot up, followed by the after-part of the deck, and then came hissing down into the water. The flames surrounding the other masts formed a fiery pinnacle rising into the dark sky, and immediately afterwards down they came with loud crashes, the ship looking like a huge roaring and raging cauldron of flame, while crash succeeded crash as the heated guns fell into the hold. Several of the people brought on us were severely scorched, showing the desperate efforts they had made to try and save their ship. Dr. M'Call and the assistant-surgeons had work enough in attending to them. Fortunately the soldiers had not arrived alongside the *Glasgow* before she caught fire, and when they came down the harbour they were put on board our frigate, and we received orders to carry them to their destination.

Everything was done as rapidly as possible for their accommodation. The men were berthed on the main deck. The captain received the commanding officer, the lieutenants messed in the gun-room, and we had the pleasure of entertaining the ensigns. The land breeze began blowing about eight o'clock, the time the *Glasgow* was to have sailed. We were detained some time in getting off provisions from the shore, but by dint of hard work all was ready by ten o'clock, and the night being bright, the anchor was hove up. With every sail that we could carry set, we glided out of the harbour. It was important to get a good offing, so that we might weather Portland Point, the southernmost part of the island, before the sea breeze should again begin to blow. We hoped that the land breeze, which generally begins to drop about midnight, would last longer than usual, so as to carry us well out to sea, There are ugly rocks off Portland which it is not pleasant to have under the lee at any time.

'Shure it would be hard to bate these nights out here, Mr. Terence,' said Larry, whom I met on deck, and who seemed to enjoy as much as I did the calm beauty of the scene, the stars like specks of glittering gold shining out of the heavens of the deepest blue, each one reflected in the tranquil ocean. The line of coast, seen astern and on our starboard quarter, rose into various-shaped mountains, their outlines clearly marked against the sky; while every now and then a mass of silver light was spread over the water, as some inhabitant of the deep leaped upwards, to fall again with a splash into its liquid home.

I asked Larry how Hoolan was going on after his flogging.

'He doesn't talk much, Mr. Terence, but he looks as sulky as ever, and I wouldn't trust him more than before,' was the reply.

'He can harm no one, at all events,' I observed; 'and I don't think he has much chance of making his escape, even if he still thinks of attempting it.'

'Faith, I don't fancy he could hide himself among the black fellows; and no merchant skipper would like to have him aboard his craft,' said Larry.

Going aft, I met Tom Pim, for he and I were in the first watch. We were pacing the deck together, when we were joined by one of our passengers, Ensign Duffy.

'Can't sleep, my dear fellows,' he said in a melancholy tone, which made Tom and me laugh. 'My thoughts are running on a charming little girl I met at Kingston. I was making prodigious way with her when we were ordered off to the out-of-the-way corner of the world to which you are carrying us, and the chances are we shall not meet again.'

'What's her name, Duffy?' I asked.

'Lucy Talboys,' he answered promptly. 'I don't mind telling you young fellows, as you are not likely to prove rivals;

but I say, if either of you meet her I wish you'd put in a word about me. Say how miserable I looked, and that you are sure I had left my heart at Kingston.'

'I will gladly say anything you wish; but perhaps she will think you left it with some other lady,' I observed.

'Say I was always sighing and uttering "Lucy! Lucy!" in my sleep.'

'I'll not say anything of the sort,' exclaimed Tom. 'I never heard you utter her name till now, and I don't believe she cares the snuff of a candle for you.'

Just as we were about to go below, at eight bells, we made out Portland Point broad on our starboard beam, so that we hoped, should the wind not fail us before morning, to be well to the westward of it. We were just turning into our hammocks, the other watch having been called, when we heard the canvas flap loudly against the masts, and were summoned on deck again to take in studding-sails. Still the land wind favoured us, the sails once more bulged out, and before we went below we had brought Portland Point on the quarter. When we went on deck again in the morning the frigate lay nearly becalmed off Carlisle Bay, thence we had a westerly course to Pedro Bluff. The sun, as it rose higher and higher in the cloudless sky, beat down hot and strong upon our heads, while officers and men, as they paced the deck, whistled perseveringly for a breeze. At length a dark blue line was seen extending in the south-east across the shining waters. It approached rapidly. Presently the canvas blew out, and with tacks on board we stood along the coast. Our speed increased with the rising breeze. We were not long in getting round Pedro Bluff, when we stood directly for Savannah-le-Mer, then a pretty flourishing little town at the south-west end of the island. Here we were to land some of the redcoats, and were to take the rest round to Montego Bay, at the north-west end of Jamaica. We came off it on the following morning.

As the harbour is intricate, we hove-to outside, while the soldiers were landed in the boats. I went in one, and Tom Pim in another, the second lieutenant having the command of the whole. We had a long and a hot pull, and Ensign Duffy, who was in my boat, declared that if it was proportionately hot on shore to what it was on the water, he should expect to be turned into baked meat before he had been there long. Larry was pulling bow-oar, and very well he pulled by this time, for though he was a perfect greenhorn when he came to sea, he had been accustomed to row on the Shannon.

The frigate, I should have said, was to call on her way back for some of the soldiers whom those we took out had come to relieve. Our approach had been seen by the officers at the barracks, which were situated about a mile from the town; and they came down to welcome their comrades in arms. Leaping on shore, the rocks which formed the landing-place being slippery, I fell, and came down on my knees with great force. I felt that I was severely hurt, and on attempting to rise, found it impossible to do so, even with the assistance of Larry, who sprang to my side, uttering an exclamation of sorrow. On this, one of the officers, whom I perceived by his dress to be a surgeon, came up to me, and at once examined my hurt.

'It requires to be instantly attended to,' he said, 'or inflammation may set in, and in this climate the consequences may be serious.'

My friend Duffy proposed that I should be carried to the barracks, though my lieutenant at first objected to letting me go, declaring that he should not be long in getting back to the ship.

'Long enough to allow of the young gentleman losing his leg, or perhaps his life,' remarked the surgeon. 'I'll have him at once taken to a house in the town, and when your frigate comes back, I hope he'll be in a condition to embark.'

Hearing this, the lieutenant not only gave me leave to remain, but allowed Larry to stay and attend on me. Tom Pim took my hand as Duffy and some of his men were placing me upon a door, which had been procured to carry me into the town.

'I wish that I was going to stay with you, Paddy,' he said;

9

'but it's of no use to ask leave, though I'd give a great deal if I could. We shall be very dull without you.'

'Thank you, Tom,' I answered. 'If I had my will I'd rather go off. I suppose the doctor is right; and it's safer to let him attend to me at once.'

I was carried immediately to a house which I found belonged to a Mr. Hans Ringer, an attorney, who had charge of several plantations in that flourishing neighbourhood. The doctor and he, it was evident, were on most intimate terms, for on our arrival, without any circumlocution, the latter at once said,—

'I have brought a young midshipman who requires to be looked after, and I'd be obliged to you if you'd order your people to get a room ready for him immediately.'

I could scarcely have supposed that so serious an injury could have been so easily inflicted. Soon after my arrival I nearly fainted with the pain, but the doctor's treatment at length soothed it, and he was able to set the injured bones.

I must make a long story short, however.

Mr. Ringer and his family treated me with the greatest kindness; indeed, nothing could surpass the hospitality of the inhabitants of Jamaica; and it was with the utmost difficulty, when I got better, that the doctor could get him to allow me to be carried to the barracks, where the fresher air would assist me in regaining my strength. Larry, of course, spent most of his time with me; indeed, had I not insisted on his going out, he never would have left my bedside.

I was now every day expecting the return of the frigate, when I believed that, well or ill, I should have to go on board her.

'That must depend on circumstances, my lad,' said Dr. M'Manus. 'For if you can't go, you can't. The captain must find another opportunity of getting you on board.'

'But suppose the frigate has to fight an action, I would not be absent on any account,' I exclaimed.

'With a fractured tibia, and the inflammation which would be sure to supervene, you would not render much service to your country,' observed the doctor. 'When you have suffi-

ciently recovered you can get back to Port Royal, and rejoin
your ship; she's not likely to be sent to a distance while
the enemy's fleet threaten the island. Indeed, we require all
the forces on shore and afloat we can collect. I don't quite
understand what we shall do if we are attacked here, though
I'm very sure we shall fight to the last before we let the French
and Spanish land.'

I saw that there was no use in arguing the point, but I was
determined, if I could, to go off and rejoin my ship. Larry
did his best to console me.

'It's not a bad place to be in, if you only had the use of
your legs, Mr. Terence. Them nager boys and girls are mighty
funny creatures. What bothers me most is that I didn't bring
my fiddle on shore, for sure if I had, it would have been after
setting them all dancing, till they danced out of their black
skins. It's rare fun to see them laughing as if they'd split
their sides, when I sing to them. They bate us Irishmen
hollow at that fun, I'll allow. I find it a hard matter to contain myself when I see them rolling their eyes and showing
their white teeth as they stretch their mouths from ear to ear.'

I happened to tell Dr. M'Manus of Larry's talent.

'I'll try and get a fiddle for the boy, and put it to the test,'
he said good-naturedly.

In the evening I was aroused from a nap into which I had
fallen, by the sound of an Irish jig played on a violin, followed
by shouts of laughter, clapping of hands, shrieks, and merriment, while the noise of feet from the courtyard below told
me that Larry had been as good as his word. I thanked the
doctor, who came in while the revels were at their height.

'I sent into the town and borrowed a fiddle, for I was sure
that your follower's music would do as much good to the men
as the fresh air of the hills. They and the black boys and girls
are all toeing and heeling it together. The niggers, I confess,
beat them hollow in agility and endurance.'

I asked the doctor to wheel me to the window, that I might
look out and see the fun. He good-naturedly complied, and
assisted me to sit up. There were forty or fifty white men,

and almost double the number of blacks of both sexes,—the women dressed in gay-coloured petticoats, with handkerchiefs round their heads; the men in white or striped cotton—the light colour contrasting with their dark skins,—one and all clapping their hands, snapping their fingers, and moving here and there in figures it was difficult to follow, but all evidently enjoying themselves immensely, judging by their grinning countenances and rolling eyes.

After this Larry became an immense favourite with the soldiers, as he found not a few of our countrymen among them. The officers of the little garrison were very kind to me, and I was never in want of society, as one or other was constantly by my bedside.

Notwithstanding this, as I got better I became more and more anxious to receive news of the frigate, and began to wonder what had become of her. Though I could not walk, I saw no reason why I should not return on board. The doctor, however, was still of a different opinion; and I was greatly disappointed when, on returning from the town one day, he told me that she had come off the harbour, and that he had sent on board to say that I was not yet fit to be moved, but would rejoin my ship by the first opportunity after I was convalescent. I could only thank him for his kindness, keeping my feelings to myself.

At length I was able to get out of bed, and walk with the assistance of a crutch. Had the doctor and Larry not held me up, however, the first time I made the attempt, I should have fallen down again. I felt just as, I suppose, an infant does on his first trying to toddle. After this I got rapidly better, and was soon able to join the officers in the mess-room, and in a short time to throw away my crutches.

The first walk I proposed to take was into Savannah-le-Mer to inquire about vessels proceeding to Port Royal. I was accompanied by Ensign Duffy and Larry. With their help I got on better than I expected; and though I didn't feel inclined to take a leap, I fancied that if put to it I could run as well as ever.

We repaired to the house of Mr. Ringer, who received us cordially, and from him I learnt that a fine vessel, the *Princess Royal*, would sail for Kingston the next day. He insisted on my remaining at his house, promising to drive me back to the barracks in the evening, that I might wish the kind doctor and my other friends there good-bye. We accordingly returned as he proposed. It was a difficult matter to get Larry away from his late companions, who seemed inclined to detain him *vi et armis*, the men grasping his hands, and the black girls hanging round him, many of them blubbering outright at the thoughts of parting from the ' lubly Irish boy dat play de fiddle,' —as for pronouncing his name, that they found beyond their power.

The officers drank my health in overflowing bumpers, and had I not remembered my uncle's advice, and prevented my own glass from being filled, I should not have been in a fit state to present myself at Mr. Ringer's hospitable mansion. I remember thinking the night oppressively hot, and was thankful that Mr. Ringer was good enough to drive me from the barracks into the town.

'I don't know what to make of the weather,' said my host the next morning, when we met at breakfast.

Not a breath of wind stirred the atmosphere, and it seemed as if all nature was asleep; while the sky, instead of being of a cerulean blue, was suffused, as the sun rose, with a fiery red tinge.

The hour—about noon—at which it was arranged that I should go on board was approaching. My host offered to accompany me down to the harbour, but before we reached it we encountered a violent squall, which almost took us off our legs, and sent Larry's hat flying up the street. He made chase after it, and we stopped to let him overtake us, while a number of other people, caught by the wind, passed us running off in the same direction. At length his hat, driven into a doorway, was recovered, and Larry came battling against the wind to rejoin us.

'You'll not put to sea to-day, ' said my friend; 'nor for

many a day to come, if I mistake not; but we'll make our way
to the harbour, and see how things are going on there.'

On reaching it we found the sea already lashed into a
mass of seething foam. The larger vessels strained at their
anchors, some tossing and tumbling about, others already
overwhelmed by the waves. It was with difficulty we could
stand our ground.

'Unless the hurricane passes by, for hurricane it is, not one
of those vessels will escape destruction,' said Mr. Ringer. As
he spoke, one of them parted from her cables and drove towards the shore.

'We must beat a rapid retreat if we wish to save our lives,'
he continued; 'the tempest is down upon us!'

The wind, which had previously blown from the south-east,
suddenly shifted to the southward.

Grasping my arm, he hurried me off from the spot on which
we were standing. At the same time down came a deluge of
rain—not in mere drops, but in regular sheets of water. It
wetted us to the skin in a few moments. Larry, now seizing
my other arm, dragged me forward. As we looked back for a
moment, we observed the sea rising in a mountain billow, hiss-
ing and foaming, and approaching the shore. It was but the
first, however, of others still larger which were to follow. It
broke with a thundering roar,—the water rushed on, flowing by
the spot we had already reached; but even though we were
nearly up to our knees, I couldn't resist taking another glance
behind. The whole ocean was covered with wreck; and one
of the larger vessels I had seen just before, had disappeared
beneath the surface.

As we hurried on, crash succeeded crash. First one house
fell, then another, and another, and from some bright flames
burst forth, which even the descending rain failed to quench.
It was useless to attempt saving the lives of our fellow-creatures,
for the same destruction would have overtaken us. Our great
object was to reach the higher country in the direction of the
barracks. Had Larry and I been alone, we should in all probability have lost our lives; but Mr. Ringer, knowing the

town, led us quickly through it by the shortest route. As we dashed through the streets, scarcely looking to the right hand or to the left, piercing cries of agony and despair struck on our ears. The smaller and more lightly built houses were levelled in a moment, and many even of the larger were crumbling away.

'Don't you wish to go to your own house? if so, we must not stop you; we will go with you,' I said to Mr. Ringer.

'We should only be crushed by the falling ruins if we made the attempt,' he answered at the top of his voice, and even then I could scarcely hear what he said 'I'll try and get to it from the rear when I have seen you out of the town.'

Not far off from where we then were was a fine house, that had hitherto withstood the hurricane. Presently a blast struck us which, had we not clung together, would have blown us down. At the same time, looking up, I saw the house literally rocking. Down came one wall, and then another, the roof fell in, and in one instant it was a heap of shapeless ruins.

'I trust the inmates have escaped,' cried Mr. Ringer.

Just then loud shrieks and cries for help struck on our ears. They came, it seemed, from beneath the ruins. We could not withstand the appeal for assistance, and calculating as well as we could in what direction the still standing walls would fall, we sprang forward, taking a course to avoid them across the mass of ruins. An arch, which had apparently formed the centre of a passage, was yet uninjured, though blocked up. The cries seemed to us to come from thence. We should find, we knew, great difficulty in removing the *débris* which encumbered it, and the walls might at any moment fall down and crush us. Still Larry and I, having climbed to the top of the heap, began pulling away the beams and planks and rubbish which stopped up the entrance. Mr. Ringer joined us, though evidently considering our occupation a very dangerous one. However, we persevered, and at length had made an opening sufficiently large to look in. We could see two ladies, an old gentleman, and a mulatto servant.

'We have come to help you,' I cried out. 'If you'll climb up here you'll be free, and there may yet be time, Mr. Ringer thinks, to reach the open country.'

Mr. Ringer joining us, the two gentlemen recognized each other.

'What, Martin! Glad to see you safe,' said the former. 'Come, get out of that place as fast as possible.'

Encouraged by us, the youngest of the ladies first made the attempt, and succeeded in getting high enough to reach our hands. The old lady followed, though unless Mr. Martin and the mulatto girl had shoved behind, we should have found it impossible to have got her through. Mr. Martin and the girl followed.

As may be supposed, we didn't stop longer on the ruins than was necessary, but scrambling over them, again reached the open street. Scarcely were we there before down came the remaining wall, with a crash which broke in the arch. It would certainly have destroyed Mr. Martin and his family had they been there. The event showed us clearly the importance of getting out of the town. It seemed scarcely possible that any one passing through the narrow streets could escape being killed. Even in the broader ones the danger of being crushed was fearful. Mr. Ringer assisted Mrs. Martin, I offered my aid to the young lady, and Larry took charge of the old gentleman, who required helping as much as his wife and daughter. I had forgotten all about my lameness. We of course were somewhat delayed in our progress. Now we had to scramble over fallen walls—now we narrowly escaped being killed by masses of masonry and timber falling around us.

At length the open was reached, and we made our way to some higher ground overlooking the bay. We had reason to be thankful that we were out of the town. Providentially we reached a small stone building, which afforded us some shelter from the driving rain and furious wind, against which it was impossible to stand alone. The bay, as we looked down upon it, presented a fearful scene. The whole shore was strewn with masses of wreck. Not a small craft had escaped, and the largest, with all anchors down, were tossing about, and seemed every moment likely to be engulfed. The town itself was a heap of ruins, scarcely a house was standing, and none had escaped injury. In some places flames were raging, which would have set fire to other houses had it not been for the mass of water descending on them, while even amid the up-roar of the elements we could hear the shrieks and cries of the inhabitants who still survived. Presently another immense wave rolled into sight, out of the dense mist which now shrouded the ocean. On it came with a tremendous roar. The first vessel it reached was in a moment buried beneath it. We thought the others would share the same fate, but the cables parted, and they were borne on the summit of the wave high up above the beach. On, on it came. Mr. Ringer shouted out to us to escape; and he had reason to do so, for it seemed as if the wave would overwhelm the spot where we stood. Though the water swept up a portion of the height, the wave broke before it reached it, leaving the *Princess Royal* high and dry on the shore, while it receded, roaring and hiss-ing, carrying off everything in its course. The crew of the stranded ship had good cause to be thankful for their escape. On again looking towards the town, we saw that the sea had swept away many of the houses in the lower part, while the water rushed through the streets, extinguishing some of the fires, and must have overwhelmed all caught in its embrace. Mr. Ringer proposed that we should make our way to the barracks, but the ladies were unwilling to encounter the storm, and begged to remain where they were. Evening was now approaching, but the hurricane gave no signs of abating. In whatever direction we looked we could see its dire effects. Not a shrub, not a cane, remained standing. Every tree had been blown down. It seemed as if a vast scythe had passed over the land. The uproar continued as loud as before.

'This is a mighty curious country,' shouted Larry to me. 'It beats a faction fight in Tipperary hollow. I was after thinking it was the most peaceable disposed part of the world, seeing how quiet it has been since we came out here. Hullo! what's that?'

There was a loud rumbling sound. The earth shook beneath our feet.

'It's an earthquake,' cried Mr. Ringer. 'Heaven forbid that it should increase.'

The ladies clung to Mr. Martin with looks of terror. Again there came that fearful shaking of the earth; many of the remaining buildings toppled over. Flashes of lightning, brighter than I had ever before beheld, darted from the sky and lighted up the sea. Even the night scarcely added to the horrors of those moments, as far as we were concerned, though it must have done so to the miserable people still within the precincts of the town. At one time the water seemed to recede altogether out of the bay, but presently, as if gathered up in a heap, it once more rolled over the land.

Hour after hour went by, till about midnight, almost as suddenly as it had commenced, the hurricane passed away from us on its devastating course; and in a short time, excepting the roar of the surf upon the shore, scarcely a sound was heard. On this we set out for the barracks, hoping that they had withstood the tempest. Although they had suffered considerably, the larger portion had escaped.

Mr. Martin and his wife and daughter warmly expressed their gratitude to us for having rescued them from their perilous position, saying that they must have perished had we not come to their assistance.

'I wish that I had a home to which to invite you,' said Mr. Martin, with a melancholy smile; 'but I trust that my house may ere long be rebuilt, and that I may have the means of showing my gratitude better than I can now.'

'I shall be very happy to stay with you if I have the chance,' I answered; 'but I suspect it will be a long time before I again get leave.'

The officers, as might have been expected, received us in the kindest way possible. Duffy was delighted to see us. He

fancied I might have gone on board, and sailed before the
hurricane came on.

Next morning the commanding officer marched the whole of
the men down, to render such assistance as they could to the
survivors among the suffering inhabitants. I have never since
witnessed a more fearful scene of destruction than the town
presented. Numbers were lying about in the streets, where
they had been crushed to death by the falling masses, many
among them being the principal people in the place. In
all directions the survivors were rushing about in quest of
relatives or friends; while the larger number of the dead
lay concealed beneath the ruins.

The appearance of the *Princess Royal* was extraordinary.
We had seen her cast on shore and left on her beam-ends. At
present she was perfectly upright, the ground beneath her keel,
during the earthquake, having given way: and there she lay,
securely embedded, without the possibility of ever being set
afloat again, about a quarter of a mile from the beach. Two
other vessels had been driven higher on shore, but lay on their
beam-ends. It was at once proposed to utilize the vessel, by
making her the home of the houseless inhabitants; and forthwith the women and children, and men unable to labour, were
collected on board her. As I surveyed the effects of the
hurricane, I naturally felt very anxious about my ship, fearing that she might have been at sea, and been lost. I afterwards learned that it was only the eastern wing of the hurricane
that had swept by the western end of Jamaica, but that its
influence in a less degree had been felt over the whole island.

As soon as the news reached Kingston, vessels were despatched with provisions, and such relief as could be afforded,
for the sufferers. As I was anxious to get back, I took my
passage with Larry on board the *Rose* schooner. The captain
promised to land us at Port Royal in a couple of days;
'always providing that we are not snapped up by the enemy,
or that another hurricane doesn't come on,' he observed.

As we sailed out of the harbour, I could see at one glance,
more clearly than before, the destruction worked by the hurri-

cane and earthquake. The whole town appeared to be reduced to heaps of ruins, with here and there a few shattered
walls standing up in their midst. The skipper of the *Rose*
could give me no information about the *Liffy*. There were
a considerable number of men-of-war in the harbour, and he
had not taken especial note of any of them.

'If she was at sea during the hurricane, it is a hundred to
one that she escaped,' he observed.

We made all sail, and kept in shore as much as we could,
lest the enemy's privateers might spy us out, and carry us off to
St. Domingo, or elsewhere. We, however, escaped all dangers;
and, to my great joy, on entering Port Royal I made out the
Liffy among the other men-of-war at anchor. The *Rose's*
boat took me alongside. Mr. Saunders was on deck, so I
went up to him.

'Come aboard, sir,' I said, touching my hat.

'What, my lad! is it you?' he exclaimed. 'I'm glad to
see you. There was a report that you had perished during
the hurricane at Savannah. How is your leg? Able to return to your duty, I hope?'

'As able and willing as ever, sir,' I answered.

'That's all right; there'll be work for us all, ere long.'

As I entered the berth there was a regular shout, 'Hurrah,
Paddy Finn!'

'Glad to have you back, youngster,' cried Nettleship.

Tom Pim grasped my hand, and seemed unwilling to let it
go, though he didn't say as much as many of the others. I
had to answer whole volleys of questions from my messmates,
who were all eager to know what had happened to me. I
described our narrow escape from the town, and modestly
touched on the part I had taken in rescuing Mr. Martin and
his wife and daughter.

'Glad to see you uphold the honour of the cloth,' said
Nettleship; 'we should never see anybody in danger, and not
try to help them at the risk of our lives.'

I was amply repaid by the praises my messmates bestowed
upon me, for they knew that I had only told them the truth

without exaggeration. I asked what they expected we should do next.

'Look out for the French and Spanish fleets, which have long been threatening to pay the island a visit, and take possession of it, if they can,' answered Nettleship. 'Why they have not come before now I don't know; but there's some reason for it, I suppose.'

The sound of music, and the stamp of feet, as I went forward in the evening, showed me that Larry's fiddle had been taken care of; and there he was, scraping away in high glee, setting his messmates dancing merrily to his music, they not troubling their heads about the fierce work which was in store for them. He had received, he afterwards told me, a hearty welcome from all hands, who were delighted to get him back among them.

The next morning Nettleship went on shore. We were most of us in the berth when he returned.

'I have grand news, boys; not so much for us, though, as for the people of Jamaica. The governor has received information that the Spanish and French fleets were caught in the late hurricane, as they were cruising off Cape François. Two Spanish ships foundered, two more were driven no one knows where, and four were dismasted. Two Frenchmen were dismasted, one went to the bottom, and another was driven on shore, while the rest, considerably battered, had to bear away to Havanna.'

'How do you know that it's all true?' asked several of the mess.

'I heard it from the captain himself, and, what's more, we're to sail forthwith to carry the information to Sir Samuel Hood, who is supposed to be at Barbadoes. He sent me on to direct Mr. Saunders to get the ship ready for sea, so that we may sail the moment he comes on board.'

The boatswain's call, summoning all hands on deck, prevented us from asking any further questions. It not being known at what moment the ship might be sent to sea, she was kept well provided with water and fresh provisions, so that we had nothing to wait for from the shore, except a few of the officers, who had gone to Port Royal.

Blue Peter was hoisted and a gun fired, as a signal for them to come off. The top-sails were loosed, the cable hove short, and we were ready to start at the first puff of the land breeze that might come off the mountains. We were all anxiously looking out for the appearance of the captain. The moment his gig came alongside, she was hoisted up, the anchor hove in, the sails let fall, and we glided out of the harbour. Under the influence of the land breeze, with studding-sails set below and aloft, we ran on at a rapid rate, expecting that we should reach Barbadoes in about a week at the furthest. When once away from the land, the wind dropped, and for hours we lay becalmed. The next morning we got a light breeze, which enabled us to steer our course. A constant look-out was kept for the enemy, for though the main body of the French fleet was said to be in harbour, it was likely that their cruisers would be met with.

Nettleship, Tom Pim, and I were in the morning watch. The first ruddy streaks, harbingers of the rising sun, had appeared in the eastern sky, when the look-out who had been sent aloft shouted, ' A sail on the lee-bow.'

CHAPTER XIII.

THERE had been a stark calm since the commencement of the middle watch. The sails still hung up and down against the masts.

'What does she look like?' inquired Mr. Bramston, the lieutenant of the watch.

'A ship, sir,' was the answer.

Nettleship, with his glass at his back, sprang up the rigging to take a look at the stranger.

'She's a ship, sir, but appears to me to be a small one,' he observed as he came down. 'The chances are that it's all we shall know about her. If she gets a breeze before us she'll soon be out of sight.

Soon after, some catspaws began to play across the water.

'Hurrah! we shall get the breeze before the stranger feels it,' cried Nettleship.

Now the canvas began to bulge out; now it again dropped. The royals and top-gallant sails filled, and the frigate moved slowly through the water. Her speed soon increased, however, as the breeze freshened. At length we could see the stranger from the decks, for, as she still lay becalmed, we were quickly coming up with her. Nettleship again went aloft, and I followed him.

'What do you think of her?' I asked.

'She's Spanish or French; I'm pretty certain of that. A

flush-decked ship, probably carrying twenty to six-and-twenty guns.'

'If she can't escape, will she fight, do you think?' I inquired.

'If her captain has any pluck in him, he may hope to knock away some of our spars, though he can't expect to take us,' he said.

When we again came below, and Nettleship made his report, the drum beat to quarters. Every stitch of canvas we could carry had been set, below and aloft. We were carrying down the breeze as we glided on towards the stranger. She also made all sail, though she still lay becalmed; but every moment we expected to see her canvas blow out, when, if she was a fast vessel, she might lead us a long chase before we could come up to her. As our object was to get down to Barbadoes with all speed, the captain might consider it his duty to let her go, rather than be led out of his course. As we approached, our bow chasers were got ready, to send her an unmistakeable message that she must strike, or run for it. Hitherto she had shown no colours. Presently the French ensign was run up at her peak. Immediately afterwards a flash issued from her stern, and a shot came bounding over the water towards us; but we were not yet within range.'

'That's a long gun,' observed Nettleship. 'If she keeps ahead, she may do us some damage with it before we get alongside of her.'

'Give her the starboard bow gun, Mr. Saunders,' cried the captain.

The gun being trained as far forward as possible, we yawed slightly to port. We watched the shot as it flew across the water. It was well aimed, for it struck the counter of the chase; but its force must have been nearly expended, for it fell back into the sea.

All the sails of the chase were now drawing, and away she went before the wind.

'She may still lead us a long dance, unless we can knock away some of her spars,' observed Nettleship. 'She's evidently a fast craft, or her commander would not attempt to escape. We are, however, as yet gaining on her ; and, if we can once get her under our broadside, we shall soon bring down her colours.'

While he was speaking, another shot was fired from the Frenchman's stern. Ricochetting over the surface, it passed close to our side. After this she continued firing shot after shot. Two went through our canvas, others missed us. At last one came on board, and carried off a man's head.

Captain Macnamara, anxious to get up to her, would not lose way by again yawing to fire ; and we had to receive her shot without returning the compliment.

' It's very annoying to be bothered by a small craft like that,' said Tom. 'However, we'll pay her off when we do get up with her.'

Fast as she was, our wider spread of canvas enabled us before long to bring our foremost guns to bear. They were fired in rapid succession. The first discharge produced no apparent damage ; but at the second, down came her mizen-yard. On seeing this, our crew cheered lustily, and our guns were quickly run in and reloaded. The enemy, however, showed no intention of striking.

Just as we were again about to fire, putting her helm to starboard, she brought the whole of her larboard broadside to bear on us, and a dozen round shot came crashing aboard the frigate.

Three of our men fell, and several others were wounded, mostly by the splinters which flew about the deck. None of our spars, however, were shot away.

Before she could again keep before the wind the whole of our starboard broadside was poured into her. It was better aimed even than hers. The sound of the shrieks and cries rising from her deck told us of its fearful effects. Still her colours were flying.

Again keeping before the wind, she stood on, blazing away at us from two long guns in her stern. The loss of her mizen told on her sailing. Slowly but surely we got nearer and nearer.

10

'Shall we not soon be up with her?' I asked Nettleship; for it was trying work to be peppered at without being able to return more than a single shot occasionally.

'As surely as the sun sets and rises again, unless she knocks away one of our masts, or brings down our main or foreyard; and then it's possible that she may get off after all.'

'I made sure we should have her before many minutes were over,' I observed.

I remarked the eager countenances of the men as they stood at their guns, expecting every moment the order to fire. It came at last. Once more we kept away.

'Give it them now!' cried the captain, and every gun sent forth a sheet of flame.

Our shot told with fearful effect on the enemy's deck. There seemed to be confusion on board, and then a man was seen to spring aft, and down came the colours.

A cheer rose from our men at the sight. We stood on, however, till we were close enough to hail, when the captain ordered through the speaking-trumpet the Frenchman to heave to, threatening to fire another broadside if he failed to do so. The order was obeyed; and we also having hove to, a boat was lowered to send on board and take possession. Mr. Bramston went in her, and I accompanied him.

On reaching the deck of the prize, a glance showed me the fearful damage our guns had produced. In all directions lay numbers of dead seamen, the deck slippery with gore. The bulwarks were shattered, two of the boats knocked to pieces, and the ship was otherwise severely damaged.

A lieutenant stepped up to us.

'My captain lies there,' he said, and he pointed to a body concealed beneath a flag; 'another of my brother officers is killed, the rest are wounded, and I alone am unhurt.'

Mr. Bramston complimented him on his bravery, and told him to prepare for going on board the frigate.

Meantime other boats came alongside and removed the crew of the prize, which proved to be the *Soleil*, carrying eighteen guns and six carronades, with a crew of one hundred and eighty men, upwards of thirty of whom were killed or wounded.

Mr. Bramston sent me back with this information. The captain at once decided to remove the prisoners, and send the prize to Port Royal.

As no time was to be lost, the boats were lowered, and the prisoners soon brought on board.

The captain at once sent for Nettleship, Tom, and me.

'I intend to send you in charge of the prize, Mr. Nettleship,' he said, 'and these two youngsters can accompany you. Fifteen men are all I can spare you, so you must make the most of them. All the prisoners will be removed, with the exception of about a dozen, who may volunteer to assist in working the ship, so that you'll easily look after them.'

'Thank you, sir, for the confidence you place in me,' said Nettleship, who would gladly have accepted the command, even if he had had but half a dozen men.

Tom and I promised to do our best, and hurried below to get our traps ready.

I took care to apply for Larry, and to remind him to bring his fiddle with him, but I didn't hear what other men were selected to form the prize crew. Ten of the Frenchmen only could be induced to promise their assistance. Tom and I, without loss of time, accompanied Nettleship on board. As soon as the dead were put overboard, the decks washed down, and the damages the prize had received were repaired, the men who had come from the frigate to assist us returned to her. She stood to the southward, and we made sail for Port Royal. Among the first men on whom my eyes fell was Dan Hoolan, looking as sulky and morose as ever, though he was going about his work with more activity than he generally displayed. As I caught sight of the rest of the crew, I found that three more of the Irishmen pressed with him were among them.

'I hope that by this time they are content with their lot, and will do their duty like men,' I thought to myself; 'still I would rather have had any others.'

'We are terribly short-handed, I must confess,' said Nettleship, as he and I were seated at dinner in the captain's cabin,
while Tom Pim was acting as officer of the watch. I know I
can trust you two fellows, however, and we must make the
most of the men we've got. There are many of them about
the worst on board; but if we have fine weather, they won't
have much to do, and we may hope not to catch a Tartar on
the way. We must take to our heels if we see a suspicious
stranger, and the *Soleil* appears to have a fast pair, at all events,
so we may hope to escape. Though I would rather be in a
condition to fight than have to run away.'

'The Frenchmen only promised to assist in navigating the
ship. We mustn't trust them to man the guns,' I said.

'We'll see what our own men can do without them, then,'
said Nettleship in a cheery tone.

We hurried over our dinner to let Tom come down and
take his, while Nettleship and I went on deck. The weather
looked favourable, and Nettleship was in high spirits at finding
himself in command of a fine ship. Should he take her to
Port Royal in safety, he might reasonably expect to obtain his
long waited-for promotion. Although the majority of the men
sent with us were the least reliable of the crew, we had an old
quartermaster, Ben Nash, and three other seamen, who were
first-rate hands, and we took care to put two of them into each
watch. Of course there was plenty of work to do in getting
the ship to rights. As soon as the men knocked off we heard
Larry's fiddle going. Stepping forward, I found that he had
set all the Frenchmen dancing, and some of our own men, too,
who were enjoying themselves to their hearts' content. 'Larry
will take good care to keep the people in good temper,' I
thought to myself, as I turned aft.

When night came on, Nettleship thought it prudent to
shorten sail, as is the custom of careful merchant skippers, who
can't perform that operation in a hurry. We lost nothing by
so doing, as for some hours it was a stark calm. Tom and Ben
Nash were in one watch, Nettleship and I in another. Night
passed quickly away. Towards morning we got a breeze, and

were once more standing on our course. We kept a bright look out, not, as we should have liked, to watch for a prize, but to run away should a suspicious sail be sighted. We kept no colours flying, for should a Frenchman see us, we might have a better chance of avoiding an encounter. At daylight, as we had a fair breeze, all sail was again set, and we stood gaily on our course.

'If this weather holds, we shall be safe at anchor in a couple of days in Port Royal,' said Nettleship.

'A sail ahead!' shouted the look-out, from aloft.

'We must continue on our course till we see what she is,' said Nettleship.

Tom Pim, who went aloft to have a look at her, on his return said that she was a brig, standing to the westward, but too far off at the time to judge of her size. She appeared to be almost becalmed, while we, carrying the breeze along with us, rapidly neared her. At length we could see her clearly from the deck.

'She has hoisted her colours,' observed Nettleship. 'Though from the cut of her canvas she's English, as far as I can make out, her flag is French.'

We had not yet hoisted our colours; indeed, as we were standing, the Frenchman could not have seen them even if we had.

'There's no doubt about the flag,' observed Tom, who had taken the glass; 'that is French, though she's an English merchantman, if I ever saw one. The people on board her recognize this ship as one of their own cruisers, and take us for a friend.'

'I believe you're right, Tom,' said Nettleship, 'and we'll not undeceive them.'

The stranger, having now got a breeze, hove to, apparently wishing to speak us. We had to luff up a little to reach her.

'Hoist the French ensign,' said Nettleship to me; and I ran it up to the peak.

As we got nearer it became necessary to shorten sail, that we might lower a boat to send on board and take possession, should it be found that the brig had been captured by the French. Whether or not it was from the slow way in which we performed the operation, the suspicions of the Frenchmen were aroused, and putting up their helm, they filled their sails and ran off before the wind. We immediately let fall our courses, and hauling down the French flag and hoisting the English, stood away in chase.

'Give her a shot, Tom,' said Nettleship. 'We mustn't let her lead us out of our course.'

Tom and I hurried forward, and, training the gun ourselves, fired. The chase took no notice of the first shot, but we quickly again loaded, and managed to send a second plump on board her. To our satisfaction, she immediately rounded to, when we were soon up to her, we also heaving to to windward.

'You shall board her, Paddy,' said Nettleship. 'Take care to let the Frenchmen understand that it was fortunate for them we didn't sink the brig.'

Larry, Hoolan, and four other men, formed my boat's crew, all of us of course being armed to the teeth. We found only ten men on board, three of whom were blacks, the rest French, under the command of a young French midshipman. He at once handed me his sword, with a polite bow. As I understood French,—I forget if I before said so,—I learnt from him that the brig was, as we supposed, English; that she had been captured a week before by a French corvette; and that he was on his way to St. Domingo. He looked a little downcast on losing his command, but shrugged his shoulders, and observed that it was '*la fortune de la guerre.*' I requested him and five of his white crew to accompany me on board my ship. He replied that he was ready, and begged that he might be allowed to carry his traps with him.

'Certainly, monsieur,' I replied; and he dived down below, as he said, to pack them up. As he was much longer in the cabin than I considered necessary, I grew impatient, and followed him. I found him talking to a person in bed in one of the side berths.

'I ought, monsieur, to have told you that I have a brother aspirant, who is very ill; and I fear that it might cause his death were he to be removed. Your captain would be conferring a great favour on us both, were he to allow me to remain with him, as no one else is so well able to nurse him as I am.'

'I'll ask him,' I said, looking at the sick youth, who certainly appeared very ill. 'I regret, however, that I cannot delay longer, so you must come with me.'

'I'll obey you, monsieur,' said the midshipman; and exchanging a few more words with his sick companion, he followed me on deck.

Leaving Larry and two other men on board, I made three of the Frenchmen take their places in the boat, and returned to the *Soleil* with the young Frenchman. I told Nettleship of the request he had made.

'I don't like to refuse him, as what he says is no doubt true,' said Nettleship; 'but we must take care that he plays us no tricks.'

'Then am I to tell him that he may return on board the brig?' I asked.

'Yes, you may take him with you, for I intend to send you in charge of the prize, as I can't spare Tom; but Nash shall go with you,—you couldn't have a better man;—and so with five hands, and the help of the blacks you speak of, and a couple of the Frenchmen, you'll be able to work the vessel, and by keeping in our wake you'll easily find your way to Port Royal.'

I was highly pleased at the confidence Nettleship placed in me, especially as Tom was not a bit jealous.

'Nettleship thinks that as I'm a little chap I shouldn't inspire the same respect among the Frenchmen that you will,' he said, as we shook hands before I went down the side.

The brig was the *Good Luck*, bound from Barbadoes to Halifax when she had been captured. The French midshipman, who was profuse in his expressions of gratitude for being allowed to return to look after his sick messmate, told me that his name was La Touche.

As soon as the boat which had brought me on board had
gone back to the *Soleil* she made sail, and I followed in
her wake. I at once mustered my crew. The two Frenchmen said that they were perfectly ready to do as their officer
wished.

'I desire you, then, to obey monsieur, who is in command
of this vessel,' said La Touche.

'Certainly we will obey him,' answered the Frenchmen,
making flourishing bows.

The blacks, two of whom spoke English, said also that
they were ready to obey me.

On looking at the men, I saw that not only Dan Hoolan,
but two of the men who had been pressed with him, had also
been sent; but then I had Ben and Larry, on whom I could
thoroughly rely; and the others, while we kept close to the
Soleil, would not venture to attempt any treachery.

In less than an hour the wind fell very light. I saw, notwithstanding this, by the way in which the brig slipped through
the water, that she was remarkably fast for an English merchant
vessel. This was satisfactory, as I felt sure that during the
night I was not likely to fall behind the *Soleil*.

As the day drew on the wind fell altogether, and we lay
becalmed at a short distance from each other. I divided my
crew into two watches. I took one with Larry, two of our
own crew, a Frenchman, and a black. Ben had charge of the
other, with the remainder. I did not think it prudent to let
La Touche take a watch, though he politely offered to do so.
The night was excessively hot, and I felt more inclined to
remain on deck than below. After La Touche and I had
had supper, he said he would remain in the cabin to look
after his sick friend. One of the Frenchmen acted as steward,
and the other as cook. The former frequently came into the
cabin to bring us our meals, and to take food to the sick
midshipman.

I kept the first watch, and Ben relieved me at midnight,
when I lay down on deck, on a mattress I had brought up
from the cabin, under a small awning rigged near the after part

of the vessel. I had been asleep for a couple of hours or more, when I was awakened by feeling the vessel heel suddenly over.

'All hands on deck! Shorten sail!' shouted Ben in a lusty voice.

I sprang to my feet. There was not a moment to lose. La Touche, who had been awakened at the same time, rushed up on deck, followed by another person, who appeared to be as active as any one. As rapidly as we could, we let fly the top-gallant sheets, lowered the peak, and brailed up the fore-sail, while the helm was put up. The brig righted, fortunately not carrying away the masts, and off we flew before the wind. The Frenchmen and blacks behaved remarkably well, and ran aloft to reef the topsails, and stow the lighter sails, which were flapping loudly as they blew out with the wind.

The sky had become overcast ; the scud flew rapidly along, just above our heads, as it seemed, while the spoon-drift, blown off from rising seas, covered the ocean with a sheet of white.

When all immediate danger was over, the stranger who had so mysteriously shown himself slipped down the companion ladder, and I was too busy to ask La Touche who he was. I naturally concluded that he was the sick midshipman La Touche had been so tenderly nursing.

As soon as we had got the brig to rights, I looked out for the *Soleil*, but could nowhere distinguish her. Had she borne up? or having shortened sail in time, was she still keeping her course? I hoped that the latter was the case, and resolved to attempt hauling to the wind, and steering for Port Royal. I told Ben of my intention, as he, I considered, was the best seaman among my crew.

'It will be as much as we can do, sir, if we could do it at all,' he answered. 'The brig is not particularly stiff, or she would not have heeled over as sharply as she did just now.'

'The French officer knows better than we can what sail the brig will bear. I might ask his opinion,' I remarked.

'Beg pardon, sir, but I would not ask him if I were you,' said Ben. 'He'll of course say, Keep before the wind; but he won't say that if we do we shall chance to run right into the midst of a Spanish or French fleet, or up to one of their cruisers, if so be this is only a passing gale.'

'I fear that it is not merely a passing gale; but still, if we can keep the brig on a wind, we'll try and do it,' I said.

I gave the order to man the braces, waiting for an oppor-tunity to put the helm down and bring the brig up to the wind. Scarcely was the order given, however, than a blast more furious than before struck the brig, and which, had I not delayed carrying out my intention, would either have hove her on her beam-ends or carried away the masts. On we flew before the wind, which was every moment increasing; while the seas rose higher and higher, and came roaring up around us. Even now we had more sail set than we could safely carry, and I at once ordered the hands aloft to furl the main-topsail, and to closely reef the fore-topsail. Yet even when this was done, the brig flew on at a tremendous pace.

'To my mind, we've got old Harry Cane on board, sir,' said Ben; 'and the sooner we get our fore-topsail stowed the better, to save it from being blown out of the bolt ropes, and the less likely we shall be to lose the masts. If the foremast goes, the mainmast will be pretty sure to follow.'

'You're right, Ben,' I answered, and I gave the order to furl the fore-topsail.

Ben and Larry led the way aloft, and most of our own men followed; but the two Frenchmen didn't seem to like the look of things, and remained on deck. I ordered them up, but they stood holding on to the bulwarks without moving, and I had no power to compel them. My own men, however, were able to perform the operation without their aid, and at length, having stowed the sail, they came down on deck.

Even now the brig dashed on at a furious rate, while the sea, roaring up astern, threatened constantly to poop her. Fortunately, we had plenty of sea-room, and unless the wind should suddenly shift round to the opposite quarter, as I knew it might do, I hoped that we should keep afloat till the hurricane had abated.

Consulting with Ben, I did everything he advised to secure the masts and spars.

When La Touche saw how we were employed, he went to the Frenchmen and blacks, and induced them to assist; indeed, without their help we could scarcely have done what was necessary.

As soon as we had finished all that was required, I went into the cabin, and asked La Touche to find me a chart, and calculating where we had been when the hurricane first struck us, I marked down as well as I could the course we had since run, that I might better be able to find my way back to Port Royal. I was not a very experienced navigator, still, having the exercise of my wits, I hoped to succeed, and I felt not a little proud at the thought that I must trust to my own resources. I could not expect assistance from La Touche, and no one else on board, except the sick midshipman knew anything about navigation.

Expecting to follow close in the wake of the *Soleil*, I had not brought a quadrant with me, but I found one in the cabin, as well as a French nautical almanack; and I hoped, when the hurricane was over and the sky had cleared, to be able to use them.

La Touche had hitherto occupied the state-room, but supposing that I should turn him out, he had removed his things to a berth on the opposite side, close to that of his messmate.

Having placed the chart and quadrant with the almanack in what was now my cabin, I locked the door, and returned on deck.

The hurricane showed no signs of abating; but the brig, which was fortunately not fully laden, behaved beautifully, and literally bounded over the waves as she ran before the wind. The crew continued on deck, holding fast on to the stanchions, belaying-pins, and the rigging, to save themselves from being washed away; for every now and then a sea tumbled on board, and swept along the deck, sometimes over one quarter, sometimes over another, and frequently over the bows; but the hatches had been battened down, and no water got below.

'We shall do well, I hope, and carry the brig safely into Port Royal,' I observed to La Touche.

He shrugged his shoulders, and answered,—

'For your sake I may wish it, though I shall not be sorry if we fall in with one of our own cruisers before the voyage is ended.'

'Very naturally; but should she appear, we will try our best to get away from her,' I said, laughing.

At length daylight broke. A wild scene the ocean presented; the foaming seas dancing up on all sides, through which the brig was struggling onwards. It seemed to me that the wind was blowing stronger than ever, and I began to fear that we should be driven over towards the reefs and shoals upon the American coast before it had ceased. If so, ship-wreck was almost certain, and the chance of saving our lives would be small indeed. Still I kept up my spirits, and took care not to express my fears to my shipmates.

Suddenly about noon the wind dropped, but whether or not it was gaining strength for a fresh blow I was not certain. I asked La Touche. He replied that he could not tell, but that it might be so, and that it would be wise to be prepared for it. The seas tumbled about so much that I could not bring the brig to the wind. I, however, first set the fore, and then the main-topsail, and kept her before it to avoid the risk of the seas pooping us. The clouds at length began to disperse, and in a short time the sea itself went down.

I lost no time in bringing the brig to the wind, making more sail, and shaping a course for Jamaica. Before nightfall the clouds had entirely disappeared; and the setting sun cast a radiant glow over the sky and sea, as the brig, heeling over to the breeze, sped on her way.

'I congratulate you, monsieur, on the change of weather, for I should have been grieved as much as you would, had he brig been lost,' said La Touche, coming up to me. 'Still here's many a slip between the cup and the lip,'—he gave an equivalent proverb in French. 'If one of our cruisers appears, you'll have to congratulate me, though I hope you'll receive the same courteous treatment that I have enjoyed from you, and for which I have to thank you.'

'I have no fear of that,' I replied. 'Your cruiser has not yet appeared. The *Good Luck* is fortunately a fast craft, and we'll do all we can to put her at her best speed.'

We had been unable to sit down to table during the hurricane, and had had no time to take a regular meal since; but one of the French seamen, who acted as steward, now placed a very substantial one on the table. I played the part of host, and La Touche that of guest. His messmate was too ill to get up, he said, but notwithstanding, though a sick man, he managed to consume a fair quantity of the viands La Touche took to him.

'There ought to be some good wine in this locker, if the bottles were not broken during the hurricane,' said La Touche, rising and lifting up the lid. Groping about, he produced a couple of bottles of claret, and another of cognac.

'There are several more here, so that we need not stint ourselves,' he said, laughing.

A corkscrew was soon found. I took a couple of glasses. The wine was excellent, there was no doubt about that. La Touche pressed me to take a third. 'Come, we must pledge each other,' he said, replenishing my glass, and filling up his own. 'Here's to the continuance of our friendship.'

I felt pretty well tired, as I had been up the whole of the last night, and a good portion of the previous one, so I was not sorry to have something to set me up. We struck our glasses together, and wished each other health, prosperity, and promotion.

'You like the wine,' said La Touche. 'Come—another glass; now we must finish the bottle, and I don't wish to take a larger share than you have.'

'No, no, my friend,' I answered, thinking there was something peculiar in his manner. 'I command this craft, and must keep a cool head on my shoulders, but I have no objection to your finishing the bottle, and taking a second, if you like.'

In vain he pressed me, for the more he pressed, the more determined I became not to take another drop. I found the wine indeed stronger than I had supposed it was. Besides which, I recollected the major's advice, which strengthened me in my resolution.

CHAPTER XIV.

TREACHERY.

AFTER supper we rose to go on deck. I observed as we did so, that La Touche replaced the bottle in the locker. I felt more inclined to go to sleep than to pace the deck, but I resolved to take the first watch, that Nash might have the middle one. The wind had fallen still more, the moonbeams cast a silvery light over the ocean. La Touche, who had followed me out of the cabin, joined me, and we walked up and down for some time. At length, giving a yawn, he said,—

'If monsieur does not wish me to keep watch, which I shall be happy to do, I shall turn in, for I can scarcely keep my eyes open.'

'Thank you,' I said; 'but I cannot disobey my orders, though I should place perfect confidence in your honour.'

'I am much obliged to you for the compliment,' he replied in a hesitating tone; and wishing me good-night, and a pleasant watch, he dived below.

I continued walking up and down the deck, doing my utmost to keep myself awake. Seeing Larry, I called to him to come to me. One of our men was at the helm. I asked Larry how the people were getting on forward.

'We're all as friendly as bees, Mr. Terence. Shure the Frenchmen are mighty pleasant fellows, though I wouldn't be after trusting to them too much. The steward has got some bottles of the crathur, and he's been serving it out pretty freely. I have been afraid that Dan Hoolan and Mat would be after taking more than is good for them, though Dan's head, to be sure, could stand lashins of liquor, and be none the worse for it.'

'Take care, and not be tempted yourself, Larry,' I said.

'No, no, Mr. Terence, I know my duty too well for that, though the Frenchmen in their love of me tried to force it down my throat.'

'I wish you could manage to find the bottles of liquor, and bring them aft, or heave them overboard; it would be putting temptation out of the men's way,' I said.

'Shure, Mr. Terence, I'll obey your orders, though the Frenchmen won't be loving me so much, if they find out it was myself that did it.'

While Larry went forward to carry out my directions, I continued my solitary walk. I was afraid even to rest against the bulwarks for a moment, or I should have been off to sleep like a shot. Even as it was, as I stood on deck watching the canvas, to see that the man at the helm was steering properly, I more than once became unconscious of where I was. Though my eyes might not have closed, I lost the power of seeing, now fancying myself on the deck of the frigate, now on board the *Soleil*, and I heard the voices of Nettleship and Tom Pim talking to each other, though except that they were speaking about me, I could not make out what they said. Now I opened my eyes. 'No higher!' I sang out, as I saw the head sails almost aback. The helmsman turned the spokes of the wheel, and the sails filled. I continued my walk, but soon again stopped. I went to the binnacle lamp to look at my watch. It still wanted half an hour to midnight. I would have given much to have had that half hour over; and it was with the greatest difficulty that I managed to stand upright. Once more as I stood, now looking out forward, now at the sails, strange voices sounded in my ears, and my senses wandered.

'Faith, Mr. Terence, the spalpeens have been too sharp for me; I could only find one bottle of spirits, and that was empty.

The blacks are as drunk as fiddlers, and the Frenchmen seem to have lost their senses, while Dan Hoolan and the rest of our men are much the same, barrin' Tim Logan here, at the helm, and Ben Nash, and he's fast asleep, waiting for me to call him, and relieve you.'

'Well, then, Larry, go and rouse him up at once, for if he doesn't come down soon there'll be only you and Logan to look after the ship, as I'm pretty well done up.'

'Hush, Mr. Terence! I'd like to see Logan kept at the helm,' said Larry, putting his hand to his mouth; 'for when he goes forward I am after thinking that the Frenchmen will be tempting him with the liquor, and he's not the boy to refuse a glass of the crathur when it's put before his nose.'

'I'll speak to Nash when he comes,' I said. 'Take a look-out ahead before you go below.'

In a short time Ben Nash came aft, hitching up his trousers and rubbing his eyes as if just awakened out of sleep. I gave him my directions, and inquired about the rest of the crew.

'Why, sir, the watch below don't seem inclined to turn out and the men forward seem more asleep than awake,' he answered. 'It seems to me that they have been having a drop too much; I only hope we shan't have to shorten sail, or there won't be many of them fit to go aloft.'

Ben's reply confirmed what Larry told me. It made me very unwilling to turn in, but so overpowerful was my sleepiness, that I knew it would be impossible for me to keep awake much longer.

'I must lie down for half an hour or so,' I said, 'and if you observe anything unusual, send Larry down to call me. Let him stay by you if he can manage to keep awake, while Logan remains at the helm a short while longer.'

'Never fear, sir,' answered Nash. 'I'll do as you order me.'

Under other circumstances I should have myself gone forward and roused up the watch, but from the reports Nash and Larry had given me, I knew that it would be useless, as I had no power to enforce obedience. I therefore very unwillingly went below, and threw myself on the bed all standing, and in half a minute was fast asleep.

I didn't dream ; not a thought passed through my brain till I was at length partly awakened by a noise overhead. What it was I couldn't make out. Presently I heard some one come down, as I supposed, to call me. Now fully awake, I was on the point of jumping up to hurry on deck, when I became aware that two persons were standing close to my berth.

'*Soyez tranquille, monsieur*,' said the voice of La Touche. 'The brig is no longer under your command; most of your people have joined my men, and they insist on carrying her into the Havanna.'

'Impossible !' I exclaimed. 'My men would not have turned traitors. I'll go on deck and see how matters stand.'

'That we cannot allow. I did not instigate my men to recapture the vessel, they managed it themselves ; but now that they have possession, I dare not order them to give her up.'

'I know that two of my people would have fought to the death rather than have turned traitors,' I exclaimed.

'Those two you speak of—the old man and the Irish lad—were overpowered, and are stowed safely below, with handcuffs on their wrists,' he answered. 'Have I your word that you'll not interfere ? You treated me with courtesy, and I wish you to be allowed to remain at liberty ; but if you decline to give me your word, I cannot prevent you being treated as they are.'

While he was speaking, I felt for my pistols, which I had placed at the head of the berth, intending to spring up suddenly, knock him and his companion over, and gain the deck, but they were gone. My sword had also been taken away.

I observed by the light of the lantern that his companion held, that both of them were fully armed, and prepared to resist any attack I might make on them. The countenance of the other person, who wore the uniform of a lieutenant, I did not recognize, but I guessed he must be the sick messmate to whom La Touche had been so attentive. I could not help thinking also that La Touche was not so ignorant altogether of the intentions of his crew as he asserted.

'I'll consider the subject, and let you know in the course of a few minutes, if you 'll give me that time for reflection,' I answered.

I was anxious to gain time, for I still had a lingering hope that Nash and Larry had managed to retain their liberty, and that if I could once get on deck, we might recover possession of the brig.

'I'll not hurry you, monsieur, but shall be very much grieved if you will not give me your word, as I shall be under the painful necessity of subjecting you to an indignity such as I would willingly avoid,' observed the lieutenant.

I spent the time in considering what I would do, and finally came to the conclusion that it would be useless to refuse the freedom offered me, as, were I handcuffed and imprisoned below, I could not assist my two faithful men, or make any attempt to recover the brig.

I therefore said, with as good a grace as I could command, 'I accept your offer, Monsieur La Touche.'

'You must give your word to this gentleman, who is my superior officer,' said La Touche, turning to the supposed sick man.

I said nothing; but I had a shrewd suspicion that he had remained on board for the purpose of carrying out the plan which had been so completely successful. I felt, however, very much downcast, and very foolish at being outwitted, and indignant at the treacherous conduct of my own men. Yet what more could I have expected from Hoolan and his associates?

'Monsieur, I promise not to interfere with the discipline of the brig, provided I am allowed to retain my liberty,' I at length said, addressing the lieutenant.

'That is well,' he replied. 'I would advise you to lie down again and finish your sleep. You will be in better heart to-

morrow to bear your misfortune, and we wish to return the
courtesy which we have received at your hands. It is the
fortune of war, and we have acted fairly.'

I was not so clear about that, but there was no use in complaining, so I at once threw myself into the berth, and in a
minute was in happy forgetfulness of all that had occurred.

Next morning, when I went on deck, I found the brig was
steering to the north-west. How different I felt to the day
before ; then I was in command, now I was a prisoner. As I
cast my eye along the deck, I caught sight of Hoolan and
the other mutineers. He scowled at me maliciously, but did
not approach, and the others continued the work on which
they were engaged. La Touche had charge of the deck. I
had my misgivings as to how it had fared with Larry and
Nash.

I turned to the French midshipman, and said,—

'I should like to see my people who did not mutiny.
Where are they ?'

'Two are in the hold, and the one who was at the wheel
was struck down and killed with an axe, and is overboard. It
was a case of necessity, and the fortune of war.'

I made no answer, for I was too indignant to speak. At
last I said,—

'Will you give me permission to go down and see my poor
men ? It will be a consolation to them to know that I am
safe, for one who is my foster-brother is much attached to me,
and the other is a faithful fellow.'

The midshipman seemed struck at hearing this, and at once
said that he would obtain permission from his lieutenant. He
went into the cabin, and quickly returned, saying that I might
go and see the men. Taking a lantern which he ordered one
of the crew to bring me, I went down into the hold, and
there, in a small space on some planks placed on the cargo,
and surrounded by casks, I found Larry and Ben Nash, with
handcuffs on their wrists, and their legs tied, seated side by
side.

'Is it yourself, Mr. Terence ?' exclaimed Larry, as I

appeared. 'Have you come to set us free? Have you got the brig again?'

'I wish that I had,' I answered, 'but there's no such good luck for us. I'm a prisoner at large, and I have obtained permission to come and see you, as I wanted to know how you're getting on, and how it all happened.'

'Shure it's bad enough for myself, Mr. Terence, but it's worse for poor Ben here, for just look at him,—he's got a mighty ugly prong in his side, another in his shoulder, and a knock in his head, which was enough to do for him. Tim Logan was killed entirely; but don't mind me, just look to Ben, he can scarcely speak.'

Ben's face was pale as death.

'Where are you hurt, Nash?' I asked.

He groaned as he told me.

'But it's water I want, sir; the fellows haven't brought us any since we were down here. Once Dan Hoolan came to look at us, and when I asked him for some, he turned away with a growl, swearing I might die of thirst before he would bring me any.'

Immediately on hearing this I sprang on deck, and begged La Touche to let me have a jug of water. He ordered one of the Frenchmen to bring it to me, and I returned with it. I first gave some to Nash, who, though he eagerly bent forward his head as I lifted the jug to his lips, seemed to have a difficulty in swallowing. I next put it to Larry's mouth, and he quickly gulped down the contents.

'Shure, that does a boy good,' he exclaimed, drawing breath. 'I wouldn't have taken it all, if I had been after thinking that Ben would have been wanting it.'

'I hope easily to get some more if he requires it,' I said; but on looking at poor Ben it appeared to me that neither water nor food would restore him. He was leaning back, gasping violently. His eyes, as I held the lantern to them, appeared to have lost all animation. I put the lantern down on the deck, and supported him in my arms.

'It's cruel in those fellows to keep the manacles on him

while he's suffering thus,' I exclaimed. 'I'll ask La Touche to have them taken off. He could no longer, even if he had a will, interfere with them.'

Springing on deck, I made my request to La Touche; he replied that he would go below and consult his commanding officer. He soon returned.

'If you think that the man is really dying, Lieutenant Dubois will give you leave to do as you desire,' he said, 'but you must be answerable for him.'

'I feel certain that he will die unless he is properly cared for,' I answered.

He called to one of the blacks who belonged to the armourer's crew on board the French frigate, and told him to go below and knock off the Englishman's irons. I thought I might put in a word for Larry.

'May they release my foster-brother?' I asked. 'Poor fellow, he did but his duty in defending the brig, and I'll be responsible for his good conduct.'

'Yes. Lieutenant Dubois fancied that I spoke of both of them, and for my part, I am very willing to do as you wish,' he answered.

I hurried below, accompanied by the black. Nash was still breathing hard, and scarcely had the armourer commenced operations, when the poor fellow fell back in my arms, his spirit set free before his body was liberated from the irons. The black continued knocking away, quite indifferent to what had occurred.

'It's all over with poor Ben,' exclaimed Larry, who was eagerly watching the operation.

'Yes, he's gone,' I answered, as I felt the honest seaman's wrist.

The black finished his work, and then stretched the body out on the deck.

'And now, my friend, I'll beg of you to release this young fellow,' I said. 'You wouldn't like to have irons on your wrists longer than you could help.'

'Not de first time I hab dem on, and big chain too; but dis

nuttin',' said the black, and a few blows sufficed to set Larry free.

He sprang to his feet, knocking his head against the deck above him with a force which brought him down again, but fortunately the crown of an Irishman's head is thicker than that of most people, and he quickly recovered himself.

Telling him to sit quiet till I got leave for him to appear, I went on deck to report the death of Nash.

'Ah, they told me the man was badly hurt,' said La Touche. 'He was a brave fellow, for he fought desperately. We will bury him forthwith.'

'And my follower, may he return on deck?' I asked. 'Both of us will be glad to assist in navigating the ship, if our services are required.'

'Yes, you can do so; but I do not think that you will return the compliment we paid you, by attempting to retake the brig from us,' he answered, laughing.

'You are right, monsieur,' I answered. 'I have given you my word to that effect, and the word of an English officer is never broken.'

La Touche winced. 'I took no part,' he observed, 'in capturing the brig; you'll understand that.'

I made no reply, though I was convinced that all along he was cognizant of the plot and plans of his lieutenant. The treachery of Hoolan and his companions enabled him to succeed with greater ease than he could otherwise have expected.

With the assistance of the black armourer, Larry and I sewed Ben up in a piece of canvas which he obtained for us, with a shot at the feet. We then together carried the body to a port, and launched it overboard, no one offering to render assistance, but at the same time not interfering with our proceedings. When Lieutenant Dubois came on deck, he bowed politely to me, and we exchanged a few words, but he didn't appear inclined to enter into conversation. Perhaps he felt conscious that he was guilty of treachery in allowing his men to mutiny, even if he had not instigated them to do so, after

the kind way in which he had been treated. Of course Nettleship made a great mistake in allowing him and the midshipman
to remain on board ; but judging them by his own sense of
honour, he could not suppose it possible they would take
advantage of his generosity, and even dream of attempting to
recapture the brig.

Larry, when I was on deck, always kept close to me, and
he asked whether I could obtain permission for him to sleep
under the companion ladder, or anywhere aft, so that he might
be within call.

'In truth, Mr. Terence, I'm not fond of the looks Dan
Hoolan casts at me when I go forward,' he said. 'I shouldn't
be surprised on waking some night to find him after cutting
my throat or giving me a knock on the head, for he knows
that if it hadn't been for poor Ben and Tim Logan and me,
he would have tried to kill you, Mr. Terence, that you might
not appear against him ; but we fought as long as we could,
till the French lieutenant came on deck, and there was only
myself remaining unhurt.'

I felt very certain that what Larry said was true, and La
Touche afterwards corroborated the account. How Larry had
escaped seemed a wonder, till I heard that he had seized a
handspike, and using it as a shillelah, or rather as a single-
stick, had kept his enemies at bay, and defended himself.
Whenever I saw Hoolan on deck, I observed that he cast
sinister looks at Larry and me, and I felt very sure that if he
had an opportunity he would carry out his threat of putting an
end to us.   When I told La Touche of Larry's wish, and his
reason for it, after speaking to the lieutenant, he said it should
be complied with.   At meal-time the officers invited me into
the cabin, and, to do them justice, treated me with as much
courtesy as if I had been a willing guest.

'We have changed places, but we hope that you don't bear
us any ill-will,' said La Touche, filling up my glass with claret.
'Here's to your health, and may our friendship endure as long
as our lives. When peace is established between our two
countries which I suppose will be some day or other, I shall

be enchanted if you will pay me a visit at my father's chateau in Normandy.'

'With the greatest pleasure in the world,' I answered; 'though I confess I didn't think you would play me so cruel a trick.' I didn't wish to use a harsher expression.

'Believe me, monsieur, that it was from no design of mine. I but performed my duty. Until the vessel was in the hands of the mutineers, I was not aware myself of what was going to happen. Monsieur Dubois will corroborate what I state.'

'La Touche speaks but the truth,' said the lieutenant. 'He acted under my orders, for, knowing his sense of honour, I didn't confide my plan to him.'

I was very glad to hear this, as I was much inclined to like La Touche, and was grieved to suppose that I had been disappointed in him.

The weather, after the hurricane which had been the chief cause of my misfortune, rapidly moderated, and became very fine; and though the wind was generally light, the brig made good way to the south-westward. During the day one of the Frenchmen, or La Touche himself, was constantly at the masthead, on the look-out for vessels, either to avoid suspicious strangers, or hoping to fall in with one of their cruisers. The lieutenant had at first intended to steer for Havanna, on the northern coast of Cuba; but just as we passed the latitude of Jamaica the wind shifted to the westward, and he determined to run for Port-au-Prince, at the westward end of St. Domingo. He didn't conceal his intentions from me; indeed there was no object in his doing so. He asked me whether we were likely to fall in with English cruisers between Jamaica and Cuba. I told him what I believed to be the case, that they would most probably be found on the south or west side of the island, looking out for the French and Spanish fleets expected to be coming from Havanna.

'I am surprised, indeed, that we have not fallen in with one of our cruisers already,' I said.

'There is a reason for that,' he remarked. 'The hurricane, of which we only felt the edge, will have driven them into port, or have sent them ashore, or to the bottom. I thought of that before I ventured here, and calculated that it must have been some days before they could put to sea again.'

I believed that the lieutenant was right, and it lessened my hopes of the brig being retaken; still I did not abandon them altogether, and the thought contributed to keep up my spirits.

Supper over, after a few turns on deck I begged leave to turn in and finish out the sleep which had been so disagreeably interrupted the previous morning. Both the officers begged I would return to the berth I had previously occupied. I thought it best to accept their courtesy. When Larry saw me go below, he came down the companion ladder, and after attending on me, as I told him he might do, he stowed himself away under it. When I awoke next morning, finding myself in my old berth, for a few seconds I forgot all that had occurred, and fancied myself still in command of the brig, but the reality soon came back to me. With anything but pleasant feelings I turned out, and having dressed, went on deck. Larry, who had slept undisturbed, followed me up.

'I'm after thinking, Mr. Terence, that Dan was looking for me, but, as good fortune would have it, I found an empty biscuit cask, so what did I do but poke my head into it, and cover my neck up with a thick handkerchief,' said Larry, as he stood by my side. 'Thinks I to myself, if Master Dan wants to be after giving me a whack on the skull, I shall have had time to jump up before he has done for me; but the spalpeen did not find me out, I've a notion, and I'll be on the watch for him if he does, another night.'

I found La Touche on deck, and we exchanged salutations. The brig was under all sail, standing to the eastward. I cast my eye eagerly astern, half hoping to see a British man-of-war in chase of us; but I found that the Frenchmen were carrying all sail, as was but natural, to reach their destination as fast as possible. I could just distinguish to the southward the distant mountains of Jamaica, rising like a blue irregular line above the horizon. Nothing could be more beautiful than the weather. The sky was bright; the ocean glittered in the rays of the rising sun.

In spite of this, I could not keep my spirits up, and put away the thoughts of the fate in store for me. Instead of serving my country, gaining honour and promotion, and passing my time in the society of shipmates to whom I was much attached, I was doomed to be imprisoned in some out-of-the-way part of St. Domingo, or sent across the Atlantic to be shut up in a French fortress, as I knew that other officers had been.

Now that their hopes of escaping increased, the Frenchmen became still more courteous, and did their best to make my stay on board pleasant. I should have been glad to have regained my liberty, but certainly should have pitied them if we had been captured.

At length we made the west side of St. Domingo, and, entering the Bay of Gonavez, ran up to the harbour at its eastern extremity. Here we found a considerable number of men-of-war at anchor. We were at once visited by several officers, who seemed surprised to hear that we had been at sea and escaped being wrecked, every ship in the harbour having lost masts or spars, or received other serious damage.

Lieutenant Dubois had promised that he would keep us on board as long as possible, as we should, on being landed, have been moved away into the interior. I was, of course, very glad to take advantage of his kind offer.

We had not been long at anchor before an officer came off from the shore with an official-looking packet. I was in the cabin when he delivered it to Lieutenant Dubois.

'The governor has heard of your arrival, and of the undamaged condition of your vessel,' said the officer. 'He is desirous of sending important information to Admiral the Count de Grasse, who will probably be found at the island of Guadaloupe, and he desires that you will sail forthwith, and convey these despatches. There is no vessel in harbour fit to go, and he considers your arrival a fortunate circumstance.'

Dubois at once expressed his satisfaction, and promised to

sail without a moment's delay. I was afraid that he might consider it necessary to send Larry and me on shore; but I thought it prudent to say nothing, and continued seated as if I belonged to the vessel. The French officer from the shore made no remark, and having performed his commission, speedily took his departure.

'All right,' said Dubois to me; 'I'm not compelled to land you, and if you like we can continue our voyage together. It will give you a better chance of escape if the fortune of war should throw me into the hands of one of your ships; but I have no intention of being caught if I can help it.

I thanked him very much, and assured him that nothing would give me greater pleasure than being once more able to play the host to him.

Before we sailed, however, six more hands, whom he had asked for, were sent on board to strengthen his crew; but Hoolan and the other mutineers were allowed to remain, for which I was sorry. Perhaps they would rather have gone on shore, for if the brig were recaptured, they would, to a certainty, have to grace her yard-arms before many days had passed over their heads.

We had to beat out of the harbour, but rounding Cape Tiburon we got a fair wind, and stood away for Guadaloupe.

We had a long passage before us, and I was continually thinking of what the fortune of war might bring about. My fear was that we might fall in with a French cruiser, to which Lieutenant Dubois might consider it his duty to deliver up his despatches, that they might be conveyed more speedily to their destination, and that we might have to return to St. Domingo. Still I did my utmost to look at the bright side of the picture; and I fancied how pleasant it would be to find the brig under the guns of an English frigate,—perhaps the *Liffy* herself.

I had another secret source of satisfaction: I had given my word to La Touche simply not to interfere with the discipline of the ship, and I had made myself answerable that Larry would not; although I had said nothing about not attempting to make my escape, should an opportunity occur, though that was very remote indeed. In a French port it would be useless, as I should only tumble out of the frying-pan into the fire, or find myself among enemies. I could not speak French well enough to pass for a Frenchmen, and Larry's tongue would at once have betrayed him. Still hope kept me up, although what to hope for was indistinct and uncertain.

Larry, having somewhat got over his unpleasant suspicions of Hoolan's intentions, was as merry as usual, and in the evening kept his fiddle going, and the Frenchman and blacks dancing to their heart's content. He, however, was disinclined to remain forward after dark, and came back to his hiding-place under the companion ladder, where he was allowed to sleep under the supposition that he was there to attend on me.

I should have said that when the officer from the shore had delivered his despatches to Lieutenant Dubois, the latter, instead of locking them up in his own berth, put them into a drawer in the cabin table. Of their contents I, of course, was kept in ignorance,—indeed, I was not certain that Lieutenant Dubois himself knew their purport.

I do not even now like to speak of the thoughts which passed through my mind about these despatches. I was greatly troubled by them. Sometimes the idea occurred to me that when no one was in the cabin, I might throw them out of the stern port, and take the consequences of my act; but then I should be making an ungrateful return to the young French officers who had treated me so courteously. I dreaded to commit an act which might be dishonourable; at the same time, it was evident that by destroying the despatches I should be benefiting my country. From the eagerness which the officer who brought the packet had shown to get it off, I was convinced that it was of great importance, and that perhaps the fate of some of our islands might depend on its delivery. I was surprised at Dubois' carelessness at leaving it exposed. though less at La Touche, who, though a good-natured fellow, was harum-scarum and thoughtless in the extreme. Perhaps he might have returned me the compliment.

The wind was light; and there seemed every probability that we should make a long passage. So much the better, I thought. While we were at sea I was in good spirits, for I knew that there was a good chance of the brig being recaptured. Larry kept the crew alive with his fiddle forward, and even Dan Hoolan looked somewhat less surly than usual; at the same time Larry kept out of his way, and never trusted himself at night on deck when I was not there. Whether he was right in his suspicions or not was uncertain, but at all events Hoolan was a ruffian, and a traitor to his country.

I treated Larry as, of course, an officer does not usually treat an ordinary seaman. He was one night walking the deck with me, and we were talking of Ballinahone and our early days, when he suddenly said, 'Shure, Mr. Terence, there's something on your mind. I've thought so more than once. Just say now what it is.'

'You are clever, Larry, to find that out,' I answered. 'It's your love for me enables you to do it. It's nothing you would think much about. I'm troubled with the thoughts that we are carrying despatches to the French admiral, which, if delivered, may cause some serious injury to our country. They are kept in the drawer of the cabin table, and I might at any moment throw them overboard, and defeat the Frenchmen's object.'

The moment I said this I regretted it, as it struck me that it was like instigating Larry to do what I would not do myself. The effect on him was what I supposed my words would produce, for he at once replied, 'Thin, shure, overboard they go before the world's many hours older.'

'No, no, Larry! you mistake me,' I exclaimed. 'That's just what I don't want you to do. If it has to be done, I'll do it myself, and I forbid you to touch the packet. I insist on your promising me that you will not.'

Very unwillingly Larry gave the promise, and I knew that I could trust him. I then let the subject drop, regretting that I had broached it to my faithful follower.

'If the Frenchman choose to hang me, I will not bring the same fate on him,' I thought.

CHAPTER XV.

DAY after day went by. Though we occasionally saw a sail, we kept out of her way.

At length, one morning the look-out shouted, 'A sail on the starboard quarter!'

We were just then setting royals, which we did not carry at night. We watched the stranger. 'She has borne up in chase,' cried La Touche, who had gone aloft.

Dubois immediately ordered the brig to be kept before the wind, and studding-sails to be set on either side. The wind freshened, and away we flew before it. The brig being lightly laden, it was her best point of sailing, as I had observed. It took us out of our course, however. I sincerely hoped that the wind would increase, and that it should carry away some of our spars, and thus enable our pursuer to come up with us, for I took it for granted that she was English. The Frenchmen watched her eagerly, for we could see her top-sails from the deck.

'Do you think we shall get away from her?' I asked La Touche in an indifferent tone, as if it were a matter of no consequence to me.

'I hope so,' he replied. 'This brig is a regular little fly-away, and your frigates are not generally fast sailers.'

'But why do you think she is one of our frigates?' I asked. 'She may be French after all, and you may be running away from a friend.'

'I think she is English, because none of our cruisers are likely to be hereabouts at present,' he answered; and then, as if he had said something without thought, correcting himself, he added, 'Of course she may be French; but we think it safest to keep out of the way of all men-of-war.'

The topsails of the stranger rose gradually above the horizon; she was evidently a large vessel—a frigate, if not a line-of-battle ship. The little brig flew on gaily, as if feeling as eager to get away as were those on board.

'Ah, my friend! a stern chase is a long chase,' observed Dubois, who saw me watching the stranger. 'You are not going to rejoin your ship just yet.'

'I have made up my mind to be content with whatever happens,' I said.

'You are wise,' answered Dubois. 'It is the best thing under all circumstances.'

Still I did not despair of being overtaken. Perhaps she might be the *Liffy* herself, which had gone back to Jamaica, and was now returning to the south. We had a brisk breeze, though it did not increase, and the brig continued running on at her utmost speed. When I looked again, some time afterwards, it did not appear to me that the stranger had gained on us. The hours passed slowly on; evening, however, at length approached, and I was afraid that during the night Dubois would alter the brig's course, and that we should manage to escape. When I went below for our meals, I endeavoured to maintain as calm a countenance as I could, and to appear as cheerful as usual.

'You are a brave *garçon*,' said Dubois, as we sat at supper. 'We should be very sorry to lose your society, and I'll endeavour to keep you on board as long as I can.'

I thanked him, and said that I hoped to have the satisfaction of returning his courtesy, should the tables once more be turned. At last darkness came on, and our pursuer was lost to sight. As it was useless to remain on deck, I turned in, and Larry as usual followed me below. Whether it was from the excitement I had gone through, or from

12

having remained on deck all day, I cannot say; but I fell asleep immediately my head touched the pillow, and slept as soundly as a top. When I awoke, I saw by the dim light coming through the bull's-eye that the day had broken, and I hurried on deck, anxious to know if our pursuer was still in sight. Dubois and La Touche were there. I saluted them as usual. They did not appear quite as cheerful as they did on the previous day. The brig was still before the wind, with every stitch of canvas she could carry set. On looking astern, there was our pursuer, though hull down, but considerably nearer than before.

'Do not be too sanguine that she will come up with us. When the breeze freshens, we shall again get away from her,' said Dubois.

'It is of course what you wish, monsieur,' I observed.

'I've been after dreaming, Mr. Terence, that that craft is the *Liffy*, and that we were again on board her, as merry as crickets,' said Larry, coming to my side.

'But dreams, they say, go by contraries,' I answered. 'It would have been better not to have dreamed that.'

'Shure, thin, I wish that I had dreamed that we had run her out of sight,' he answered.

Soon after the wind got up, and was soon blowing as freshly as on the day before. The Frenchmen's spirits once more rose. Larry's and mine fell. The big ship, however, continued about the same distance off; but as long as she did not gain on us, our captors did not mind. At length it seemed to me that we were actually drawing ahead. Perhaps we might be leading our pursuer further out of her course than she wished to go, and she would give up the chase. The Frenchmen, from their remarks, seemed to think so.

Mid-day arrived; an observation was taken. I found that we were in the latitude of the Virgin Islands, still a long way from Guadaloupe. When once among the islands, we should very easily escape during the night. Dubois and La Touche were congratulating themselves, when the look-out aloft shouted, 'Several sail in sight to the south-east!'

La Touche, immediately on hearing this, went to the masthead. I should have liked to have followed him, eager to know what they were. He said nothing till he came down. I then saw by the way he spoke to Dubois that he considered them to be enemies. After a short consultation the helm was put to starboard, and the brig headed more to the north; the yards were braced up, though the studding-sails were still set. In my eagerness to ascertain what the strangers were, I sprang aloft without waiting to ask leave of Dubois. He did not, however, call me down. As I got to the top-gallant masthead I looked eagerly to the southward, and I made out what I took to be a large fleet standing to the eastward, while here and there ships were scattered about, which I took to be frigates. I had no doubt that Dubois concluded they were English, and had therefore no wish to run in among them. We had heard before we left Jamaica that Sir George Rodney was expected out to join Sir Samuel Hood, and I had little doubt but that the fleet in sight was that of either the one or the other of those admirals. Whether the brig would escape them or not was doubtful, and I expected every instant to see either a frigate or corvette coming in chase of us. Our other pursuer could not have seen the ships visible from our masthead, and would therefore not understand the reason for our change of course. Had it been earlier in the day, our capture by either one or the other would have been certain; but Dubois might now manage, by good seamanship, to slip between the two. The wind increased, and our starboard studding-sails were taken in; we carried those on our larboard side to the last. Having satisfied myself, I returned on deck.

'Do you know what those ships are away to the southward?' asked Dubois.

'Yes, monsieur, I believe them to be English,' I answered.

'And you expect them to catch us, do you?' he said.

'That depends on circumstances,' I replied; 'but I know your determination, and believe that you will make every effort to escape.'

'You may be sure of that,' he said, laughing. 'See how I'm carrying on. Many would have shortened sail before this.'

I made no reply, but looked aloft. The brig was literally tearing through the water; the breeze was increasing; the sails were bulging out, every rope stretched out to its utmost tension; the studding-sails pulled and tugged as if eager to fly away. Presently there came a loud crack, and both studding-sail booms broke off close to the irons. The men attempted to get in the fluttering canvas.

'Cut! cut!' cried Dubois. 'Let them go!'

The wind shifted a point or two, and we had to haul still more up. As I had been unable lately to look at the chart, I could not make out exactly for what place we were steering, but I could distinguish several blue hillocks rising out of the ocean, which I knew must be small islands, either the Virgin Islands or others in their neighbourhood. We were now steering due north. I again went aloft. The main body of the fleet was no longer in sight, but three or four white sails could be seen shining brightly in the rays of the setting sun far away astern, while our pursuer could still be distinguished over our larboard quarter, yet apparently no nearer than before. On returning on deck Dubois looked at me with a smile of satisfaction.

'We are not caught yet,' he said. 'But bear it patiently, my young friend. We all have our trials.'

I made no reply, but walked to the other side of the deck. It was again night; the steward came and invited me down to supper, in which I joined Dubois, while La Touche remained on deck. He did not think fit to tell me what were his intentions, and though I should have liked to have known, I did not ask him. At last I turned in, and tried to go to sleep. I should not have minded hearing the brig go crash on shore, so vexed did I feel at the idea of her having escaped. Still I could not but admire the determination of the two young French officers, and again better feelings rose in my breast. At length I fell fast asleep. As I had no watch to keep, I slept on, as usual, until daylight streamed in through the bull's-eye over my head, when, to my surprise, I heard the sound of the cable slipping out, and knew that the brig had come to an anchor. I dressed as speedily as I could, and went on deck. We were in a fine harbour with numerous vessels of all sizes and nations—Spanish, French, Dutch, and Danish (the latter predominating)—floating on its bosom, and among them a frigate, with the colours of England flying at her peak. I knew, therefore, that we were in a neutral port, for which Dubois had steered when he found he could not otherwise escape. On examining the frigate more narrowly, my heart gave a bound, for I felt almost sure that she was the *Liffy*, but as several vessels were between us I could not make her out very clearly.

Dubois, who had probably been on deck most of the night, had gone below; and La Touche was engaged in issuing his orders to the crew. I took care to conceal my feelings, and on speaking to Larry I found he had not suspected that the frigate was the *Liffy*. Still he might do so, and I told him that I believed her to be our ship, charging him on no account to exhibit his feelings.

'Shure, Mr. Terence, that's a hard matter,' he exclaimed. 'I half feel inclined to leap out of my skin and get aboard her.'

'We must try to do that by some means or other,' I said; 'but how to accomplish it is the question. Even if Captain Macnamara knew that we were on board this brig, he could not come and take us by force.'

'Why not, Mr. Terence?' exclaimed Larry in surprise. 'Shure if I see one of our boats pulling by, I'll be after shouting at the top of my voice, to tell them we're here, and to ax them to come and take us off. Our captain's not the man to desert us, nor Mr. Saunders either; and as soon as they know that we're prisoners, they'll be after sending a couple of boats to release us; or maybe they'll bring the frigate round, and blaze away at the brig till they sink her.'

'That would be an unpleasant way of proceeding for us, at all events,' I answered, laughing. 'The reason they can't take us by force is, that this is a neutral port, and all vessels in here must keep the peace towards each other; so that if Monsieur Dubois refuses to give us up, our captain can't compel him. We must therefore manage to get away by ourselves if we are to be free.'

'Thin, Mr. Terence, that's just what we will be after doing,' said Larry, taking off his hat and scratching his head while he considered how the undertaking could be accomplished. 'Couldn't we just slip overboard at night and swim to the frigate? It wouldn't be further than I have swum many a time in the Shannon.'

'But the Shannon and this place are very different,' I answered. 'Jack Shark keeps as sharp a look-out here as he does in Port Royal harbour; and we may chance to have our legs nipped off before we can get up the side of the frigate.'

'Shure, Mr. Terence, thin I never thought of that,' said Larry; 'but maybe the officers will go on shore, and they don't keep very strict watch aboard here, so I might just manage to slip a grating and a spar or two over the side, to make a raft; then we might paddle on it to the frigate.'

'I don't see any better plan than you propose,' I answered; 'though I would risk a swim and the chances of encountering a shark rather than not make the attempt to escape; for, even supposing the frigate on the other side of those merchantmen should not prove to be the *Liffy*, we should be welcome on board. It is of the greatest importance that the captain should know of the despatches the brig is carrying to Guadaloupe, so that a watch may be kept on her movements, and that she may be pursued and captured outside the harbour.'

'Thin, Mr. Terence, let me go alone; I'd have no difficulty in slipping overboard, and there's less chance of my being missed,' said Larry. 'When her captain knows that you're aboard the brig, he'll be after her in a jiffy.'

'No, no, Larry; I can never let you go alone. Whatever we do, we'll do together.'

'That's like you, Mr. Terence. Just trust to me, thin; only do you be ready for a start directly it's dark, and I'll be keeping a look-out on deck for the chance of one of the *Liffy's* boats coming near, to let them know that we're aboard.'

Tantalizing as it was to see the ship, as I supposed, to which I belonged within a short distance of me, and yet not be able to communicate with her, I felt that I could do nothing for the present, and that it was prudent not to be seen talking too much with Larry. I therefore told him to keep away from me during the day, unless he had something particular to say, while I went below again, to finish my toilet and wait for breakfast.

La Touche had been too busy to speak to me, and Dubois was still asleep. I remained in my berth until the steward announced that breakfast was ready, when I met the two officers, who had just come below. They politely invited me to take a seat at the table.

'Well, you see, we have managed to escape your cruisers,' said Dubois, as he poured me out a cup of coffee. 'We have reason to congratulate ourselves, as we were very hard pressed.'

'I must compliment you, monsieur, on your skilful seamanship,' I said. 'I do so with sincerity, although I should have been very glad had you been caught. However, I am prepared to bear my disappointment philosophically. We have not yet reached Guadaloupe, and I don't despair of regaining my liberty, though I conclude you'll not consider yourself justified in letting me leave the brig?'

'For your sake I wish that we could,' said La Touche; 'but you are known to be on board, and we should have to account for you; so I'm afraid you must exercise the philosophy you speak of.' Imitating the Frenchman, I shrugged my shoulders, as if I was perfectly resigned to my fate. I made no remark about the English frigate in the harbour, as the Frenchmen didn't allude to her, though they could not have supposed that I was ignorant of her being there.

I saw that the brig was riding at single anchor and hove short, and I expected that Dubois was waiting for an opportunity of slipping out of the harbour before the frigate was prepared to follow him. That she would do so, should the brig be discovered to be an English vessel, a prize to the French, there could be no doubt, unless detained by some matter of more importance.

After breakfast we walked the deck for some time, and then Dubois ordered La Touche to take a boat and pull round the harbour.

'See as you pass yonder frigate there, how she's riding,' he said; 'whether she appears to be ready to put to sea, and learn, if you can ascertain, what brought her in here. I wouldn't have come in had I known that we should have found so unpleasant a neighbour.'

'Do you know what frigate she is?' he asked, turning to me.

'As I can't see her hull clearly, were I perfectly acquainted with her I should be unable to answer your questions, monsieur,' I replied.

'Well, then, favour me by going aloft with my telescope, and you'll then, by looking down on her deck, be able to tell me whether you recognize any of those on board, or have to your knowledge seen the frigate before.'

From his manner I believed he had not an idea that I suspected the frigate to be the *Liffy*.

I willingly agreed; and, taking the glass, went aloft. All my doubts were at an end. I at once made out Captain

Macnamara walking the starboard side of the quarter-deck with Mr. Saunders. On the opposite side, I distinguished several of my messmates by their figures. Some of the men were forward, but the greater number were below, and I could see no signs of any intentions of getting under way. I waited a considerable time, and heartily I wished for a pair of wings, that I might fly over the masts of the other vessels, and pitch down on her deck. No sight could have been more tantalizing. I descended at last, and returning the telescope to Dubois, said,—

'I confess frankly that I know the frigate. She is the one to which I belong.'

'Is she a fast vessel?' inquired Dubois.

'She is considered so, monsieur,' I answered.

'Faster than this brig?' he asked.

'Certainly, unless in a very light wind,' I said. 'If you expect to be chased, you have very little chance of escape from her, I should think.'

'I must hope for the best,' he said. 'There's a fine breeze out of the harbour, and we may be off again before the frigate finds we are moving. We have the advantage of being concealed from her sight, and she dare not fire a gun or send a boat after us, even should she wish it, till we're three leagues outside the harbour.'

Dubois spoke in a confident tone, as if he did not think that there was the slightest chance I should even try to make my escape. I was dreading all the time that he would ask me to give my word not to do so. He didn't, however, appear to think of that. In a short time La Touche came back, and reported, as I knew he would, that the frigate didn't appear to be preparing to sail. Scarcely had he come on board than the wind began to drop, till it became a stark calm. I saw the officers exchange looks with each other as they observed the dog vane hanging right up and down. It was very certain that we could not move, for we had not boats sufficient to tow the brig out of the harbour. There was every prospect of the calm continuing for many hours. The Frenchmen, by the way they paced the deck, showed their vexation, every now and then giving an impatient stamp with their feet.

At last La Touche stopped and said,—

'Wouldn't it be well to go on shore and try and pick up some news? We may gain intelligence which may be of importance; at all events, we shall pass the time more pleasantly than on board.'

'A good idea,' answered Dubois. 'We will go. You'll be content to remain on board?' he added, turning to me. 'It might be inconvenient to take you with us, as we might meet some of your brother officers; but I brought a few books of light literature in my portmanteau, besides my nautical almanack, and you can read them while we're on shore.'

I thanked him, and was very glad to find that he didn't wish me to go; as, although by landing I might have a chance of making my escape, I would not do so without Larry.

They did not wait for dinner; but telling the steward to bring me mine at the usual hour, pulled away in one of the boats, leaving the brig under the charge of a quartermaster, who had come on board at Gonavez Bay. He was a sharp-eyed old fellow, and had evidently been directed to keep a watch on Larry and me. Several shore-boats came alongside, but after some fresh provisions had been purchased, the others were ordered to keep off.

Soon after the officers had gone Larry came up to me.

'Hwist, Mr. Terence,' he said in a low voice. 'Dan Hoolan and the other boys know that the frigate out there is the *Liffy*, and I heard Dan say to one of them that they must take care we don't get away to her, for he's afraid, if we do, that Captain Macnamara, when he hears of the mutiny, will consider that he has a right to retake the brig, and that they'll all be triced up to the yard-arm before many hours are over afterwards.'

'We must try, then, to throw them off their guard,

Larry,' I said. 'Have you thought of any other plan for escaping?'

'Not just yet, Mr. Terence; but I'm still hoping that something will turn up. I'll tell you all about it presently; but I mustn't stop long aft, for I have a notion that Dan and the rest have got something into their heads, and that they won't be stopping aboard if they can help it, to run the risk of hanging.'

Larry again went forward, and I returned to the cabin. I cannot say that the books Dubois left me were edifying; and after I had turned over a few pages, I threw them aside as abominable trash, not fit for any gentleman's eyes to rest on. They were such works as contributed to prepare the way for the French Revolution. The steward brought me an excellent dinner, and placed a bottle of claret on the table, of which, however, I partook very moderately. I passed the afternoon as best I could, now and then going on deck to have the pleasure of taking a look at the *Liffy*, and hoping to see one of her boats passing. I determined, should one pull by, to hail her and say who I was; for I was afraid that Nettleship might suppose the brig had been lost, and that the report of my death might, by ill luck, reach Ballinahone. I watched, however, in vain. As evening approached I expected that Dubois and La Touche would return. Something kept them on shore; probably, finding the calm continue, they were carrying out their intentions of amusing themselves. At last darkness came on, and I went back into the cabin. I should have said that the brig carried a small boat hoisted up astern, but which was in a dilapidated condition, and considered not fit to put into the water. As we had no carpenter on board able to repair her, she was allowed to remain hoisted up. I had been in the cabin some time, and I believe I must have dropped off into a doze, when I heard a sound of blocks creaking, and presently there was a splash in the water. Springing up, I looked out of one of the stern ports, which was open, and could distinguish a boat just below me with a man in her, moving round the quarter. At first I thought he was Larry, and then I felt sure that Larry would not have taken a boat without first giving me notice of his intentions. In less than a minute afterwards, however, he poked his head into the cabin.

'Hwist, Mr. Terence, it's just as I thought it would be,' he whispered. 'Dan Hoolan and the rest are going to pull on shore. They have made the watch below drunk, and they have seized the anchor watch and put them in limbo. They fancy that if they can get away up the country, they'll be safe, and I have a mind to go with them and pull the boat back, and take you off. Keep a look-out of the cabin window, Mr. Terence; maybe I'll come under the counter, and you can squeeze through the port without anybody on deck finding us out. Now I'm off.'

Larry hurried out of the cabin, leaving me in a state of anxious doubt as to whether he would succeed. I was afraid of going on deck lest I should be seen by the mutineers, and I at once therefore went to the port, hoping that I might catch a glimpse of them pulling away. Even if Larry got off with them, there might be many chances against his returning. The boat even might fill before she could reach the shore, or she might encounter the French officers returning to the brig, and be seized. I wondered at their carelessness in leaving the vessel with such a crew as theirs; for those who had proved traitors to me might have been expected to turn traitors to them.

Scarcely a minute had elapsed before, to my surprise, I heard a 'hwist' come from under the counter, and Larry's voice saying,—

'Lend a hand, Mr. Terence, and catch the painter as I chuck it up.'

I did as he desired, and presently he climbed up in at the port.

'Hold fast there, Mr. Terence,' he said, as he squeezed through, and springing forward locked the cabin door. 'I'll tell you all about it when we're free of the brig,' he whispered.

Quick as thought he made the painter fast to an eye-bolt, used to secure the dead-light. 'Now jump into the boat, Mr. Terence, and we'll be off,' he added.

As he bid me, I slid down the painter, expecting him to follow immediately. For a few seconds he didn't come, and I feared that something had happened to him; but he soon appeared, and slid down as I had done, holding in his mouth a knife, with which he quickly cut the rope.

I had taken one of the oars, he seized another, and giving a shove against the counter, sent the boat off from the brig. We paddled away with might and main, making, however, as little noise as we could. Scarcely, however, had we gone half a cable's length than I heard a gruff voice, which I recognized as Dan Hoolan's, uttering a fearful oath, and inquiring what had become of the boat. Several others replied in the same tones; and one of them, who had apparently run aft, exclaimed, 'Shure there she is, and that —— Larry Harrigan has gone off with her.'

'Come back, come back, you villain!' shouted the men.

'It's mighty likely we'll be after doing that,' Larry was on the point of shouting out, when I told him to be silent; and there being now less necessity for caution, we bent to our oars with all our might.

'I wonder the villains don't fire at us,' I said.

'Shure the cabin door's locked, and they can't get at the muskets, or they would be after doing the same,' answered Larry.

We had ample reason to pull hard, for the water was leaking in through every seam in the boat; but I hoped that she might keep afloat long enough to enable us to reach the side of the frigate. Hoolan and his companions, finding that it was of no use, had ceased hailing us. We had gone a short way when I saw a boat coming off from the shore. 'A hundred to one the French officers are in her,' I thought; 'and if they have heard the shouting from the brig, they

will fancy that something has happened, and be on the
look-out. However, we are in for it.' We were at first
pulling ahead of the vessels which were at anchor between
us and the frigate; but, on seeing the boat, I told Larry
we would pass under the stern of the one nearest us, and
thread our way in and out among them, so that we might be
concealed from the sight of those coming off from the shore,
in case they should make chase after us. In a short time,
however, the boat was half full of water.

'We must get this out, or we shall be sinking,' I said.

There was no bailer; but I had seized my hat before I
had got out of the cabin window, and putting in our oars
we bailed away as hard as we could. We had succeeded
in partly freeing the boat of water, when we heard the
splash of oars coming from the direction of the brig. Once
more we gave way, the water still coming in. I very much
doubted that we should reach the frigate without having
again to stop. The boat, however, was gaining on us.
Should she come up before we could get under our own
flag, we might lawfully be recaptured; the water was already
up to the thwarts, and the boat pulled heavily; our pursuers
were getting closer and closer. We were nearing the frigate.

I looked round. I saw her high sides and tall masts
against the sky.

I shouted at the top of my voice, '*Liffy* ahoy! help, help
here!'

Larry shouted still louder, for he had a voice of his own
when he tried to exert it. The boat pulled more heavily
than ever. If it had not been for the dread of the sharks, I
should have jumped overboard and tried to swim to the
frigate. Still we made her move. I can't say what a leap
my heart gave as we ran up against her side. Some ropes
were hove to us, for our shouts had attracted attention, and,
swimming up them, we each reached a port in time to see our
boat's gunwale flush with the water, and our pursuers turning
round to pull away. As we got on deck the quartermaster
brought a lantern, which he held so as to throw a light

on our faces, and at the same time a midshipman ran
up.

'Who have we here?' he exclaimed, and I recognized
Chaffey's voice. 'What! Paddy Finn, my boy, where in the
world have you come from?'

'From a brig—a prize to the French,' I answered. 'But
I say, Chaffey, I want to see the captain at once. If there
comes a breeze she'll be slipping out of the harbour, and we
must be ready to go after her.'

'Why, we thought you were on board the *Soleil,* and
expected she would be put into commission, and be sent
out to rejoin us, as we want small craft to watch the
movements of the French.'

I briefly told him what had happened. He in return
told me what I was sorry to hear, that nothing had been
heard of the *Soleil,* though the idea was that she had got
safely into Port Royal harbour.

'The captain doesn't like to be roused up; but I suppose
as your information is of importance, he won't give me a
wigging for disturbing him,' he said, as we reached the
cabin door. Mentioning his object, the sentry stationed
there allowed him to pass, and I stood for a time outside,
trying to squeeze the water out of my nether garments. I
had formed a little pool round my feet by the time Chaffey
returned.

'You're to go into the captain, Paddy,' he said. 'He
fired off his great guns and small arms at me, so he'll receive
you pleasantly, I hope.'

Giving a final wring to my coat tails, I made my way to
the after cabin. The captain, with night-cap on head, had
just got into his breeches.

'Glad to see you safe on board, Finnahan,' he said.
'Now give me the information you have brought. I'll
hear about your adventures afterwards.'

'I have just escaped from a brig, sir, that is carrying
despatches to the French admiral at Guadaloupe, and as she
may at any moment slip out of the harbour, I thought you

would like to know of it, that you may follow and capture her as soon as she gets to a sufficient distance from this place.'

'How do you know she has despatches?' he asked.

'I heard the French officer who came on board tell the lieutenant in command of the brig what they were, and I saw them in the drawer of the cabin table. I supposed that the lieutenant put them there that they might be handy to throw overboard, should he find at any time that the brig was likely to be recaptured.'

'Then why didn't you bring them away with you?' asked the captain. 'You made your own escape—you might easily, I should have thought, have got hold of them.'

'I felt in honour bound not to do so, sir. I was trusted on board; but as I had not given my word not to escape, I felt justified in getting away when the opportunity offered.'

'I consider you acted rightly,' said the captain. 'A man cannot have too nice a sense of honour; at the same time I believe you would have gained great credit if you had brought them off. Much may depend on our getting hold of them. However, we must do our best to capture the brig, and prevent her delivering them to the French admiral. You deserve credit as it is for making your escape, and I'm glad you got off without breaking your parole. I should have regretted to find that you had done that. Now call Mr. Saunders, and—hillo! my lad, you're dripping wet! Go and shift into dry clothes, or rather, if you're not wanted, turn into your hammock and get some sleep. You have not had much of that to-night, I conclude.'

Getting a lantern from the sentry, I at once repaired to old 'Rough-and-Ready's' cabin.

'Mr. Saunders,' I shouted, 'the captain wants to see you.'

He jumped up in a moment wide awake—a good first lieutenant always sleeps with one eye open.

'Why, where do you come from, youngster?' he asked, as, throwing his night-cap on the pillow, he rapidly slipped into his clothes.

I very briefly told him while he finished dressing, which took him scarcely a minute, and he then hastened to the captain's cabin, while I gladly went below and had my marine roused up to get me out some dry clothes from my chest and to sling my hammock. I inquired for Larry, who I found had gone forward. In a short time he came aft, having also got into dry clothes.

'Mighty glad we've got away from the brig, Mr. Terence,' he said; 'but still I'm as sorrowful as a pig in a gale of wind. The first thing the men axed me for was my fiddle, and bedad I left it aboard the brig; so if she gets away I'll never be after seeing it again.'

'We must hope to take her,' I said. 'Depend on it the captain will keep a look-out on her movements, and we shall then recover your fiddle, though I'm afraid we shall not get hold of the despatches.'

'Is it them bundle of papers in the drawer you're speaking of?' asked Larry. 'I was after thinking it would be as well to bring them away, in case the captain should like to have a look at them, so I just put them in my shirt before I slipped out of the cabin window. I hope I won't be called a thief for taking them. Here they are, Mr. Terence;' and he handed me the packet which I had seen in the drawer.

I hurried aft with it to the captain. I found him and the first lieutenant in the cabin.

'Why, what's this?' exclaimed the captain, as I gave him the packet.

I told him that I believed it contained the despatches sent from Port-au-Prince; and that my companion, Larry Harrigan, unknown to me, had brought them away.

'What! and you gave him a hint to do so?' said the captain.

'No, indeed I didn't, sir,' I answered firmly, though I blushed as I then explained, that although I had spoken to Larry about them, it was with no intention of inducing him to do what I was unwilling to do myself. 'I had told him of them, sir,' I said; 'but I give you my word of honour that I had no thought at the time of his getting hold of them. I did meditate, I confess, throwing them overboard; but under the circumstances I came to the conclusion that I had no right to do that, independent of the risk of being severely dealt with by the Frenchmen, should my act be discovered.'

'Well, well, I believe you, Finnahan,' said the captain in a kind tone. 'We have got them, and we must take them at once to Sir Samuel Hood. We need care very little about the brig now.'

CHAPTER XVI.

OLD FRIENDS.

'HADN'T you better, sir, see what they contain?' observed Mr. Saunders. 'It's just possible, too, that the commander of the brig knows their contents, and will communicate it verbally to the French admiral, or perhaps he may have duplicates on board.'

'I don't think he has that, sir,' I remarked. 'I saw the packet delivered to the French lieutenant, and he certainly did not open it, though I can't say whether he knows the purport of the despatches.'

'It's likely enough that he does, though; and at all events we must prevent him, if we can, from communicating with his admiral,' said Captain Macnamara. 'When he finds that you have made your escape, he'll be eager to be off, and still more so if he discovers that the despatches are missing. Send a boat, Mr. Saunders, at once to watch the movements of the brig. Heave the cable short, and be ready to sail the moment we get a breeze.'

Mr. Saunders left the cabin to carry out the orders he had received. I hadn't yet told the captain of the way the brig was taken from me, and of the mutiny. I now, by his desire, gave him a detailed account of the circumstances.

'There's no blame attached to you, Finnahan,' he said; 'though as far as I can make out, the French officers didn't behave in an honourable way, and I hope those mutinous scoundrels will get their deserts before long. I'm sorry they are our countrymen, but I can show them no favour on that account. If we take the brig, every one of them will be hanged.'

'I rather think, sir, that the French officers will have saved us the trouble; for when they get on board and find what Hoolan and his mates have been about, they won't be inclined to treat them leniently.'

'I wish that we had left them ashore at Cork,' observed the captain. 'We should have been better without such scoundrels. Now, with regard to these despatches. I don't understand a word of French, nor does the first lieutenant, nor any other officer in the ship except yourself, Finnahan; still it may be necessary to act immediately on them. I'll open them, and you must translate their contents.'

I would thankfully have excused myself; for though I could jabber French pretty glibly, I was very little accustomed to write or translate it. The captain got out pens and paper from his desk; and, telling me to sit down, opened the packet, and put it into my hands. The hand-writing greatly puzzled me, for it was not a style to which I was accustomed. I spelt out the words, however, as well as I could, and tried to get at the sense. It contained an account of the intended sailing of the Marquis de Boullie with four thousand troops for the relief of Guadaloupe, which was at that time being attacked by the English under General Prescott. There were also various directions for the guidance of the French forces in those seas; but the most important was a plan for the concentration of the fleet, carrying a large body of soldiers, so that they might pounce down on Jamaica while the English squadrons were being led away in opposite directions. It was some time before I arrived at the gist of the matter.

'This is important,' exclaimed the captain. 'You would have rendered essential service to the country by bringing these on board, and I must see that Harrigan is rewarded;

while the part you have played must not be forgotten, as, though your sense of honour prevented you from taking the packet, it is owing to your courage and determination that we have obtained it. However, we will talk of that by and by. We must look out, in the meantime, that the brig doesn't escape us; for though I have got the information to put Sir Samuel Hood on his guard, the French may obtain it also, and act accordingly.'

While we were speaking, Mr. Saunders came in to say the boat was ready, and the cable hove short; but that, as it was still a stark calm, there was no chance at present of the brig getting under weigh.

'You must go in the boat, Finnahan, and make sure that we watch the right brig. As we can't see her from the ship, we may be following the wrong vessel,' said the captain.

Though I would much rather have turned in and gone to sleep, I of course obeyed orders.

Mr. Harvey, the third lieutenant, was in charge of the boat, and as I stepped into her, I found that Larry Harrigan formed one of the crew. They pulled away under my directions, and soon gained sight of the brig.

'It's mighty hard that we can't jump aboard and take her,' I heard Larry say to the stroke oar, behind whom he was sitting. 'I'd be after getting back my fiddle, at all events, if we could.'

'It's agen' the law of nations,' answered the man; 'though I should like to punish the rascal Hoolan for murdering poor Ben Nash and Tim Logan.'

'Silence, men,' said Mr. Harvey; 'we must not let the people on board the brig find out that we are watching them. They'll probably take us for a guard-boat, but if they hear our English voices, they'll know who we are.'

We kept under the shade of one of the neighbouring vessels. All was quiet on board the brig. There were no signs of her being about to trip her anchor. I wondered whether Dubois had put Hoolan and the rest in irons when he discovered how they had behaved. I could scarcely suppose that they would have contrived to seize him and his boat's crew when they returned on board; yet such was possible, and would have been retributive justice on him for having taken the brig from us. Still I should have been very sorry indeed to hear that he and La Touche had met with any injury.

We waited and waited, till it appeared that we were not likely to wait to any purpose.

At last Larry, who seemed to have forgotten the order he had received to keep silence, suddenly exclaimed,—

'Couldn't we go aboard just to ax the Frenchmen to give me back my fiddle. That wouldn't be agen' the law of nations, would it, Mr. Terence?'

'Silence there,' said Mr. Harvey, scarcely able to restrain his laughter. 'I ordered you men not to speak.'

'Shure I forgot the same,' said Larry in a suppressed tone. 'Och! my fiddle, my fiddle! what will I be after doing without it!'

At length daylight dawned; and according to the orders Mr. Harvey had received, we returned on board. As the sun rose, a light breeze began to play over the surface of the harbour. A look-out was sent aloft to keep watch on the brig, while every preparation was made for heaving up the anchor and making sail, should she be seen to get under weigh.

Dubois, knowing that Larry and I had gone aboard the frigate, must have been aware that the captain was acquainted with the character of his vessel, and also that she was carrying despatches. He would certainly, I thought, suppose that we should follow him, should he put to sea. I therefore scarcely fancied that he would venture out of the harbour during daylight, but fully expected that he would wait another night, on the chance of there being a breeze during the time to enable him to get away. I was therefore greatly surprised when the look-out hailed,—

'The brig is loosing her topsails, and heaving up her anchor.'

The breeze at this time had freshened considerably. Scarcely had the words been uttered than I saw, between the other vessels, the brig, with her topsails and courses set, steering towards the narrow entrance, through which only small or light vessels could venture.

The capstan was instantly manned; the hands were ordered aloft, and topsails, and top-gallant-sails were let fall; but before we could cant the right way, the brig had passed us, and had already reached the passage, when, the head-sails filling, the anchor was tripped, and being run up to the bows, we steered for the broader and only safe channel.

What had induced Dubois to put to sea, and leave the safe shelter of the harbour, I could not divine. It made me suspect that he had not discovered the loss of the despatches, and knowing the importance of delivering them without delay, he had determined to run every risk for that object. He probably expected, by getting the first of the breeze, to be a long way ahead before we could follow, trusting to the various chances which might occur to effect his escape. Had we been able to go through the narrow passage, he must have known that he would to a certainty have been caught; but our captain, from remarks I heard, seemed to think that the brig might possibly succeed in getting off, though he was resolved to use every exertion to overtake her, provided we were not led out of our course, for it was of still greater importance to get down to Barbadoes, or wherever the English admiral might be.

During the stay of the *Liffy* in the harbour, information had been obtained of the movements of the French fleet, as also that they had a large number of troops on board. Their object was to capture as many of our West India Islands as they could, and several had already fallen into their hands. St. Christopher's, however, had hitherto held out; Jamaica was prepared to resist to the last; and Barbadoes, our pet island, was strongly protected by Sir Samuel Hood's fleet.

The French were, I should have said, vastly superior

in numbers to the English. We had, however, brave and vigilant commanders, who took good care not to let the grass grow beneath their feet.

Had Captain Macnamara been certain that Lieutenant Dubois was ignorant of the contents of the packet Larry had carried off, he would have cared very little about letting the brig escape. He thought, however, that Dubois might possibly have duplicates, or might have learned the information they contained.

The wind freshened as we got outside. We could now see the brig about five or six miles away to the southward, for she had got the first of the breeze, and had carried it along while we were getting under weigh. All sail being made, however, we rapidly gained on her.

'It'll be a bad job for Dan Hoolan if we come up with the little hooker, Mr. Terence,' said Larry. 'If the Frenchmen haven't shot him already, our captain will be shure to run him up to the yard-arm, with the poor fellows he decaived.'

'It's what he richly deserves,' I replied; 'but I wish that he had never been pressed. It would have been better to have left him on shore, to stand his chance of hanging, or turning honest.'

'Ah, shure there's but little honesty likely to come out of Dan Hoolan,' observed Larry, who disliked him more than ever since he had caused the deaths of Tim Logan and Ben Nash.

The brig was steering south-east directly for Guadaloupe, and we followed in the same direction; but as there were numerous islands in her course, she might, if she could retain her distance ahead till dark, escape by keeping round them, or if hard pressed, run on shore, when the French officers would probably endeavour to forward the information they were conveying by some other vessel. She was, as I have said, very fast, and she was now carrying every stitch of canvas she could set. The *Liffy* was no laggard, and we pressed after her. The chase was as exciting as it could

well be. Scarcely any of the officers left the deck, except
to take a hurried breakfast, and every glass on board was
in requisition. Now, when the breeze freshened, we appeared
to be gaining on her; now, when it fell, she seemed to
draw ahead of us. We passed between the islands of St.
John and Tortola; we sighted the east end of Santa Cruz,
and then made out the curious conical hill of Saba, to the
north of St. Eustatia. Noon had passed, and the wind
again freshening, we gained rapidly on the chase. The look-
out aloft hailed that he saw several sail right ahead. It was
a question whether they were English or French. If the
latter, the brig might lead us under their guns, and it was
necessary to be cautious. Dubois must have seen them
also, but probably was as uncertain about their character as
we were. He might, after all, be captured should he stand
on. At length he altered his course, and appeared to be
making for St. Eustatia, and from this it was pretty evident
that he took the fleet ahead to be English. Whether he was
right in that respect or not we could not tell, but he made
a mistake in hauling his wind. In another half hour we
got near enough to send a shot, which fell aboard him;
another and another followed, when, letting fly his head
sheets, he put his helm to starboard, and hauled down his
colours. We at once hove to. A boat was lowered, and I,
being able to speak French, was sent with Mr. Harvey to
take possession. We were soon alongside. Dubois must
have recognized me when in the boat. As we stepped on
deck he and La Touche advanced, and presented their swords
to Mr. Harvey, at the same time each of them made me a
very formal bow. I returned it, and said, as I stepped
forward,—

'What is the meaning of this, Monsieur Dubois? You
have made a gallant attempt to escape. It's the fortune of
war that you have failed; but why do you treat me as a
stranger? I wish to behave towards you as old friends, and
will do all in my power to help you.'

'We do not desire the friendship of one who has been guilty

of such an act as you have committed,' answered Dubois stiffly.

'What act do you speak of?' I asked, suspecting, however, to what he alluded.

'You were trusted. You made your escape, and carried off the despatches,' he answered.

'I had a right to make my escape, for I had not given you my word to remain,' I said. 'I did not carry off the despatches, nor did I instigate any one to do so. You'll find that I speak the truth.'

'I have, then, to beg your pardon,' said Dubois, with French politeness, though he looked doubtfully at me.

There was little time for conversation, however. Mr. Harvey desired the two French officers to prepare for going on board the frigate. 'I understand that you have some English seamen on board. Where are they?' he asked.

'Two of them lie there,' said Dubois, 'and the third, in trying to swim on shore, was seized by a shark. We are well rid of them, for they were mutinous rascals.'

I looked forward; there, on the deck, lay Dan Hoolan and the other mutineer. A shot had struck him on the chest, and nearly knocked the upper part of his body to pieces, while it had cut his companion almost in two, but I recognized his features, grim and stern, even in death. One of the French seamen had also been killed, and his countrymen, without ceremony, hove his body overboard. Mr. Harvey ordered our men to dispose of the mutineers in the same manner, and to wash down the deck, for the sight was not such as any of us cared to look at longer than was necessary. Dubois and La Touche, who had gone below to get their valises, now returning with them, stepped into the boat, and Mr. Harvey left me in charge of the brig. I felt somewhat elated at finding myself on board the craft of the command of which I had been so suddenly deprived, and began to hope that I was to retain it. I resolved, at all events, should any of the Frenchmen be left in her, to be careful that they didn't again take her out of my hands.

I was sorry that I didn't know rather more about navigation, but I thought that I could manage, by carrying on, to
keep in sight of the frigate. I was especially thankful that we
had not been compelled to hang Dan Hoolan and the other
men, for ruffians as they were, and outlaws as they had been,
I felt for them as countrymen, and should have been sorry
to see them suffer so ignominious a fate. The brig was still
hove to, and I was pacing the deck with all the dignity of a
commanding officer, when I saw another boat come off from
the frigate, full of men. In a short time, Sinnet stepped up
the side.

'I have come to supersede you, Paddy,' he said. 'The
captain doubts your capabilities as a navigator ; besides which,
he wants you as an interpreter, so you need not consider
yourself slighted.'

'Not a bit of it,' I answered. 'Only look out that the
Frenchmen don't take the brig from you.'

'The captain has made sure that that won't be the case, by
ordering all the prisoners to be sent to the frigate,' he replied.

I saw Larry step on deck with the new arrivals, and fancied
that he had been sent to form part of the brig's crew. I asked
him if we were to be separated.

'No, Mr. Terence, I'm thankful to say ; but I axed leave of
Mr. Saunders to come and look for my fiddle. "To be shure,"
said he ; "it puts life into the men, and you may go." So I've
come, Mr. Terence. If Dan Hoolan hasn't hove it overboard,
I'll be after setting the men a-jigging this very evening,
supposing we haven't to fight the French, or do any other
trifle of that sort !'

'Be smart, then, Larry, about it,' I said, 'for I have to be
off ;' and Larry dived below. I ordered the Frenchmen to
tumble into the boat,—they obeying in their usual light-hearted
manner, not in any way looking as if they were prisoners.
The last man had got into the boat, when Larry came up from
below with his fiddle-case under his arm.

'Hooray, Mr. Terence ! shure I'm in luck, for I've got
back my Cremona !' he exclaimed, as he came down the side.

'I'll set your heels going, mounseers, so don't be down-hearted, my boys,' he said, addressing the French prisoners.

They seemed to understand him. Some exclaimed, '*Bon garçon!*' snapping their fingers, and moving their feet, to show that they were ready enough to dance notwithstanding that they were prisoners.

'It's a wonder, Mr. Terence: I've been after looking for Dan Hoolan, but never a sight could I get of him, or Phelan, or Casey,' said Larry.

When he heard of their fate, he'd scarcely believe it, till I told him that I had seen two of them dead on the deck, and that Dubois had accounted for the other.

'Well, I'm mighty thankful, for they might have had a worse ending, and it wasn't to be supposed that they'd come to a good one,' he remarked.

Soon after I got back to the ship the captain sent for me into the cabin.

'I wish you, Finnahan,' he said, 'to try and ascertain from these two young French officers what they know about the proceedings of their fleet, and also learn whether they suppose the ships ahead are those of our country or theirs.'

I promised to do as he desired. I found Dubois walking the deck, looking somewhat disconsolate. He received me as before, in a cold manner, though La Touche held out his hand when I offered him mine.

'It's of little consequence now,' he said; 'but I confess that we suspect you of carrying off the packet. We only discovered that it was gone after we left the harbour.'

I told him exactly how it had happened, and that I myself considered that under the circumstances I should not have been justified in taking it.

'You have acted honourably, monsieur. I apologize for our wrong suspicions, and I hope Dubois will do the same,' he said.

'Certainly,' said Dubois. 'I vowed, when I discovered our loss, that I would never trust an English officer again.'

'You will now acknowledge, then, that though we are compelled to be enemies, we act honourably towards you,' I remarked. 'However, all is said by you to be fair in love or war—is it not?'

'We have got the saying, though it may not be a true one, for all that,' he answered.

I now tried to carry out the captain's instructions, but I confess that I could gain very little either from Dubois or La Touche. Perhaps they didn't know much about the movements of their own fleet. Their opinion was that the ships they had seen ahead were English, or they would not have gone out of their course to avoid them. Captain Macnamara was not quite satisfied on that point.

We continued standing to the southward, with the brig following in our wake, while a bright look-out was kept aloft, that we might haul our wind, and get out of their way, in case they should prove enemies. It was fortunate that we were cautious, for, just before dark, the ships in sight were made out to be certainly French, and we immediately stood away to the southward to avoid them. Two frigates were seen coming in chase, but we made all sail, and night hid them from our sight. Whether or not they were still pursuing us we could not tell, but no lights were shown, and it was important to avoid an engagement, especially with enemies of a superior force. A careful look-out, however, was kept, lest they should come up with us during the night. When morning dawned we found that we had run them out of sight, and we now once more steered our course for Barbadoes.

On reaching Carlisle Bay, we found the fleet under Sir Samuel Hood moored in order of battle. It was evident from this that the admiral expected an attack from the French fleet, and we afterwards learned that he had gained information that it had sailed from Martinique in great force for the purpose of attacking the island. In an hour afterwards Sinnet brought in the brig in safety, when he had to deliver her up to the prize agents.

It was a fine sight to me, for I had never seen so many line-of-battle ships together, with their broadsides pointed in the same direction, sufficient, it seemed, to blow the whole navy of France into the air. Captain Macnamara, immediately on bringing up, sent Mr. Harvey with the despatches to the admiral, and directed him to ask for instructions as to our future course.

We waited hour after hour in expectation of the French fleet.

'We shall have a good stand-up fight for it,' observed Sinnet to me. 'I only wish that I had kept command of the brig, and I would have blazed away at the Frenchmen with my pop-guns.'

The night passed away. Early the next morning a sail was seen in the offing, standing towards the bay. We all supposed her to be one of the advance frigates of the French, sent ahead to ascertain our strength ; but as the light increased she was seen to be a corvette, though at the same time she had a French appearance. She came steering directly for the admiral, and hove to inside him.

'Why, I do believe it's the craft we took soon after we left Jamaica, and Nettleship and you were sent away in charge of,' exclaimed Sinnet, who had been watching her.

I had also been examining her minutely, and had come to the same conclusion.

Directly she had furled sails, a boat went off from her to the admiral, and remained alongside for some time. We were thus left in doubt as to whether we were right. At length the boat, which had returned to the corvette, came pulling towards us.

Sinnet was watching her through a telescope.

'Why, I say, Paddy, I'm nearly certain I see old Nettleship in the stern sheets, and Tom Pim alongside him,' he said.

'Then there can be no doubt that the corvette is the *Soleil ;* but Nettleship hoped to get his promotion, and if so, he has been made one of her lieutenants,' I remarked.

'He hasn't got on a lieutenant's uniform, at all events,' said Sinnet, looking through the telescope.

In a short time the boat was alongside, and our doubts were

solved, by seeing Tom Pim and Nettleship come on deck. They went aft at once, and reported themselves to Captain Macnamara. As soon as they were dismissed they joined us. They both gave a start of surprise at seeing me.

Tom grasped my hand and said, 'Well, I am glad, Paddy, to find you safe aboard. We fully believed that the brig was lost in the hurricane, and never expected to set eyes on you again.'

Nettleship also greeted me warmly, though he looked somewhat down in the mouth. The cause of this soon came out.

'Why, Nettleship,' I said, 'I thought you would have been made long before this.'

'It's my ill-luck that I'm not, Paddy,' he answered. 'I thought so to. I got highly complimented for bringing the prize into Port Royal, and I was then told to rejoin my ship as soon as possible; while the *Soleil* was commissioned, and a commander and two lieutenants, who had just come out from England with strong recommendations from the Admiralty, were appointed to her.'

'Well, cheer up, old fellow; we are very glad to have you still with us,' said Sinnet.

Tom afterwards told me that Nettleship got blamed by the admiral at Jamaica for sending me aboard the brig with so few hands, and for allowing the prisoners to remain on board, as he shrewdly suspected what had really happened, that if we had managed to escape the hurricane, they had risen on us and taken possession of the vessel.

The *Soleil* had brought intelligence which she had gained from the crew of a prize she had captured a few days before, that the Count de Grasse had borne away for St. Christopher's, where he had landed a force under the Marquis de Boullie, which it was feared would overpower General Fraser. The news soon ran through the fleet that, instead of waiting to be attacked, we were forthwith to sail in search of the French, to attack them. In a short time, at a signal thrown out from the flag-ship, the fleet, consisting of twenty-two sail of the line and several frigates, got under way, and stood out from Carlisle

Bay. We first proceeded to Antigua, where we obtained fresh provisions, and took on board the 28th regiment of foot and two companies of the 13th, under the command of General Prescott; and on the evening of the same day we sailed for St. John's Roads, and stood under easy sail for Basse Terre, two of our frigates going ahead to give timely notice of what the French were about. We and the *Nymph* frigate were on one flank, and two others on the opposite side. We were fully expecting that we should have warm work in the morning. Few of the officers turned in. When a large fleet is sailing together, it is necessary to keep a very bright look-out. We could dimly see the other ships, with their lights burning, as we glided over the water.

Presently Nettleship, near whom I was standing, remarked,—

'There are two of them closer together than they should be;' and the next instant he exclaimed, 'They're foul of each other! I feared that it would be the case.'

Signals of distress were now thrown out from both the ships. We on this closed with them; and Captain Macnamara ordered the boats to be lowered, to ascertain what had happened, and to render assistance. I went in one of them with our second lieutenant. The first we boarded proved to be the *Nymph*. She had been run into by the *Alfred*. She was dreadfully knocked about, being almost cut in two. We heard aboard her that the *Alfred* herself had also been severely damaged. A boat was at once sent to report what had happened to the admiral, and as soon as daylight dawned he threw out signals to the whole fleet to lay to while the injuries the *Alfred* had received were being repaired. The *Nymph* herself was too severely damaged to proceed, and was ordered at once to return to Antigua.

While we were lying to, a sail was seen in the distance, when the admiral ordered by signal the *Liffy* to chase. Before long we came up with her. She proved to be a large French cutter, laden with shells and ordnance stores for the besieging army.

Nearly the whole day was spent in repairing the damages the *Alfred* had received, and on our approaching Basse Terre, to our bitter disappointment, we found that the Count de Grasse had put to sea. The next night was spent in doubt as to what had become of him, but in the morning the French fleet, consisting of about twenty-nine sail of the line, was perceived about three leagues to leeward, formed in order of battle. Sir Samuel Hood immediately ordered the British fleet to bear down as if to attack him. This had the effect of driving him still farther to leeward, when, to our surprise, the admiral threw out another signal, directing the fleet to stand for Basse Terre.

In the evening we entered Frigate Bay, and anchored in line of battle. The object of this was to cut off the French from all communication with their forces on shore. Before we had brought up, the Count de Grasse stood towards us, and commenced a furious attack on the rear of our fleet, commanded by Commodore Affleck. He, supported by the *Canada*, Captain Cornwallis, and the *Resolution*, Lord Robert Manners, kept up so incessant a fire on the French, that, finding they could make no impression on us, their squadron bore up and stood again to sea. I mention these events to show the sort of work in which we were engaged.

The night passed quietly, but in the morning the French fleet was seen again approaching. On they came, passing along our line, and pouring their broadsides into us. Though superior to us in numbers, we returned so furious a fire, that after a time, finding we remained firm, they wore, and again stood out to sea. In the afternoon the French again appeared, but we again pounded them so severely that they at length, having had enough of it, once more retired, evidently having suffered severe loss.

The French flagship, the *Ville de Paris*, was seen to be upon the heel, blocking up the shot-holes she had received between wind and water.

All this time on shore the French were attacking General

14

Fraser, who had been compelled to retire to a fort o
Brimstone Hill, and with whom it had become exceeding
difficult to communicate. I was in the berth when I receive
a message from the captain, to go to his cabin.

'I have just come from the admiral,' he said. 'He wishe
to send some one on shore to communicate with Genera
Fraser at Brimstone Hill. I told him at once that yo
would be able to succeed if any one could; though
warn you that the risk of being shot or captured by th
enemy is considerable. Are you, notwithstanding, read
to go?'

'With all the pleasure in the world, sir,' I answered, 'i
I am likely to be able to find my way to the fort.'

'You'll not have much difficulty in doing that,' he said
'unless you're stopped, for you'll be furnished with a
exact plan.'

'Am I to go in uniform, sir, or in disguise?' I asked.

'I wouldn't have you risk your life by going in disguise
he replied. 'If you were caught you would be shot a
a spy. You must make the attempt at night, and by wearin
a cloak you may escape detection, unless you happen t
encounter any of the French soldiers; in that case you'll hav
to yield yourself a prisoner.'

'Whatever the difficulties, I'm ready to go through wit
them, sir,' I said; 'and as I speak French, though no
very well, should I meet any French soldiers, I may perhap
be able to make my escape from them.'

The captain told me that the object of the admiral wa
to establish a communication between the fleet and Brimston
Hill, by means of signals, which I was to carry with me
the general not being supplied with them. 'It will be safe
to take a man with you to convey the flags, while you carr
the code of signals, which you must endeavour to destro
should you be made prisoner,' he said.

I had still some hours to wait, however, before it was dar
enough for me to land. I soon afterwards met La Touche
Both he and Dubois made themselves very happy on board

caring apparently very little about being prisoners. I told him of my intended expedition.

'If you succeed, well and good,' he said; 'but if you are taken prisoner, I hope you'll mention Dubois and me to the Marquis de Boullie, and suggest that he should make an offer to exchange you for me. Perhaps he has captured another English officer, who would gladly be exchanged for Dubois. Not that we are weary of our captivity, as you all do your best to make it as light and agreeable as possible.'

I told La Touche that I should be happy to carry out his wishes should I be taken prisoner, though I had no intention of being made one if I could help it.

When I told Tom Pim of what I had to do, he declared that he was jealous of me, and that he thought he should try to get leave to go. I said that I should like to have his company, and accordingly we went together to the captain to ask leave. He, however, refused, saying that he would not risk the loss of two midshipmen at the same time.

'You may, however, take Harrigan with you,' he said; 'he is a sharp lad, and will serve you better than any other man in the ship.'

Though I should have been unwilling to ask for Larry, for fear of exposing him to danger, I was very glad to have him with me.

Just before dark a boat was lowered and manned, and Nettleship was ordered to take me and Harrigan on shore. I shook hands with my messmates.

'We hope you'll get back, Paddy,' said Sinnet. 'If you're killed or taken prisoner, we will mourn over your hard fate. However, you're too sharp to be caught, and we shall see you back again before long, I daresay.'

The captain desired to see me before I started, and gave me further instructions, making me study well a plan of the road to the fort, so I did not fear that I should lose my way. At length we shoved off. Instead, however, of pulling directly for the shore, we steered over to the opposite side of the bay to that where the enemy were encamped.

Nettleship seemed very anxious about me.

'I wish that an older man had been sent, Paddy,' he said; 'and I'm ashamed of myself that I don't understand French, or I might have been employed in the service. I envy you for the opportunity you have of distinguishing yourself.'

'I don't see that I shall have much to boast of, having only to creep along in the dark up to the fort and back again. There's no great difficulty in the undertaking, besides having to keep out of the way of the French pickets.'

'It's not so much what you have to do, as the object to be attained, and the danger of doing it, which will bring credit on you,' he answered.

It was perfectly dark before we reached the place which had been fixed on for landing, so that we ran no risk of being observed from the shore. It was arranged that Nettleship was to wait off it until I made the signal for him to come in and take me aboard. Not a word was spoken as Larry and I stepped on to the beach, he carrying the signals and I the book and the admiral's letter. We kept first to our right till we found a path leading inland through a wood We went on as rapidly as the nature of the ground would allow. The snake-like roots ran across the path, and creepers hung low down in festoons, forming nooses, which might have brought us sharply up if we had run our heads into them. Now and then I fancied that I saw a huge snake winding its way along before me; and tree-frogs, crickets, and other nocturnal insects, kept up a noisy chorus as we went on. Sometimes it was so dark that it was with the greatest difficulty I could make my way with the stick I carried. I was very glad when, getting out of the wood, we found ourselves on the borders of a sugar-cane plantation. This I knew I should have to skirt till I reached another path leading almost directly up to the fort.

CHAPTER XVII

WE had proceeded some distance when the voice of a sentry hailing a passer-by struck my ear. The challenge was in French, as was the answer. It appeared to be some way off, and I hoped might come from one of the extreme outposts. Still I knew that it was necessary to proceed with caution, or we might suddenly find ourselves close upon another. We went on and on, occasionally stopping to listen. No other sounds besides those of noisy insects broke the silence of night. Already we could see the top of Brimstone Hill rising against the dark sky. In another quarter of an hour or so we might reach it. I hoped that we might find nothing to stop us in passing over the intervening space. We continued on, concealing ourselves as much as possible beneath the hedges of cacti, or the trunks of trees. We had got close to a thick copse, as we should call it, only that the plants were of a very different character, when I heard a sound of feet passing apparently before us. Then I heard a remark made in French by one person to another, who answered it in the same tongue. Grasping Larry's arm, I dragged him towards the wood. Fortunately we found some thick bushes, behind which we crouched down. Presently the sounds of the footsteps grew louder, and I could just distinguish the dim outline of a party of men and several officers, passing along the road towards the left, where the French army were supposed to be encamped.

They had evidently been out on a reconnoitring expedition, and were now returning. Had we gone on we should certainly have fallen into their hands. I waited until they were out of hearing, and then, whispering to Larry, we got up and made our way directly towards the fort, with much less fear than before of meeting any one. Still I knew that we were not safe until we had actually gained our destination.

At last we were hurrying on, when I heard a voice say, 'Who goes there?' and I answered, 'A friend from the fleet, with a letter for the general.' The sentry told us to pass on. In another minute we reached the picket, a soldier from which was sent up with us to the fort. We were at once admitted into the presence of General Fraser, to whom I delivered the despatches and signals.

'You have performed your service well, young gentleman,' said the general. 'Are you to remain here, or to return to the fleet?'

I told him that my directions were to get back as soon as possible.

'I'll detain you, then, but a short time, while I write a letter to Sir Samuel Hood,' he said. 'I hope that you'll be as successful on your journey back, as you were in coming here.'

Before he began to write, he ordered a servant to bring me refreshments, and to look after my companion. The walk had given me an appetite; and I did justice to the food placed before me.

The general had soon finished his letter; and, giving it to me, with a warm shake of the hand, told me that I was at liberty to set out when I was ready.

'My orders are to return without delay, sir,' I answered, and took my leave.

The sentry accompanied Larry and me to the outer picket, thence we hurried on as fast as we could manage to get along. Still I maintained the same caution as in coming, for at any moment we might fall in with some of the enemy, who might be watching the fort from a distance. The

farther we got, the more my hopes of succeeding increased.
I could already make out the lights of the ships in the bay,
and the sheen of the intermediate water. We reached the
wood through which we had before passed, and had just
made our way to the outside, when I caught sight of a
body of men, apparently a patrol, a short distance to the
right. We were still under the shade of the trees, and I
hoped that we should not be discovered. We drew back to see
in what direction they were coming. It appeared to me
that they had already passed, and that we might gain the
landing-place, even should they see us making towards it. We
accordingly, after waiting a short time, darted forward, running
at our full speed. Scarcely, however, had we begun to run,
than I heard a shout of,—

'*Arrêtez là!*'—'Stop there, stop!'

It was an order we were not likely to obey. It was too late
to return to the wood, so, scampering as fast as our feet
could move, we ran on to where we expected to find the boat.

Again the Frenchmen shouted to us, and presently a shot
came whistling by my ear.

'Stoop down, Larry,' I cried, 'as low as you can; it
doesn't do to present a larger target to the enemy than is
necessary.'

I hoped that the shots would attract the attention of
Nettleship, and that he would pull in to take us aboard.
I turned my head for a moment, and saw the soldiers
running towards us; still, as we were some way ahead, I
expected that we should have time to reach the boat, and
to shove off to a distance before they came up.

To make sure, I shouted out,—

'Nettleship, ahoy! Pull in as hard as you can.'

Though I could see lights on board the ships, close to the
water as it was, I could not distinguish the boat, and I was
afraid that, not expecting us so soon, Nettleship had pulled to
a distance. Should he not arrive our capture was certain.
We had nearly gained the rocks on which we had landed,
when I made out a dark object on the water approaching.

That must be the boat, I thought, and again hailed. Nettle-ship, recognising my voice, answered, and I guessed by the sound of the oars that the men were bending to them with all their might. Larry and I stood ready to spring in. We could hear the footsteps of the Frenchmen approaching rapidly. By stooping down we managed to conceal ourselves, and to avoid several more shots which were fired. The moment the bow-man touched the rock with his boat-hook, Larry and I sprang on board. I scrambled aft, while Nettleship shouted out,—

'Back oars all. Now, starboard oars, give way.'

The boat was quickly got round, but we had pulled to no great distance before the Frenchmen, reaching the beach, began to blaze away at us. We returned the compliment by firing the only two muskets which had been brought. The Frenchmen standing up on the rock presented a good target. First one shot struck the stern, and another the blade of an oar, but no one was hurt, and the Frenchmen, finding that they were the greatest sufferers, prudently retired from the beach.

After a long pull we got back to the frigate. The captain, to whom I delivered General Fraser's letter, complimented me on having performed the duty.

'Your conduct will be noted, Finnahan, and you may depend upon obtaining your promotion as soon as you are old enough.'

I expected to be able to turn in, but he sent me with the letter at once on board the flagship, and I delivered it in person to Sir Samuel Hood.

The admiral almost repeated what the captain had said; and I had good reason to congratulate myself at the success of my adventure.

Next day, General Prescott's division was re-embarked, as it was not a sufficient force to fight its way to General Fraser at Brimstone Hill. Other attempts were made to com-municate with him, and two officers were captured; so that I had good cause to be thankful that I had escaped.

Dubois and La Touche confessed that they were very sorry to see me back.

'I felt sure that you would be made prisoner, and fully expected to have had the satisfaction of being exchanged for you,' said the latter. 'But we have to practise patience and laugh at our misfortunes, to get on in this world.'

'I'm very glad you were not caught, Paddy,' said Tom Pim. 'I envy you your success, and only wish that I could talk French as you do, to be employed on the same sort of service. La Touche is teaching me, and I'm trying to teach him English, but we make rum work of it without a grammar or dictionary, or any other book. I suspect he gets more out of me than I do out of him, though I try very hard to pronounce the words he says.'

We could hear the French guns thundering away at the fort, and those of the fort replying, hour after hour, without intermission, but the signals made by General Fraser were not supposed to be satisfactory.

At last, one day, we saw the flag hauled down; the guns at the same time ceased, and we knew that all was over, and the gallant garrison had been compelled to capitulate. Information of this was sent on board to the admiral, with a flag of truce, by the Marquis de Boullie.

That evening we sailed on a cruise to ascertain the movements of the French fleet. We had not been to sea many hours when we saw them standing in for Nevis Point, where they came to an anchor; and counting them, we found that they numbered no less than twenty-four sail of the line, several ships having lately joined them. We at once returned with the information to Sir Samuel Hood. It was now discovered that the French had been throwing up gun and mortar batteries on a hill, which would completely command the fleet.

We were seated in the berth after we had brought up, discussing the state of affairs.

'We're in a nice position,' said Chaffey. 'We shall be pounded at from the shore, and shall have the French fleet,

with half as many more ships as we possess, down upon us
before long, and it will be a tough job to fight our way out
from among them.'

'Just trust our admiral,' answered Tom; 'he knows what
he's about, depend on that; he won't let us be caught like
rats in a trap.'

As he was speaking, Nettleship came into the berth.

'The captain was sent for on board the flag-ship, and he's
just returned,' he said. 'I hear that he met all the captains
of the fleet on board, and the admiral told them to set their
watches by his timepiece, and directed all the ships to slip
or cut their cables at eleven o'clock. The sternmost and
leewardmost ships are to get under weigh first, and so on in
succession, and we're to stand on under easy sail, in sight
of each other, till we receive further orders from the
admiral.'

No one turned in; the crews were at their stations; not
a sign was shown which might allow the French—who were
of course watching us from the shore—to discover that any
movement was in contemplation. At the appointed time,
the *Alfred*, the most leeward of our ships, was seen to get
under weigh, followed in rapid succession by the *Canada*,
the *President*, and the rest of the line-of-battle ships, which
stood out of the bay, accompanied by the frigates, before
probably the French were aware what we were about.

It was a masterly movement, as it would have been madness to have stopped to be attacked by so superior a force
as the French possessed; for though we might have driven
them off, we must have suffered severely, and have had to
return into harbour to refit. At this time we were out-
numbered, and even out-manœuvred, by the French, who
took possession of several of our islands, which we were
unable to protect.

We were not to be idle, for there was plenty of work
for the frigates in watching the enemy, and occasionally in
engaging their frigates.

We had not been long at sea when our captain received

orders from Sir Samuel Hood to stand in towards where the French fleet were supposed to be, and ascertain what they were about.

We had sighted the island of Antigua on our starboard bow, and were standing in towards Nevis, when three sail appeared to the westward. One of the lieutenants went aloft to examine them. On returning on deck, he reported that one was a line-of-battle ship, and the other two frigates. As there could be no doubt, from their position, that they were enemies, the captain ordered our course to be altered, intending to pass to the northward of Antigua. We had been seen by the enemy, who were making all sail in chase. I saw Dubois and La Touche watching them eagerly.

'You expect this time to gain your liberty, my friend?' I said to La Touche. 'Don't be too sure that your country-men will come up with us, or if they do, that they will make the *Liffy* strike her flag.'

'I would rather be set at liberty in any other way,' he answered, in his usual cordial tone; 'but they appear to me to be gaining on us.'

'Perhaps they are, and if so we must fight them, and drive them off,' I observed.

'It would be madness to do that,' he remarked. 'You cannot cope with a line-of-battle ship alone, independent of two frigates, each of which is a match for the *Liffy*.'

It was soon seen that our captain had no intention of striking his flag without striking very hard first at the enemy. The strangers appeared to have a stronger breeze than filled our sails, and were coming up hand over hand with us. Still we might get the wind, and run into an English harbour. It was the first time the *Liffy* ever had to run, and we didn't like it. I asked Nettleship what he thought about the matter.

'We shall have a tough fight, at all events; but if we can save our spars, I don't think, notwithstanding, the enemy will take us.'

This was the general feeling of all on board.

We had sighted Nevis, when two other ships were made out to the south-east. Presently several more appeared in that direction. It was a question, however, whether they were friends or foes. Had we been certain that they were friends, we should have stood towards them, but our captain was unwilling to run the risk of finding that he had made a mistake. A look-out was kept on them from aloft; and before long they were pronounced to be enemies. I saw by the looks of our captain that he didn't like it, though he tried to appear as confident as usual. The rest of the officers kept up their spirits.

It was very evident that we were now in a difficult position. The line-of-battle ship was the closest; the two frigates, one to the north of us, the other some way to the south of her; while the new enemies we had discovered prevented us escaping in the opposite direction. Our only hope was to knock away some of the spars of the line-of-battle ship, and then fight our way past the two frigates. The line-of-battle ship was rapidly approaching. A single broadside, should we be exposed to it, would almost sink us.

Every preparation had been made for fighting; and not a man flinched from his gun. The officers were at their stations; the powder-monkeys seated on their tubs; the surgeons below, preparing for the wounded; and we, the younger midshipmen, ready for any duty we might be called on to perform.

At length a puff of smoke was seen issuing from the line-of-battle ship. The shot fell close to our counter.

'That was fired from her forecastle,' observed Nettleship, 'from a long gun, too. It will play Old Harry with us if well served, before we can return the compliment.'

A second shot quickly followed, and struck the hammock nettings on the starboard side, knocking several overboard.

We at length luffed up; and the captain ordered the whole of our starboard broadside to be fired. Our guns were well aimed, and immediately we had fired we again kept away. Our shot did considerable damage to our pursuer, but she still kept on, while we expected every moment to have her broadside crashing into us.

Fortunately for us the wind fell, and our light frigate moved rapidly through the water. The other frigates were, however, coming up.

'What does the captain intend to do?' I asked of Nettleship.

He pointed ahead where the island of Nevis rose green and smiling out of the blue water.

'Depend on it he won't let the enemy have our tight little frigate if he can help it,' he answered. 'My idea is that he'll try and get close in, and stand round the island, to give a chance to our big enemy to run on shore.'

Shortly after this I heard Nettleship involuntarily exclaim, 'See! see! here it comes!' and as I looked aft I saw the line-of-battle ship luffing up, and as she did so her whole broadside was discharged at us.

With a fearful uproar the shot came crashing on board. Cries and shrieks arose from all sides. Well-nigh a dozen of our men were struck down, and many more were wounded. The most severely hurt of the latter were carried below. Comparatively little damage, however, had been done to our spars and rigging, though the rents in our sails showed where the shot had passed through; while blocks came rattling down on deck, and several ropes hung in festoons from the yards. Still our stout-hearted captain held on.

To return the enemy's fire would have been useless, and only the sooner insure our destruction. We got nearer and nearer the island. The men were ordered into the chains to heave the lead. The captain and master examined the chart, which had been brought from the cabin. We had no doubt of what their intentions were, but we couldn't hear a word they said. We were gaining on our pursuer, but at the same time the two frigates were not far astern, while the other ships, which had last been seen, were coming up rapidly. The men in the chains were heaving the lead. We were shoaling our water.

'By the mark, nine,' was called, and immediately followed
by 'By the mark, eight.' Before the men in the chains
could again cry out, a loud crash was heard,—every timber
in the ship trembled,—the tall masts quivered.

'We're on shore,' I cried out.

'No doubt about that,' said Nettleship, 'and likely to
remain there too.'

The captain at once ordered the men aloft to furl sails.

Our pursuer, not wishing to meet with the same fate,
hauled her wind, and stood to a distance, which left us
beyond the reach of her guns.

'Roll them up anyhow. Be smart about it,' cried Mr.
Saunders.

It was done. Then the order came,—'Out boats!'

Every boat was got into the water, and brought over to
the starboard side, with a few hands in each.

'We shall have to cut away the masts,' said Nettleship,
whom I again passed.

The ship was still forging over the ledge on which she
had struck, closer and closer towards the shore. The order
which he expected quickly came.

'Stand from under,' shouted Mr. Saunders. Some of
the men sprang below, others forward. We, the officers,
rushed aft. The carpenter, with his mates, and the boatswain, stood ready, with their gleaming axes in their
hands.

'Cut!' cried the captain.

The shrouds were severed at one side, then the axes
descended. A few strokes, and the masts in rapid succession
fell overboard. We had all been so engaged in this operation that we had not watched our enemies. We now saw
the line-of-battle ship signalling the frigates. Shortly after
they were seen to stand in, apparently for the object of
attacking us.

'It must be done,' cried Captain Macnamara. 'Lads,
I'm sorry to say we must leave our stout ship. We must
not allow her, however, to fall into the hands of the enemy.

Get your clothes, and anything you value most, as I have resolved to destroy her.'

Every one now hurried below to get their clothes, and such other things as they desired to preserve. The purser appeared with the ship's papers, the master with the ship's log, and the captain with a few instruments. Muskets and ammunition, pistols and cutlasses, were then served out, so that we might have the means of resisting the enemy should they attempt to land. All were now ready for embarking. He would allow none of us to take larger sized packages than the men were permitted to carry away. The crew were now all told off to take their places in the boats. The midshipmen and boys, as in the case of fire or shipwreck, were sent first. Larry was in my boat.

'It's a sad day this, Mr. Terence, which I never thought to see,' he said; 'but arrah! I've not forgotten my fiddle, and it will be mighty convenient to cheer the hearts of our poor fellows when we get ashore.'

Most of the men took the matter very philosophically. Those who suffered most were the unfortunate wounded, who had previously been lowered into the boats, with the surgeons to look after them. Our two prisoners, Dubois and La Touche, had, I fancied, formed some plan for remaining on board, but a hint from Rough-and-Ready made them very quickly follow me into the boat, accompanied by a marine.

'Take care, Finnahan, those two foreigners don't give you the slip,' shouted the first lieutenant. 'Let them understand that they must remain under charge of the sentry, and that if they give leg-bail he has orders to shoot them. Now shove off.'

I told my friends what Mr. Saunders had said.

'Ah, that lieutenant of yours is very suspicious,' remarked Dubois. 'We wish to get away! What folly to think of it.'

I said nothing more, but there was a twinkle in Dubois' eye, which made me fancy he did think of it.

The shore was soon reached; providentially there was no surf, and the men quickly landed. On this the boats at once put off to bring away the remainder of the crew. The men bent to their oars. There was no time to be lost, for the French frigates were approaching, and would soon be blazing away at our ship. On they came under all sail.

'We'll have them right enough if they run ashore,' cried one of the men; 'there'll then be fair play maybe.'

'I wish that our captain would only just let us go back and fight them,' exclaimed another; 'we'd soon show them that the saucy *Liffy* hasn't done barking yet.'

But the Frenchmen seemed to have no intention of running ashore if they could help it. As we got alongside they had come almost within range of our guns. The remainder of the crew and officers stood ready to embark. Just at that moment I recollected that I had come away without my grandfather's sword, which was hung up in the berth. I sprang on deck and rushed down below to obtain it. Having got it in my hand, I was hurrying out of the berth, when I saw the captain, accompanied by Mr. Saunders with the gunner and his crew, just coming aft. At the same time I observed a dense smoke issuing from the forehold. They had matches in their hands, with which they had lighted some trains which had been laid leading to the after part of the ship. I sprang back into the boat, into which the gunner and his crew followed me, the captain's gig still waiting alongside. Mr. Saunders came down and took his seat. The captain stood for some moments gazing along the deck, then, lifting up his hat, he also descended. 'Shove off!' I heard him cry out, in a husky voice, just as we were pulling away.

He was the last man to leave the frigate. As he did so several shot came crashing aboard her from the opposite side. We pulled away as fast as we could lay our backs to the oars, for we had a good chance of being hit. The shot dropped round us pretty thickly, but we escaped uninjured. As we looked astern thick wreaths of smoke were issuing from every part of our gallant frigate.

'Her fighting days are over,' I observed.

'Not just yet, sir,—not just yet. Wait a minute and you'll see,' exclaimed the coxswain.

He was right. Before we landed the flames had reached the guns, and her whole broadside, pointed towards the Frenchmen, went off in rapid succession.

'Hurrah! hurrah!' shouted all the men; 'the old girl dies game to the last.'

What damage the guns of our ship effected on the French frigates we could not discover, but they were seen to haul their wind and to stand off as fast as they could from the land. We soon gained the shore, which was as captivating in appearance as any shipwrecked mariner has ever landed on. It seemed like a perfect garden, with churches and planters' houses peeping out from among the trees, in the midst of the most picturesque scenery. In the centre rose a lofty cone, surrounded by a ruff of trees, below which all was one mass of verdure. We had little time or inclination just then to admire the beauties of nature. The crew having been mustered, none being missing except the poor fellows who were known to have been killed, the wounded were placed on litters formed of sails, and we were set off to march towards Charlestown, the smart little capital of the island, whence Captain Macnamara expected to be able to send intelligence of the disaster to the admiral.

We had gone some distance, and were all feeling hungry and thirsty, when we came in sight of the house of a planter. Our approach was perceived. The master of the mansion came forth, and, addressing Captain Macnamara, insisted on our halting, and taking such refreshment as he could provide. His offer was gladly accepted. As the house wouldn't hold us all, we youngsters stopped in the shade of of a grove of trees close to it, the captain and gun-room officers being invited inside. The men threw themselves on the ground, in every variety of attitude, waiting for the expected feast. We of the midshipmen's berth formed a group by ourselves a little way from the men, close to a fountain, which sent up a jet of water into the quivering air. The sight of it alone was calculated to cool us, and we needed cooling, for our march had been hot and fatiguing. Some of the men suffering most from thirst rushed to the fountain, and baled the water into their mouths, or lapped it up like dogs.

'I say, Paddy, what has become of your French friends?' asked Nettleship, looking round. 'I thought La Touche would at all events have been with us, though Dubois might have considered himself privileged to go in with the gunroom officers.'

'I haven't set eyes on them—since—since—let me see—not since we left the shore,' I answered. 'I suppose they must be in the house.'

Just then I saw the marine who had had charge of the prisoners. I asked him what had become of them. He had been ordered to fall into the ranks with his comrades, and had handed them over, he said, to the second lieutenant,—Simon Silk,—known among us as Softy. I told Nettleship this.

'Oh, then of course they are in the house,' he remarked.

'Not so sure of that, if Softy had charge of them,' said Tom.

In a short time a number of blacks came out, bringing provisions of all sorts. Huge jugs of sangaree, baskets of pink shaddocks, bananas, oranges, pomegranates, figs, and grapes, in addition to the more substantial fare. How we did peg into the fruit, which we enjoyed the more from having been lately on salt provisions. To the poor wounded fellows the fruit was especially refreshing, and I believe the lives of several were saved who would otherwise have succumbed.

'Well, I shouldn't mind being shipwrecked occasionally, if I could always land in such a place as this,' said Chaffey, devouring a superb shaddock, while the rest of us were similarly employed, or sucking oranges, or popping grapes into our mouths.

As we were at no great distance from Charlestown, our kind host advised the captain to remain, and to pursue his march in the cool of the evening, undertaking to send on to the authorities that quarters might be provided for us. We were not at all sorry to hear this, as all of us needed rest. We ate the delicious fruit till we could eat no more, and then threw ourselves on the ground. Our host came out and invited us into the house, but Nettleship, who considered that he might have done so at first, declined his offer; indeed, we were far better off under the trees than between walls, and certainly more at our ease. At length Mr. Saunders came out, and ordered us to get ready for marching; the men were formed in ranks, and, giving a cheer for our host, we set out.

I had been looking about for Dubois and La Touche, when I saw Lieutenant Silk. I asked him if he knew where they were.

'Bless me! why, have they not been with you all this time?' he exclaimed. 'I understood them to say that they would join you when we arrived at Mr. Ballahoo's, and I never dreamed of their not doing so.'

The marine officer looked somewhat aghast on hearing that we had not even seen the Frenchmen.

'Whether he dreamed it or not, they are off as sure as a gun,' observed Nettleship, when I told him.

Such proved to be the case; and though Softy had to march back with a party of his men to look for them, they were nowhere to be found. I do not think that the captain was very much put out, though I was sorry to part from my polite friends without saying good-bye. As the enemy were in the neighbouring island, it was probable that they would send a force across to capture Nevis, so that we fully expected to have work to do, as the governor was resolved to oppose them.

We arrived at Charlestown just at sunset, and were

hospitably received by the inhabitants, among whom we were billeted, the wounded being sent to the hospital. We were expecting to have a pleasant stay in the town, but next day a frigate appeared off the place and sent her boat ashore, when our captain applied for a passage for himself and men to join the admiral. We had at once, therefore, to embark on board the *Thisbe*. Next day we stood across to Antigua, and, having passed that island, we beat to the southward, when a large fleet was seen ahead. We approached cautiously till we got within signalling distance, when the fleet was found to be that of Sir Samuel Hood, steering for Antigua. We were ordered to join it, and the next day brought up in St. John's roads. We here remained at anchor for some time, till we were joined by Sir George Rodney, who had come out from England with several sail of the line. Sir George Rodney became commander-in-chief, and now considered himself strong enough to cope with the French and Spanish.

While the officers and crew of the *Liffy* were together, we were merry enough ; but after we had undergone the trial for her loss, and our captain and his subordinates had been honourably acquitted, the time came for our separation. We were distributed among the different ships of the fleet. Nettleship, Tom Pim, and I were ordered to join the *Cerberus*, 74, with a portion of our men, among whom was Larry. Tom and I agreed that we felt lost in so big a ship. We soon, however, got accustomed to her, and became intimate with our new messmates, several of whom were very good fellows. Tom declared that he should never like the gun-room after our snug little berth, for, should he once fetch away, he shouldn't bring up again until he had cracked his head against a gun or against the ship's side. For some time we had fine weather, so that he had no opportunity of experiencing the inconvenience he anticipated. We heard that the very day we left Nevis the French had thrown an overwhelming force across and taken possession of the island.

'I don't know that we should have prevented that,' said Tom, 'so I am glad that we got away, or we might have been killed or made prisoners.'

The fleet being strengthened as I have described, we proceeded to St. Lucia to complete our water. We now had to sail in search of a large French convoy which was expected to arrive from Europe, and anticipated a rich prize; but the French were too sharp for us, for though a vigilant lookout was kept by the frigates, they managed, by sailing close under Dominique and Guadaloupe, to reach Port Royal Bay unperceived by any of our ships. When Sir Samuel Hood got information of this unlucky event, the line-of-battle ships returned to St. Lucia to refit, while the frigates were employed in watching the movements of the enemy. The object of the French and Spaniards was well known. It was to unite their fleets, and thus, forming a powerful force, to proceed to the conquest of Jamaica. Our object was to prevent them from doing this. The frigates had ample work in watching their movements, and many ran a great risk of being captured in the anxiety of their captains to keep a vigilant watch on them. Our fleet lay ready for a start as soon as information was brought of the enemy having put to sea.

CHAPTER XVIII

T length, at daylight on the 8th of April, when I, acting as signal midshipman, was on the look-out, I saw a frigate standing towards us and making signals. I immediately communicated the information to the commander, who was on deck.

'The *Andromache*, Captain Byron,' he exclaimed. 'She tells us that she has seen the enemy's fleet with a large convoy coming out of Port Royal Bay, and standing to the north-west.'

Tom Pim was immediately sent down to call the captain, and, as he appeared, the admiral threw out a signal from the *Formidable* to put to sea in chase of the enemy. Cheers resounded from ship to ship, and never did fleet get under weigh with more alacrity. By noon we were clear of Gros Islet Bay, when we stretched over to Port Royal, but, finding none of the French ships there or at St. Pierre, we stood after them in the direction they were supposed to have taken. We continued on for some hours during the night, still uncertain as to whether we should overtake the enemy, when, to our joy, we discovered their lights right ahead.

As morning broke, a large portion of the convoy was discovered under Dominique, while to windward we could see the French fleet forming the line of battle. As the light increased, the admiral threw out signals to prepare for action and to form the line.

It was welcomed by a hearty cheer from ten thousand
throats. As, however, we got under Dominique, to our bitter
disappointment the sails flapped against the masts, and most
of the ships lay becalmed, unable to obey the orders which
had been received. It was tantalizing in the extreme. At
length, however, the lighter canvas filled, and the sea-breeze
freshened. The *Barfleur*, Sir Samuel Hood's flag-ship, then
our ship, then the *Monarch* and *Warrior*, the *Valiant* and
Alfred, got the wind, and the whole of the van division, of
which we formed a part, stretched to the northward on the
starboard tack in chase, while the central and rear divisions,
under Sir George Rodney, lay still becalmed and unable to
join us. Our gallant admiral, however, anxious to bring on an
action, continued his course, when we saw the French fleet
also forming their line on the starboard tack, in the hope of
attacking us before we could be joined by Sir George Rodney.

'Now, Paddy, we shall see what a real fight is like,' said
Tom Pim, as we stood on the quarter-deck.

'I hope we shall see what a victory is like, too,' I answered,
as I eyed the approaching enemy, numbering fifteen ships, to
oppose which we had but eight. Sir Samuel Hood, however,
knew what he was about, and the order was given to heave to,
which brought our broadsides to bear upon the French, and at
the same time would allow the other two frigates to come up
with us as soon as they could get the wind. The first shot
was fired from the *Barfleur* a few minutes before 10 A.M., and
then all our eight stout ships began blazing away at the
French, as they stood down intending to break our line ; but
so tremendous was the fire with which they were received,
that they found the attempt hopeless. They, however, returned it vigorously, and for a full hour we were pounding
away at each other, not a few of our brave fellows being killed,
and many more wounded. Towards the end of the time, as
the smoke cleared away, I saw the rest of our fleet coming up
with the breeze, which had at length reached them. The
French admiral also saw them, and, having had a taste of how
eight ships could treat him, he stood away under all sail after

the remainder of his fleet. Sir George Rodney now threw out a signal for a general chase, but the Frenchmen beat us hollow in running away, and we in vain attempted to come up with them. For two whole days we were engaged in chasing.

'I'm afraid, after all, the mounseers will get off, and reach Jamaica before us,' said Tom Pim to me; 'and if they do, what will become of Mr. Talboys and his family? Poor Lucy! she will be marrying a French count, perhaps, and I shall never see her again.'

'They are not quite out of sight, and though they're gaining on us, the wind may change, or some other accident may occur, and we shall have another stand-up fight,' I answered.

This was soon after sunrise on the 12th of April, when our fleet was standing to the northward, about five leagues north-west of Prince Rupert's Bay, with a light breeze. The French were upon the same tack to windward of the Saintes, with a fresh sea-breeze. The light increasing, we saw a ship which had lost her foremast and bowsprit, in tow of a frigate standing in for Guadaloupe. On perceiving this the admiral threw out a signal for us and three other ships to chase; and, disabled as the French line-of-battle ship was, we made sure of capturing her.

'We shall get hold of one ship, at all events, and the frigate too, if she doesn't up stick and run,' said Nettleship, as he watched the two Frenchmen ahead.

Presently he exclaimed, 'Not so sure of that, though. I see the French admiral making signals, and we shall know what he has been saying presently.'

A short time afterwards he added, 'His fleet is bearing up for the purpose of protecting the wounded bird.'

We stood on, however. The captain told Tom Pim, who was signal midshipman, to keep a sharp eye on our admiral.

'If he keeps on that course he'll give us the weather gage, and we shall catch him as sure as his name is De Grasse,' cried Nettleship.

Our crew of course were at their quarters, and we expected ere long to be exchanging broadsides with the enemy.

Presently the French again altered their course, and formed their line on the larboard tack.

'The admiral has hoisted the recall signal,' cried Tom. Directly afterwards we saw the signal made for our ships to form the line of battle on the starboard tack. Rear-Admiral Drake's division was now leading, the *Marlborough* being ahead. The island of Dominique was on our starboard hand, the wind coming off the land, and the French between us and it. Thus they were to windward of us, standing almost directly for Guadaloupe. We were now gradually nearing each other. Just at 8 A.M. the *Marlborough*, in gallant style, opened fire on the rear of the French. At the same time Rodney made the signal for close action. Soon after it was hoisted all the other ships and Rear-Admiral Drake's division commenced firing their broadsides. For a time Admiral Hood's division was almost becalmed, as were many of Sir George Rodney's ships, but as they drew ahead they got the wind much stronger clear of the land. After the action had continued for some time, the wind shifted, enabling us to get to windward of the enemy.

'Look out there, Paddy, at the *Duke*. See, that gallant fellow Gardner is endeavouring to force the Frenchman's line,' cried Nettleship.

We watched for some minutes, when a shot carried away the *Duke's* maintopmast, and she dropped to leeward, and Sir George Rodney, followed by the *Namur* and *Canada*, stood right in between the enemy's ships, not far from the *Ville de Paris*, carrying their admiral's flag. Others quickly followed, when Rodney wore and doubled upon the enemy, all the time, it must be understood, keeping up a tremendous and incessant fire. By this gallant manœuvre the French line was completely broken, and thrown into the utmost confusion. Their van bore away, and endeavoured to form to leeward, but our division, under Sir Samuel Hood, now getting the breeze, came up, and joined in the close fight which had long been going on. To describe it so that my account should be understood would be difficult in the extreme. All the time the shot of

the enemy came crashing aboard. Our object was to catch
sight of the hulls of the Frenchmen amid the clouds of smoke,
and to pound away at them. Each of our ships did the same.
Amongst the ships was the *Glorieux*, commanded by the
Vicomte d'Escar. Though surrounded by enemies, he continued to fire his broadsides until his masts and bowsprit were
shot away by the board, and not till he saw that he must
abandon all hope of rescue did he haul down his colours. We
almost immediately afterwards came up with another ship,
which we found to be the *Cæsar*, Captain M. de Marigney.
We got so close up to her that our guns almost touched, and
began furiously pounding away at her sides. She had already
been severely battered before we attacked her. The gallant
Frenchman, however, continued to engage us, and, looking up,
as for an instant the smoke was blown aside, we saw that he
had nailed his colours to the mast.

'We must knock them away notwithstanding,' said Nettleship.

Soon afterwards down came the enemy's mainmast, followed
by her mizzenmast, fortunately falling over on the opposite
side.

Still the Frenchmen continued working their guns, but one
after the other ceased firing, and at last an officer waved a
handkerchief, to show that they surrendered. As he did so
the foremast went by the board. We immediately ceased
firing, and our second lieutenant was sent to take possession
in one of the few of our boats which could swim. I accompanied him. I by this time had seen a good deal of fighting,
but I had never yet witnessed any scene so dreadful as the
decks of the *Cæsar* presented. On reaching the upper deck,
one of the first objects which met our eyes was the body of
the gallant captain, who had just breathed his last. Near him
lay three or four other officers, and a little farther off two
young midshipmen; while fore and aft lay the dead and
wounded, their shipmates having had no time as yet to carry
the latter below. Everywhere there was wreck and confusion,
masts and rigging trailing overboard, the stumps alone remain-

ing, the bulwarks shattered, the guns upset, the carriages of some knocked to pieces, every boat damaged, while it was impossible, as we stepped along, to avoid the pools of blood and gore. The third lieutenant, his head bound up, stepped forward, saying that he was the officer of the highest rank remaining, and offered his sword. In the meantime the fight continued raging: the *Ardent* struck to the *Belliqueux*, and the *Hector* to the *Canada*; but the gallant Cornwallis, leaving his prize, made sail after the Count de Grasse, who, together with his second, was endeavouring to rejoin his flying and scattered ships. We were fast approaching. Notwithstanding this, the Count de Grasse held out till the *Barfleur* came up, and poured in so tremendous and destructive a fire, that at length the gallant Frenchman, deserted by his ships, was compelled to haul down his flag, just as the sun sank beneath the horizon.

The French fleet were now going off before the wind, pursued by some of our ships. Others would have joined in the chase, but Sir George Rodney, wishing to collect the fleet and secure his prizes, made the signal to the fleet to bring to.

Our captain meantime had ordered us at once to commence removing the prisoners.

I had shoved off with one boat-load, and just got alongside the *Cerberus*, when I heard the cry, 'The *Cæsar* is on fire!' I hurried the prisoners up the side, eager to assist in extinguishing the flames, or to bring away as many as I could of those on board. Several of the other ships were also sending their uninjured boats to the rescue; but before they could reach the blazing ship, we heard a fearfully loud explosion. Up went her decks. Fragments of planks and timbers, and even heavy guns, with human bodies torn and rent asunder, rose in the air; the whole ship blazed furiously, lighting up the surrounding vessels with a lurid glare, when suddenly her hull sank, and all was dark around. In her perished our third lieutenant and boatswain, and fifty of our gallant crew, besides four hundred Frenchmen.

Our most valuable prize was the *Ville de Paris*, as she had
on board a quantity of specie, and she was considered the
finest ship afloat; but we had a heavy price to pay for our
victory: Captain Bayne, of the *Alfred*, and Captain Blair, of
the *Anson*, were killed, besides several lieutenants and other
officers.   Altogether we lost two hundred and fifty-three men
killed, and eight hundred and sixteen wounded.   The French
ships, having numerous troops on board, and carrying more
men than ours, suffered more severely in proportion, and it
was generally believed that three thousand were killed, and
double the number wounded.   On board the *Ville de Paris*
alone four hundred were slain.

We remained three days under Guadaloupe, repairing
damages, when Sir George Rodney ordered Sir Samuel Hood
to proceed with his division in search of stragglers.   In spite
of the fighting we had had, with cheerful alacrity we stood
away; and on the 19th sighted five of the enemy's ships.
They were standing for the Mona passage.

'They hope to escape us,' said Nettleship.   'But never
fear, if they can get through, so can we.'

This proved to be the case.   Just then Sir Samuel Hood
threw out the signal for a general chase.   A shout rose from
our deck when it was seen that the wind had died away, and
that the enemy lay becalmed.

The *Valiant* early in the afternoon got alongside the *Caton*,
which immediately struck.   Captain Goodall then stood on,
leaving us to pick her up, and attacked the *Jason*, of the same
force, with so much impetuosity, that after a stout resistance
of twenty minutes she also hauled down her colours.   Two
other smaller ships were shortly afterwards captured, and only
one, which got through the passage, effected her escape.

A few days afterwards we rejoined Sir George Rodney under
Cape Tiberoon, and with him proceeded to Jamaica.

Great was the rejoicing of the inhabitants.   Guns were
thundering, flags flying on steeples and houses and hundreds
of flagstaffs; and the whole town of Kingston turned out, with
the military and civic authorities at their head, to receive the

conqueror as he landed, accompanied by the Count de Grasse, the admiral who had threatened their subjugation.

We aboard the *Cerberus* saw little of the festivities which took place, as we were engaged in repairing her, and fitting her for sea,—it being understood that in consequence of the damages she had received she was to be sent home.

Tom and I got leave only for one day to go up to Kingston, in the hopes of seeing our friends the Talboys. Tom was in a great state of excitement.

'I say, Paddy, I wonder whether Lucy still cares for me,' he said. 'Perhaps she'll have forgotten all about me by this time; and if that fellow Duffy has been stationed at Kingston, as soon as we left he'll have done his best to cut me out.'

'I don't think her papa, at all events, would prefer an ensign to a midshipman; and depend upon it, that if she has transferred her affections, it would be to a post-captain or a colonel,' I answered. 'But cheer up, Tom, don't be down-hearted; we'll hope for the best.'

Almost the first gentlemen we saw on landing were two French officers, strolling along arm in arm. As we got close to them they turned their heads, and I recognised Lieutenant Dubois and La Touche. They knew me in a moment, and held out their hands with more cordiality than I should have expected.

'You see us again prisoners to your brave nation; but we have given our parole, and are allowed to be at large during the day,' said Dubois.

'You'll come to our lodgings, I hope, and allow us to show you some hospitality,' added La Touche. 'In this life we have many ups and downs. One day you are prisoners to us, and the next day we are prisoners to you. What matters it if we retain our honour and our lives. It's a miracle that we're alive.'

'How is that?' I asked.

'We were aboard the *Ville de Paris*,' he said, 'and were doing duty on the lower deck. We fought to the last, and fully believed that the ship would go down. At one time the admiral was the only person left unwounded on the upper deck. Officer after officer was killed as they went up to join him. We were about to follow, when our flag was hauled down. However, we expect to be exchanged soon, when, for my part, I intend to return to France.'

This was said as we walked along with the young Frenchmen.

The lodgings to which they introduced us consisted of a single room, in which they slept and took their meals; but they didn't seem a bit ashamed of it, and did the honours with as great an air as if they were receiving us in a magnificent saloon. They had evidently won the heart of their mulatto landlady, who placed an elegant repast on the table,—indeed, in a country where fruits and delicacies are abundant, that is not any difficult matter.

'The English are very polite to us here; and some of the young ladies are charming,' observed Dubois. 'There is one family especially polite,—that of a Monsieur Talboys. Ah! *ma foi!* his little daughter is perfectly charming.'

On hearing the name of Talboys, Tom Pim pricked up his ears and looked at me, for he was not able to understand all that was said.

'We are acquainted with Mr. Talboys,' I observed, 'and all must admire his daughter. Is she not engaged to be married yet?'

'Ah, yes, there's the pity,' said Dubois, shrugging his shoulders; 'to a military officer, I'm told,—the Capitaine Duffy. He has lately obtained his promotion, and appeared at a ball in a bright new uniform, which completely captivated the young lady's heart.'

'I'll not believe it until I see her, and she tells me so,' exclaimed Tom, starting up. 'You must have been misinformed, monsieur.'

'*Ma foi!* I hope so,' said Dubois; 'for I thought I was making great way, and resolved, if her father would accept me as his son-in-law, to give up the sea and settle down as a planter in Jamaica.'

On hearing this Tom became very fidgety, and proposed that we should go in search of our friends. As I was afraid that he might say something which might annoy our hosts, I agreed, and, wishing them good-bye, Tom and I started for Mr. Talboys' town house.

We had no great difficulty in finding it. Just as we reached the entrance, who should I see but Duffy himself, strutting out in a captain's uniform. He didn't know me at first, until I hailed him.

'What, Duffy!' I exclaimed. 'It must be yourself or your elder brother. Let me congratulate you on obtaining your captain's commission. You have faster promotion in your service than we have in the navy.'

'Ah, Paddy! is it you?' he cried, taking me by the hand. 'It's myself, I can assure you. Thanks to this torrid climate, sangaree, and Yellow Jack, you're right, my boy. All the fine fellows you knew at Savannah are invalided home, or are under the sod; but as I eschew strong drinks, and keep in the shade as much as I can, I have hitherto escaped the fell foe. I suppose you're going to call on my friends the Talboys? They will be very glad to see you. We often talk about you, for the gallant way in which you, Pim, and your other messmates behaved when the house was attacked.'

'Here is Pim,' I said.

'What! I beg your pardon,' said he; 'I really did not recognise you;' and he put out his hand, which Tom took rather coldly. 'We all owe you a debt of gratitude which none of us know how to repay.'

'I don't require payment,' said Tom, drawing himself up stiffly. 'Good morning, Captain Duffy! I don't wish to detain you.'

'Well, as I have to go on guard, I mustn't stop, or I should like to go back and join Lucy in thanking you.'

'I don't require thanks,' said Tom, gulping down his rising anger. 'Come along, Paddy.'

As I saw that the sooner the interview was brought to

an end the better, we entered the house. Tom was even half inclined to turn back, and I think he would have done so had not Mr. Talboys seen us, and insisted on our coming into the drawing-room.

Both of us followed him over the slippery floor, and nearly pitched down on our noses, making a somewhat eccentric entrance into the room.

Mrs. Talboys, with Lucy and her younger girls, were seated on cane-bottomed sofas, dressed in white, with fans in their hands. The weather was unusually hot. A blush rose to Lucy's cheek as she saw Tom. She, however, came frankly forward, and we all shook hands. Nothing was said about Duffy. They were all eager to hear our adventures, which we narrated as briefly as we could. They knew Dubois and La Touche, and Mr. Talboys thought them very agreeable Frenchmen, but they didn't appear to be much in Lucy's good graces. I was much inclined to speak of Duffy, but Lucy evidently didn't wish to mention him. We had observed the marks of fire on some of the houses as we came along, and Mr. Talboys told us that since we had been there there had been a fearful conflagration; and had not the wind shifted, the whole town would have been burned down. He and his family were at that time in the country, and so escaped the alarm which the fire caused.

Mrs. Talboys invited us to spend the evening at the house, but Tom at once answered for himself and me, and said that we had to return on board, and we were not pressed to stay. At last we got up to take our leave.

'Lucy is very anxious again to thank you, Mr. Pim, for your brave conduct in saving her from the blacks. Perhaps you'll meet in England, as she expects to go there shortly, should peace be established; but we are unwilling to allow her to risk the danger of the passage in war time.'

Lucy had managed to get Tom to the window, so I didn't hear what she said, but he looked far from happy.

'I must tell you, Mr. Finnahan, that my daughter will

probably be soon married. Captain Duffy,' said Mrs. Talboys, 'her intended, is an excellent young man, and heir to a good estate, with a sufficient fortune already in possession; and she could not expect to make a more satisfactory match. It has our entire approval. You know him well, he tells me?'

I of course said that I did, that he had treated me very kindly at Savannah, and that I must congratulate him on his good fortune.

While we were speaking, Tom came up, and said somewhat abruptly, 'Paddy, we must not delay longer.' He didn't again turn towards Miss Lucy, to whom I went up and wished good-bye. Tom and I then paid our adieus to the rest of the family. Lucy was well nigh crying, I thought, but the yellow light admitted through the blinds prevented me from seeing clearly.

'It's all over,' cried Tom, as we got outside. 'I thought it would happen. I've been and made a fool of myself, and I'll never do so again as long as I live; no, never— never!'

I comforted Tom as well as I could, and indeed he soon recovered his equanimity. I told him I was sure that Miss Lucy was very grateful, though she was not inclined to wait till he had become a post-captain, or even a commander, to marry him.

We looked in on our way down to the harbour on our two French friends. We found them in high spirits, for they had just received information that they were to accompany the Count de Grasse, and other French officers, who were about to return home, on board the *Sandwich*, Sir Peter Parker's flag-ship, on their parole. As Sir Peter was on the point of sailing in charge of a homeward-bound convoy, Sir George Rodney remained as commander-in-chief at Jamaica. A short time after, Admiral Pigot arrived out from England to supersede him, and Sir George returned home in the *Montague*.

At length, after lying idle for some time, Admiral Pigot,

16

with his flag on board the *Formidable*, made the signal for the whole fleet to put to sea.

A report reached us just before this that we and the other ships were to return to England, and highly delighted every one was at the thoughts of going home. We were, however, kept cruising for some time, till we fell in with the fleet of Admiral Graves off Havanna; thence we proceeded to Bluefields, on the south coast of Jamaica, towards its western end.

Here Admiral Graves, whose flag was flying aboard the *Ramilies*, received orders to convoy a hundred sail of merchantmen, together with the French prizes, consisting of the *Ville de Paris*, 110 guns, the *Glorieux* and *Hector*, of 74 guns each, and the *Ardent* and *Jason*, of 64 guns each. The men-of-war accompanying them were the *Canada*, our ship the *Cerberus*, of 74 guns each, and the *Pallas*, of 36 guns.

'It's to be hoped that we shall have fine weather,' said Nettleship one day at mess. 'Even now we're obliged to keep the pumps going every watch. It's a wonder the hull and rigging hold together; while we're terribly short-handed, and, as far as I can judge, the rest of the ships are in no better condition, and the prizes are still more battered.'

'What an old croaker you've become,' cried Tom. 'I thought you would have been the last person to talk in that way.'

Others, joining Tom, made the same sort of remarks.

'I'm not croaking. I only say that never fleet put to sea in a worse condition; but I do hope we shall be blessed with fine weather, and not meet with a heavy gale, or have to encounter an enemy of superior force.'

Those watching us from the shore could certainly not have supposed that the fine-looking fleet sailing along the coast of Jamaica was unable to cope with the fiercest gale that it was likely to encounter.

As we got away from land we found that the *Jason*

had not joined us, being employed in completing her water, while during a calm the officers of the *Ardent* sent a memorial to the admiral stating that she was totally unseaworthy; and they had therefore the good fortune to be ordered back to Jamaica to refit.

For some time the fine weather lasted, and few doubted that we should convoy the merchantmen committed to our charge, and the trophies of our hard-earned victory, in safety to England. We had got about the latitude of the Bermudas, when some of the convoy parted company, on their way to New York, leaving us, including the men-of-war and merchantmen, with only ninety-two sail,—the *Ville de Paris*, under an experienced navigator, leading the van through the Gulf Stream. The wind and sea, however, shortly after this got up, and two ships, the *Caton* and *Pallas*, made signals of distress, each having sprung a leak. The admiral therefore ordered them to bear away for Halifax, then less than a hundred leagues distant. Scarcely were they out of sight than the wind shifted to the southeast, blowing strongly, while a still heavier sea got up. The admiral on this made signals for the whole fleet to collect together, and prepare for a heavy gale. He hove to on the larboard tack under his mainsail, with top-gallant masts struck. We and the other ships followed his example, with all our other canvas furled.

Nettleship, Tom Pim, and I, being in the same watch, were on deck together. We had just got the ship snug, and, our duties for the moment performed, were standing together, watching the fast-rising seas.

'I say, Nettleship, we have got that gale you hoped we should escape, and no mistake about it,' said Tom Pim; 'but the old barkie rides easily, and the wind must blow a good deal harder than it does yet to hurt her.'

'But we can't say that it won't blow harder, youngster,' said Nettleship, who was much graver than usual. 'To my mind the weather looks as threatening as it well can be, and those in authority would have shown more wisdom had they waited

till the equinox was over to send us to sea. Just look round;
now did you ever see a wilder sky?'

Nettleship was right. The clouds were rushing madly on
overhead, while to the southward and east it had a peculiarly
angry appearance. Foam-capped waves were tossing and
tumbling, the spoon-drift flying off their heads covering the
ocean with a sheet of white, while a lurid light occasionally
gleamed forth from the point where the sun was going down,
tinging for a moment the crests of the seas and here and
there a tossing ship on which it fell. The sea with thundering
blows struck our bows and washed along our high sides, the
blocks rattled, the wind whistled in the rigging, the masts
groaned, the bulkheads creaked. We had to speak at the top
of our voices to make each other hear, while the lieutenants
had to shout their loudest through their speaking-trumpets as
they issued their orders. We were the leewardmost of the
men-of-war who were in sight, the merchantmen scattered
around, all pitching and rolling together, in a way which
threatened to send their masts overboard. The latter we
could see had now a yard, now a topmast carried away, but as
far as we could make out, no great damage had been done.
Each dog-watch the pumps were manned. Their clanking
was heard amid the uproar as night closed in. My old shipmates and I had to keep the morning watch, so as soon as
the hammocks were piped down, we turned in to get some
sleep first. Seldom that I had my head on the pillow many
seconds before my eyes closed, but this night the fearful
uproar, the violent swinging of my hammock, and the plunges
which I felt the ship making, kept me awake. My watch
below seemed twice as long as usual. At length I heard eight
bells strike. I turned out, and with my two messmates went
on deck.

'Things haven't mended since sundown,' observed Nettleship, as he, Pim, and I were together on the quarter-deck.

Indeed, the wind was howling more furiously than ever, and
the big ship plunged and rolled in a way which made it
difficult to keep our feet.

'We've plenty of sea-room, that's one satisfaction, at all events,' said Nettleship. 'I shouldn't like to be on a lee shore on a night like this.'

'Faith, nor should I, unless there was a good harbour to run into,' said I.

'It must have a broad entrance, and be well lighted, then,' he answered, 'or we shouldn't be much better off than we are at present.'

Two—four bells struck in the morning watch, and there appeared to be no improvement in the weather. The captain and second and third lieutenants came on deck, and, by the way they stood talking together, I saw that they considered matters growing serious. The pumps were kept going twice as long as usual. Six bells had just struck, when there came a sound like thunder breaking over our heads. Looking up, I saw the mainsail aback.

The captain shouted out, 'Man the clew garnets, let fly tacks and sheets;' but the words were scarcely out of his mouth before the ship heeled over, with a suddenness which nearly took us all off our feet.

There was no need for the officers to cry out, 'Hold on for your lives.' We struggled to windward, grasping whatever we could clutch. More and more the ship heeled over; then there came another loud report, the mainmast went by the board, the fore-topmast fell over the starboard bow, and the next instant the mizzenmast was carried away half up from the deck, while the sound of repeated blows which came from the afterpart of the ship, showed us that the rudder had been wrenched from the pintles, and was battering away under the counter. All these accidents happened in such rapid succession that it was impossible to do anything to avert them. The utmost vigilance was required to save ourselves from being crushed by falling yards and blocks, while cries and shrieks arose from many of our poor fellows, some of whom had been struck down, and others carried overboard, vainly endeavouring to regain the ship. Suddenly she righted, with a violence which tore away the guns from their lashings, and jerked the shot out of the lockers. The captain, not for a moment losing his self-possession, shouted to the crew to clear away the wreck of the masts,—himself, axe in hand, setting the example. Before, however, many strokes had been given, the sea came roaring up astern, and, bursting into the captain's cabin, swept everything before it. The doctor, purser, and several other officers who had remained below, came rushing up, some only in their shirts and trousers, others in their shirts alone, believing very naturally that the ship was going down. Tom Pim and I, with the other midshipmen, were exerting ourselves to see that the men obeyed the orders received. I met Larry, axe in hand, chopping away vigorously at the shrouds.

'Ah, then, Mr. Terence, things have come to a bad pass, I'm after fearing,' he exclaimed. 'Will you be letting me keep by you, if you please? If the ship goes down, I'd like to see how we could save ourselves on a boat, or a raft, or one of the masts, if we can't get into a boat.'

'If it comes to that, Larry, I'm afraid we shall have little chance of saving our lives,' I answered; 'at all events, however, I should like to have you near me.'

I can scarcely find words to describe the fearful condition of the ship. Gun after gun broke loose, crushing several of the men against whom they were cast; shot, hove out of the lockers, were rolling about between decks, injuring many others. The water from below rushed from side to side, making a clean sweep of everything it encountered, doing almost as much mischief as the seas which broke aboard on the upper deck. The officers who had last come from below were unable to return, and stood shivering in their scanty clothing, no one having even a coat to spare. While some of the crew were clearing away the masts, which were striking with every surge against the ship's side, tearing off the copper, and, as the oakum washed out, increasing the leaks, others, encouraged by their officers, were labouring at the pumps, while a third party was endeavouring to bale out the water with buckets. I didn't expect to see another dawn ; but the morning came notwithstanding, and a fearful sight it presented to us. Away to leeward we discovered the *Canada*, with her main-topmast and mizzenmast gone. The flag-ship, more to windward, seemed in no better condition. The *Glorieux* had lost her foremast, bowsprit, and main-topmast. The *Ville de Paris* still proudly rode the waves, as far as we could judge, uninjured, yet ere long she was to share the fate of many others, for after that day she was never again seen, and must have foundered with all her crew. Of the merchantmen several had already gone down, others had lost many of their spars, and some their masts, while out of the whole fleet not twenty remained in sight. Not far off from us lay a large ship on her beam-ends. Nettleship pointed her out to me. 'Poor fellows, they're worse off than we are,' he said. The crew were attempting to wear her. First they cut away the mizzenmast, then shortly the mainmast went ; still she lay helpless.

'See, she's hoisting the ensign, Union downwards,' said Nettleship. 'It's her last despairing signal for help.'

No help could any one give her. We watched her for a few minutes, when her stern rose, the sea rolled up and plunged into it ; down she went, the fly of her ensign the last object visible.

She was the *Dutton*, formerly an East Indiaman, and then a storeship. Her fate might soon be ours.

'Some of her poor fellows have escaped,' cried Nettle-ship.

He pointed out to me a boat under sail, not far from where the *Dutton* had foundered. We watched the boat. Now she was hid from sight in the trough of the sea, now she rose to the summit of a billow. Still it seemed impossible that she could escape being swamped. Yet on she went, driving before the gale.

'That boat is well handled, or she would have been under water before this time,' observed my messmate. 'What she can do others can do, and some of us may have a chance for our lives if our old ship goes down. Paddy, my boy, if that happens, do you try and get aboard a boat. You're young, with a good chance of promotion. I'm old, and have none; and I should like to have you and Tom Pim save yourselves.'

'But I can't go without Larry,' I answered; 'and you too, Nettleship, if you have any hope of a boat living in this sea, you must try to get off.'

He shook his head.

'No, no, Paddy. I have long made up my mind for the worst, and am ready for it. I should be thankful, though, to see you and Pim escape, and your honest fellow, Larry. There are two or three boats still uninjured. It's a pity that the lives of some of us should not be saved, if we can but manage to launch them.'

While he was speaking I was watching the progress of the *Dutton's* boat. First she steered for a ship some way to the eastward, but those on board at length saw that they should have to haul up to reach her, and again she kept away for a large merchantman to leeward. Presently the boat ran alongside the merchantman, from whose deck a number of ropes were hove into her, and the men, clutching them as the boat surged by, were hauled up, and, as far as we could see, none were lost, though the boat herself almost immediately filled and disappeared. In other directions most melancholy spectacles met our sight. The whole sea was literally covered with pieces of wreck and human beings clinging to them, among whom we observed several women lashed to spars or gratings, probably by brave fellows who themselves had perished after in vain attempting to preserve those they loved. No help could be given to the unfortunate wretches; and even had we been able to haul some who came near us on board our ship, it would only have been to prolong their lives for a few short hours.

Our captain and officers were making all possible efforts to save our ship, but from the first, I suspect, they must have seen they were hopeless. Every possible weight was got rid of. The anchors were cut away; then the upper deck guns were hove overboard, though the operation in itself was a dangerous one, for, after the gun tackles were cut loose, there was the risk of the guns upsetting and crushing those standing near. All this time the pumps were being worked. The captain ordered all hands not otherwise engaged to bale, and we were formed in gangs 'o pass the buckets up and down and along the deck.

CHAPTER XIX.

THE WRECK OF THE 'CERBERUS.'

WE were thus employed when the carpenter came to the captain with consternation in his countenance, and told him that the pumps would no longer work, for, the shot-lockers being destroyed, the shot as well as the ballast had got into the well, and completely choked it up.

'Well, my lads,' cried the captain, 'we must try what baling will do, and lightening the ship by every means in our power.'

Those who had been working at the pumps, and some others, were now divided into gangs under different officers, and were employed in getting rid of the heaviest things which could be reached. Some hove the guns overboard, others got up the weightier stores, the boatswain's party being engaged in chopping up the cables and throwing them into the sea.

While my messmates and I were hard at work with the rest, I saw the captain beckon Nettleship to him. They talked for a minute or more. Directly afterwards Nettleship came to where Tom and I were at work with Larry and some of the men. 'The captain has given me charge to try and save some of you youngsters,' he said. 'Life is sweet, and I won't deny that I am glad to have the chance of preserving my own with honour. You tell Tom Pim and

your boy Larry. I'll speak to some of our other messmates, and try to pick out a few trusty men who I know
are cool hands, and we will try and get a boat into the water.
It will be no easy matter,—it may, I warn you, hasten our
deaths ; but the captain is satisfied that the ship can't float
many hours longer. He argued the point, and showed me
that if we don't get off as he directed, we shall not escape
at all, as numbers will be rushing for the boats when they
discover that the ship must go down.'

Matters were growing rapidly worse. Even now I don't
like to think of that dreadful night which followed. When
morning broke, the number of ships in sight had much
diminished. The sea raged as furiously as ever, the wind
blew with fearful force. All hands had been toiling away.
Nearly every one began to see that our efforts had been
in vain. A loud noise was heard like that of an explosion
coming from far down in the depths of the ship. The
carpenter reported that the water in the hold had blown
up the orlop deck. It was very evident that the ship
was settling down. Many of the men who had been looked
upon as the bravest now gave way to despair, and went below,
crying out to their messmates to come and lash them into
their hammocks. Other stout fellows were in tears as they
thought of their country and those dear to them, whom they
were never to see again. Some, though they must have
known it would be of no use, were lashing themselves to
gratings and small rafts, which they had formed of spars.
Larry wanted me to do the same.

'Shure, Mr. Terence, you and Mr. Pim and I will be
able to manage a raft between us, and we'll get aboard one
of the ships in better plight than we are,' he said.

I pointed out to him the distance the ships were from
us, and the impossibility of reaching one of them. Some
of the poor fellows launched their rafts overboard, but were
quickly swallowed up by the sea. Even the lieutenants
went below; and, strange as it may seem, few of the men
remained on deck. Tom Pim and I, however, kept together,

with Larry, who would not leave me. Presently Nettleship came up.

'Now is our time, lads, if we're to save our lives. I have spoken to those whom the captain named, but none of them will come. They shake their heads, and declare it useless.

One of the quarter boats still remained uninjured. We went to her and found six of our men, one of whom was Larry, standing by the falls ready to lower her. Nettleship told us to jump in, there was not a moment to be lost. We found that he had put masts, and sails, and oars, and provisions aboard. Waiting till a sea surged up alongside, he and the men sprang into her.

'Cut, cut!' he cried.

The next instant I found that the boat was some fathoms from the ship. All was done so rapidly, and it seemed only by a miracle we got clear, that I can scarcely explain how it happened. I looked around, when what was my dismay to find that Tom was not with us. Looking up, I saw him on the deck.

'Leap! leap!' shouted Nettleship, though in the uproar his voice could not have been heard so far. Next instant Tom was in the water, striking out towards us.

'We have already as many aboard as the boat will carry,' cried some of the men.

What we had been about had been discovered by our unfortunate shipmates, who were now crowding to the side and shouting to us to return. Several in their fear leaped into the sea, but immediately disappeared. I caught sight of one head still above water. It was Tom Pim.

'Oh, take him in—take him in!' I cried out.

The men were getting out the oars. We were still, it must be understood, under the lee of the ship, or we should instantly have been swamped.

'We must have that lad aboard,' exclaimed Nettleship sternly. 'I'll not try to save you if you desert him.

Tom struck out bravely. Larry and I stretched out our arms, and, catching hold of him, hauled him on board the boat. Several others, now leaping into the water, tried to reach us, but, had we attempted to save them, we should to a certainty have perished together.

Nettleship sprang aft to the helm.

'Now, lads, step the mast and hoist the sail,' he shouted. 'Get out the starboard oars.'

In another instant the boat was before the wind, a cable's length from the ship. We could scarcely believe that we were saved; indeed, every moment it seemed as if the fierce foaming seas would break aboard us and send us to the bottom. I could not resist still looking at the ship, nor could Tom Pim. He presently exclaimed,—

'There's another boat being launched.'

We both saw her for a moment, but she presently disappeared.

'She's gone,' cried Tom.

'No—no, there she is,' I exclaimed, as I caught sight of her on the summit of a sea, and again she sank out of view. As far as I could make out, there were several people in her, but she had no sail hoisted, and consequently in those foaming seas rising up between us was scarcely visible.

We ran on, steering to the southward. Most of the hands were employed all the time in baling out the water, while Nettleship's whole attention was engaged in steering the boat, for he well knew that with the slightest want of care she would have filled in an instant. It seemed a wonder, indeed, that she could float in the midst of those foaming seas. Tom and I still kept looking at the ship.

'She is sinking lower and lower,' said Tom.

I hoped that he was mistaken, and that she appeared to be so only because we were getting farther from her.

Not many minutes afterwards, as I looked, a huge sea rolled up towards her.

The next instant Tom cried out, 'She's gone!' I rubbed my eyes. The foaming waters raged over the spot where the old *Cerberus* had floated; and I knew too well that every one of our helpless shipmates had perished, unless the other boat had got safely off. Their fate might be ours before long, we all knew, though we did not despair.

Nettleship's first care was to see what provisions we had got. We found that we had but two quart bottles of water, a bag of biscuits, a small ham, a single piece of pork, and three bottles of French cordials. These he had placed in the stern-sheets, that they might be kept dry, and that none of the men might be tempted to take more than their share. We might be days, or even weeks, before we were picked up or reached land. Nettleship pointed out to us the importance of husbanding our stores. The afternoon was far gone before we left the ship, and night was now approaching, while the gale had shown no signs of abating.

Humanly speaking, our lives depended on Nettleship's steering. There was everything to try the skill and nerves of a man; but it was difficult in the darkness to watch the seas coming up so as to avoid those likely to break aboard.

He sat in the stern-sheets like a figure of iron, his countenance fixed, his eyes turned now ahead, now on one, now on the other side. He seldom spoke, for his attention was occupied with the task he had undertaken. Older seamen had given in, while his courage and resolution had remained unshaken.

I had always liked him, ever since I joined the *Liffy*, but now I admired and respected him above all men, barring my uncle the major, who would, I am sure, have acted in the same way, though he might not have had the nautical skill to steer the boat.

'Stretch yourselves as best you can, youngsters, in the stern-sheets, and go to sleep,' said Nettleship; ' I intend to steer till daylight, and then let either Hunt or Ray (they were two quartermasters) take the helm.'

'But I don't like to leave you without company,' I said.

'Don't trouble yourself about that, Paddy,' he answered; 'the seas are my company, and precious rough company they are too ; they'll prevent me nodding.'

He laughed at his own remark.

At last Tom and I did as he advised us; indeed, we couldn't keep our eyes open longer, for we had had no sleep, lashed as we had been to the bulwarks on the previous night.

We both of us slept on right through the night. I awoke with a weary heart-sinking feeling. Dawn was already casting a grey light over the still troubled ocean. Clouds hung thickly overhead; the seas seemed to reach them as they rose up on either side.

There sat Nettleship, wide awake, his hand on the tiller, his eyes wearing a pained expression, as well they might, looking round watching the waves as they hissed up, threatening to overwhelm us. No one was speaking. Most of the men sat with their arms folded and their heads bent down, still fast asleep. I believe that Nettleship had been the only one awake among us during the night.

'The wind has fallen, and the sea has gone down considerably, Paddy,' he said, looking at me. 'Cheer up, lad; we shall save our lives after all, I believe.'

Tom, hearing him speak, awoke.

'I wish you would let me take the helm, Nettleship,' he said.

'No, no, Tom! The responsibility is too much to impose on you; I'll let Hunt steer presently.'

First one man woke up, then another, and another; but they all looked round with lack-lustre eyes and gloomy countenances. After some time, Tom shouted out that there was a break in the clouds to the eastward.

Just then a ray of bright light streamed across the ocean, tinging the foam-topped seas with a ruddy hue.

'It's the harbinger of better weather,' I said.

'You're right, sir,' observed Hunt. 'It will be our own fault if we don't manage to keep the boat afloat.'

I saw Nettleship for the first time showing signs of sleepiness. He aroused himself for the moment, and called to Hunt to take the helm. The quartermaster stepped aft, and

Nettleship, resigning his seat to him, a moment afterwards was fast asleep.

The men now cried out that they were very hungry, and Pim and I agreed that it would be better to serve out some food without awaking Nettleship. We gave each man a biscuit and a small piece of ham. The neck of a broken bottle was the only measure we had for serving out the water. The quantity was but just sufficient to moisten our lips, but not to quench our thirst. The men asked for more, but Tom told them that until Nettleship awoke he couldn't give them any.

Though the weather was moderating, the wind went down very slowly, and the seas tossed and tumbled with almost as much violence as before. It was noon when Nettleship awoke. He approved of the allowance Tom and I had served out.

'But, my lads,' he said, 'you see these two bottles of water. We don't know how long we may have to go before we get more, so you must make up your minds to do with the allowance you have already had to-day. I'll take no more.'

He then told Tom and me to give him what we had given the rest; and, after eating the biscuit and bit of ham, he drank the bottle-neck full of water. My own sensations made me hope that we should not have many days to live on so small an allowance. Still, though my throat felt like a dust-bin, I determined to support Nettleship, and I knew Tom would do so, in whatever he thought necessary. We ran on all day, the wind going down very slowly. At noon, Ray took the helm. Whether he steered with less care, or, as I think, the seas broke in a different way, two in succession came aboard, and we had to bale as fast as we could, to get the water out of the boat. As it came in, it washed right aft and wetted through our bag of biscuits, which Tom and I in vain tried to save. Nettleship didn't blame Ray, but warned him to be more careful.

'I intend to steer to-night,' he said, 'so I'll finish out my snooze, and call me at sundown.'

Both Hunt and Ray asked him to let them steer during part of the night, but he was firm.

'No,' he answered; 'your lives are entrusted to me, and it's my duty to keep at the helm while there's most likely to be danger.'

Tom and I, however, determined to have our eyes open, so as to make company for him during part of the night, which, it being summer time, was fortunately not long. Had it been in the winter, none of us could have survived. Nettleship appeared to have completely recovered himself. I sat up through part of the night, and Tom through the remainder. We talked cheerfully and hopefully. When I lay down, I slept as soundly as I ever did in my bed. Towards morning, I suppose it was, I dreamed of the various scenes I had gone through since I came to sea, among others of the earthquake at Savannah, and then I was looking out into the barrack-yard, and there was Larry fiddling away, with soldiers and blacks dancing to his music,—everything seemed so vivid that I had no doubt about its reality. Then Mr. Talboys and Lucy and Captain Duffy came in and joined in the dance. I thought it very good fun, so I ran down and began to dance, and who should I see but the admiral and captain and old Rough-and-Ready, each with a black partner, and there we were jigging away right merrily, till I awoke, to find myself in the stern-sheet of the boat, and to see Nettleship steering, while the notes of Larry's fiddle sounded in my ears. There, sure enough, he was, seated on the after-thwart, with the fiddle at his chin, working away with right good-will. I sat up and looked at him with amazement.

'Shure, Mr. Terence, I wasn't going to leave that behind after it had been saved from fire and water, so I took it into the boat the first thing, and Mr. Nettleship gave me leave to play it, just to cheer up the boys a bit.'

The music had certainly had that effect, for all the people wore more cheerful countenances than they did the day before. Larry, however, put his fiddle back in its case while

17

breakfast was served out. It consisted only of wet biscuit, a modicum of ham, and a small taste of liquor. The water Nettleship said he should keep till mid-day, to serve out with the pork.

The sea was still rough, though there was much less than on the previous day, and careful steering was necessary to keep the boat free from water. As there was nothing for the men to do, Nettleship advised us to spin yarns and sing songs in the intervals of Larry's playing. He was ready enough to go on moving his bow as long as he had leave.

During the day the clouds cleared away, and the sea went down still more. We were thankful for this, as we could now dry our clothes, and, what was of more importance, our biscuits, and move about in the boat to stretch our limbs. But then, again, with a calm we might be delayed, and, after all, perish from hunger and thirst. Nettleship, I daresay, thought this, but notwithstanding cheered us up with the hopes of reaching land or being taken on board some vessel. Next night passed much as the others had done. The sun rose in a clear sky, and as it got above the horizon the wind dropped, and there appeared every likelihood of a perfect calm. Our scanty provisions were served out, and then Nettleship, as he had done the day before, set us to spinning yarns and singing; but even those who had the best voices could scarcely bring out a note, and several appeared but little inclined to talk. Larry, however, kept his fiddle going, and Tom and I talked, and tried to draw out the men to tell something about themselves. At last my throat felt like a dust-bin, and I suspect the rest were very much in the same condition. There we were, floating out in the Atlantic, hundreds of miles away from help, as far as we could tell, and the calm might continue after the gale for a week or more. At last Nettleship ordered the men to get out the oars.

'We may pull into a breeze, lads, perhaps,' he said. 'At all events, we shall get so much nearer land.'

Tom and I each took an oar to encourage the rest, half of us pulling at a time. We had been at the oars for some five or six hours, when towards evening, Nettleship, who had been standing up shading his eyes, said,—

'Lads, there's a sail in sight; she has a light breeze, and is standing to the northward. We shall, I hope, get up to her; but mark you, she may be English, but she may be French, and in that case we shall be made prisoners.'

'That won't be much odds,' said one of the men; 'better be made prisoners than die of hunger and thirst out here.'

That was true enough, but I didn't like the thoughts of the alternative. When Nettleship, however, said that he was determined to try and come up with the stranger, the men bent to their oars. Tom and I, at the time, were now pulling, and I was surprised to see the strength the men still possessed.

Gradually the stranger's top-gallant-sails, and then the heads of her topsails, rose above the horizon.

'She's a large ship, no doubt about that,' said Nettleship. 'Cheer up, lads! my belief is she's English, but we shall be better able to judge when we see her courses.'

We were now steering west-and-by-north, so as to cut her off. After going some distance, Nettleship called to Tom Pim to stand up in the stern-sheets, and take a look at the stranger.

'What do you think of the cut of her canvas, Tom?' he asked. 'Is that English or French?'

'I should say English,' answered Tom, 'but we must get nearer to be certain.'

'Have you made up your minds to a French prison, lads, if we're mistaken?' again said Nettleship.

'Better a French prison with food and water, than out here starving to death,' answered the men. 'And we'll ask you, Mr. Nettleship, for a drink of water apiece. We'll get aboard her before dark, and our throats are terribly dry.'

'I warn you, lads, that a breeze may spring up, and that even now we may miss her; and what shall we do if we have no water left?' said Nettleship.

Still the men cried out for water. I could judge how my companions felt by my own sensations. Nettleship reluctantly served out a double allowance, leaving scarcely a quarter of a bottleful,—the other had before been exhausted. The sun was sinking low, and we had not yet seen the hull of the ship. Nettleship looked more anxious than before. The men strained every nerve, for they believed that their lives depended on their getting up to the ship before dark.

Some of them now called out for food, and declared that they could pull no longer without it; others asked for the remainder of the water.

Accordingly, while one half rested, Nettleship served out a portion of our remaining stock of provisions. The other half then took a meal. This, however, only made us all more thirsty, and again the cry rose of—

'Water! water! We must have it, or we shall have to give in!'

Nettleship seemed to think that it would be useless to resist their entreaties, and with a look of desperation he divided the remainder of the water, leaving not a drop at the bottom of the last bottle.

Rapidly the sun sank towards the horizon. In a short time it would be dark, and we should have no chance of being seen from the ship. The men cried out for the remainder of the liquor, saying that they could pull all the better if they could get it. This, also, to my surprise, Nettleship served out to them,—the bottle-neck full to each of us, for we all shared alike,—and again they pulled as lustily as before for a short time; but we all felt our thirst increased. Few of them spoke; but Larry every now and then gave a shout, or made some comic remark to encourage his companions. Nettleship also did his best to keep up our spirits.

Darkness, however, was fast approaching; the wind appeared to be freshening, and, should a strong breeze fill the stranger's sails, all hope of getting alongside her before she passed us would be lost. Not a word was now uttered; but every now and then the men turned their heads to ascertain what progress we were making.

Nettleship now steered the boat rather more to the northward.

Presently a light streamed out towards us across the water. Again our hopes of getting on board increased. The wind once more dropped.

'We shall reach her, lads! cried Nettleship at length, in a confident tone.

The men cheered, though their voices sounded husky, the ring of a British seaman's voice sadly wanting. They pulled bravely on, however.

The light rose higher above the surface. It was now almost ahead. Then another streamed forth from a port. Presently Nettleship's voice rang out clear and loud,—

'Ship ahoy! What ship is it?'

'His Britannic Majesty's ship *Hector*. What boat is that?' came over the water.

Nettleship replied.

Presently the order sounded out from aboard the ship,—

'Raise tacks and sheets! clew up mainsail and foresail! Let fly top-gallant-sheets!'

The wind having fallen, the ship soon lost her way, and we pulled up alongside. A light gleamed through the entrance port, and ready hands, coming down, quickly assisted us up on deck, while the boat was secured, for none of us had much strength left to help ourselves.

Nettleship, Tom, and I were at once conducted to the upper deck, where we found the gallant commander of the *Hector*, Captain Bouchier, to whom Nettleship at once gave a brief account of what had happened.

'We have reason to be thankful that we escaped the

gale, Drury,' said the captain, turning to an officer in a captain's uniform standing near him. 'We should to a certainty have shared the fate of many others.'

Captain Bouchier made this remark, I found, in consequence of the unseaworthy condition of his ship. To enable her to perform the voyage, before she sailed from Jamaica she had had twenty-two of her guns taken out of her, and her masts replaced by others of smaller dimensions. Her crew amounted in all to scarcely three hundred men, many of whom were invalids, and others French and American prisoners, who had volunteered to assist in working the ship.

As soon as Nettleship had finished his account, the captain directed that we should be taken below, and hammocks slung for us.

'I would advise you to turn in, young gentlemen, as soon as you have had some food,' he said, as we were leaving.

He also ordered that our boat's crew should be well looked after. The surgeon, who was summoned, went to attend to them, and to prevent them from being overfed, or overdosed with grog, which to a certainty they would otherwise have been by the seamen of the ship. As I was going down to the orlop deck, Larry came aft, supported by two men, with his fiddle-case under his arm.

'Och, Mr. Terence,' he said, 'I'm mighty glad to find ourselves safe aboard a big ship again, and to see you all right. It is more than I thought to do since our own went down with all her brave boys, barrin' ourselves.'

The doctor, finding that we did not require much of his assistance, attended to Larry and the other men, who appeared far more knocked up than we were, and they were at once sent to their hammocks. We were ushered into the gun-room by the master's mate, who accompanied us. Here we found a number of midshipmen seated at a table, employed in various ways. They greeted us warmly, and were all eager to know our adventures, which we told them while discussing the meat placed before us. Scarcely, however, had I finished eating, when my head dropped on the table, and there I should have sat, had not one of the assistant-surgeons aroused me and advised me to turn in. I slept on, as did Nettleship and Tom, till the hammocks were piped up next morning, and, if left alone, should not have awoke for hours afterwards.

We all three, though still weak, felt pretty well able to get about, and were in reality in a better state than many of the officers and men, who were suffering from the effect of the West Indian climate. I never saw so pale and haggard a crew. We were treated with the greatest kindness by our new messmates, and Nettleship was asked into the ward-room, to give a further account of what had happened to us. We had indeed ample reason to be thankful for our preservation, when so many on board our own and other ships had perished.

In a couple of days we were as well as ever, and, as many of the mates and midshipmen were too ill to do duty, we were directed to take their places. Larry, as usual, made himself at home with his fiddle, and soon set the seamen and French prisoners jigging away, as he had done on board other ships.

We were standing on with all the canvas the battered old *Hector* could carry, with the wind from the southward, when the look-out aloft announced two sail away to leeward. One of the lieutenants, with his telescope on his back, immediately went to the main-topmast crosstrees to have a look at them.

'As far as I can make out, they are two frigates, sir, coming up before the wind,' he said to the captain when he came down.

'Are they English or French?' asked the captain.

'According to my judgment, sir, they are French,' was the answer.

The captain took a few turns on deck, and then again sent aloft. The lieutenant, on his return, pronounced his opinion more decidedly that they were French, and both large frigates. The captain on this ordered the drum to beat to quarters, and the usual preparations were made for battle. Evening was approaching, and it might be well on in the night before the enemy could be up to us.

Although the *Hector* was a 74-gun ship, she in reality only carried fifty-two guns, and, from her battered condition, was not fit to cope even with a single frigate. Still our brave captain determined to struggle to the last. She being a heavy sailer, the two frigates came rapidly up with us, and there was no doubt from their appearance that they were enemies, although we could not as yet see their ensigns. All doubt on that score was dissipated, when, in a short time, French flags were run up at their peaks. The prisoners were accordingly ordered below and placed under sentries, while the captain went along the decks encouraging the men. They received him with cheerful countenances as he appeared, promising to do their best to beat the enemy. I asked Nettleship what he thought would be the result of the contest.

'Heaven only knows!' he answered; 'but there's one thing, I'm certain that our fellows will fight to the last. I never saw a crew, though so many of them are sick, more resolute or full of pluck.'

The leading frigate, now coming up on our starboard quarter, opened fire, and we, luffing up, returned it with our aftermost guns. She then ranged up abeam, while her consort placed herself on our larboard quarter, so that we could not luff up again without being raked by the other. We, however, could fight our starboard broadside, and occasionally could bring some of our larboard guns to bear on the enemy on that side. We could now see that each frigate mounted forty guns, their decks being crowded with men; indeed, they together mustered more than double our complement. These were fearful odds, but Captain Bouchier and his crew seemed in no way daunted. The men ran the guns in and out as fast as they could load them, but the enemy's shot came crashing aboard, committing fearful havoc in all parts of the ship. The French must have known, from our smaller masts and spars, that we were likely to be short-handed, and also soon discovered the small number of guns we carried.

Though I saw numbers struck down around me, I never for one instant thought of myself or expected to be killed. The surgeons below soon had their hands full, as one poor fellow after another was carried down to the cockpit. The dead were left where they fell, for all were too busy to remove them. The enemy generally fired at our hull rather than at our spars.

I was standing near Nettleship, when I heard him exclaim,—

'Here comes one of them alongside us.'

I looked out of a port, and there saw the frigate on the starboard beam dropping so close that I could distinguish the countenances of the people on her deck.

Presently the voice of the captain sounded loud and clear,—

'Boarders! repel boarders!'

Our crew, leaving the guns on the starboard side, seized their weapons; some stood armed with cutlasses and pistols, others with pikes, at the place where the Frenchmen were likely to try and gain a footing on our deck. Our larboard guns were still replying to the fire of the frigate on that quarter; but she now making sail, ranged up alongside, receiving, however, a heavy fire from our guns as she did so. A large body of her men, with the soldiers, stood on the forecastle, ready to leap aboard.

'You must drive those fellows back,' cried Nettleship. 'Come on, my lads,' he shouted to such of the men as were near him, among whom was Larry. Tom also, who saw what we were about, quickly joined us.

Just as the first Frenchman sprang on to our deck, Nettleship's sword cut him down. Others, however, followed, but our men fought desperately. Though the enemy came rushing on board, not an inch of ground did they gain.

Presently, a big fellow—the boatswain, apparently, from his dress—joined his shipmates, and attacked Nettleship. I saw another close behind him, aiming a pistol at his head. I sprang forward and knocked it up just as it exploded, and the next moment dealt the Frenchman a blow on his sword arm, which saved Nettleship's life. The fellow whose pistol I had knocked up, however, had his cutlass uplifted to strike me down, when Larry, who was by my side, parried the blow with his cutlass, and, though he got a severe wound, he brought the man to the deck by a blow which he gave the next moment. Others of our crew now coming to our assistance, we drove back the enemy, who had nearly gained a footing.

The fight all the time was going on fiercely on the starboard side, and we could not tell whether the Frenchmen were getting the best of it.

As we had begun the action with but three hundred men, many of whom had been killed or wounded, and invalids who had scarcely strength to handle their weapons, and the French had upwards of six hundred, it might be seen that our chance of success was very small indeed. Our men, however, fought with the most desperate courage. Captain Bouchier, with Captain Drury—who was a passenger—and several of the lieutenants, headed the men on the starboard side in repelling the enemy; while the master and two of the other lieutenants and the purser encouraged those on our side of the deck.

Directly the Frenchmen had been driven back, the second lieutenant, calling off a portion of the men, hurried to the guns, when their thundering roar, with the crashing sounds which followed, showed us that their shot were creating a dire effect on the bows of our antagonist. All this time a withering fire of musketry had been kept up on us from a body of troops stationed on the forecastles of the French frigates, and many of our poor fellows had been struck down.

Again and again the Frenchmen attempted to gain a footing on our deck, some springing down from the fore-rigging, others clambering up from the forecastle, and all the time the guns roaring, the musketry and pistols rattling, the cutlasses clashing, the men shouting and shrieking, while the ships surged against each other with tremendous crashes,—many of the Frenchmen who were driven overboard being crushed to death between them. This continued, not for the few minutes which it has taken me to describe the scene, but for an hour or more, and it seemed sometimes that all the three ships must go down together.

Our marines were not idle, for some stationed on the fore-castle, and others on the poop, kept up a hot fire on the enemy.

At length our ship tore herself from her two antagonists almost at the same moment; and they apparently gave up all hopes of taking us by boarding, as they didn't attempt again to come close alongside, though their fire was even more destructive than at first, for now one passed under our stern and raked us, now the other performed the same manœuvre; while we, with our braces shot away, our masts and yards injured, and our sails shot through and torn, were unable to move with sufficient swiftness to avoid them.

Already numbers of our men had fallen. I frequently looked round to see how it fared with Larry, Tom Pim, and Nettleship, and was thankful to find them still actively engaged at the guns, at which most of the officers were assisting the men.

CHAPTER XX

OLD ENGLAND AGAIN.

OCCASIONALLY, as the French ships were man-œuvring, alternately passing either ahead or astern of us, there was a cessation of firing, but it was only for a short time. Again their shot came crashing aboard.

I observed Captain Bouchier not far from me, when, just as we were receiving a raking broadside, he staggered, and would have fallen to the deck, had not the purser sprang forward and caught him. Directly afterwards, the latter, summoning two men, the captain was carried below.

On this, Captain Drury, shouting 'Keep at it, my lads! We'll beat them off yet!' took his place, and issued the necessary orders.

Again the Frenchmen ranged up as before,—one on our beam and the other on our quarter,—and made another attempt to board. Captain Drury, leading our men on the starboard side, while our first lieutenant commanded those on the other, drove them back, many falling dead on our deck and others overboard. In a few minutes we again separated.

For four hours the action had continued (it appeared to me to be much longer), when, as the smoke from the guns cleared away, I saw that day was breaking.

As it showed the enemy more clearly than before our shattered and weak condition, I could not help fearing that they would again renew the attack, with every prospect of success.

From the numbers of the poor fellows who had been carried below wounded, and the many who lay stretched dead on the deck in all directions, I fancied that we must have lost half of our crew, while it seemed to me that at any moment our shattered spars would come tumbling down on deck. The fore-topmast hung over the bows, the main-yard was nearly cut in two, and not a sail remained whole. Still Captain Drury and the other officers went about encouraging the men to persevere.

When daylight increased, however, and we saw our two antagonists in comparison to our ship but slightly injured, we knew how desperate was our condition, yet our men stood sturdily to their guns, and blazed away as they could be brought to bear.

While watching the two frigates, I observed signals ex-changed between them, and almost immediately afterwards, to our astonishment, they hauled their tacks aboard, and stood away from us. Our nearly exhausted crew, on seeing this, cheered again and again.

'We must not be too sure that they don't intend to come back again when they have repaired damages, and renew the fight,' said Nettleship to me.

'We will hope for the best, and if they do, try to beat them off again,' I answered.

'That's the right spirit, Paddy,' said Nettleship. 'Please Heaven, we shall do so.'

'Hurrah! hurrah! We've licked the Frenchmen,' I heard Larry shouting. 'Give them another cheer, boys! Hurrah! hurrah!' and the men round him joined in his hurrahs.

The men were still allowed to remain at their quarters, for it was yet difficult to say what the enemy would do next. We watched them anxiously, for even the most fire-eating of our men had no wish for more fighting, as by no possi-bility could we hope to capture either of the frigates. When some way astern they joined company, and we saw them standing to the westward. They got farther and farther off, and gradually their hulls sank below the horizon. We were now ordered to secure the guns. This done, the dead hove overboard, and the decks washed down, all hands were employed in knotting and securing the running and standing rigging, and strengthening the wounded spars. I asked one of the assistant-surgeons, who came on deck to get a little fresh air, if he knew how the captain was going on.

'He has a desperate wound in the arm, but is likely to do well,' he answered.

He told me, besides, that there were six - and - twenty wounded men below, while nineteen had been killed. From the number of shot the Frenchmen fired at us, I supposed that we had lost many more. A large proportion of the shot, however, had flown over our heads, and injured only our sails and rigging. The ship was but partially put to rights when another night closed in. I found it difficult enough even during my watch to keep my eyes open, and the moment I turned in to my hammock I was fast asleep. I suspect that all on board, both officers and men, were equally drowsy. I had not to turn out again till the hammocks were piped up.

When I came on deck I found that the weather had changed. Dark clouds were rushing across the sky, the sea had got up, and the ship was rolling and pitching into it. The wind was from the southward. Two reefs had been taken in the topsails, but from the way the ship heeled over it was evident that she had more canvas on her than she could carry.

Captain Drury had just come on deck.

'We must shorten sail,' he said to the first lieutenant.

'Hands aloft,' he shouted.

Just at that moment, as the men were about to spring into the rigging, a tremendous blast struck the ship, and over she heeled.

'Up with the helm!' cried Captain Drury.

The ship did not answer it, but heeled over more and more. I thought she was about to share the fate of the *Cerberus*. The moment afterwards a heavy sea came roaring up, a succession of crashes was heard, the masts went by the board, and she rose on an even keel, the wheel flying round and sending the men at it across the deck. The rudder had been carried away, and the ship lay a helpless wreck on the stormy ocean.

The men looked at each other, with blank dismay in their countenances, but our brave commander did his best to conceal his anxiety, and the officers followed his example.

'Clear away the wreck, lads; the gale won't last long, and when the wind goes down we must try to get up jury-masts and repair the rudder,' he cried out.

All hands were now employed in trying to save some of the spars, and to cut the masts clear, for their butts were striking with fearful force on our larboard side, already shattered by the shot of the enemy. While we were thus employed, the carpenter and his mates, who had been below, came on deck, and went up to the captain. I saw by his looks as he passed me that something was the matter. Directly afterwards the order was given to man the pumps, and they were set clanging away as fast as they could be made to work. The quantity of water gushing out showed that the ship must be leaking at a rapid rate. There was so much work to do that but few words were spoken. I happened to meet Larry.

'Cheer up, Mr. Terence,' he exclaimed. 'Things look mighty bad; but though our ship went to the bottom we were saved, and I'm after hoping that we'll be saved again. It would be hard to have beaten the enemy and yet to lose her.'

'I don't expect that we shall do that,' I answered. 'The wind is fair for Nova Scotia, and when we get up jury-masts and rig a new rudder, we may be able to get her along.'

Though I said this, I confess that I was not very sure about it. Things didn't improve. The sea increased, the wind blew stronger and stronger, and though the pumps were kept going without cessation, we could not get the water under. It came in faster and faster. The reports from the sick bay were also disheartening. Several of the poor fellows who had left their hammocks to fight had since succumbed, and many others were following them. The wounded, who might have done well under other circumstances, dropped off one by one. The only satisfactory intelligence was the state of the captain, who, though so badly wounded, was progressing favourably. The day after the gale commenced ten men died, and the following a still larger number. It was sad to see them lashed in their hammocks as they were slid overboard. There was no time for any funeral ceremonies. Even the healthiest among us looked pale and broken in spirits. On the fourth or fifth day, I think it was, from that on which the gale commenced, the purser's steward, on getting up provisions, found that the salt water had spoiled all the bread, while many of the casks with fresh water had broken loose and their contents were lost.

To try and stop the leaks, Captain Drury ordered the only spare mainsail to be fothered and drawn under the ship's bottom. To prepare it a quantity of oakum was spread over the sail, and stitched down by the sail-makers, thus forming what seemed like an enormous mat. This was lowered over the bows, and gradually hauled under the ship's bottom, where the leaks were supposed to be the worst. We all looked anxiously for the result. Though, in addition to the pumps, a gang of men were set to bale, the water still continued to gain on us. In spite of this, neither officers nor men appeared to lose heart.

'The gale will come to an end some day,' cried Captain Drury, 'and we must keep the ship afloat till then. We should be cowards to give in.'

He did his best to speak in his usual cheery tone, but even his voice was more husky than usual, and it was easy to see that he didn't say what he thought. At last many of the men were seen to desert the pumps.

'Come, Paddy,' said Tom Pim, 'we must not let them do that. You and I will take their places and shame them back.'

We turned to, and worked away till our arms ached. 'Spell ho!' we cried, and, catching hold of two men, we dragged them back to the pumps. Nettleship did the same with others. The lieutenants were constantly going about trying to keep the crew at work. Some of them behaved exactly as those aboard the *Cerberus* had done before she was lost, and were about to lash themselves into their hammocks. The first lieutenant and the boatswain, going round, quickly routed them out, and they returned to their duty, either to pump or bale.

The carpenter and his mates, assisted by the boatswain, were attempting to get at the leaks, but even they at last abandoned their efforts on finding them hopeless.

Captain Drury, who had been to visit Captain Bouchier, now returned on deck, and ordered the guns to be hove overboard to lighten the ship. All hands not engaged in pumping were employed in this duty. One by one they were sent plunging into the sea, and the big seventy-four was left at the mercy of the smallest privateer afloat. This gave the ship relief, and our hopes rose of saving her. Of late we had been on the smallest possible allowance of water, and now, to our dismay, the purser announced that the last cask was expended. Nor could wine or spirits be got at owing to the quantity of water in the hold. We had beef and pork, but the bread was all spoiled; thus, even should we keep the ship afloat, we ran the risk of dying of hunger and thirst. Of the crew of the *Hector*, which had consisted of three hundred men when my companions and I got on board, nearly one hundred had been killed in action, or had since died, and still others were dropping off fast.

Day after day went by. We had known when in the boat what it was to suffer from thirst, but I now felt it more

18

severely. Even Nettleship owned to me that he didn't think he could get through another day.

'I don't know whether either of us will survive, Paddy,' he said, 'but if you do, I want you to write to my mother and sister, who live near Plymouth, to tell them what happened to me, and that I thought of them to the last ; and should be thankful if you could just get some one to let the Admiralty know that Jack Nettleship did his duty while life remained.'

I tried to cheer him up, at the same time promising to carry out his wishes if I should survive him. I fancy a good many, both of officers and men, were feeling as he did. Still, no one I saw showed any signs of cowardly apprehension. Our chief work was now to keep the men at the pumps and baling. It was only by the constant efforts of the officers that they could be induced to remain at their stations ; and when ' Spell ho !' was cried, and a fresh gang was ordered to take their places, the people relieved staggered away, and fell down on the deck like drunken men. The others, after labouring away for some time, relaxed in their exertions. Nettleship and I were standing near, occasionally taking a turn to help them. One poor fellow fell down. We ran forward to lift him up, but he was dead. We could only just drag him out of the way and call to another to take his place. Before many minutes were over another fell in the same way, dying at the post of duty, as heroically as if he had been standing at his gun. One of the lieutenants, who just then came up, called the surgeon to examine them. He came at once, but his efforts proved ineffectual to restore the men, and they were soon sent to join a number of their shipmates in their ocean grave. Two or three others, I heard, died in the same manner, when I was not present. The gun-room had become uninhabitable from the water washing through it. We had to move up to the ward-room. The deck below us was fast sinking. The carpenter reported that some of the beams of the orlop deck had fallen into the hold, though they must have done so gradually, for we had heard no sound to account for what had taken place. Indeed, the loud noise of the seas beating against the ship, and the water washing about in the hold, prevented any noises except the loudest from being heard. We all now knew that the ship was sinking. Only by the greatest exertions could she be kept afloat to prolong our lives for a few hours. Still no one talked of giving in.

Captain Bouchier, wounded as he was, got up and went about, encouraging both officers and men. The spirit he and Captain Drury displayed encouraged us all. For three days we had none of us tasted a drop of water or spirits. We could judge by our own sufferings the fearful agonies the sick and wounded must be enduring. Not one would have survived, had not the surgeon discovered a few bottles of claret, which the captain insisted should be reserved for them, and though he required it as much as any one, he would not touch a drop himself.

The third day since the water had been exhausted came to an end, and few of us expected to see another sunrise. That night was a dreadful one. The loud lashing of the sea against the side, the creaking of the bulkheads, the ominous sounds which came from the depths of the ship, the groans and cries of the sick and dying, heard at intervals, the ceaseless clanging of the pumps, rang in our ears as we lay, during our watch below, on our damp beds extended on the wardroom deck. The night, however, did come to an end, and we found ourselves still alive, though the ship had evidently sunk lower since the previous day. I joined Nettleship on deck, for we naturally kept together as much as we could. I found that the wind was still blowing strongly, and the sea running high, although it had lately somewhat gone down. Nothing could be seen around but the leaden-coloured foaming seas rising and sinking between us and the horizon. On comparing notes, my two messmates and I agreed that we didn't suffer nearly so much from thirst as we had done in the boat. Such provisions as could be got at were served out, but none of us cared much for food, though we ate what we could to keep up our strength. We were soon summoned to watch and assist the men at the pumps and buckets, for even now, not for an instant were they allowed to relax in their exertions. Captain Bouchier, weak as he was, went frequently amongst them.

'Keep at it, my lads!' cried Nettleship; 'while there's life there's hope. If we can keep the ship afloat for a short time longer, it may make all the difference whether we save our lives or perish. Cheer up, lads, cheer up! Show that you're British seamen to the last!'

The men uttered a faint cheer when the captain, leaning on the purser's arm, returned.

Captain Drury, who had fought the ship so bravely after Captain Bouchier was wounded, was the life and soul of all on board.

Noon had passed, and still the stout ship lay rolling in the trough of the sea. Inch by inch the water was rising, and we knew that if we were to cease pumping and baling, it would gain upon us still more rapidly.

Already despair could be seen on nearly every countenance. Notwithstanding, few, if any, flinched from their work. Those who spoke, talked of home and friends whom they never expected to see again. Some shook hands, believing that at any moment the ship might make the last fatal plunge, and sink beneath the waves.

Larry was now like my shadow, wherever I went, he followed, no one preventing him, except when he had to take his turn at the pumps or buckets.

Some of the officers had written letters addressed to friends or relatives, and were enclosing them in bottles headed up in small casks, so that some record might be preserved of our fate. Nettleship had prepared one.

'Have you anything to say to your friends at Ballinahone, Paddy?' he asked.

'Yes; beg your mother to write to them, and say that I send my love to all, not forgetting my uncle the major, and that I have been thinking much of them to-day,' I answered, as well as I could speak with the choking sensation in my throat.

'And please, Mr. Nettleship, may I be so bold as to ax you to put in a word about Larry Harrigan, and to say that he stuck to Mr. Terence to the last, and that if he couldn't save him, it wasn't the will that was wanting, but the cruel say was too much for us at last.'

'And put in a word to my family,—you know their address,' said Tom; 'just my love, and that I was thinking of them. They'll know that I was likely to have done my duty as far as I could, so I won't trouble you with a longer message.'

Just as Nettleship had returned to the gun-room to add the messages to his letter, there came a shout from the poop,—

'A sail! a sail!'

Many of the officers rushed up to take a look at her. Tom Pim and I followed them. We could make her out clearly,— a small vessel, right away to windward. The question was whether she would see us.

Captain Drury also had his telescope on her.

Now she was hidden by the seas which rose up between us; now she came clearly into view, her hull almost visible.

'She's standing this way,' said Captain Drury, 'and I believe has made us out, but of that we can't be certain. However, we must not relax in our efforts to keep the ship afloat, for it may be many hours before we can get aboard her.'

I should have said that we had had a spar secured to the stump of the mainmast, to which an ensign with a jack downwards had been nailed from the first, in the hopes of attracting the attention of any passing vessel.

Captain Bouchier, who had been informed that a sail was in sight, now came up to have a look at her, but almost immediately went down again among the men.

'Lads,' he said, 'your exertions will be rewarded, I hope; but you must not slacken in them, or your labours may be thrown away. We may keep the ship afloat many hours longer if you bale and pump as sturdily as heretofore. By that time the sea may have gone down, and we may manage to get aboard the vessel in her boats, though she probably will not venture alongside.'

The men received his address with a faint cheer, and turned to again at the pumps, while those employed in baling passed the buckets to and fro with greater alacrity even than before.

I occasionally ran up on deck to see how near she was getting. I know my heart bounded when I saw the English flag flying out at her peak. She appeared to be a good-sized merchantman, a ' snow,' and I heard some of the officers who had been looking through their glasses say that she had guns aboard.

On hearing my report when I returned, some of the men burst into tears, others shouted for joy and shook each other by the hand, believing that our deliverance was near.

Night was now coming on. The sea still ran too high to allow of boats laden with men to pass from one vessel to the other. For the same reason it was impossible for the stranger to come near enough to take any of us off. Many would very probably perish in the attempt, even if the snow should escape being hove against us and stove in.

Again I ran up. All those on deck were now stretching out their hands towards her. She came close enough for the voice of her captain—who stood on the poop—to be heard through his speaking-trumpet.

' I'll stay by you during the night,' he shouted. ' The sea is going down. In the morning I'll take you off,—please God.'

The last words reached us as the stranger surged by, close under our lee. She then hove to at a safe distance. Eager eyes were turned towards her before the light altogether faded away, and many looked as if they were tempted to leap overboard and swim to her. Thirsty, hungry, and weary as we were, we would gladly have knocked off baling; but the captain wisely ordered us to keep at it as long as we remained on board.

'You can't tell, my lads, when the bucketful will leak in that will send her to the bottom,' he said, and the men again turned to. He ordered, however, the carpenter to patch up such of the boats as could be made serviceable enough to float even for a short time, so that they might be employed in carrying us aboard the snow. Without the masts the launch could not be got off the deck, but we had three other boats fit to be repaired ; all the others had been completely knocked to pieces. No one slept at all events during that night, for we were all kept spell and spell at the pumps and buckets. The certainty that relief was at hand if we kept afloat, inspired us with renewed strength. When morning dawned the snow came as close as she could venture. Three of her boats approached and pulled towards us. The order was now given for the men to prepare for leaving the ship. Sentries were placed at the gangways to prevent any crowding in till they received the order to go down the side, but this was unnecessary. The few survivors of the sick and wounded were first lowered into the boats, with the surgeons to attend them. The boys and midshipmen were then ordered to go down the side, the names of all being called in succession. As soon as the snow's boats were filled and had pulled away, ours were lowered. Tom Pim and I went, with Larry, in one of them, Nettleship having charge of her. I looked up at the old ship. She seemed to be settling fast. The water came out of the scuppers, showing that, according to the captain's orders, the hands were still at the pumps. There was no hurry, yet all was done rapidly. The moment we shoved off our crew gave way, and we were soon aboard the snow. While Nettleship returned for more men, Tom and I stood watching them anxiously. It seemed even now that before they could escape the ship would go down. Though the sea had much decreased, there was no little danger, while the boats were alongside the *Hector*, of their being swamped. As fast as they could the boats went backwards and forwards, taking their cargoes in through the lower ports. I saw Captain Drury and the first lieutenant pressing Captain

Bouchier to leave the ship, but in spite of his wound he insisted on remaining to the last. Our men, as they arrived, stood watching the ship from the deck of the snow, and gave a cheer as they saw him descending, the last man, into the cutter, for they knew that not a soul was left on board the gallant *Hector*. Scarcely had the captain been helped up the side, than we saw the ship's head begin to sink. Lower and lower it went, then down she plunged, her ensign flying from the spar secured to the stump of her mainmast, streaming upwards, alone showing us the spot where she was sinking into the depths of the ocean. A groan escaped from the breasts of many of those who had long sailed in her. We found that we were on board the *Hawk* snow, a letter-of-marque belonging to Dartmouth, Captain John Hill, and bound from Lisbon to St. John's, Newfoundland. When Captain Bouchier expressed his gratitude to the master for receiving him and his people, the reply was,—

'Don't talk of it, sir; I'm but doing my duty. I would wish to be treated the same way by others.'

Besides his own crew of five-and-twenty men, he had now two hundred of the *Hector's* on board. We had brought neither provisions nor water, and were still many a long league from our port. The *Hawk* had fortunately hitherto had a quick passage. We had, therefore, more provisions and water on board than would otherwise have been the case. Still two hundred mouths in addition was a large number to feed, yet neither the captain nor his ship's company grumbled or made the slightest complaint. To stow us all away was the difficulty. To solve it, the captain at once ordered his men to heave overboard the more bulky portion of his cargo. His owners, he said, would not complain, for he himself was the principal one, and he trusted to the justice of his country to replace his loss. We were, of course, put on an allowance, but after the starvation we had endured, it appeared abundance. Even when the cargo had been got rid of it was unpleasantly close stowing for most of us, but we had great reason to be thankful to Heaven for having escaped with our lives. The officers and crew of the *Hawk* treated us with the greatest kindness; most of our poor fellows, indeed, required help, and were unable to move about the deck by themselves. The wind, however, continued fair, and those who had abundant sleep recovered their spirits. Still several died, worn out by fatigue and sickness. We were safe for the present, and we did not allow ourselves to recollect that another gale might spring up before we could reach St. John's, to which port we were bound, or that contrary winds might keep us from our port, and that, after all, we might perish from hunger and thirst. I was talking of what we should do when we got ashore.

'Wait till we are there, Paddy,' said Nettleship. 'I don't say that we shall not reach it, but we may not. That noble fellow, Hill, knows that such may be the case as well as I do; and I admire his calmness, and the care he takes not to show us that he fears he and his people may suffer the fate from which they rescued our ship's company. You see they are all put on the same allowance that we are, yet not one of them complains.'

I heartily agreed with him. Shortly afterwards I asked Nettleship what he had done with his letter.

'I left it in the cask aboard, Paddy,' he answered. 'So in case we're lost, our friends will know our whereabouts, though they'll not hear of our being rescued, and the chance we have had of escaping; but that won't matter much, though I should like to have made Hill's conduct known.'

Never, perhaps, did seamen watch the weather more anxiously than we did. Our lives, as far as we could see, depended on the winds. Already the stock of provisions and water was getting low, and it was necessary to diminish the allowance of both. Still the crew of the *Hawk* would only receive the same quantity that we did. The sun rose and set, and again rose, and we sailed on. Mr. Hill met us each morning at breakfast, his honest countenance beaming with kindness, and jocularly apologized for the scantiness of the fare. Even he, however, one morning looked grave; the wind had fallen, and we lay becalmed. He had good reason to be grave, for he knew what we did not, that he had only one cask of water left, and provisions scarcely sufficient for a couple of days.

'I have come away without fish-hooks,' he observed. 'If I had had them, gentlemen, I might have given you cod for dinner; and I promise you I'll never be without them again, when I make this voyage.'

'Then I only hope, captain, that you'll take us up again if we happen to have our ship sinking under us,' I said, at which there was a general laugh.

As we had nothing else to do, all hands employed themselves in whistling for a breeze. Just before the sun again rose, a cheering shout was heard from the masthead,—

'Land! land!'

In a short time the rocky coast of Newfoundland rose on the larboard bow, and we stood along to the northward for St. John's harbour, on the east coast. Before evening we were passing through the Narrows, a passage leading to the harbour, with perpendicular precipices rising to a considerable height on either side. Passing under Fort Amhurst, a voice came off hailing,—

'Where are you from? What length of passage?'

The answer announcing, 'We have on board the officers and crew of H.M.S. *Hector*,' evidently caused considerable excitement, and signals were made to a post on the top of a lofty hill on the right side, whence the information was conveyed to the town.

Before we dropped our anchor, the last cask of water was emptied, the last particle of food consumed.

The moment we brought up, the vessel was surrounded by boats, the news of our arrival having preceded us. Before landing, all the officers again expressed their thanks to our gallant preserver, who, I hope, received the reward he so well merited, from our Government, we ourselves being unable to offer him any. None of us, indeed, had more than the clothes we wore, and a few articles we had been able to carry off with us from the wreck.

We were received with the greatest kindness and hospitality by the inhabitants of St John's. Nettleship, Tom, and I were lodged together in the house of a merchant, whose wife and daughters, pitying our condition, did everything they could to restore us to health. Certainly we were very unlike the gay midshipmen we appeared when we sailed from Jamaica. Both the young ladies were very nice girls; but Tom confided to me that his heart had become hard as adamant since Lucy's cruel treatment of him.

'It will soften by and by, Tom,' I answered, laughing, though I could not say that I felt mine inclined to yield to their attractions.

We agreed, however, that Nettleship, as we thought, would knock under. What might have been the case I don't know; but as soon as the men had somewhat recovered from their hardships,—there being no man-o'-war likely to call off the place,—the captain chartered two merchant brigs to convey himself and the survivors of the *Hector* to Halifax, Nova Scotia, whence he expected to get a passage home for us to England. Nettleship, Tom, and I, accompanied by Larry, had to go on board the *Jane*, one of the vessels, of which Captain Drury went in charge; while Captain Bouchier, though still not recovered from his wound, went in the other, the *John Thomas.*

I did not mention it at the time, but Larry had managed to save his fiddle uninjured when he left the *Hector*, and his appearance with it under his arm afforded no small amount of satisfaction to the crew of the *Jane*.

The *John Thomas* proved a much faster sailer than the brig, and soon ran ahead of us. We had just lost sight of Cape Race when a sail was made out, standing towards us from the southward.

'I don't like her looks,' observed Nettleship to me, as she approached. 'I shouldn't be surprised if she proves to be a French privateer.'

The captain appeared to be of this opinion, for, after examining the stranger through his glass, he ordered all the sail we could carry to be set, and stood away right before the wind, to the north-west. The stranger, however, came up with us hand over hand. In a short time the French ensign was seen blowing out at her peak, leaving no doubt as to her character.

'We must not be taken, lads. I trust to you to fight to the last, before we strike our flag,' cried the captain.

The crew cheered, and promised to do their best.

The *Jane* had six nine-pounders, while the enemy carried twice as many guns, evidently of much heavier metal. As a few men only were required to work them, the captain ordered the rest to go under shelter. Tom and I were among those ordered below. In a short time we heard our guns go off, and the shot of the enemy came rattling on board. Presently there came a crash, and we guessed that the privateer had run us alongside.

'On deck, lads!' cried the captain. 'Boarders, repel boarders.'

At the summons we eagerly rushed up through every hatchway, to see a number of Frenchmen swarming on board; but they didn't get far beyond the bulwarks before they were driven back, we in return boarding them. Tom and I led our men into the fore part of the vessel. More and more of our fellows followed. The Frenchmen gave way, some leaped below, others ran aft, where they encountered Nettleship and his party; in less than five minutes the privateer was ours, and Larry, shouting,—

'Wallop-a-hoo-aboo! Erin go bragh!' hauled down her colours.

The enemy had so completely been taken by surprise, that they had offered but a slight resistance, and few, therefore, had lost their lives, while we had only half a dozen wounded. Captain Drury, with two-thirds of our men, went on board the prize, retaining the larger number of our prisoners; while Nettleship, Tom, and I remained in the *Jane*, with orders to follow close astern.

'We must take care, Paddy, that our prisoners don't play us the same trick yours played you,' said Nettleship. 'They would like to try it, no doubt.'

We had thirty prisoners to look after.

'I'll take remarkably good care that they don't do that,' I answered; 'and to make sure, it would be as well to keep them in durance vile till we reach Halifax.'

The Frenchmen grumbled at finding that they were to have their arms lashed behind them, and be kept below under charge of a couple of sentries. They were somewhat more contented when we fed them carefully, and told them that it was because we considered them brave fellows, and felt sure that if they had the opportunity they would take the brig from us, that we were obliged to treat them so unceremoniously. Fortunately the wind held fair, and we had a quick passage to Halifax, where we arrived before the harbour was frozen up. Of course we gained great credit for our last exploit at that favourite naval station.

We found the *Maidstone* frigate just about to sail for England, on board of which all who were well enough were ordered home. We were pretty considerably crowded, but we were a merry set, and had plenty to talk about. The midshipmen of the *Maidstone*, which had been for some time at Halifax, spoke warmly of the kindness they had received, and of the fascinations of the young ladies of the place, except an old mate and an assistant-surgeon, who declared that they had been abominably treated, and jilted by half-a-dozen whose hearts they thought they had won.

Old Grumpus, the master's mate, was especially bitter. 'Look here,' he said, producing a sketch which he had made. 'See these old ladies seated on chairs on the quay, watching their daughters fishing. There are a dozen girls at least, with long rods and hooks, baited with all sorts of odds and ends. And see what sort of fish they're after,— naval officers—marine officers—and of all ranks, from an admiral down to a young midshipman. And there's a stout dame—she can't be called a young lady exactly —casting her hook towards a sturdy boatswain.

'"Look here," one of them cries out, "mother, mother, I've got a bite."

'"Play him, my dear," cries the mother, "till you see what he is."

'"Oh, mother, mother!" she cries out presently, "I've caught a midshipman."

'"Throw him in, my dear, he's no good," answered the old lady.

'Presently another sings out, "Mother, I've got a bite. I'm sure it's from a lieutenant, from the way he pulls."

'"Let him hang on a little, my dear," says the mother; "may be if you see a commander or a post-captain swimming by, you may cast him off, and hook one of the others instead."

'Presently a fourth cries out, "Oh, mother, I've hooked a captain!"

'"Run, Jane, run, and help your sister to land him," cries Mrs. Thingamebob; and just see the way they're doing it, so as not to frighten him, and make him turn tail.

'At last another shouts, "Mother, I've hooked a master's mate."

'"Then go and cut the line, Susan. Don't let Nancy land that brute, on any account. He's the worst of the lot."

'And so it goes on,' exclaimed old Grumpus. 'However, to my mind they're all alike. Why, while we have been there a dozen officers from different ships have been and got spliced. It's lucky for you fellows that you were not there long, or you would have been and done it, and repented it all your lives afterwards.'

During the voyage old Grumpus brought out his sketch a score of times, and repeated his story as often, with numerous variations, which afforded us all much amusement. He had anecdotes of other descriptions without end to tell, most of them hinging on the bad way the junior officers of the service were treated. He didn't say that most of those junior officers were rough diamonds like himself, who would have been much better off if they had not been placed on the quarter-deck.

We had a somewhat long and stormy passage, and were half frozen to death before it was over, most of us who had been for years in the West Indies being little prepared for cold weather. We should have been much worse off, however, in a line-of-battle ship, but in the midshipmen's berth we managed to keep ourselves tolerably warm when below. At length we sighted the coast of Ireland.

'Hurrah, Mr. Terence! There's the old country,' said Larry, throwing up his hat in his excitement, and nearly losing it overboard. 'If the captain would only put into Cork harbour, we would be at home in two or three days, and shure they'd be mighty pleased to see us at Ballinahone. What lashings of whisky, and pigs, and praties they'd be after eating and drinking in our honour, just come home from the wars. Och! I wish we were there, before a blazing turf fire, with the peat piled up, and every one of them red and burning, instead of being out here with these cold winds almost blowing our teeth down our throats.'

The picture Larry drew made me more than ever wish to get home. Not that I was tired of a sea life, though I had found it a pretty hard one in some respects; but I longed to see my father, and mother, and brothers, and sisters again, and my kind uncle the major, as I had not heard from them for many a long day. Letters in those days were conveyed to distant stations very irregularly. I had only received two all the time I had been away. Indeed, friends, knowing the great uncertainty which existed of letters reaching, thought it scarcely worth while to write them. We could just see the land, blue and indistinct, over our larboard bow, when the wind veered to the eastward, and instead of standing for Plymouth, as we expected to do, we were kept knocking about in the Chops of the Channel for three long weeks, till our water was nearly exhausted, and our provisions had run short. There we were, day after day, now standing on one tack, now on another, never gaining an inch of ground. Every morning the same question was put, and the same answer given,—

'Blowing as hard as ever, and right in our teeth.'

We sighted a number of merchant vessels, and occasionally a man-of-war, homeward bound from other stations, but all were as badly off as we were.

At last one morning the look-out at the masthead shouted, 'A sail to the eastward coming down before the wind.' It was just possible she might be an enemy. The drum beat to quarters, and the ship was got ready for action. On getting nearer, however, she showed English colours, and we then made out her number to be that of the *Thetis* frigate. As soon as we got near each other we both hove to. Though there was a good deal of sea running, two of our boats were soon alongside her to obtain water, and some casks of bread and beef, for, as far as we could tell to the contrary, we might be another month knocking about where we were. In the meantime, one of her boats brought a lieutenant on board us.

'Peace has been signed between Great Britain and France,' were almost the first words he uttered when he stepped on deck. 'I can't give particulars, but all I know is, that everything we have been fighting for is to remain much as it was before. We are to give up what we have taken from the French, and the French what they have taken from us, and we are to shake hands and be very good friends. There has been great rejoicing on shore, and bonfires and feasts in honour of the event.'

I can't say that the news produced any amount of satisfaction to those on board the *Maidstone*.

'Then my hope of promotion has gone,' groaned Nettleship; 'and you, Paddy, will have very little chance of getting yours, for which I'm heartily sorry; for after the creditable way in which you have behaved since you came to sea, I fully expected to see you rise in your profession, and be an honour to it.'

'What's the use of talking to sucking babies like Paddy and Tom here about their promotion, in these piping times of peace which are coming on us,' cried old Grumpus, 'if we couldn't get ours while the war was going on?'

CHAPTER XXI.

THE news of peace was received perhaps with more satisfaction by the men who had no promotion to look for, and who now expected to visit their families, or enjoy themselves in spending their prize-money according to their own fashion on shore.

Parting from the *Thetis*, we continued beating backwards and forwards for another week, when the wind shifting suddenly to the southward, we ran up to Plymouth, and at last dropped anchor in Hamoaze. We lived on board till the ship was paid off. In the meantime, I wrote home to say that Larry and I would return as soon as we could manage to get a passage to Cork. Tom Pim was uncertain of the whereabouts of his family, so he also waited till he could hear from them. Nettleship had told us that his mother and sister lived near Plymouth, and he got leave to run over and see them.

'It won't be a good thing for you youngsters to be knocking about this place by yourselves,' he said, on his returning; 'and so, having told my mother this, she has invited both of you, with Larry, to come up and stay with us till you can go home. You'll be much better off than in lodgings, or stopping at an inn, even though you may find it somewhat dull.'

Tom at once accepted the invitation, and persuaded me to do so, though I wanted to see some of the fun of

Plymouth, which my other shipmates had talked about. I won't describe the scenes which took place on board,—the noise and uproar,—the characters of all descriptions who crowded the ship, eager to take possession of the sailors, or rather of the money which lined their pockets. I saw very much the contrary of fun in it. We had then a midshipman's paying-off dinner on shore, to which some of the ward-room officers were invited. The wine flowed freely. Healths were drunk and sentiments given, and in a short time most of the party became very uproarious, those who were sober enough on shore being as bad as the rest.

'Come, Paddy,' said Nettleship, 'we have to get home to my mother's house to-night, and I can't introduce you, remember, if you're not quite yourself.'

Tom Pim was ready.

'So am I,' I said. 'I'll not take another drop.'

Our intended departure being discovered, we were assailed with hoots, and shouts, and groans.

'Never mind them,' said Nettleship. 'If we were to be moved by that sort of stuff, those very fellows would be the first to laugh at us another day.'

On seeing us gaining the door, several jumped up, intending to bring us back.

'Run for it, Paddy; run, Tom,' cried Nettleship. 'I'll guard your retreat. They'll not stop me.'

'Hands off,' he shouted, as Grumpus and some others attempted to seize him. 'I have made up my mind to go, and go I will, though every one in the room were to jump up and try to bar my passage.'

Tom and I got safe into the street, where we were joined by Larry, who had been waiting for us; and Nettleship came up, saying that he had got clear off, at the cost of flooring two or three of his assailants.

'Not a satisfactory way of parting from old friends,' he said, 'but the only one which circumstances would permit.'

We at once set off, walking briskly, to get as soon as

possible away from the scene of our shipmates' revels. We at length reached a pretty little cottage, a short way out of Plymouth, where Mrs. Nettleship and her daughter received us in the kindest manner possible. I was struck by the appearance of the two ladies, so nicely dressed, and quiet in their manners, while the house seemed wonderfully neat and fresh, greatly differing from the appearance of Ballinahone. It was the first time in my life that I had ever been in an English house. When Nettleship talked of his mother's cottage, I had expected to see something like the residence of an Irish squireen. Both inside and out the house was the same,—the garden full of sweetly-scented flowers, the gravel walks without a weed in them, and the hedges carefully trimmed. Then when Tom and I were shown to the room we were to occupy, I was struck by the white dimity hangings to the beds, the fresh curtains and blinds, the little grate polished to perfection, and a bouquet of flowers on the dressing-table. Tom was not so impressed as I was, though he said it reminded him of his own home. Miss Fanny was considerably younger than Nettleship, a fair-haired, blue-eyed, sweetly-smiling, modest-looking girl, who treated Tom and me as if we were her brothers.

Nettleship and Tom accompanied me into Plymouth each morning, that I might learn if any vessel was sailing for Cork, and thus be saved the journey to Bristol, with which place and Ireland, as there was a considerable amount of trade carried on, I was told that I should have no difficulty in obtaining a vessel across. I was so happy where I was, however, that I was less in a hurry than might have been supposed. I had no want of funds for the purpose, for I had received my pay; and a good share of prize-money for the vessels we had captured was also due to me, though, as Nettleship told me, I must not count upon getting that in a hurry.

At last, one morning, on going to a shipbroker, who had promised to let me know of any vessel putting into Plymouth on her way to Cork, he told me that one had just arrived, and would sail again in a few hours. I at once went on board the *Nancy* schooner, and engaged a passage for Larry and myself, and then hurried back to wish Mrs. Nettleship and her daughter good-bye. My old shipmates returned with me, and Larry carried our few traps over his shoulder, as I had not possessed a chest since mine was lost in the *Liffy*.

'Good-bye, Paddy, old fellow,' cried Nettleship. 'If I get appointed to a ship I'll let you know, and you must exert your interest to join her; and I hope Tom also will find his way aboard. We have been four years together without so much as a shadow of a quarrel; and if we were to spend another four years in each other's company, I'm sure it would be the same.'

Tom merely wrung my hand; his heart was too full to speak.

'Good-bye, Mr. Pim,' said Larry, as the schooner's boat was waiting for us at the quay. 'Your honour saved my life, and I would have been after saving yours, if I had had the chance, a dozen times over.'

'You saved it once, at least, Larry, when you helped to get me out of the water as the boat was leaving the *Cerberus*, and I hope that we may be again together, to give you another chance.'

'There's nothing I'd like better. May Heaven's blessing go with your honour,' said Larry, as Tom held out his hand and shook his warmly.

Our friends stood on the shore as we pulled across the Catwater to the schooner, which lay at the entrance. Directly we were on board she got under weigh, and with a fair breeze we stood down Plymouth Sound. She was a terribly slow sailer, and we had a much longer passage to Cork than I had expected. We had no longer any fear of being snapped up by a privateer, but, seeing her style of sailing, I hoped that we should not be caught in a gale on a lee shore. or we should have run a great chance of being wrecked.

Larry made friends with all on board, keeping them alive with his fiddle, which he was excessively proud of having saved through so many and various dangers.

'Shure, I wouldn't change it for all the gold in the *Ville de Paris*, if it could be fished up from the bottom of the say,' he exclaimed, 'for that couldn't cheer up the hearts of my shipmates as my old fiddle can be doing. Won't I be after setting them toeing and heeling it when we get back to Ballinahone!'

At length our eyes were rejoiced by a sight of the entrance to Cork Harbour, and the wind being fair, we at once ran up to Passage, where I engaged a boat to take us to Cork. As we had no luggage except what Larry could carry, and he wouldn't let me lift an article, we proceeded at once to the inn at which my uncle and I had put up.

I was just about to enter through the doorway, when I saw a tall figure standing before me, not older by a wrinkle than when I, a stripling, had last seen him, standing on the quay waving me a farewell; his hat and coat, the curl of his wig, every article of dress, was the same. For a moment he looked at me as if I were a stranger; then, recognising my features, though in height and breadth I was so changed, he stretched out his arms, exclaiming,—

'Terence, my nephew! Is it you, indeed?' and embracing me, his feelings overcame him, and he could say no more for some minutes. 'I came on the chance of meeting you, though I knew not when you would arrive,' he said at length. 'I have been waiting day after day, every hour in expectation of seeing you; but faith, when my eyes first fell on your figure I forgot the change that four years would have produced in you, and took you for a stranger. And you have brought back Larry safe from the wars? Glad to see you, boy. I thought you would be taking care of the young master.'

'Faith, your honour, I should have been mighty grieved at myself if I hadn't done the best I could; and it's a pleasure to hand him back to you, major, without a wound or a scratch, though the round shot and bullets have been flying about pretty quickly round him; and we've escaped from fire and hurricane, and shipwrecks and earthquakes, and a mighty lot of other things besides.'

'And you, uncle, don't look a day older than when I went away,' I said.

'You must not trust too much to appearances, Terence,' he answered, shaking his head. 'The enemy has been sapping the foundations, though he has not as yet taken the fortress. I have a good many things to try me. Matters at home are not in a satisfactory state.'

'It was about them all I was going to ask, uncle,' I said. 'How are my father and mother, the girls and the boys?'

'Your mother is not so strong as she was, though she bears up bravely; but your poor father has greatly changed. Though he has given up his claret, he still sticks to his potations of rum shrub and whisky punch, which are rapidly bringing him to his grave, though he won't believe it. Kathleen and Nora are married; Kathleen to Eustace Fitzgerald, and Nora to Tim Daley. I would rather they had found steadier husbands, but they'll bring the boys into order, I hope, in time. Your brother Maurice got his commission soon after you left home, and, having seen some service in America, has lately returned home on leave. I was in hopes that he would have fallen in with you. Denis stops at home to help me mind the house and keep things in order. The rest have grown into strapping lads, and it's time to be sending them out into the world to seek their fortunes. The Fitzgeralds and the Daleys are staying at the Castle, and they'll be mightily pleased to see you. We will start to-morrow morning at daylight. I brought horses for you and Larry, with Tim Sweeney to look after them, for I suppose that Larry will scarcely know the head from the tail of one by this time.'

'Och, your honour, I'll soon be after remembering which is which when I see the bastes again, though I haven't crossed a horse's back since I left,' said Larry, in answer to my uncle's remark.

'I'll trust you for that, my lad,' said the major; 'and now, Terence, we will go in and order supper, and while it's coming, you shall give me an account of your adventures.'

I was soon seated before the fire, briefly describing what I had gone through, in as clear a way as I could. My uncle was deeply interested, and constantly stopped me to put questions, when he did not clearly understand my descriptions. Even when we were at supper he made me talk on, appearing scarcely to think about what he was eating, so eager was he to listen to me. He was much struck on hearing of Dan Hoolan's fate.

'I can't say the country is much the quieter, for unfortunately there are too many boys of the same character to take his place,' he remarked, 'but I hope we shall reach Ballinahone without meeting any of them.'

At last, seeing that I was getting sleepy, he advised me to turn in, to be ready to start in the morning.

Larry in the meantime had been well taken care of by Tim Sweeney,—indeed, too much taken care of; for when he came into my room to see if I wanted anything, he stood balancing himself with difficulty, and talking away, until I was obliged to turn him out and bid him go to bed as fast as he could.

The next morning we were on the road, the major sitting his horse as firmly as ever; and indeed, except that we were going in an opposite direction, I might have fancied, until I looked at Larry and felt the change that had come over myself, that we were but continuing our journey of four years back.

Having plenty to talk about, I rode alongside my uncle, Larry and Tim following us, the latter listening with eager ears to the wonderful accounts Larry was giving him. We pushed on as fast as our horses would carry us, but as the roads were none of the best, our progress was much slower than I liked.

The afternoon of the second day my uncle proposed that, instead of stopping at the village through which we were then passing, we should push on to a little roadside inn, that we might be so much the further on our way next morning. It was almost dark when we arrived, but the landlord, Pat Casey, who knew my uncle well, received us warmly, promising to give us all the accommodation we could desire, and a supper and breakfast not to be despised. Pat at once fulfilled his promise by placing some rashers of bacon and fresh eggs, and actually a white loaf, which with several others he said he had received that morning, on the table.

'I would be after having some tay for breakfast, but I wouldn't dream of giving it to your honours for supper,' he said, as he placed instead on the table a bottle of the cratur, from which, he observed with a wink, the revenue had not in any way benefited, while a bowl of smoking hot potatoes formed the chief dish of the feast. I remember doing good justice to it, and was not sorry when my uncle proposed that we should retire to our downy couches. Unpretending as was the outside of the inn, they were far superior to what I should have expected; mine was a feather bed to which many hundreds of geese must have contributed, while the curtains were of silk, faded and patched, to be sure, but showing that they had come from some grand mansion. I slept like a top, till my uncle roused me up in the morning with the announcement that breakfast was nearly ready. To that I was prepared to do more ample justice than I did to the supper.

'Come, Terence, let us take our seats,' said my uncle. 'Biddy has just placed the things on the table, and they will be getting cold.'

The breakfast looked tempting. There was a pile of buttered toast, plenty of new-laid eggs, a beautiful griskin broiled to perfection, and water boiling on the hot turf fire in a saucepan. The teapot having taken to leaking, as Biddy said, she had made the tea in the potheen jug.

I was just about to follow my uncle's example, when there came a rap at the outside door of the paved parlour in which we were sitting.

'Come in,' said my uncle.

No one answered.

'Go and see who it is, Terence; maybe it's some modest fellow who doesn't like to open the door.'

No sooner had I lifted the latch than I felt a heavy shove. The door flew open, and before I could get out of the way, in rushed a huge sow, knocking me over in a moment; and while I was kicking my heels in the air, over my body came nearly a dozen young pigs, their amiable mother making her way round the room, grunting, snorting, and catching the air through her enormous proboscis.

'Jump up, Terence! jump up, or she'll be at you!' said my uncle, coming to my assistance; but the sow was too rapid in her movements, and, ere he could reach me, charged furiously at his legs. Fortunately he escaped her by springing with wonderful agility out of her way, and, mounting on a chair, got up on the top of a chest of drawers, which formed a convenient place of retreat. In the meantime I got on my legs, and, seeing the savage sow was inclined to attack me, I sprang on to the chest of drawers, the only safe place I could discover. Here we sat, regularly besieged, for our weapons of offence and defence had been left on the table. The sow, seeming to know the advantage she had gained, kept eyeing us savagely. Indeed, unless we had thought it worth while to run the risk of an attack from her, we saw that we must make up our minds to remain where we were. The louder we shouted for help, the more enraged the sow became, thirsting, as we had reason to believe, for our blood. She was the lankiest, the tallest, and grisliest beast I ever saw; her back, arching higher than a donkey's, resembled a rustic bridge; her loose-flapping ears nearly hid her small sunken, fiery eyes, their ends just covering one half of her mouth, which divided her head, as it were, into an upper and under storey, clearly showing that she had the means of taking a huge bite out of our legs, could she get at them. Her tusks, like those of a boar, projected from under her nostrils, and the ring and hook in her nose was a formidable weapon of offence, though intended to prevent her from digging up the ground. Her promising family were not little pigs, but had nearly attained the age when they would be turned out to shift for themselves, regular hobbledehoys of swinehood.

After rampaging round the room, sniffing the air, and vainly attempting to get at us, the sow ran under the table, which she unceremoniously upset, when, with a peculiar grunt summoning her progeny to the feast, she and they immediately commenced gobbling up our viands. Seeing this, I jumped down, intending to drive her away, but scarcely had I reached the ground when she made so savage a rush at me that I was glad to regain my former position.

'This is too bad,' cried the major; and, slipping off the drawers, he seized a chair, with the intention of belabouring our assailant, when just at that moment one of the young pigs, of an inquisitive disposition, hearing the bubbling water on the fire, attempting to look into the pot, brought the scalding contents down upon itself. On feeling its tender bristles getting loose, it set up the most terrific cries, louder even than the most obstinate of its race when the butcher is making preparations for manufacturing it into corned pork. The sow, attributing the cries of her darling to some torture inflicted by us, rushed to the drawers, making several savage attempts to rear up against them so that she could seize us by the legs. Every moment we expected to be caught hold of by the hook in her nose, when we should have inevitably been brought down. In vain we kicked and stamped at her to drive her off, while we shouted loudly for assistance.

As it turned out, Larry and Tim were in the stables attending to the horses, while the landlord and his family, having performed, as they supposed, all their required duties in attending on us, had gone to the potato garden. Not for some minutes did Pat hear our voices, and then in he rushed, with astonishment depicted on his countenance. Seizing a stick, he began belabouring the sow, bestowing on her epithets numberless and profuse.

'Och! the curse of Crummell light on you for a greedy old sow as ye are,' he exclaimed, whacking away at the creature, who didn't care for his blows, though she dared not attack him. At length Tim and Larry came in, and, seizing the sow by the tail, attempted to drag her out; she, supposing that they wanted her to go into the room, in the usual swinish spirit of contradiction turned to snap at their legs, and, followed by her hopeful progeny, bolted out of the door. My uncle and I burst into fits of laughter, though in reality it was no laughing business as far as our breakfast was concerned. Pat expressed his fear that there was not another morsel of food in the house; however, Biddy and her assistant, coming in from the potato garden, soon set matters to rights, and put some water on to boil, hunted up some fresh eggs, and produced another loaf. We were too hungry to let them toast and butter it, however. We made a very good breakfast after all, our appetites being sharpened by the exercise of our lungs, not to speak of the alarm we had been in. The occurrence delayed our departure till a later hour than we intended, and we pushed on to try and make up for lost time.

I confess that I occasionally looked round, half expecting to see some of Dan Hoolan's successors come out from behind the rocks or bushes, and demand our valuables; but if any were lying in wait in the neighbourhood, they probably thought four well-armed men too formidable to be assailed, and we proceeded towards our journey's end without molestation. I had at first felt a sort of callousness about reaching home, and should have been indifferent had any delay occurred; but as I approached Castle Ballinahone I became more and more eager to be there, and could scarcely restrain my feelings when I saw the towers rising beyond the trees in the distance, and the

Shannon shining brightly in the rays of the setting sun. My uncle and I gave our horses the rein, and our two attendants clattered after us. The gate of the park was open, and as we dashed up the avenue at full speed, the sounds of our horses' hoofs attracted the attention of the inmates of the castle. The door was thrown open, and my mother and sisters, and Maurice and Denis and my two brothers-in-law, appeared on the steps, down which the younger boys came springing towards us; while from the servants' wing out rushed a whole posse of men and girls and dogs,—tumbling over each other, the dogs barking, the girls shrieking, and the men shouting with delight, as they surrounded Larry, and half pulled him off his horse. Dismounting, I sprang up the steps into my mother's arms, where she held me for some time before she was willing to let me go. I received a similar welcome from my sisters. 'You see I have brought him back safe after all,' said the major, benignantly smiling. My hands were next seized by my brothers and brothers-in-law, who wrung their fingers after receiving the grips which I unconsciously bestowed upon them.

'And my father?' I asked, not seeing him.

'He is in the parlour,' answered my mother in an altered tone; and she led me in. He was seated in his wheel-chair, a look of dull imbecility on his countenance.

'What! are you Terence?' he asked in a quavering tone. 'Come back from the wars, eh? I suppose you are Terence, though I shouldn't have known you. We will drink your health, though, at supper in whisky punch, if he'll let me have it, for we can't afford claret now,—at least so he says, and he knows better than I do.'

I was much pained, but tried to conceal my feelings from my mother, though my father's changed appearance haunted me, and prevented me from being as happy as otherwise would have been the case. His state had been that of many of his neighbours, whom he was fond of boasting he had seen under the sod,—once fine intelligent men, who

might have lived out their natural course of years in health
and happiness, with everything to make their lives pleasant,
had it not been for the drinking habits so general among
their class.   After the greetings with my family were over,
I went into the servants' hall to have a talk with the old
domestics.   Larry was in the height of his glory, just getting
out his fiddle to give them a tune in honour of our return.
They all crowded round me, each eager to grasp my hand,
and congratulate me on having escaped the dangers of the
wars.   I felt myself more of a hero than I had ever done
before.   The moment I retired I heard Larry's fiddle going,
and the boys and girls beginning to make use of their feet,
for it was impossible to keep them quiet while such notes
sounded in their ears.   After a visit to my chamber, which
had long been prepared for me, accompanied by Denis, who
wanted to hear all I had got to tell him, I returned to the
drawing-room.   I there found the family assembled, fully as
anxious as my brother to have a narrative of my adventures.
My mother, taking my hand, which she held in hers, led me
to the sofa, and fondly looked in my face as I described the
battles I had been engaged in and the shipwrecks I had
encountered.   My uncle nodded approvingly as I described
the actions in which I had taken a prominent part.   My poor
father, who had been wheeled into the room, stared with lack-
lustre eyes, evidently only comprehending a portion of what
I said.   The rest of the family occasionally uttered exclamations of surprise and astonishment, now and then putting
questions to help me along, when I stopped for want of
breath or to recollect myself.   I had never in my life
talked so much at a stretch.

At last we went in to supper.   My poor father, lifting his
glass with trembling hands to his lips, drank my health.   My
brothers-in-law, Maurice and Denis, followed his example.
The major kindly nodded.

'You have done well, Terence, and I'm proud of you,' he
exclaimed; 'and though the war is over, I hope you'll still
find means to climb up the rattlings, as you say at sea.'

Several neighbours looked in, hearing of my arrival, to congratulate me and my family. The whisky toddy flowed fast. I as usual drank but little; in truth, I had no taste for the stuff, though probably it would have grown upon me, as it does upon others.

My uncle looked at me approvingly. 'I'm glad to see, Terence,' he said, 'that you possess one of the qualities of a good officer, and that even when off duty you retain the habit of sobriety.'

My brothers-in-law glanced at each other and laughed, but took care that the major should not observe them. The guests took no notice of my uncle's remark, evidently intending to make the whisky punch flow freely, the great object for which they had come. Toasts and sentiments, according to the fashion of the day, were given. My father tried to sing one of his old songs, but soon broke down. Several of the other gentlemen, however, took up his stave, and soon began to be uproarious. My mother on this got up, and beckoned to my sisters to follow her. They whispered to their husbands, who, however, only nodded and laughed. My uncle's object was rather to guide than to suppress the hilarity, and when he observed anything like a dispute arising, he put in a word or two nipping it in the bud, in a calm, determined way, to soothe irritated feelings. In a short time Dan Bourke came in, and, putting his hands on the back of my father's chair, said, 'By your leave, gentlemen, I'm come to wheel the master away;' and without more ado, though my poor father stretched out his hand trying to grasp his glass, before he could reach it he was at a distance from the table. It was a melancholy spectacle, and I almost burst into tears as I saw him moving his arms like a child, and trying to kick out with his gouty feet. As Dan wheeled him round towards the door, he shouted and cried, 'Just let me have one glass more, Dan, only one; that can't be after doing me harm.'

One of the guests exclaimed, 'Can't you be leaving the

master alone, and let him have a glass to comfort his soul? Just one glass can make no matter of difference.'

But Dan was obdurate, and, looking over his shoulder, he said, 'It's the orders of the mistress, and they're to be obeyed.'

Had the major's eye not been upon him, I don't know how Dan would have behaved, but without another word he wheeled my poor father out of the room, and closed the door behind him. It was almost the last time he appeared at table. His state made a deep and lasting impression on me.

As soon as he was gone, the guests went on talking and singing as before, and would probably have kept up their revels till a late hour, had not my uncle reminded them that he and I had just come off a long journey.

'As I've been playing the part of host, I can't be so rude as to leave you at table, gentlemen.'

The hint, as he intended it to be, was too broad not to be taken, and those whose brains had still some sense left in them rose to take their departure, hoisting the others in a friendly way out of their seats, when arm-in-arm they staggered to the door.

'The ladies have retired, so you need not stop to pay your farewell respects to them,' said my uncle; and he told Dan Bourke, who was in the hall, to order the gossoons to bring round the gentlemen's horses. Some mounted without difficulty, but others had to be helped up on their steeds by my brothers-in-law and Denis. I thought they would have tumbled off.

'They'll be all to rights when once in their saddles,' said Denis. 'They're accustomed to ride home in that state. To be shure, one of them now and then dislocates his neck or breaks his head, but that's a trifle. It's too common a way for an Irish gentleman to end his mortal career for anything to be thought of it.'

'I hope, Denis, that you'll not be after following their example,' I remarked.

'Faith, the major keeps me in too strict order for that at present,' he said; 'I don't know what I should do if I hadn't his eye upon me, but I'll acknowledge I have no wish to become a brute beast, as some of them are.'

My first day at home was over. I felt less happy than I had expected. My father's melancholy condition,—my mother's sorrow, which she in vain tried to conceal,—and the fallen fortunes of the family, damped my spirits. My brothers-in-law were fine young fellows, but not altogether what I liked; and my sisters were graver than they used to be. Everything about the house looked in a dilapidated condition. My mother and sisters wore old dresses; the furniture was faded; the servants, if not ragged, were but poorly habited. Had it not been for the major, the family, I suspect, would long ere this have been turned out of house and home. I must not spend much time in describing my life at Castle Ballinahone. I soon got tired of it, and began to wish myself at sea again, for I knew that my only chance of promotion was to keep afloat. I told the major. He said that he perfectly agreed with me, and that he would at once write to Captain Macnamara, who was in London, and to two or three other friends, and ask them to try and get me appointed to a ship without delay. After I had been at home a few days, Fitzgerald and Daley invited me to accompany them to the fair at Mullyspeleen, where they wished to dispose of some horses they had bred on my father's property. Larry begged that he might come, just to see the fun. I observed, as he mounted, that he had strapped his fiddle-case on his back. My journey had made me as much at home as ever on horseback, so that I was enabled to keep up with my brothers. The distance we had to go was about fifteen miles, through beautiful country, with a range of hills in the distance, below which is situated the old castle of Tullinhoe, once the seat of a powerful family, many of the descendants of whom were now probably selling pigs at the fair. We met people wending their way towards the place of meeting, some on foot,

20

some on horseback, others in cars and carts of primitive construction, all grinning and shouting in high glee at the thoughts of the fun to be enjoyed. What that fun was we were soon to witness. Not only were there men, but women and children, down to small babies in arms,—the men with frieze coats, with shillelahs in hands, the women in cloaks and hoods, and caps under them. Others had gaily-coloured handkerchiefs tied over their heads. As we got near the fair the crowd increased, till we sometimes had a difficulty in making our way among the people. As we pushed them aside, however, they were in no way offended, but good-humouredly saluted us with jokes of all sorts. There were tents and booths of various descriptions, the most common among them being formed of wattles,— that is, young saplings cut from some neighbouring estate, the thick ends stuck in the ground some distance apart, and the thin ends bent down till they met, when they were fastened together with haybands. Some twenty or thirty of such arches having been formed, and, further secured by a long pole at the top, were covered over with blankets, sheets, and quilts, borrowed from the nearest cottages, occasionally eked out with petticoats and cloaks of varied hue; the quilts, being of every variety of pattern, and of all the colours of the rainbow, had a very gay appearance. The tables were composed of doors carried off from farm buildings and cottages, elevated on hillocks of clay dug from underneath. The benches on either side generally consisted of doors cut longitudinally in two or three parts, and to be nailed together again when done with. Outside several of the tents were huge turf fires, on which pots were boiling, some containing lumps of salt beef and cabbage, while fried herrings were sending up a fragrant odour attractive to hungry visitors. There were cold viands also displayed, to tempt those disposed for a snack, rounds or rumps of beef, hams, bread and cheese, and whisky enough to make every soul in the fair moderately drunk if equally divided. Here and there were booths containing toys and trinkets; but the great object of the fair was for the sale of horses, cows, pigs, and poultry. Besides these were the more pretentious booths of the frieze merchants, who were likely to run a good trade to supply the place of the garments which would be torn into shreds before the fair was over. In other booths, earthenware, knives, and agricultural implements were to be procured. My brothers-in-law having disposed of their horses at a good price,—especially good to them, as the animals had cost them nothing since they were foals,—we agreed to ride round the fair and see the fun, which had now been going on for some time, while, as the eating and drinking booths had been constantly filled and emptied, a large portion of the visitors were already in a hilarious condition. We were passing a booth, when a man came out, who, taking off his long frieze coat, which he trailed along behind him on the ground, at the same time flourishing his shillelah, shouted out,—

'Who'd be after daring to put a foot on that, I should like to know?'

He hadn't gone far, when from another tent out sprang a stout fellow, holding a cudgel big enough to fell an ox with. Rapidly whirling it in the air, he exclaimed,—

'That's what I'll dare to do!' and he made a fierce blow at the head of the owner of the coat, which would have felled him in a moment, had he not been prepared to defend himself with his shillelah. A clatter of blows succeeded, when the owner of the coat fell, stunned, to the ground.

At the same instant numbers of fellows in frieze coats, brogues, and battered hats, rushed forth from the various tents, flourishing their shillelahs, and shouting at the tops of their voices, some siding with the fallen man, others with the victor, till a hundred or more were ranged on either side, all battering away, as fast as they could move their arms, at each other's heads. Now one party would scamper off as if in flight; then they would meet again, and begin cudgelling each other, apparently with the most savage fury, while the women and children stood around, the latter forming a squalling orchestra, which kept time to the blows. When matters were becoming serious, a number of the women, handing their babies to their companions, sprang into the fight, shrieking out, 'Come out o' that, Pat!' 'Come out o' that, Tim!' and dragged their husbands, or sons, or lovers, away from each other.

The men mostly, however, endeavoured to release themselves by leaving their coats in the women's hands, exclaiming,—

'Let me get at them, Biddy. I'll not be held back!'

The women succeeded in dragging but a very few out of the fray, and again the combatants went at it, till one after the other was stretched on the ground.

At length a priest arrived, and exhorted those who were of his flock to desist; and, rushing in among them, where words were ineffectual, dealt them pretty hard blows with his own cudgel. I was inclined to go and assist his reverence, but Fitzgerald advised me to do nothing of the sort.

'They treat him with some sort of respect,' he observed, 'but they would treat you with none, and a broken head would be the consequence.'

The tumult and uproar had made our horses restive; and as a party of the combatants, with loud shrieks and clashing of shillelahs, came rushing against mine, he began to kick and plunge, and at length bolted with me, scattering the people in his course right and left.

Shouts and imprecations followed me, but though I pulled at the rein with all my might, I could not stop him. On he went, upsetting a booth of crockery and scattering the contents; he dashed in among a herd of pigs, which scampered off in all directions; when finally, attempting to leap over a tent in our course, he went through one side of it, pitching me before him, and down he came on to the middle of the table, with his hind legs under the bench, and very nearly on the top of me.

I scrambled out of the way, bruised and scratched, receiving no very friendly greeting from the owner of the booth. Larry, who had seen what was going on, followed, and assisted to extricate my steed as well as me.

Its knees were cut and hind legs sprained, and I felt as if every bone in my body was broken, though I managed to get on my feet, and, giving myself a shake, had the satisfaction of discovering that nothing of the sort had occurred.

My brothers-in-law, coming up, paid the men for the damage done to the crockery booth and the tent my steed had upset, out of the proceeds of their sale; and I, to show that I was not daunted, remounted my horse.

'Have you sufficiently enjoyed the humours of the fair, Terence?' asked Fitzgerald.

'Faith, indeed I have, and sufficient to last me a mighty long time,' I answered.

In one place there were a dozen fellows piled up, one upon another, struggling and kicking, with their heads cut and their noses bleeding; but few of them had lost their voices, and not one of them was mortally wounded.

I had charged Larry not to join in any of the fights; and though he confessed that he had been sorely tempted, he had become too well disciplined at sea to disobey me. He came out of the fair, therefore, with a whole skin, having employed himself for a good portion of the time in amusing the boys and girls with some tunes on his fiddle. I took care to see him clear of the fair, and free from danger, before we put our horses into a trot.

The whole scene gave me some idea of the state of my native country, to become still more unhappy before many more years were over, owing to the misguiding of hot-headed men, and the cruel treatment of a Government whose only notion of ruling was by stern suppression and terrorism.

We rode too fast to allow of Larry playing his fiddle, so he was obliged to put it in its case, and trot after us.

I felt dreadfully stiff for several days after this ad·
venture, and but little inclined to ride, though I managed
to walk about.

Denis begged me to go with him to fish in a stream
which ran into the Shannon three or four miles from the
house. I agreed, for the sake of having his society,
although no adept in the art of throwing a fly. Larry
acccompanied us, to carry our baskets, and the fish we
intended to bring home. We started later in the day
than we had intended, so that the best part of it had
gone by before we could reach the stream.

I was more successful than I had expected, and succeeded
in hooking and landing a brace of tolerably-sized salmon,
—Denis having caught twice as many. This encouraged
us to go on, and the shades of evening had already begun
to spread over the beautiful landscape before we thought
of giving in. At length Larry came up to me.

'I wouldn't be after wishing to frighten you, Mr.
Terence,' he said in a whisper, 'but I have just now
seen something I don't like.'

'What is it, Larry?' I asked. 'Is it in human shape, or
with four legs, a couple of horns, and a tail?'

'Don't be laughing at it, Mr. Terence. I'm thinking
you don't know where we are, or you wouldn't be after
doing that,' he whispered.

'We are fishing in the stream of Corregan,' I said.

'But does your honour know what happened here?' he
asked, in a low voice. 'It's his ghost I've seen, as sure as
I'm a living man, just behind yon clump of trees there
hanging over the water; and I'm thinking he'll be showing
himself again if we stop here longer.'

'I shall be very happy to make his acquaintance, whoever
he is,' I said. 'Does Mr. Denis know anything about
him?'

'Master Denis would be only laughing at me if I were
to speak to him about it,' said Larry.

I called to Denis, and said that I was ready to put up my

rod, as I wished to make the acquaintance of a suspicious individual who was said to be lurking about the stream. He replied that he would be ready to come as soon as he had landed a salmon he had lately hooked.

'Come, Larry, tell me all about this ghost, or spirit, or whatever it was, you fancy you saw just now,' I said, while engaged in winding up my line.

'Hish! your honour; we mustn't speak loud about him, if you plaise, and I'll tell you,' he answered. 'It's just this, your honour: while we were away in foreign parts, there was a broth of a boy,—I knew him well,—Dominic Brian. Well, Nick w··· one evening going home from reaping, along this very part of the stream, when what did he do but cut his own head off. Why he did it no one to this day can tell; but certain sure his body was found on the bank, with his bloody scythe beside him, but his head was gone. They say he comes every evening at the same hour to look out for his head, since he doesn't rest quiet in his grave without it. When they told me about it I laughed, thinking it couldn't be true; but seeing's believing, and as sure as I'm a living man, I saw Dominic Brian this very evening with his head under his arm.'

'I thought you said that he always came to look for his head?' I observed.

'Shure so I did, Mr. Terence; but the ghost I saw had his head tucked under his arm, just as if it had been a keg of potheen.'

'Whether he has his head under his arm or has got it on at all, I'll rout him out,' I exclaimed.

'Oh, don't, Mr. Terence, don't!' cried Larry. 'No one can tell what he'll be after doing to you. Shure it will be safer for us to be away from this as fast as our legs can carry us. Just shout to Master Denis to make haste, or we don't know what will be happening.'

CHAPTER XXII.

A GHOST AND A WEDDING.

LAUGHING at Larry's fears, I, having just finished winding up my line and disconnecting my rod, bade him take up the fish, while I walked towards the clump of trees where he had seen the headless ghost.

I didn't feel altogether sure that something would not appear. I had not gone many paces before I caught sight of a white object. Larry saw it also, and my gallant follower, who would have tackled a dozen Frenchmen with a cutlass in his hand, fairly turned tail and scampered away, shouting out,—

'The ghost! the ghost! It's Nick Brian himself, barring his head. Run, Mr. Terence! Run, Mr. Denis! or he'll be taking hold of us, and carrying us off into the river to help him to look for it.'

In spite of Larry's shouts, I still went on, although not feeling over comfortable, when, as I got nearer, out flew, with a loud hiss, a large white swan, whose nest was probably thereabouts. Though I might have defended myself with the end of my rod, I thought it prudent to beat a retreat and leave her in quiet possession of the locality. On seeing this she also returned to her nest. When I overtook Larry,—who, finding that I was not following him, had halted,—I assured him that the ghost was only a swan. He, however, still remained incredulous, declaring that it might have appeared like a swan to me in the gloom of the evening, but he felt sure it was Nick Brian, and no one else. In vain I endeavoured to induce him to return with me.

'I'd rather not, Mr. Terence, if it's the same to you,' he answered. 'It's not wise to be hunting up them sorts of things.'

Denis now joined us, and though he laughed at the idea of a ghost, he remarked that it would be as well, while there was sufficient light to see our way, to commence our return home, which, as it was, we should not reach till long after dark. I saw Larry every now and then turning his head round, evidently expecting that Nick Brian the headless would be following us.

We got home without any other adventure, where Larry gave a full account of our encounter with Nick Brian's ghost, and the gallant way in which Mr. Terence had faced him, though he was not ashamed to confess that he had not backed me up as he should have done, had I been attacked by a human foe.

Though Denis had not seen the ghost, and I assured every one that it was only a white swan, I found that Larry's account was believed in preference to mine; the general opinion being that I fancied I had seen the bird, though it was a ghost notwithstanding.

To do honour to my return, and to keep up the dignity of the family, my mother and sisters considered it necessary to give a ball to the neighbours, and invitations were issued accordingly. The major was rather against the matter, on the score of expense, but he didn't hold out as stoutly as usual. The preparations, however, were not on a very extensive scale. Such flags and banners as were to be found in the castle—many of them tattered and torn—were arranged so as to decorate the entrance hall. The furniture was carried out of the dining-room—the largest room in the house—and piled up in the dingy study. Supper-tables were placed on one side of the hall; and my mother and sisters, and all the females in the establishment, were engaged for some days in manufacturing pasties, tarts, and jellies; while at the same time sundry pieces of beef, ham, turkeys, and poultry were boiling and roasting at the kitchen fire.

At the usual hour the guests began to arrive,—some in family coaches, once covered with paint and gilt, but now battered and dingy; others came in cars and gigs, and a considerable number of the fair sex on horseback, having sent their ball dresses on before, by the invitation of my sisters, who had promised their assistance in bedecking them. My father complained that he was hurried away from the dinner-table that due time might be obtained for making the necessary preparations. He was left in his chair in the corner of the room, whence he watched the proceedings with an expression which showed that he could not make out exactly what was being done. I went up to him several times and tried to make him understand.

At last the O'Maleys, the O'Flahertys, the Frenches, the Fitzgeralds, the Burkes, the Geraldines, and the members of numerous other families began to arrive, and Larry, habited in a sky-blue coat, a huge frill to his shirt, pink breeches and green stockings, with four or five other musicians, similarly attired, playing various instruments, took their places on a raised platform which served as an orchestra.

A country dance was speedily formed, the couples stand-ing opposite each other, reaching from the top to the bottom of the room, and I had the honour of leading out Miss Nora O'Flaherty, who was considered one of the beauties of the county, though in many respects I doubt whether Tom Pim would have looked upon her with the same eyes as he had done on Lucy Talboys. Taking my partner, I led her prancing down the centre, and proud enough I felt as I heard the remarks made upon us. Then we had to come back and turn each couple, and so on in succession till we reached the bottom. It was pretty hard

work, though my fair partner seemed to enjoy it amazingly.
Of course, as was the custom of those days, I could not
take another partner, and I had every reason to congratulate
myself on having obtained so good a one. I suspect that
many envied me. I was naturally over head and ears in
love with her before the evening was over. There was
very little rest between the dances. As soon as one was
over another was started, the musicians playing away with
might and main. We got through a few minuets, but
such dances were too tame for my fair countrywomen;
indeed, but few of the men were able to perform them,
whereas all took to the country dances as if by instinct.

While we younger ones were thus amusing ourselves,
the older people passed the time playing cards, and afterwards did ample justice to the supper. Indeed, very few
of the young ladies were very backward at that. Even
Nora managed to discuss the wing and breast of a chicken,
with ham and a slice of beef, not to speak of tartlets
and other delicacies, without the slightest difficulty.

I saw her to her family coach, which conveyed her
mamma, two sisters, and a he cousin besides, of whom
I felt prodigiously jealous. I could think of nothing and
talk of nobody but Nora O'Flaherty all the next day, and
proposed riding over to pay my respects to the family.

'You'll do nothing of the sort, Terence!' said my uncle.
'I should be the first to say "Go," if I thought it would
add to your happiness; but, to the best of my belief, the
young lady is engaged to her cousin; and even supposing
that she cared for you, and would consent to wait till you
became a post-captain, you would then only have your
pay, and she has not a stiver in the world, and you would
thus be doing her a great injustice. Talk of her as you
like, think of her as a perfect angel; but angels don't
make good wives down here on earth, whatever they might
do in ethereal regions.'

In fine, my uncle talked and laughed me out of my
first love. Instead of going over to Castle Moirty, I em-

ployed myself in fishing, shooting, and other rural sports with my brothers and my brothers-in-law, and occasionally with the major. This sort of life, however, didn't suit my taste, and I began to wish myself once more afloat.

Among the young ladies present at the ball given in honour of my return was a Miss Kathleen O'Brien, to whom I observed my brother Maurice paid the most devoted attention, and I guessed, as I afterwards discovered, that he was over head and ears in love with her. It was not a matter of surprise, considering that she was among the prettiest of the very pretty girls present. As she was an only daughter, and heiress of a very fine estate, my family were highly delighted at the prospect of his winning her; and as he was supposed to be crowned with laurels, had a couple of honourable wounds in his arms, and our family was equal to hers, it was hoped that no impediment would be thrown in the way of their marriage, provided the young lady would accept him. Young ladies in those days in Ireland had a free will of their own, and Maurice acknowledged that he was not certain what way he had made in her affections. My mother and sisters, however, encouraged him, and, considering that there was no young man like him in that part of the country, assured him that he had no cause to fear. Thus it appeared to me that the battle was half won, and I had no doubt, when he set out the next morning, attired in his red military suit, to pay his respects at Castle Blatherbrook, that he would return back an accepted lover. We cheered him as he set forth.

'Good luck go with you,' cried Denis. 'We will welcome you as an intended Benedict when you come back again. Kathleen's tender heart will never stand that gay coat and clashing sword. Talk of your laurels, Maurice, and tell her how beautiful she will look with a wreath of orange-blossoms across that fair brow of hers.'

Maurice, a good-natured fellow, took all our jokes in good humour, and, waving his hand as he put spurs to his steed, galloped off; while Denis and I went to amuse ourselves with our fishing rods, in hopes of obtaining some variety to our usual fare. On our return we found that Maurice had not come back from his wooing. This was considered a good sign, as it was hoped that he was detained at the castle as an accepted suitor. Our own meal was over, and evening was approaching; still Maurice did not appear. My mother and sisters were very positive that he had won the lady. At length, just as it grew dark, his horse's hoofs were heard clattering up the avenue.

'You must not be disappointed,' said the major, as we were all rushing out to welcome him. 'Girls are not always to be won by once asking.'

Maurice threw his rein to Larry, who had taken up his old office of groom, with what we thought a disconsolate air.

'Well, my dear boy, has she accepted you?'

'Yes, I'm sure she has. She could not have said no,' exclaimed my mother, taking him by the hand.

'Faith, then, she has,' cried Maurice, 'and I ought to be, and fancy I am, the happiest man under the sun. But I am to quit the army, and turn my sword into a ploughshare, and gather oats instead of laurels; and I am not quite certain how I shall take to that sort of life.'

We all congratulated him on his good fortune, and assured him that he would soon get accustomed to a domestic state of existence.

After this I had very little of his society, as he rode off every morning to Blatherbrook. He used to look bright and happy enough when he came back, and Denis and I agreed that he was by degrees getting accustomed to the thoughts of his expected change of life. This was very good fun for Maurice, but I began to find it rather dull, and even to wish myself afloat again. However, I wanted to wait for the wedding, which, to my great satisfaction, I found was fixed for an early day. I managed to spend the intermediate time much as before,—fishing or sailing and shooting on the Shannon, with Larry as crew and old Mike O'Hagan as pilot, when we explored not only the banks of the beautiful river, but the various lochs which opened out of it. At last the happy day

arrived which was to see my brother united to his lady love.
The ceremony was to take place at her father's house, as was
the custom of those days among people of rank and fashion.
Everything was arranged on a splendid scale. All our neighbours from far and near assembled at Castle Ballinahone, to
see the bridal party set off, and to wish us good luck. We
had wedding favours down from Dublin, and wedding clothes
of resplendent hue, no one just then troubling themselves
much as to how they were to be paid for. My sisters were
adorned with silks and satins, and looked unusually handsome ;
but my mother, as became her position, was attired in a
costume of silver satin, so that when she put it on the evening
before, the light of the lamps made her resemble a moving
constellation. My brother, as became his military character,
was habited in a scarlet uniform, to which the tailor had added
a sufficient amount of gold lace to adorn the coats of half a
dozen field-marshals, white satin breeches, silk stockings, and
diamond buckles in his shoes, setting him off to great advantage, and we all agreed that a more gallant bridegroom never
set forth on a matrimonial expedition. The family coach had
been burnished up for the occasion, and was drawn by four
of the sleekest steeds in the stable, Larry and the other boys
having been employed for many a day previously in currying
them down. Dan Bourke was turned into coachman for the
occasion, dressed in a magnificent bright blue coat and hat
adorned with gold lace. The footboys, Mick Kelly and Tim
Daley, were habited in new liveries, of the same colour as
Dan's, and stood behind the coach, in which were ensconced
my mother, two sisters, and the happy bridegroom. My
uncle, disdaining to enter a coach, led the way on horseback,
dressed also in full uniform ; and amid the shouts and good
wishes of the assembled spectators, the family coach set off,
those who had horses or vehicles immediately following at a
respectful distance. Denis, my two brothers-in-law, and I had
a vehicle to ourselves, which it had not been thought necessary
to furbish up. It was an old travelling chaise, which had long
rested in an out-house, covered with dust and cobwebs, and

often the roosting-place of poultry. It was drawn by two
sorry hacks, and driven by Phil Kearney, the gamekeeper, for
so he was called, though there was but little game on the
estate to keep, he being our usual attendant on all sporting
expeditions; while Larry, dressed in the attire in which he
had appeared at our ball, mounted the rumble with his beloved
fiddle, all ready, as he said, for setting the heels of the boys
and girls going in the kitchen, while their betters were dancing
in the hall. Denis and our two brothers-in-law were habited,
as became the attendants of the happy bridegroom, in white
cloth coats with blue capes, waistcoats and breeches of blue
satin, spangled and laced all over, while their heads were
adorned with large paste curls, white as snow, and scented
with bergamot. I was more modestly attired in a new naval
uniform, carefully made from the pattern of my last old one
under my uncle's inspection. As we wished to reach Blatherbrook Castle before the rest of the party, we took a short cut
across the country, so as to get into another high road, which
would lead us directly to our destination. Phil lashed on
our steeds, when, with a pull and a jerk, our horses, not
being accustomed to work together, dashed forward at a
rapid pace over the stones, in a way calculated not only to
dislocate our limbs, but to shake the vehicle to pieces, but
we held on to the sides, trying to keep it together as best
we could.

When we settled to take this route, we forgot that there
existed a turnpike on the road, an institution to which Irishmen have a decided objection. The old turnpike-keeper, a
discharged soldier, who had only lately been sent there, and
was thus unacquainted with any of us, cautiously closed the
gate, knowing that travellers often forgot to pull up and pay.
We, as loyal subjects of His Majesty, were ready to disburse
whatever was demanded of us. I accordingly put my hand in
my pocket, but not a coin could I find in it, and, knowing that
my brothers-in-law were not over-willing to draw their purse-
strings if there was any one else ready to do it, I desired
Denis to give the gatekeeper the toll.

'I quite forgot to put any money in my pocket,' he observed. 'But you can pay him, Daley.'

'I have not a stiver,' said Daley, feeling first in one pocket, then in the other.

'Well, we must come upon you, Fitz,' I said.

'Faith, I left my purse in my other small-clothes,' he answered.

'Is there any cash in it?' asked Daley, with a wink.

'Well, but the man must be paid,' I said. 'I'll tell Phil Kearney,' and, looking out of the window, I called to him.

'Sorra a ha'p'orth of coppers there are in my pocket, seeing not a sight of coin have I got from the master this many a day,' he answered.

I then turned to Larry, hoping that he might be better off than the rest of us.

'Faith, Mr. Terence, it's a long time since I have had a coin to boast of, and if I had that same, I'd not be after chucking it to an old spalpeen for just opening a gate.'

Phil at this juncture, observing that the gate was swinging slowly back, lashed on his horses, and attempted to pass through, on which the old soldier seized them by their heads; but Phil, not inclined to be stopped, furiously flourishing his whip, bestowed his lashes, not only on their backs, but on the shoulders of the gatekeeper. Fitzgerald, who was the most peppery of the party, tried to get out to join in the fight, but fortunately could not open the carriage door. Just then the gatekeeper's wife hurried out, and joined her husband in hurling abuse at us.

'I see who you are,' she exclaimed, 'a party of vagabond stage-players running away from Cork, where you haven't paid your bills, and going to wheedle the people at Limerick out of their money.'

'That's true enough, mistress,' said Fitzgerald, who had a soft tongue in his head when he chose to use it; 'but we're coming back soon, and we'll pay you double for the beating your husband has got, and remember, the next time he deserves it you'll pardon him for our sakes, and it will save you

the trouble of giving it to him. It's not to Limerick we're
going, but only to Castle Blatherbrook, where we're to play for
the entertainment of the wedding guests, for it's Mr. Maurice
O'Finnahan is to marry Miss Kathleen O'Brien; and Mr.
O'Brien, the lady's father, will be after paying us well, for he's
as rich as Crœsus, and we'll bring away a bottle or two of the
cratur to comfort your old soul.'

As Phil had by this time ceased beating his horses, which
stood quietly enough while Fitz was giving this address, the
old man let go their heads and came to listen.

'Shure then you look like dacent stage-players, for
certain; and as I'm mighty fond of a good tune, now just
give us one, and maybe if I like it, I'll let you off this time,
and thank you into the bargain,' said the old soldier.

'With all the pleasure in the world,' answered Fitz.
'There's our musician sitting behind the coach, and he'll
tune up his fiddle while we tune up our pipes, and just
consider what's likely to please you.'

Larry, on hearing this, shouted out,—

'I'll be after giving you what'll make your old hearts
bump right merrily, if it doesn't set your heels agoing,' and,
putting his fiddle to his chin, he began playing one of his
merriest airs.

'Arrah now, but that's a brave tune,' cried the old woman,
beginning to shuffle her feet, though she hadn't much
elasticity in her limbs.

'It's a song we're after wanting,' cried the gate-keeper;
'shure you'll give us a song, gentlemen?'

'Well, you shall have one to begin with, and you shall
have a dozen when we come back from the wedding,' cried
Fitz, and he struck up,—

> 'As beautiful Kitty one morning was tripping
> With a pitcher of milk from the fair of Coleraine,
> When she saw me she stumbled,
> The pitcher it tumbled,
> And all the sweet buttermilk water'd the plain.

21

'"Och ! what shall I do now?
'Twas looking at you now ;
Sure, sure, such a pitcher I'll ne'er meet again ;
'Twas the pride of my dairy,
Och, Barney M'Cleary,
You're sent as a plague to the girls of Coleraine."'

So Fitz ran on, verse after verse, and tune after tune, till
he stopped for want of breath.

Highly delighted, the old pikeman insisted on shaking
us all round by the hand, and then, running in, brought us
out a glass of whisky each. He was much surprised to find
Denis and I declined taking it. Daley, however, prevented
his feelings being offended by singing another song. Then
Larry gave them a second tune on the fiddle, which pleased
him still more, and he set to work with Phil to put to rights
the harness, which had been considerably disarranged by
the prancing of our steeds.

Then he exclaimed,—

'Good luck to you. You'll give us some more tunes
when you come back. Off with you now. Success !
success !'

Phil lashing on the horses, away we went, laughing
heartily at our adventure. We soon arrived at the castle,
where we found the guests rapidly assembling. I won't
describe the ceremony. My brother and Kathleen O'Brien
were indissolubly united. No sooner was it over than every
one rushed forward to kiss the blushing bride, and then we
all heartily congratulated each other at the happy event.
My mother took charge of her new daughter-in-law, who
cried a little, but, soon recovering, looked as bright and
blooming as any of her fair bridesmaids.

Plum-cake and wine were then handed round, just to
stay our appetites till dinner was announced,—a substantial
repast, to which all did good justice. Then the ball commenced, the bride leading off the dance. It was kept up,
with an interval for a hot supper, until three or four in the
morning. It was lucky for me that Nora O'Flaherty, for

some reason or other, was not present, or I believe that in spite of my uncle's advice I should have forgotten my poverty and confessed my love. But there's luck in odd numbers, and there were so many charming girls present that my heart was pretty evenly divided among them. The whole of the guests were put up in the house,—and pretty close stowing it was, but no one complained,—and, after a breakfast as substantial as the supper, we set off to return home. We purposely went back by the way we came, and greatly astonished the old pike-keeper by not only paying him his toll, but treble the value of the whisky he had bestowed on us, as well as two or three additional songs. He had by this time discovered who we were, and was profuse in his apologies for the way in which he had behaved. We assured him that he had but done his duty, and as we had chosen to pass for stage-players we could not complain of him for believing us. For a few days things went on much as usual. At last my uncle received a letter from Captain Macnamara, saying that he had not been appointed to a ship himself, but had applied to Lord Robert Altamont, who had just commissioned the *Jason* at Plymouth, and who had agreed to receive me on board on his recommendation. 'Your nephew will meet some of his old shipmates, who, I have no doubt, will be glad to have him among them,' he added.

At first I was highly delighted at this news, but when the time came for parting I wished that I had been able to remain longer at home. It appeared to me very unlikely that I should ever see my father again, and the state of our pecuniary affairs was evidently telling on my mother, though my brave uncle was doing his utmost to keep things together. It was settled, of course, that Larry was to accompany me.

'I should like to go with you,' said my uncle; 'but you're old enough to take care of yourself, and affairs at home require my presence. Two men will, however, attend you, to look after the horses and bring them back.'

I will not describe our leave-takings a second time, or my journey to Cork. I found there was a vessel just about to sail for Plymouth, and I therefore secured berths on board her for myself and Larry. Nothing particular occurred during the passage. We dropped anchor in the Catwater at Plymouth five days after leaving Cork. I at once repaired on board the *Jason*, lying in Hamoaze.

Who should I find walking the deck as first lieutenant but old Rough-and-Ready. He put out his hand and shook mine cordially.

'Glad to have you aboard, my lad,' he said. 'You see, their Lordships, knowing my value as a first lieutenant, have taken good care not to promote me, lest my peculiar qualities should be lost to the service.'

'I should have been glad to have served under you, had you been in command of a corvette, sir,' I said; 'and I'm very happy to be with you again.'

'You'll find two or three old shipmates on board, for Lord Robert, being a friend of Captain Macnamara, applied to him to recommend such officers as he thought well of. He has immense interest, and I hope that we shall all get our promotion when he's done with us, though he'll take very good care it will not be till then.'

I begged Mr. Saunders to let me go ashore again to procure an outfit, as I had not got one at Cork.

'Have you brought another family chest with you?' he asked.

'No, sir; I'll get one of the proper dimensions this time, knowing the size you approve of,' I answered.

On going into the berth, I found, to my infinite satisfaction, my old friends Nettleship and Tom Pim.

'Glad to see you, Paddy,' they exclaimed in the same voice, each grasping a hand.

'We heard rumours that you were appointed to the *Jason*, but could not ascertain the fact for certain,' said Nettleship. 'Well, here you see me, after all the actions I have taken part in, still an old mate. Lord Robert assures me that he

will look after my interests; but he has said the same to
everybody else, and will probably tell you so likewise.'

Tom Pim accompanied me on shore, and assisted me by
his advice in getting the outfit I required, and I took care
to choose the smallest chest I could find, that there might
be no risk of its being cut down. In the evening Nettleship
joined us, and we accompanied him to pay his respects to
his mother and sister. I was more than ever struck by
the sedate manner of the young lady, after having been
so lately accustomed to those of Irish girls. Though Miss
Nettleship was very pretty, I didn't lose my heart to her.
Tom Pim, however, seemed to admire her greatly, though
it was impossible to judge of how her feelings were affected
towards him. We spent a very pleasant evening, and I took
greatly to Mrs. Nettleship, who seemed to me to be a very
kind and sensible old lady. We had to return on board
at night, to be ready for duty the next morning, for the
frigate was now being rapidly fitted out. Old Rough-and-
Ready was in his true element, with a marline-spike hung
round his neck, directing everywhere, and working away
with his own hands. He made us do the same.

'We don't want dainty young gentlemen on board,' he
said, 'but fellows who are not afraid of the tar-bucket.'

Though not pleasant, this was useful, and I learned a
good many things which I had before not known perfectly.
The ship was completely fitted for sea before Lord Robert
Altamont made his appearance on board. We all turned
out in full fig to receive him as he came up the side. He
had sent down a pattern of the dress he wished his crew
to wear, and the men as they joined had to put it on. It
consisted of a blue jacket, a red waistcoat, white or blue
trousers, slippers of white leather, and a hat with the ship's
name in gold letters under a crown and anchor. All the
men wore pigtails, to the arrangement of which they devoted
a considerable portion of Sunday morning. They might
then be seen in groups, combing and brushing each other's
hair, which hung down very long behind, and then tying

up the tails with a bit of blue cotton tape. The captain was a young man, tall and slight, with a very effeminate air, and as unlike his first lieutenant as he well could be. Still his countenance was not bad, and he smiled in a pleasant way as he returned our salutes.

'Very well done, Mr. Saunders,' he said, looking aloft, and then glancing round the deck. 'You have got the ship into good order, and I hope to find the crew in the same satisfactory state. If not, we must take measures to make them so. Though it's peace time, we must maintain the discipline of the service.'

After a few more remarks he retired to his cabin, where he had ordered dinner to be prepared. He now sent to invite the first and second lieutenants, the lieutenant of marines, the doctor, and three of the young gentlemen, to dine with him. Such an invitation was like a royal command. Nettleship and I, with Dick Larcom, who had just joined the frigate, and who was a *protégé* of the captain, were the favoured ones. The repast was sumptuous in my eyes, and unlike anything I had seen before. Lord Robert was all courtesy and kindness. He inquired of each of us what service we had seen, and particulars about our family history.

'My father was a lieutenant, killed in action, and my mother lives in a cottage near Plymouth,' answered Nettleship.

'And I came in at the hawse-holes, and worked my way up. I have been in ten general actions, and five-and-twenty engagements with single ships, or cutting-out expeditions in boats,' said Mr. Saunders. 'Here I am a first lieutenant; and a first lieutenant I suppose I shall remain until I'm too old to keep at sea, when perhaps I shall be rewarded with my master's and commander's commission.'

'Long before that period arrives, I hope,' said Lord Robert, smiling blandly. 'I trust before many years are over to see you posted to a ship like this.'

I answered his lordship's questions with all due modesty,

and he seemed well pleased at hearing about my family. His lordship happened to look at Dicky Larcom, who, supposing that he had to give an account of himself, said,—

'I haven't done anything yet, Lord Robert, because I have only been two days in the navy; but I intend to do as much as Admiral Benbow, Lord Rodney, or Sir Samuel Hood, if I have the chance.'

'No doubt about it, youngster,' said his lordship, laughing. 'While I think of it, I wish two of you young gentlemen to breakfast with me every morning. I wish you all to learn manners, in which I find occasionally a great deficiency among the junior officers of the service. I'll say nothing about their seniors. You'll let it be known in the berth, Finnahan. You can all come in rotation.'

'Thank you, my lord,' I answered, for I found that he always liked to be thus addressed.

The announcement did not afford as much pleasure as I had expected. The oldsters voted it a great bore, though Dicky Larcom and the other youngsters looked upon the invitation as an especial honour, and anticipated the good breakfasts they were to enjoy several times a week.

Where we were to be sent to was now the question, for as yet that important information had not transpired. The bumboat-woman, the great authority as far as midshipmen were concerned, could not enlighten us, though some of the more knowing expressed an opinion that we should be attached to the Channel squadron, which, in other words, meant that Lord Robert intended to remain in harbour as much as possible, to save himself from the perils and discomforts he might be exposed to at sea.

We waited day after day, while the captain, it was understood, was transacting important business on shore, though it was shrewdly suspected that he was amusing himself as he thought fit. At length he received a peremptory order to proceed to sea. When he came on board, he complained to old Rough-and-Ready of the hardships to which he was subjected.

'Don't you think, Mr. Saunders, that it's a shame that men of rank like myself should be at the beck and call of such old fogies as my Lords Commissioners of the Admiralty?' he exclaimed. 'I have had positively to give up Lady Seacombe's ball on the 15th. Putting my own feelings aside, there will be several sweet girls who will be bitterly disappointed.'

'I don't know anything about balls, except round shot and musket-balls,' answered the first lieutenant. 'For my part, if I'm asked the use of a ship-of-war, I should say that it is to be afloat, looking after the interests of the country. I don't know, however, since the Government have thought fit to shake hands with the French and Spaniards, and to knock under to the Yankees, what we have got to do; only I do know that we shall never get the ship into a proper state of discipline till we're at sea, and can exercise the men at their guns, reefing and shortening sail.'

'Ah, yes, to be sure! that's a very proper matter for you to think about, Mr. Saunders,' said the captain; 'but for my part, I esteem that sort of thing as a great bore. However, understand that I want you to do whatever you consider right and proper.'

'Thank you, my lord. If you leave the matter to me, I'll do my best to make the ship's company the smartest in the service,' answered the first lieutenant.

'Well, I'm much obliged to you, and will support you to the best of my ability,' said the captain.

I overheard this conversation; indeed, his lordship was not at all particular as to what he said, or as to who was present when he expressed his opinions.

That afternoon, the wind being fair, we went out of harbour, and by dark were well to the south-west of the Eddystone. As Lord Robert said he preferred having plenty of sea-room, we at once steered out into the Atlantic.

'We may thus, you see, Mr. Saunders, be able to get a fair breeze from whatever quarter the wind blows, which is far better than having to batter away against a head-wind,

and make ourselves uncomfortable. I wrote some lines on
the subject :—

> We're rovers where'er rolls the fetterless sea,
> For the boundless blue ocean was made for the free.

They are fine, are they not ? Shall I go on with them ? '

'They may be, my lord, but I'm no judge of pottery,'
answered Mr. Saunders ; 'indeed, I never read a line in my
life, except some old sea-songs. And as to being free, we
should soon get the ship into a pretty state of disorder if the
men were to get that notion into their heads ; they may not
be slaves, but they must do what they're ordered, and pretty
smartly too, or look out for squalls, I've a notion. That's
what we must do at present.—All hands, shorten sail !' he
shouted. ' Be smart about it, lads.'

Lord Robert put his paper into his pocket, and threw
himself into an attitude of command, while he glanced up
at the straining canvas, and Mr. Saunders shouted the
necessary orders, which he did not receive from the
captain.

The hands flew aloft. My station was in the main-top, to
which I quickly ran up. Royals and top-gallant sails were
speedily taken in, two reefs in the topsails, the yards were
squared, and we ran off before the fast-rising gale. We
pitched and rolled pretty considerably as it was ; it would
have been much worse if we had been close hauled. As
the gale was from the northward, we ran south all the
night.

In the morning it was my turn, with Dicky Larcom, to
breakfast with the captain, which, according to his lordship's
orders, the young gentlemen in the berth had taken their turns
to do with considerable regularity. We had to dress in our
best, and at the appointed hour we made our appearance
at the cabin door.

The captain treated us with his usual urbanity. We took
our seats, and had got through some slices of ham and toast,
when Lord Robert told us to help ourselves to coffee. As the

ship was rolling and pitching, I, knowing what might happen if I filled my cup, poured out only a small quantity. Poor Dicky, not aware of the necessity of taking the same precaution, filled his to the brim ; when, just as he was about to lift it to his lips, out flew the contents over the fine blue damask table-cloth. On this Lord Robert jumped up, his countenance exhibiting anything but an amiable expression, and, seizing poor Dicky by the collar, he gave him a kick which sent him flying to the cabin door, with an expression which sounded very unlike a blessing, exclaiming,—

' Who is to wash breakfast-cloths for such a young powder-monkey as you ? Remember that in future you only breakfast with me once a month.' Then turning to me, he said in a gentle tone, ' You see, Finnahan, I must maintain discipline.'

I of course said nothing, but bolted the remainder of my breakfast as fast as I could, thinking it prudent to take my leave, lest his lordship should, with or without reason, find fault with anything I might do, and treat me in the same way.

CHAPTER XXIII.

N returning to the berth, I found poor Dicky blubbering, and looking very melancholy.

'It was not the loss of my breakfast, for I don't care if I never have another with him, but it was the indignity with which I was treated,' he exclaimed.

At this most of our messmates laughed.

'Indignity, do you call it, Dicky, to be kicked by a lord? It's a high honour,' said old Grumpus, who had joined us just before we sailed, and did duty as mate of the lower deck. 'Look out, youngster, that you don't get treated with greater indignity before long. I took the skipper's measure the day I first set eyes on him. With all his mincing manners and fine talk, depend upon it he'll prove a Tartar at bottom.'

Besides Dicky, another youngster had come to sea for the first time, and was related, it was supposed, to the captain. Alfred de Lisle was somewhat older than Dicky Larcom, and a refined, nice fellow. I took a great liking to him, though he had his faults. He was excessively indignant when he heard how Dicky had been treated.

'It's a great shame. I wouldn't stand it,' he exclaimed. 'If he treats me in the same way, I'll leave the ship and go home.'

'Bravo, youngster,' cried Grumpus, backing him up.

'There'll be one less in the service to be placed over my head one of these days, and so I approve of your resolution; only just stick to it. When the captain next orders you to do anything you don't like, just let it alone. Don't say you won't, or you'll be guilty of mutiny.'

De Lisle took what Grumpus said in downright earnest, though I didn't fancy he would have done so, or I should have given him better counsel.

As the gale increased, the captain, as we heard, sent for the first lieutenant, and said he should like to bear up for the Cove of Cork or Plymouth Sound.

'There's just one objection to our doing that,' observed old Rough-and-Ready. 'You see, my lord, they happen to be right away to windward, and we can no more get there until the wind shifts, than we can reach the moon. We'll heave the ship to, if your lordship pleases, and she'll be so much nearer Portsmouth than if we run on as we're doing.'

'Oh, pray heave to; it is the best thing we can do under the circumstances,' answered his lordship.

The hands were accordingly turned up, and the ship brought to the wind at the risk of carrying away some of our bulwarks and boats. We thus rode, hove to, for a couple of days, when, the gale moderating, we were able to make sail, and steer for the Channel.

As soon as the weather was fine enough, old Rough-and-Ready, according to promise, kept all hands exercising at the guns and shortening and reefing sails for hours together. He was in no hurry to get into port again, as he wanted before then to have a smart ship's company.

This evidently gave the captain great satisfaction, for he knew he would gain the credit, and he was not above wishing that for himself, if it could be obtained without too much trouble. He had come on deck with his arms akimbo to give his orders, in a voice very different from that in which he spoke when in his cabin or ashore, introducing as many expletives and adjurations as the boatswain himself could have done. No sooner had the sails been again loosed, and tacks and sheets hauled down, than he sang out once more,—

'Shorten sail. If you're not smart enough about it, I'll flog the last man in off the yards.'

The midshipmen had to furl the mizzen-topsail. We consequently flew aloft with the rest. De Lisle, though active enough in general, didn't at all like this, and chose to take his time about it. He was consequently the last on deck. The captain had marked several of the men for punishment, which they got the next morning, and took it as a matter of course. The captain, however, said nothing to De Lisle, who did not dream, therefore, that he would carry out his threats. He was in the morning watch the next day, and had to turn out at eight bells to assist in holy-stoning and washing down decks. This was always done under the supervision of the first lieutenant, who appeared on such occasions in an old sou'-wester, a jacket patched and darned, a comforter round his throat, and a pair of blue trousers tucked up at the knee, without shoes or stockings. The midshipmen had also to go about with bare feet, as of course had the men. They, with buckets in hand, were dashing the water over the decks to carry off the sand through the scuppers, and then they had to dry the decks with huge swabs, which they swung about, now bringing them down on one side, now on another, with loud flops. When old Rough-and-Ready's eye was off them, all sorts of larks would take place. One would heave a bucket of water over a messmate, the other would return it with interest, and a battle royal would ensue, till every one was soused through. Then one fellow would bring his swab across the back of another, and a swab fight would generally follow, till the first lieutenant would turn round and call them to order.

De Lisle on this morning had not made his appearance. At length Rough-and-Ready, recollecting him, sent below. He came up dressed in full uniform.

'What are you after?' exclaimed the first lieutenant, staring at him. 'Turn to at once, and attend to your duty.'

'I don't consider it my duty, sir, to engage in such dirty work as washing down decks; I should spoil my dress if I did,' answered De Lisle.

'What I order you is your duty; and if I tell you to put your hands in the tar-bucket and black down the rigging, you'll have to do it,' said the first lieutenant, for once in a way growing angry.

'I'll go and change my clothes, then, sir,' said De Lisle.

He was so long about this that when he came on deck the operations were concluded, and the men were flemishing down the ropes. Rough-and-Ready said nothing at the time, and De Lisle attended to his duty as usual. Before noon, however, the captain sent for several of us youngsters into the cabin. Though I had been so long at sea I was still considered a youngster. The master-at-arms was standing with a small cat in his hand, a weapon of punishment capable of inflicting a considerable amount of pain, but not of so formidable a character as the large cat used on delinquents among the crew. By the captain's side stood his clerk, with a printed document in his hand.

'Read the Articles of War,' said the captain, 'and do you youngsters listen.'

When he came to the part referring to obedience to the orders of superior officers, he looked at De Lisle, and exclaimed in a thundering voice,—

'Do you hear that, youngster? Prepare to receive the punishment you merit for disobedience to orders.'

On the port side was a gun which Lord Robert had chosen to have painted green, carriage and all, to make it harmonize with the furniture.

'Strip,' he said.

De Lisle, trembling, seemed disinclined to obey; but the master-at-arms seized him, and quickly had his jacket off, and his back exposed. He then, in spite of the boy's struggles, secured him to the gun.

'Give him half-a-dozen lashes,' said the captain.

The cat descended till the blood came.

'I'll tell my father and mother,' sang out poor De Lisle in his agony.

'Two more for that,' cried the captain.

'Oh! could my brothers and sisters see my disgrace!' cried out poor De Lisle, scarcely knowing what he said.

'Two more for that,' shouted Lord Robert.

Again the cat descended. He thus got ten instead of six lashes. He did not again speak. Overcome by his feelings rather than by the pain, he had fainted. The captain sent for the doctor, who soon brought him to, when he was led off to the surgery to have his wounds attended to.

'That's a lesson for you all, young gentlemen,' said Lord Robert in a subdued tone, differing greatly from that which he had lately used. 'I'm determined to maintain discipline aboard my ship; and you'll understand that though I wish to treat you all with consideration, I will certainly punish any disobedience to orders.'

We looked at each other, and then at the captain, and, supposing that we were not required to stay longer, I led the way out of the cabin, followed by the rest, my feelings boiling over with indignation, for I had never before seen a midshipman flogged. Still I could not but acknowledge that De Lisle merited punishment, and he confessed as much to me afterwards, though he did not expect to receive it in that fashion. He harboured no ill-will towards the captain in consequence, and became far smarter than he had ever been before in attending to his duties. The lesson was not thrown away on any of us, and we took good care not to run the risk of incurring the captain's displeasure. Notwithstanding the captain's effeminate looks and manners, he managed to gain the respect of the men, who liked to have a lord to rule over them, though they knew well enough that it was old Rough-and-Ready who had got the ship into such prime order; and for him they would have gone through fire and water, though they might not have wished to have him in supreme command. The captain having abundance of stores on board, our cruise continued for a longer period than we had expected, and we in the midshipmen's berth had run short of all our luxuries, and were condemned to exist on salt junk and hard biscuits. This gave old Grumpus, Nettleship, and other oldsters the opportunity of grumbling, which made them, as Tom said, perfectly happy. We enjoyed, however, an occasional blow-out, when we breakfasted or dined with the captain. We were beginning to wish, however, that another war would break out, or that we might return into port and have a spree on shore.

Besides making and shortening sail, we were constantly exercised at the guns, as well as the small arms. Our chief employment was firing at a cask with a flag at the top of it, in doing which we expended as much powder and shot as would have enabled us to fight a couple of pitched battles; but it made the men expert gunners, and would have enabled them, as old Rough-and-Ready observed, to take an enemy's frigate in half the time they would otherwise have done.

At length we sighted the coast of Ireland, and, with a westerly breeze, stood up Channel under all sail. We expected to put into Plymouth, and Nettleship invited Tom and me to come and pay his mother and sister a visit, but, to our disappointment, we found the ship passing the Eddystone, and heard that we were to go on to Portsmouth, where the captain had his reasons for wishing to remain, namely, that he might be so much the nearer to London. On a fine bright morning we stood in through the Needles, and steered for Spithead, where the fleet was lying at anchor. We carried on in fine style as we stood up the Solent, between the Isle of Wight and the mainland, exciting the admiration of all beholders on shore.

'Now, my lads, let's show the admiral how smartly we can shorten sail and bring the ship to an anchor,' said the captain, who appeared in full fig on deck.

We were all on the alert, and the moment 'Away aloft' reached our ears we flew up the rigging. The boatswain's pipe sounded shrill, the topsails came down smartly with a loud whirr. The ship was rounded to, the men lay out on the yards and briskly handed the canvas, and the anchor was let go, a short distance from the flag-ship. Directly afterwards a signal was made for Lord Robert to go aboard her. I had the honour of accompanying him. The boats were newly painted, the men wearing white trousers and shirts, the oars without a speck; and in good style we dashed alongside.

The admiral received Lord Robert on the quarter-deck, and desired to compliment him on the splendid way in which he had brought his ship to an anchor. Lord Robert bowed, and, with a self-satisfied smile, replied he was glad to find that his efforts to bring his crew into a state of good discipline met with approval, and his only regret was that, it being peace time, he was unable to bring in a prize in tow, which, as he pleasantly observed, he should otherwise without doubt have done.

I thought that he might possibly refer to the assistance he had received from old Rough-and-Ready, but not a word escaped his lips to allow the admiral to suppose that all was not due to his own admirable system. He then hinted that the ship had been in some heavy weather, and that it might be necessary to go into harbour, to have her damages made good. The admiral made no objection, and we accordingly, the next morning, got under weigh, and stood in to Portsmouth harbour, where we brought up some distance from the dock-yard. We found two or three other frigates lying there, and several sloops-of-war and corvettes and brigs.

We had not been there long before our captain received invitations from the residents in the neighbourhood, who had known him as a lieutenant and commander, and were

22

accustomed to make much of him. He was acquainted with most of the captains of the other ships, and they were constantly dining on shore in each other's company. They had all been invited to dinner at the house of a baronet some miles out of Portsmouth, and their boats were ordered to be in waiting for them at about half-an-hour after midnight. All the commanders and most of the post-captains were young men, full of life and spirits, two or three of them noted for their harum-scarum qualities.

I had been sent to bring off Lord Robert, and a midshipman was in each of the other boats belonging to the different ships. We waited and waited for our respective captains, sitting in the stern-sheets wrapped in our thick cloaks, afraid to go ashore lest our men should take the opportunity of slipping off into one of the public-houses on the Common Hard, standing temptingly open.

At last we heard the voices of a party of revellers coming along, and I recognized among them that of my captain, who seemed to be in an especially jovial mood.

In those days there stood on the Hard a sentry-box, furnished with a seat inside, on which the sentry was accustomed to sit down to rest his legs between his turns.

Presently I heard Lord Robert sing out,—

'Hillo! where's the sentry?'

He and the other captains then gathered round the box. The sentry was fast asleep. They shouted to him. He made no reply. There was a good deal of laughing and talking. Then they called several of the men, and in another minute they brought the sentry-box, with the sentry in it still fast asleep—or rather dead drunk—down to the boats. Securing two together, the sentry-box was placed across them, and, the order being given, we shoved off. Instead, however, of returning to our ships, we made our way across the harbour to the Gosport side, when the sentry-box was safely landed, and placed with the sentry, his head fortunately uppermost, and his musket by his side, on the beach.

We then left him, the boats casting off from each other amidst shouts of laughter, and we pulled back to the *Jason*. The captain didn't say much, for the best of reasons, he was not very well able to use his tongue, but rubbed his hands, chuckling at the thoughts of what he had done. I helped him up the side, and assisted him to his cabin.

I believe most of the other captains were also, as he was, three sheets in the wind, or they probably would not have engaged in the proceeding.

Next morning, soon after daybreak, Nettleship and I were sent ashore by the first lieutenant to look out for three men who had not come off on the previous evening, and who, it was supposed, might have deserted.

'Something like looking for a needle in a bundle of hay,' said Nettleship, as we pulled towards the Hard. 'The chances are we shall find them drunk in some house or other, or perhaps in the gutter with black eyes and broken heads. It's not pleasant work, but it must be done.'

I said nothing about the condition in which the captains had come off the previous evening, but I thought to myself if captains set such an example, no wonder if the men follow it in their own fashion.

On landing we found an unusual number of people on the Hard for that early hour, while parties of soldiers, headed by sergeants, were passing at the double-quick march. We inquired of one of the men we met what had happened. He said that on the relief coming to the spot where the sentry-box had stood, and finding neither box nor sentry, they had been seized with alarm. The captain of the guard had immediately reported the circumstance to the fort major, and, forgetting that peace had been established, he roundly asserted that the French squadron was at Spithead, that the Isle of Wight had been captured, and that Portsmouth would be attacked. The whole garrison was aroused, and the telegraphs on the hills set to work to communicate the intelligence far and wide. As I was the only person in the boat who knew what had actually occurred, I thought it prudent to hold my tongue and let things take their course. Nettleship and I therefore proceeded in search of the men, and before long found them, much in the condition we had expected, though sufficiently recovered to walk. Helped along by their shipmates, we got them down to the boats. The excitement was still at its height, when, just as we were shoving off, a boat arrived from the Gosport side, with the astounding intelligence that the missing sentry-box, with the sentry in it, was standing upright on the beach. Immediately a number of boats, one of which contained the captain of the guard and several other officials, pulled across to investigate the matter.

'We may as well go to see the fun,' said Nettleship; 'the first lieutenant won't find fault with us when I explain the object.'

Away we pulled with the rest, and lay off the beach, while Captain Bouncer and his party landed.

The sentry, who was standing in his box, stepped out, and saluted in due form.

'How did you get here, my man?' inquired Captain Bouncer in an angry tone.

'Faith, captain, that's more than I can be after telling you,' answered the sentry, whom I recognized as a countryman.

'You don't mean to tell me that you don't know how you and your sentry-box were transported across the harbour in the middle of the night!' exclaimed Captain Bouncer.

'That's just what I'm saying I can't do, captain dear,' replied the sentry.

'You must have been drunk as a fiddler,' shouted the captain.

'I can swear, your honour, by all the holy saints, that I was sober as a judge,' answered Pat. 'Shure it's my belief I was lifted up by a couple of witches riding on broom-sticks, and carried across without so much as wetting my feet, for my boots are as dry as if they had been roasting before the fire.'

'If witches carried the man across, they must be hunted up and punished,' cried one of the bystanders.

'Witches be hanged!' exclaimed the captain; 'the man must give a better account than that of the way he came across.'

'Then, captain, if it was not witches, it must have been a score of will-o'-the-wisps, who just upset the sentry-box and towed it across the harbour while I was sitting quiet, not dreaming of what was happening, and only just looking up at the stars shining brightly above me,' said Pat in a wheedling tone.

'You must have been asleep, at all events, or you would have discovered that your box was being moved,' said the captain.

'Asleep is it, your honour!' exclaimed the sentry; 'shure Pat Donovan, and that's myself, never went to sleep on guard since he listed in His Majesty's army.'

'Whether the sentry was drunk or asleep, whether transported across by witches or imps, we must have the sentry-box back again,' said Captain Bouncer, and he gave orders to have it lifted into a boat. This was found, from its weight, not to be an easy matter, confirming the people in their belief that the sentry had been carried across as he stated, for if heavy when empty, it must have been much heavier with him in it.

Poor Pat meantime was placed under arrest, and carried away to be further examined by the town major, and dealt with as might seem expedient, while we pulled back to our ship. There were many among the crowd who believed that Pat Donovan, of her Majesty's 3—th regiment, had been spirited across Portsmouth harbour by a couple of witches riding on broomsticks, though where they were to be found was more than one could say. We heard afterwards that a dozen old women had been seized and accused of the crime, and that had it not been for the interference of certain naval officers, whose names were not mentioned, they would have been subjected to the ordeal of being ducked in the harbour, or tossed in a blanket. It was reported that our captain had seen what he took to be a sentry-box floating across the harbour on the night in question, and he could swear that no such agency as was reported had been employed. Whatever the educated might have believed, the lower classes were still forcibly impressed with the idea that the sentry-box and sentry had been carried across by witches; but on board ship the real state of the case was soon known, and the men, who kept the secret, chuckled over the credulity of their friends on shore.

Portsmouth had become very dull, I was told, since the war was over, and we certainly at times found a difficulty in knowing how to pass our time. Our captain occasionally posted up to London, but, having no business there, received a hint from the Admiralty that he must remain on board his ship, and therefore had to post down again as fast as he could. He consoled himself by spending nearly all the day on shore, generally at the houses of people in the neighbourhood. He had one evening gone to dine at a house situated some way in the country, on the Gosport side, and he had ordered his boat to be waiting for him at the nearest landing-place to it, punctually at ten o'clock. As he had a picked crew, not likely to desert, no midshipman went in the boat. As it happened, the doctor, the second lieutenant, and the lieutenant of marines had been invited to spend the evening close to Gosport, and I was ordered to go and bring them off at half-past ten, not far from the place where the captain had intended to embark. When I got in I found his boat still there. The men had been talking and laughing, and had evidently managed to get some liquor on board. They did not see me, and as I was afraid that they might send over some to my men, I kept my boat as far off as I could get.

Presently the steward came down, and told the coxswain

that his lordship had made up his mind to stay on shore, and that the boat was to return to the ship. Just then, however, I saw an animal of some sort, but what it was I could not distinguish through the gloom of night, come close down to the water. A couple of the men instantly jumped ashore, and, catching hold of it, lifted it into the boat, laughing and chuckling loudly. I had a short time longer to wait before the officers came down.

Of course I said nothing of what I had seen. We pulled alongside the frigate, the boats were hoisted up, and my watch being over, I turned in to my hammock. I had not been long asleep when my ears were saluted by the most unearthly sounds, so it seemed to me, that ever broke the stillness of night. A universal panic seemed to be prevailing. Men were rushing up on deck, shouting out that Old Nick himself had gained possession of the ship, some carrying their clothes with them, but others only in their shirts, leaving in their terror everything else behind.

The alarm which had begun forward extended aft; the marines, headed by their sergeant and corporal,—though the sentries still remained at their posts,—ever mindful of their duty, and ready to do battle with foes human or infernal. I and the other midshipmen, thus awakened from our sleep by the fearful sounds, jumped out of our hammocks, and began dressing as fast as we could. It was not until I was half-way up the ladder, and still not quite awake, that I recollected the occurrence at the landing-place. Again the sounds which had alarmed us came forth from the lower depths of the ship. Many of the men in their terror seemed inclined to jump overboard.

Before long, however, old Rough-and-Ready came hurrying on deck, with his small-clothes over his arm and nightcap on head; his voice rang out above the uproar, inquiring what was the matter. The drum beat to quarters, the boatswain's whistle sounded shrilly, piping all hands on deck, though the greater number were there already. No one answered the first lieutenant's question.

Again the sound was heard. The men who were at their stations seemed inclined to desert them, when it struck me that only one animal in existence could make that fearful noise, and as matters were getting serious, I went up to the first lieutenant and said,—

'I fancy, sir, that it's a donkey's bray.'

'Of course it is,' exclaimed Mr. Saunders. 'How in the name of wonder came a donkey on board the ship?'

I thought it prudent not to reply; and the second lieutenant and other officers who had come off with me of course said that they knew nothing about it.

The first lieutenant, having now got into his breeches, calling the mate of the lower deck, the master-at-arms, and others, to bring lanterns, descended to the fore-hold. None of the men, however, except those who were summoned, appeared inclined to follow them. I, however, expecting to have my suspicions verified, went forward with Tom Pim. We heard old Rough-and-Ready shouting out for a tackle, and in another minute up came an unfortunate donkey. The poor brute, having fallen into the hold, had given expression to its dissatisfaction by the sounds which had driven the ship's company well-nigh out of their wits.

How the donkey had come on board was still to be discovered. My boat's crew knew nothing about the matter; and it was surprising that the captain's crew, including the coxswain, were equally unable to account for the mysterious occurrence. As they had been engaged in transporting the sentry-box across the harbour, it was just possible that they might have taken it into their heads to imitate the example of their superiors, and play a trick on their own account.

Whatever the first lieutenant might have thought on the subject, he took no steps in the matter, but awaited the return of the captain. The first thing the next morning, however, he sent the poor donkey ashore.

Late in the afternoon Lord Robert came on board, and received due information of what had occurred. Perhaps he might have suspected how the donkey had entered the ship;

at the same time it is possible that his conscience may have smote him for having set the example of practical joking. At all events, he made no strenuous attempts to discover the culprits. The next day he issued an order that, even if his satanic majesty and a thousand of his imps should come aboard, the men were not to turn out of their hammocks till piped up by the boatswain.

CHAPTER XXIV.

WHILE we lay in harbour, three ships of Sir Edward Hughes' squadron from the East Indies came home and were paid off, the crew not only receiving their pay, but large sums for prize-money. Scarcely had they dropped their anchors than the ships were boarded by hundreds of harpies in all shapes, eager to fleece the crew,—or rather, to win their confidence, in order to fleece them as soon as they had received their hard-earned wages. Pinchbeck watches, copper chains which passed for gold, huge rings for the fingers and ears, trinkets of all sorts, and cutlery made of tin, were pressed upon Jack as loans, to be paid for as soon as he landed; and the moment he got his pay, no time was lost in commencing the operation of fleecing him. Some sturdy fellows, who had been played that trick often before, attempted to resist the importunities of their pretended friends, and kept their hands in their pockets, turning scornful glances on either side, as they rolled along; but most of them, unless they could resist the grog-shop, were very soon doomed to fall into more warily-laid traps.

Tom and I were on shore the day the *Hero* was paid off, one of the ships which had so often encountered the squadron of the French Admiral de Soufryen. The whole of Portsmouth was in an uproar. We met dozens of stout fellows rolling along, with massive chains hung from their

fobs, rings on their fingers, their heads adorned with love-
locks, pigtails, and earrings, with female companions hung
on to each of their arms, rolling and shouting as they went,
paying no respect to anybody out of uniform, in the height
of good-humour as long as they could have their way, but
evidently ready to quarrel with any one whom they might
fancy wished to interfere with them.

At the door of one of the principal inns we found a
couple of coaches, with four horses each, prepared for
starting, and surrounded by some twenty or thirty seamen.
Some quickly clambered up on the roof and into the front
seats, and others behind; those who had climbed outside
shouting out that the ship would be top-heavy if the rest
did not stow themselves away below, the last half-dozen or
so got inside.

'Drive on, coachee,' cried one of the men in front; 'let's
see how fast your craft can move along.'

The coachman smacked his whip, and off galloped the
horses, the men cheering and waving their hats at the
same time, and throwing showers of silver among the boys
in the street, who had gathered to look on, and who were
soon engaged in a pretty scrimmage to pick up the coins
thus profusely bestowed on them. Tom and I could with
difficulty refrain from joining in the scramble.

The junior officers were at a paying-off dinner at the
'Blue Posts,' to which Tom and I, and Nettleship, who
afterwards joined us, were invited. The wine of course
flowed freely. Before the feast was over, the larger number
of the party scarcely knew what they were about.

At last it was proposed that we should sally forth, and
out we went, arm-in-arm, in good-humour with ourselves,
and ready for anything that might turn up. One of the
party commenced a sea song, in the chorus of which we all
joined at the top of our voices, awaking the sleeping inhabitants, who, however, were not unaccustomed to such
interruptions to their slumbers. We were becoming more
and more uproarious, when we encountered a party of

watchmen in greatcoats, carrying lanterns and rattles. Having been lately reprimanded for allowing disturbances in the streets, they took it into their heads to disperse us, telling us in no very courteous manner to return on board our ships. They were received with shouts of laughter, and, as they still persisted in interfering, our leader cried out,—

'Charge them, lads.'

At the word we rushed forward, scattering the old gentlemen right and left.

'Chase them, boys! chase them!' cried our leader.

As they went up one street, and then down another, this was no easy matter, and we became quickly dispersed.

'I say, Paddy, this sort of thing doesn't do,' said Tom. 'It may be all very well for those fellows who are paid off, and are going home, but we shall be getting into a row before long, and it would look foolish to return on board with broken heads and black eyes.'

Just then we met Nettleship, who had been looking for us, and who, being perfectly sober, fully agreed with Tom. We accordingly directed our course to the Point, where we knew we should find a boat to take us off.

Just as we were turning out of the High Street, however, we encountered three of the guardians of the night who had been assailed by our party. They instantly accused us of attacking them, and I fully expected that we should be carried off into durance vile.

'How dare you say anything of that sort?' said Nettleship. 'We belong to the *Jason*, Lord Robert Altamont, and his lordship will take very good care to bring you to justice should you venture to detain us. Make way there. Let us pass.'

The watchmen were overawed by his manner, and we walked steadily on. Seeing that we were perfectly sober, they supposed that we did not belong to the party, as they had at first fancied, and we reached the water's edge without further interruption.

'You see the dangerous consequences of being in bad company,' observed Nettleship. 'We might have been kept locked up all night, and had our leave stopped for a month when we returned on board.'

'But you joined us,' said Tom.

'I know I did,' said Nettleship, 'and I am more to blame than you are, in consequence of setting you so bad an example; but that does not prevent me from reading you a lecture. It's easier to preach than to practise.'

'You are right, I see,' said Tom; 'and I am very glad we haven't lost our senses, as most of the other fellows have done.'

We roused up a waterman who was sleeping in the bottom of his boat, and got on board the frigate in time to keep the middle watch.

Lord Robert Altamont being fond of amusing himself on shore, was willing to allow his officers the same liberty, provided a sufficient number remained on board to maintain the discipline of the ship, for which he was at all times a great stickler.

'You have never been in London, Paddy,' said Nettleship to me one day. 'I have some business that calls me up there. It's a legal affair, and if I am successful it will add some fifty pounds or more a year to my mother's income. I have obtained leave, and if you like to accompany me, I'll ask leave for you to go, and promise to take charge of you.'

It was not likely that I should refuse such an offer, and, leave being obtained, we set off by the coach as Nettleship intended. We had inside places, for there was only room outside for four persons besides the coachman, and on the hinder part, on a little box of his own, sat the guard, arrayed in a scarlet coat, a three-cornered hat, a brace of pistols in his belt, a hanger by his side suspended by a sash over his shoulder, while a couple of blunderbusses were stuck into cases on either side of him ready to his hand.

'Why does the man carry all these arms?' I asked.

'If he didn't, the chances are that the coach, when passing over Hounslow Heath, would be attacked by highwaymen or footpads, and the passengers robbed, if not murdered,' answered Nettleship. 'As it is, occasionally some bold fellows stop the coach and cry, "Your money or your lives," and the guard is either shot down or thinks it wise not to interfere, and the passengers have to deliver up their purses.'

'I hope that sort of thing won't happen to us,' I said.

'When they look in and see two naval officers, with a brace of pistols and swords by their sides, the highwaymen will probably ride on. They are generally, I fancy, arrant cowards, and prefer pillaging old dowagers, who are likely to afford good booty without any risk,' said Nettleship.

Notwithstanding Nettleship's assertions, I half expected to be stopped, but we reached London in safety. When he had time Nettleship accompanied me about to see the sights, but when he was engaged I had to go out by myself, and consequently very often lost my way. I always, however, managed to get back to our lodgings without having to obtain a guide. I will not here describe the adventures I met with. As, according to Nettleship's advice, I looked upon every one who spoke to me as a rogue, I escaped being fleeced, as some of my shipmates were who ventured into the metropolis by themselves. Our leave had nearly expired, and we had to be down at Portsmouth the following evening. When we went to the coach office to secure our places, we were told that the whole coach had been engaged, it was supposed by a gentleman who was going to take down his family.

'But we must go,' said Nettleship to me, 'even if we travel in the boot, for I've not got money enough left to pay for posting, and I should not like to expend it so even if I had.'

We waited until the coach drove up to the office, expecting to see a dignified gentleman with his wife and daughters inside, and his sons and servants on the outside. What was our surprise, then, to behold only a jovial Jack Tar, with his arms akimbo, seated on the roof, looking as dignified and independent as the Sultan on his throne.

'Come, there's plenty of room,' I said to Nettleship. 'No one else seems to be coming; the gentleman who took the coach has probably delayed his journey.'

Nettleship put the question to the coachman.

'There's the gentleman who's taken the coach,' he replied, pointing with his thumb over his shoulder. 'He says it's his, and that no one else is to ride, inside or out. He has paid his money, and we can't interfere.'

All this time Jack was regarding us with supercilious glances. I felt very indignant, and proposed opening the door and getting inside, whatever the seaman might say; but the doors were locked, and the shutters drawn up.

'That will never do,' observed Nettleship. 'Let me tackle him, though it won't do to give him soft sawder. I say, my man, you lately belonged to the *Hero*, didn't you?' he asked.

'Yes, I did, but I'm free of her now,' answered Jack.

'You fought some pretty smart actions in her, I've a notion. We have heard speak of them. My young messmate and I were out in the West Indies, and belonged to the *Liffy*. She ran ashore. Then we joined the old *Cerberus*, which went down in the Atlantic; and then we went on board the *Hector*, which fought the two French frigates. We had a narrow squeak for our lives, for she went the way of our former ship. And now we belong to the *Jason*, and shall have to keep the middle watch to-night, which is what you'll not have to do, I fancy. Now if we overstay our leave and don't get down, you know what the consequences will be.'

'I've some notion of it,' said Jack. 'What is it you're driving at?'

'If you'll just let us get inside your coach we'll say you're a mighty good fellow; and if you don't, we'll leave you to call yourself what you think you would be,' answered Nettleship.

'Come, I like an outspoken fellow,' said Jack. 'Jump in, youngsters; I'll give you a passage down, and nothing to pay for it. You guard there, with your long horn, open the door and let the young gentlemen in, but mind you, you take up nobody else, not if the First Lord and all the Admiralty come and ax for places.'

In we sprang with our valises, and we heard Jack shout,—

'Make sail, coachee, and see how many knots you can run off the reel.'

The coachman smacked his whip, and away we rattled through the villages of Knightsbridge, Kensington, and Hammersmith. The coach pulled up at the 'Green Dragon' at the latter place, and some parcels were offered, but Jack kept his eyes about him, and would not let one be taken on board. In an authoritative tone he ordered the landlord to bring us out a tankard of ale, and likewise treated the coachman and guard. As we knew it would please him, we did not refuse the draughts. He flung the landlord a sovereign.

'There's payment for you, old boy,' he cried out. 'Don't mind the change; and, I say, you may treat as many thirsty fellows as you like with it. Now drive on, coachee.'

Thus Jack went on at each stage, sitting, while the coach was in motion, with his arms folded, looking as proud as a king on his throne. I thought at one time that he would have quarrelled with us because we declined to taste any more of the ale he offered. He was pretty well half-seas over by the time we arrived at Portsmouth. When he came to the door to help us out, Nettleship began to thank him.

'I don't want your thanks, young masters,' he answered gruffly. 'I've had my spree, and maybe before long I shall be .t your beck and call; but I'm my own master now, and intend to remain so as long as the gold pieces jingle in my pocket. Maybe I'll have another ride up to London in a day or two, and if you like the trip, I'll give it you. You may thank me or not as you like.'

Nettleship and I saw that it would be no use saying more, so, wishing him good evening, we took our way down to the Hard. I turned for a moment, and saw our friend rolling up the middle of the street with his hands in his pockets, as proud as the grand bashaw.

A few nights after this Tom Pim and I, having leave on shore, took it into our heads to go to the theatre. In the front row of seats sat our friend who had given us so seasonable a lift down from London. The seats on either side of him were vacant, and when any one attempted to occupy them he told them to be off. He had taken three seats that he might enjoy himself. There he was, with his arms folded, looking as if he thought himself the most important person in the house. There were a good many more seamen on the other benches,—indeed, the house was more than half filled with them, some in the pit, others in the upper boxes and galleries. The play was 'The Brigand's Bride.' The lady evidently had a hard time of it, and appeared to be in no way reconciled to her lot, her great wish being clearly to make her escape. In this attempt she was aided by a young noble in silk attire, who made his appearance whenever the brigand, a ferocious-looking ruffian, was absent. The lady made piteous appeals to the audience for sympathy, greatly exciting the feelings of many of them, though Tom and I were much inclined to laugh when we saw the brigand and the lover hob-nobbing with each other behind a side scene, which, by some mischance, had not been shoved forward enough. At length the young count and the brigand met, and had a tremendous fight, which ended in the death of the former, who was dragged off the stage. Soon afterwards, the lady rushed on to look for him, and the brigand, with his still reeking sword, was about to put an end to her existence, when, stretching out her hands, she exclaimed,—

'Is there no help for me on earth? Am I, the hapless one, to die by the weapon of this cruel ruffian?'

23

'No, that you shan't, my pretty damsel,' cried our friend Jack, forgetting all the stern selfishness in which he had been indulging himself,—'not while I've got an arm to fight for you.'

Just as he was speaking, a dozen of the brigand's followers had appeared at the back of the stage.

'Hurrah, lads! Boarders! repel boarders!' he exclaimed, starting up. 'On, lads, and we'll soon put this big blackguard and his crew to flight.'

Suiting the action to the word, he sprang over the footlights, followed by the seamen in the pit. The lady shrieked at the top of her voice, not at all relishing the interruption to her performance, and far more afraid of the uproarious seamen than of the robber from whom she had just before been entreating protection. Bestowing a hearty box on Jack's ear, she freed herself from his arms, and rushed off the stage, while the brigand and his companions, turning tail, made their escape.

'Blow me if ever I try to rescue a young woman in distress again, if that's the way I'm to be treated,' cried Jack. 'Shiver my timbers, if she hasn't got hold of that vagabond. There they are, the whole lot of them, carrying her off. No, it's impossible that she can be wanting to go with such a set of villains. On, lads! on! and we'll soon drive them overboard, and just bring her back to learn what she really wants.'

Saying this, Jack, followed by a score of seamen, rushing up the stage, disappeared behind the side scenes. We heard a tremendous row going on of mingled cries and shouts and shrieks. Presently the seamen returned, dragging with them the perfidious heroine, and well-nigh a dozen of the brigands whom they had captured. In vain the latter protested that they were not really brigands, but simply scene-shifters and labourers, who had been hired to represent those formidable characters. The lady also asserted that she was the lawful wife of the robber chief, and the mother of six children, and that she didn't stand in the slightest fear of him, but that he was the kindest and most indulgent of husbands.

At length the manager came on the stage, leading forward the murdered youth and the brigand himself, who now, having laid aside his beard and wig, looked a very harmless individual. The manager, politely addressing the seamen, requested them to return to their seats and allow the perform-ance to continue. After some persuasion they complied, but the illusion was gone, and by the loud remarks which issued from their lips they evidently took very little interest in the plot of the piece.

'I say, Smith, how are the babies at home?' shouted one.

'You know if you was such a villain as you say, you would be triced up to the yardarm in quarter less than no time,' cried another.

The poor actress, as she reappeared, was saluted with 'How goes it with you, Mrs. Smith? Have you been to look after the babies?' while the carpenters and scene-shifters were addressed as Jones and Brown and other familiar names.

In vain the manager protested against the interruption of the performance. He was desired to dance a hornpipe or sing a sea-song. To the latter invitation he at last acceded, and at length restored somewhat like order in the theatre. Tom and I, having to return on board, left the house before the performance was concluded, so I can give no further account of what happened on that memorable evening.

Some days after this, the boatswain, with a party of men, having gone ashore to obtain some fresh hands to fill up our complement,—there was no need of the press-gang at that time,—returned on board with six stout fellows. Among them I recognised the seaman who had given us a passage down in the coach from London, and who had taken so prominent a part in the defence of the brigand's bride. They were at once entered, the man I speak of under the name of John Patchett. He looked at Nettleship and me as if he had never before seen us in his life, and I at first almost doubted whether he could really be the same man; but when I observed the independent way in which he went rolling along the deck, evidently caring for no one, and heard the tone of his voice, I was certain that he was the fellow I had supposed; so also was Nettleship, who said that he would have a talk with him some day, under pretence of learning what ships he had served aboard. He told me afterwards that he had done so, but that Patchett didn't allude to his journey in the coach. His only answer when he asked him if he knew anything about it was,—

'Well, the fellow had his spree, but he was a fool for all that.'

At last Lord Robert, whose name had appeared very frequently at balls and entertainments given in London, received peremptory orders from the Admiralty to put to sea. He came back in very ill-humour, complaining as before to Mr. Saunders of the harsh treatment he received from the Admiralty. In a cheerful tone the following day old Rough-and-Ready, who was always happier at sea than in harbour, gave the order to unmoor ship. Visitors were sent on shore, and sail being made, we stood out of Portsmouth harbour to Spithead. We there dropped our anchor near the spot where, four years before, the *Royal George*, with brave Admiral Kempenfeldt and upwards of four hundred men, went down. A large buoy marked the place where the stout ship lay beneath the waves.

Some cases of claret and other stores which Lord Robert expected had not arrived, and he declared that it would be impossible to put to sea without them. It was a matter of perfect indifference to us in the midshipmen's berth how long we remained, or where we went, for in those piping times of peace we expected to have very little to do. In that respect we were not mistaken. After waiting three days, the expected stores, which had come down from London by waggon, were brought alongside, and, going out by St. Helen's, we stood down Channel. We put into Plymouth Sound, where we remained a whole week, while Lord Robert went on shore; but as it was impossible to say at what moment we might be ordered to sea, no leave was granted. We all wished for a gale of wind from the south-west, which might compel us to run into Hamoaze, as the Sound itself afforded no shelter.

Lord Robert had better have kept at sea if he had wished to remain on the home station, for by some means or other information was sent to the Admiralty of our being at Plymouth, and a courier came down post haste from London, with despatches for the *Jason* to convey to the Mediterranean. We were well pleased when the news was brought aboard. The captain, however, looked in not very good humour at having to go so far from home. The wind being to the eastward, we immediately got under weigh, and proceeded on our course down Channel. Old Rough-and-Ready tried his best to restore the men to their former discipline, by exercising them at the guns, and repeatedly shortening and making sail. The despatches, I suppose, were of no great importance, as Lord Robert appeared not to be in a hurry to deliver them. We took it easily, therefore, and at times, when the wind was light or contrary, furling everything, and then making all sail again; that done, we had once more to reef and furl sails, and to brace the yards about. However, at last we got a strong breeze and continued our course. About a month after leaving Plymouth, we came in sight of the Rock of Gibraltar, and brought up in the bay. Lord Robert delivered the despatches he had brought out to the governor. We got leave to land and visit the wonderful galleries hewn out in the Rock, which had bid defiance to the fleets and armies of France and Spain when General Elliot was in command of the place, in 1782, while we were in the West Indies. We heard many particulars of the gallant defence. General Elliot had comparatively a small force of troops to garrison the fortress, but they were reinforced by the seamen of the fleet, who were landed, and formed into a brigade under the command of Captain Robert Curtis, of the *Brilliant* frigate. The French and Spaniards had a fleet of forty-seven sail of the line, besides floating batteries of a peculiar construction, frigates, zebecks, gun and mortar boats, and upwards of 40,000 troops, who besieged the fortress on the land side. The nava. brigade had charge of the batteries at Europa Point, and so ably did they work their guns, that they soon compelled the Spanish squadron to retire out of the reach of their shot. Besides the vessels I have mentioned, the Spaniards had 300 large boats, collected from every part of Spain, which were to be employed in landing the troops. Early in the morning on the 13th September, the fleet, under the command of Admiral Moreno, got under way, and, approaching to a distance of about a thousand yards, commenced a heavy cannonade, the troops on the land side opening fire at the same time. It was replied to by the garrison with tremendous showers of red-hot shot, which, falling on board the Spanish ships, set that of the admiral and another on fire. The Spaniards were seen in vain attempting to extinguish the flames. The fiery shower was kept up, and during the night seven more vessels took fire in succession. The Spaniards were seen making signals of distress, and the boats of their fleet came to their assistance, but were so assailed by the showers of shot, that they dared no longer approach, and were compelled to abandon their ships and friends to the flames.

CHAPTER XXV.

WHEN morning broke, a scene of fearful havoc was exhibited. Numbers of men were seen in the midst of the flames imploring relief, others floating on pieces of timber; and even those on board the ships where the fire had made but little progress were entreating to be taken off. Captain Curtis, on seeing this, regardless of the danger he was running, or that those in distress were enemies, embarked with several of his boats to their assistance. They boldly boarded the burning ships and rescued the perishing crews. While engaged in this glorious service, one of the largest of the ships blew up, scattering its fragments far and wide around. One English gunboat was sunk, and another was considerably damaged. A piece of timber falling struck a hole in the bottom of the barge in which was Captain Curtis. His coxswain was killed, and two of his crew wounded, and the boat would have sunk had not the seamen stuck their jackets into the hole. By these means she was kept afloat till other boats came to their assistance. Don Moreno left his flag flying on board his ship, and it was consumed with her. The English garrison had sixty-five killed and four hundred wounded, and the naval brigade only one killed and five wounded. Soon after this a heavy gale from the southward sprang up, dispersing the enemy's fleet. A fine seventy-four was driven close under the Rock, when, after a few shots, she struck. Others received much damage. The garrison was finally relieved by the fleet under Lord Howe, who attacked the French and Spaniards, and gave them a severe drubbing. They managed, however, to escape, and stood up the Mediterranean, where Lord Howe didn't consider it prudent to follow them. Tom Pim and I agreed that we wished we had been there. When we had gone over the place, we were not so much surprised as we might have been at its having been able, with so small a garrison, to resist the enormous force brought against it. The Spaniards received a lesson at that time which they have never since forgotten.

All now looked peaceable and quiet. The country people came jogging on their mules across the neutral ground up to the forts, and seemed on perfectly good terms with their old enemies. After spending a week at Gibraltar, we steered for the Bay of Naples, Lord Robert intending, we heard, to pay his respects to the king and queen of that very insignificant state, and to give an entertainment to their majesties. Cork harbour is a fine place, but the Bay of Naples, we all agreed, beat it hollow.

Lord Robert went on shore, and was, we suppose, received by the king and queen, for two days afterwards we were ordered to dress the ship with flags, and to rig an awning over the quarter-deck, so as to turn it into what looked very much like a tent. Old Rough-and-Ready grumbled as if he were not at all pleased at what he had to do, but he did it notwithstanding. All the officers then turned out in full uniform, and shortly afterwards we saw a magnificent barge coming off, followed by a number of smaller boats. The barge came alongside, and the captain went down the accommodation ladder which had been rigged to receive his royal guests. They seemed highly pleased with the appearance of the ship, and, it was said, did good justice to the banquet which had been prepared for them. We then very quickly unrigged the tent and hauled down the flags, and, getting under weigh, took a cruise round the bay. As the water was perfectly smooth, their majesties seemed to enjoy them-selves, and the king remarked that he was not surprised that the King of England's son should become a sailor.

'I've a notion that the prince has a very different sort of life to this,' remarked old Rough-and-Ready, 'though I have no doubt they make it as easy for him as they can.'

When we came to an anchor, their majesties, with their courtiers, went ashore, and we had the ship to ourselves. We got leave to visit a number of ruins and other places. As far as we could judge, we should have time to become well acquainted with the neighbourhood, as our captain was evidently intent on enjoying himself after his own fashion, and showed no inclination to put to sea. Lord Robert knew, however, that even he must not remain there for ever, and, fearing that the commodore might come in and send him off, with orders not to return, reluctantly came on board; the anchor was weighed, and we sailed on a cruise along the African coast. At that time the Barbary States, as they were called, were nominally at peace with England, but their cruisers didn't object to capture English merchantmen when they could fall in with them, and carry off their crews into slavery. In the day-time we stood close to the coast, and at night kept at a respectful distance. We had one night been standing to the eastward, about nine miles off the land.

Just as day dawned the look-out from aloft shouted, 'Two sail ahead!'

'What are they like?' inquired the first lieutenant.

'I can't make out, sir,' was the answer. 'One seems to me as if she had boarded the other, for she's close alongside.'

Mr. Saunders at once sent me aloft to have a look at the strangers. I was also at first puzzled, till the light increased, when I made out an English merchant vessel, and a foreign-looking ship alongside her. Soon after I came down, and had reported what I had seen, we made them out clearly from the deck.

'We must overhaul those fellows,' said the first lieutenant, and he instantly gave orders to make all sail.

The breeze was increasing, and we soon neared them. At last we saw the larger ship make sail, and stand in for the land, while the other remained, with her yards some one way some another. As she was not likely to move, we steered after the first. The captain had been called, and now made his appearance on deck. Our fear was that the stranger would run on shore, or get into some harbour before we could come up with her. That she was an Algerine pirate, and had been engaged in plundering the brig, we had no doubt. However, she was not a very fast sailer, and we soon got her within range of our guns.

'Give her a shot across the forefoot, and make her heave to,' cried the captain, who was more animated than I had ever yet seen him.

Our larboard bow-chaser was fired, but the Algerine took no notice of it. We now sent our shot as fast as our guns could be run in and loaded. Several struck her, and at last her main yard was knocked away. Still she stood on, her object being, apparently, to induce us to follow till we ran ashore. The men were sent into the chains to heave the lead. Occasionally the chase fired at us, but her shot did us no damage.

'She will escape us after all,' cried the captain, stamping with impatience.

Scarcely had he uttered the words than there came a loud roar. Up rose the masts of the Algerine, with her deck, and fragments of wreck and human bodies, and then down they fell into the water, and, except a few spars and planks, the fine vessel we had just seen vanished from sight. The frigate's head was at once put off shore; the boats were lowered, and pulled away to rescue any of the unfortunate wretches who had escaped destruction. I went in one of the boats, and we approached the scene of the catastrophe. We saw two or three people clinging to the spars, but as they perceived us they let go their hold and sank from sight, afraid, probably, of falling into our hands alive. As soon as the boats returned on board, the frigate's sails were filled, and we stood for the brig alongside which we had seen the Algerine, hoping to find that her crew had escaped with their lives, even though the vessel might have been plundered. As we again caught sight of her, however, we observed that her yards were braced, some one way, some another, and she lay like a boy's model vessel on a pond, without a hand to guide the helm.

'That looks bad,' observed Nettleship.

'Perhaps the poor fellows are below, thinking the Algerine still in sight, and are afraid to return on deck,' I remarked.

'Very little chance of that,' he replied; 'however, we shall see presently.'

On getting near the brig, the frigate was hove to, and I was sent in a boat with the second lieutenant to board her. A fearful sight met our eyes. On her deck lay stretched the bodies of her officers and crew, almost cut to pieces by the sharp scimitars of their assailants. We hurried below, hoping to find some still alive, but not a voice answered to our shouts. Finding a couple of lanterns, we explored the vessel fore and aft, but the wretches who had just met their doom had made certain work of it, having killed every human being who had attempted to resist them. Many of the sufferers whom they had captured must have perished when their vessel blew up. The lieutenant sent me back to report the state of things to the captain. After a short talk with Mr. Saunders, Lord Robert sent for Nettleship.

'I put you in charge of the brig,' he said. 'You may take Pim and Finnahan with you, and follow close in our wake. I intend to steer for Gibraltar, and will there ascertain whether it is necessary for me to send the brig to England or not.'

On receiving the captain's orders through Mr. Saunders, we immediately got our traps ready, and the boat carried us on board the brig, with eight hands to form our crew. Among them was Larry, who jumped into the boat in the place of another man, who was glad enough to escape having to go, and Jack Patchett, our coach friend, who proved himself, though a sulky, self-conceited fellow, a prime seaman. As we were short-handed we were not sorry to have him. On getting on board the brig we had first to bury the bodies of the murdered crew. Her ship's papers showed her to be the *Daisy* of London, John Edwards, master. The pirates had rifled his pockets, and those of his mates, so that we were unable to identify them. We at once, therefore, set to work to sew the murdered men up in canvas, when, without further ceremony, they were launched overboard. We then washed down decks, to try and get rid of the dark red hue which stained them; but buckets of water failed to do that.

The lieutenant and his men having assisted us in knotting and splicing the rigging, and in bracing the yards the proper way, returned on board the frigate, which directly made sail, we following in her wake. The *Daisy* was not a fast craft, and though we made all sail we could carry, we found she was dropping astern of the frigate.

'It matters very little,' said Nettleship, who had brought his quadrant and Nautical Almanac; we can find our way by ourselves.'

We saw the frigate's lights during the early part of the night, but before morning they had disappeared. This being no fault of ours, we did not trouble ourselves about the matter. As daylight approached the breeze fell, and became so light that we scarcely made more than a knot an hour. As soon as it was daylight, we turned to with the holy-stones to try and get the blood-stains out of the deck before they had sunk deeply in. We were thus

employed till breakfast.   By this time the wind had completely dropped, and it became a stark calm, such as so
often occurs in the Mediterranean.   The brig's head went
boxing round the compass, and chips of wood thrown overboard lay floating alongside, unwilling to part company.
The heat, too, was almost as great as I ever felt it in the
West Indies.   Still we tried to make ourselves as happy as
we could.   We were out of sight of the African coast, and
were not likely to be attacked by Salce, Riff, or Algerine
corsairs; and Tom observed that if we were, it would be a
pleasing variety to our day's work, as we should to a
certainty beat them off.

'We must not trust too much to that,' observed Nettleship.   'We have only six small pop-guns, and as we muster
only eleven hands, all told, we might find it a hard job to
keep a crew of one hundred ruffians or more at bay.'

We kept the men employed in putting the brig to rights,
and setting up the rigging, which had become slack from
the hot weather.   As the vessel was well provisioned, and
one of the men sent with us was a tolerable cook, we had
a good dinner placed on the table.   Nettleship and I were
below discussing it, while Tom Pim had charge of the
deck.   I hurried over mine, that I might call him down,
and was just about to do so, having a glass of wine to my
lips, when there came a roar like thunder, and over heeled
the brig, capsizing everything on the table, and sending
Nettleship and me to the lee side of the cabin.   We
picked ourselves up, and rushed to the companion ladder,
but it was upset.

While we were endeavouring to replace it, I heard Tom's
voice shouting,—

'Cut, lads, cut!'

Just as he had uttered the words, a succession of crashes
reached our ears, and the brig righted with a suddenness and
force which threw us off our legs.   We quickly, however,
had the ladder replaced, and sprang up on deck.   We found
that both the masts had been carried away by the board

and were trailing alongside. Tom Pim was holding on to the starboard bulwarks, while Jack Patchett was at the helm, steering the brig before the gale. None of the men appeared to have been lost or injured, but were standing forward, looking very much astonished at what had happened.

'The first thing to do is to clear the wreck,' cried Nettleship, and he called the men aft; while I ran down to get up some axes which we had seen in the cabin.

When I returned on deck, to my surprise I found that the wind had suddenly fallen. The brig had been struck by a white squall, which frequently occurs in the Mediterranean, and either whips the masts out of a vessel, or sends her to the bottom.

We accordingly, under Nettleship's directions, began hauling the masts alongside, to obtain such spars as we could that might serve us to form jury-masts. We could scarcely hope, with the limited strength we possessed, to get the masts on deck. We were thus employed till dark. We had saved the spars and some of the sails, though it was rather difficult to avoid staving in the boats, which had been lowered that we might effect our object. The weather might again change, and it was important to get up jury-masts as soon as possible.

During the night, however, we could do but little, as the men required rest. One half, therefore, were allowed to turn in. The night was as calm as the greater part of the day had been. At dawn we all turned out and set to work. We were thus employed, when I saw several sail standing down towards us, and bringing a breeze with them. I pointed them out to Nettleship.

'It's to be hoped the wind will continue moderate,' he said, 'or we may be driven nearer to the African coast than may be pleasant.'

We were at this time just out of sight of land, to the north-ward of Algiers. As the ships got nearer, we made them out to be a large fleet, several being line-of-battle ships, others frigates, and vessels of various rigs. In a short time many more came in sight, till we could count upwards of one hundred. These appeared not to be all. The larger number had lateen sails and long tapering yards.

'What can they be about?' asked Tom.

'That's more than I can say,' said Nettleship; 'but I suspect they are bound upon some expedition or other,— perhaps to attack the Algerines.'

As we got near enough to make out their flags, we distinguished four to be Spanish ships, two had Maltese flags flying; there were two Portuguese, and one Sicilian.

'Then I have no doubt about it,' said Nettleship, 'for the Dons and Portingales have the chief trade up the Levant, and are likely to suffer most from those rascally corsairs. Since Blake gave them a good drubbing they have generally been pretty careful how they interfere with English vessels; but we have strong proof in this unfortunate craft that they want another thrashing to keep them in order.'

As we had not as yet got up our jury-masts, we were unable to move out of their way, and there appeared to be some risk of our being run down. Every now and then Jack Patchett hailed with his stentorian voice, and warned the vessels approaching us that they might pass ahead or astern, as the case might be. At last a Spanish man-of-war, carrying an admiral's flag, was sailing quite close to us, when a voice asked from her deck in English,—

'Can we render you any assistance?'

'The best assistance you can give us, is to take us in tow, and carry us to Gibraltar,' answered Nettleship.

He said this without the slightest expectation of its being done.

'We'll heave to and send a tow-rope on board,' was the answer; and presently the line-of-battle ship, shortening sail, hove to under our lee. A couple of boats being lowered, came rowing towards us. Their object, we found, was to tow us close enough to receive a hawser on board.

As one of them came alongside, an officer stepped on to our deck, and, advancing towards Nettleship, said,—

'I am an Englishman, and have joined an expedition to

attack Algiers, for my hatred and detestation of the cruelty the Algerians inflict on the unfortunate Europeans they capture. An English vessel in which I sailed lately up the Levant was attacked, and not until we had lost several men did we succeed in beating off the Algerines.'

Nettleship explained that the *Daisy* had also been plundered and her people murdered.

'That is a good reason why you should join us in our proposed attack on Algiers,' said the officer. 'I must introduce myself to you as Henry Vernon, a name not unknown to fame. I am a nephew of the admiral, and my desire is to emulate his deeds.'

Nettleship at once agreed to accompany the fleet, and expressed his readiness to take part in the expected engagement.

'We have no help for it,' he said to Tom and me; 'and I think I am justified in agreeing to Mr. Vernon's proposal. We shall, I expect, see some heavy work. Algiers is a strong place, I'm told, and the Algerines are not likely to knock under without trying to defend themselves.'

Tom and I were of course well pleased with this.

The Spanish ship, the *Guerrero*, having taken us in tow, continued her course after the fleet. We waited just out of sight of land till nightfall, when, some of the smaller vessels piloting ahead, we stood in towards the Bay of Algiers.

Before daybreak the troops were embarked on board a number of galleys and gunboats, which landed them a short distance from the town.

By Harry Vernon's advice we dropped our anchor out of range of the Algerine guns, as the brig could not be of any assistance in the attack. Nettleship had resolved to go on board the flag-ship to assist. Tom and I asked him to take us with him. He replied that it was impossible for both of us to go, but that Tom Pim should remain in charge of the brig with four hands, while the rest of us should go on board the *Guerrero*, to assist in working her guns. Tom did not at all like this arrangement, but Nettleship replied that as he was senior to me, he was the proper person to take charge of the brig. We shook hands with him as we went down the side to go on board the flag-ship.

'Never mind, Tom,' said Nettleship, 'you're doing your duty by remaining where you are.'

The Admiral Don Antonio Barcelo expressed his pleasure, through Harry Vernon, at having the assistance of so many English officers and men, whose noted courage, he said, would animate his crew.

The wind being fair at daybreak, the line-of-battle ships stood slowly in, each having to take up an appointed position before the town. The ships were stationed as close as they could venture, the gun and mortar boats being placed in the intervals between them, but still closer to the shore.

Scarcely had the anchors been dropped and the sails furled, than the Algerines began blazing away along the whole line of their batteries, the ships discharging their broadsides at the same moment. The troops had been ordered to make an assault at the same time; and it was hoped by the combined efforts of the land and sea forces that the pirates would soon be compelled to yield.

After some hours of firing, however, news was brought to the admiral that the assault made by the troops had failed, and as far as we could judge from what we could see through the wreaths of smoke which enveloped the ships, no impression had been made on the walls of the city, though the flames bursting forth here and there showed that some of the houses inside had been set on fire. Don Antonio Barcelo, thus finding that his efforts were unavailing, the wind having shifted, ordered the ships to get under weigh, and stand out of the reach of the Algerine shot.

We had lost a few men, but had not been at sufficiently close quarters to receive much damage. Vernon was much disappointed, and so were we; but the admiral assured him that he would go at it again the next day, after the troops had had a little breathing-time.

He was as good as his word; and soon after dawn the

24

fleet again stood in, and recommenced the attack. The Algerines, however, kept up so tremendous a fire, that some of the ships, being much damaged, withdrew to a safer distance. The admiral also received information that the enemy had made a sortie on the troops, and had driven them back with fearful slaughter. Still he was undaunted, and declared his intention of succeeding.

'If he would dismiss a few of the Maltese and Sicilian ships, he would have a better chance of doing so,' said Vernon. 'The Spaniards and Portuguese are brave enough, but they are not much given to coming to close quarters, while the others would keep out of the fight altogether if they could.'

Another attack was accordingly planned, and Don Antonio ordered the smaller craft to stand closer in than before. The other ships, however, brought up at a respectful distance when they found the Algerine shot came rattling aboard them. Judging by the thunder of the guns and the amount of the smoke, it seemed to me impossible that the Algerines could long stand out against our assaults. In all directions houses were seen in flames; and I thought that the whole city must be burned down, for the flames were extending, yet the guns and batteries replied with as much briskness as at first. Again news was brought from the shore that the troops had made another assault, but that the Algerines had sallied out, and were cutting them fearfully up. On this Don Barcelo notified his intention of going himself to lead them, and invited Vernon to accompany him.

'If you like to come and see what is going on, I can give you a seat in the boat,' said Vernon, an offer I was delighted to accept.

We at once pulled off from the side of the flag-ship. The admiral had promised Vernon the command of one of the ships, the captain of which had shown the white feather, and he expected to have the honour of leading the attack and taking the ships in closer. Away we pulled, but we had not gone very far when a couple of shots struck the boat herself, killing three men. I remember hearing two distinct crashes, and the next moment found myself in the water, and about to sink. I believe I should have gone down, had not a friendly hand held me up; and, looking to see who it was, I recognised the face of my faithful follower, Larry Harrigan.

'It's all right, Mr. Terence, and I'll not let you go while I can keep my feet moving,' he cried out, energetically treading water. 'We will swim back to the big ship, and there'll be plenty of ropes hung over the sides by this time.'

The distance, however, was considerable, and, independent of the chances of being hit by the round shot which were plunging into the water around us, I doubted whether we could swim as far, even though I did my best to second his efforts to keep me afloat. We were now joined by Patchett, who came swimming up, and offered to assist Larry in supporting me.

'Hurrah! here comes a boat,' cried Patchett.

Looking round, I saw one approaching, and soon made out Nettleship standing up in the stern-sheets; but as the shots from the Algerine batteries came plunging into the water close to her, it seemed doubtful whether she would reach us. She soon, however, got up uninjured, and I and my companions were taken on board. We then went on to where two persons were still floating. The one was Vernon. He had been gallantly supporting the Spanish admiral.

'Take him aboard first,' cried Vernon; 'he's unable to help himself.'

We accordingly hauled in the Don, while Vernon held on with one hand to the gunwale of the boat. Nor till the admiral was safe would Vernon allow us to lift him in. He sat down, looking very ghastly.

'Why, my dear fellow, you are yourself wounded,' said Nettleship, examining his shoulder, from which the blood was flowing.

'Yes, I fancy I was hit,' answered Vernon, 'though I have not had time yet to think about it.'

'The sooner you're under the doctor's care the better,' said Nettleship, as he got the boat round. 'Now give way, lads.'

CHAPTER XXVI.

A MIRACULOUS ESCAPE.

THE Spanish crew understood his gestures more than his words, and with might and main pulled back to the flag-ship. As we went on, the shot fell like hail around us, but providentially none of us were hit. On getting to the opposite side of the ship, the admiral and Vernon were lifted on board. The rest of us quickly followed. Vernon was at once carried below to be placed under the care of the surgeon; while, without waiting to change our wet clothes, we hurried to the guns, to encourage the Spanish crew, some of whom appeared to think they had had enough of it. Don Barcelo, however, retired to his cabin, and, having changed his uniform, shortly afterwards reappeared. He showed no wish, however, to make another attempt to land, but sent off despatches by an officer to the commander of the land forces. What were their contents did not at the time transpire. He continued, however, pacing the deck, watching, as far as the smoke would allow, the other ships, and the forts opposed to us.

'I very much doubt whether we shall thrash the Algerines after all,' said Nettleship to me. 'The villains fight desperately, and I can't see that we have made a single breach in any part of the walls. See! two more of our galleys have sunk; and I have seen half-a-dozen gun or mortar boats go down. Several of the ships and frigates are already tremendously cut about. The old Don is a plucky fellow, or he wouldn't keep at it so long.'

While he was speaking the admiral came up, pointing first towards a sinking vessel, and then at one of the boats alongside.

'Just ask him, Paddy, if he doesn't want me to go and rescue the fellows,' said Nettleship. I addressed the admiral in French, which he understood tolerably well.

'Yes, I shall be obliged to him if he will. My officers and men are required to fight the ship,' answered the admiral.

'They don't exactly like the sort of work,' observed Nettleship; 'but I'll go willingly.'

'And I will go with you,' I said.

We ran down and got into the boat, followed by Larry and Patchett, the rest of our crew being made up of Spaniards, who were ordered by their officers to man the boat. Away we pulled, and had time to save a good many people from the vessel, which had sunk before we reached her. We were exposed all the time to the shot, which came splashing into the water close to us. I heartily hoped that none would come aboard, for, crowded as the boat was, a number of the people must have been killed. There was no necessity to tell the Spanish crew to give way, for they were eager enough to get back.

Soon after returning on board, the admiral, having received intelligence from the shore that the attack had again failed, threw out a signal to his ships to discontinue the action. Fortunately the wind enabled us to stand off the shore, in spite of the shattered condition of many of the ships, when we anchored out of range of the enemy's guns. As soon as we had brought up, Nettleship and I went down to see Vernon. Though the surgeon had told him that the wound was a bad one, he didn't complain.

'I fear, after all, that we shall not succeed, and I advise you, Nettleship, to return on board your brig, and get her into a condition to put to sea,' he said. 'The admiral may not be able to help you as I could wish, and you will have to look out for yourself.'

Nettleship thanked him for his advice, saying that he intended to follow it, as we could not further assist the cause, and that it was our duty to get the brig to Gibraltar as soon as possible.

The admiral had invited both of us to supper in the cabin. He spoke in the highest terms of Vernon, and said that he had intended to give him command of one of his ships, that he might lead the next attack.

'I wish, gentlemen, also to show you my high sense of the assistance you have rendered me by coming on board,' he added.

When I translated this to Nettleship, he said,—

'Tell the old fellow that I shall be obliged to him if he'll send a dozen of his best hands, with such spars and rigging as we require, to set up jury-masts.'

'It shall be done to-morrow,' replied the admiral. 'I intend to give the crew of my ships a short breathing time before I again renew the attack.'

Though we were ready enough to fight, we were not sorry to find the next day that the old Don was as good as his word, and had sent us on board a sufficient number of spars, which, with the aid of his men, enabled us to set up jury-masts, and to get the brig into condition for putting to sea. The Spaniards worked very well, and as soon as their task was accomplished, Larry offered to give them a tune on his fiddle.

When, however, he began scraping away, instead of jumping up, and toeing and heeling it as Frenchmen would have done, they stood with their arms folded, gravely listening to his strains.

'Arrah, now, my boys, there is no quicksilver in your heels,' he exclaimed, observing their apathy. 'What's the use of playing to such grave dons as you?' We then tried them with a song, but with no better effect. At last their officer, who took supper with us in the cabin, ordered them into the boat, and they pulled back to their ship.

'I say, Paddy,' said Tom, 'I wish that you would let me go instead of you to-morrow, if the dons make another attack on the city. I daresay Nettleship will consent, if you ask him.'

I did not like to disappoint Tom, but at the same time, as I should thereby be avoiding danger, it was just the request to which I could not well agree.

Nettleship, however, settled the matter. 'To tell you the truth,' he answered, 'I have been thinking over what is our duty, and have arrived at the conclusion that, now the brig is ready for sea, we ought to make the best of our way to Gibraltar. As far as I can judge, no impression has been made on the city; and if the Spaniards and their allies could not succeed while their ships were in good order, they are less likely to do anything now. Had the Spanish admiral requested our assistance, we should have been bound to afford it; but as he said nothing on the subject, I don't feel called upon to offer it again.'

We, however, remained at anchor during the night. The next day the fleet showed no signs of renewing the attack, though fighting was taking place on shore. Nettleship, however, having desired me to accompany him, we pulled on board the flag-ship to bid farewell to Don Barcelo and Henry Vernon. The admiral again thanked us, but, from the remarks he made, I judged that he was rather anxious than otherwise that we should go away, so as not to witness his defeat. When I wished him success, he looked very gloomy, and made no reply. Having paid him our respects, we went down into the cockpit to see Vernon, who was, we were sorry to find, suffering greatly. The surgeon, however, who was present, assured me that his wound was not mortal, though it would be some time before he recovered. When Nettleship told him his intention of leaving the fleet, he replied that it was the wisest thing he could do.

'If you could speak Spanish you might have taken the command of the ship which was to have been given to me; but as it is, the men would not place confidence in you, and you could do nothing with them ; so, to tell you the truth, I think you are well out of it. Our success is very uncertain. The troops on shore have again been defeated with heavy loss, and I suspect have been so demoralized that they'll take to flight whenever the enemy rush out upon them.'

These remarks strengthened Nettleship in his resolution, and, wishing our new friend good-bye, we pulled back to the brig. The wind was from the south-east, and Nettleship thought it prudent to get a good offing before night, lest it should again shift and blow us back towards the land. The brig sailed under her reduced canvas tolerably well, and before daybreak the next morning we had made fair progress towards Gibraltar. As the sun rose, however, the weather gave signs of changing. The wind veered round to the north-west, and blew heavily directly towards the Bay of Algiers.

'Don Barcelo and his fleet will catch it, I'm afraid, if they don't manage to get out of the bay before this gale reaches them,' remarked Nettleship. 'I'm very thankful that we put to sea, or we should have fared ill.'

As it was, we ran a great risk of losing our masts ; but they were well set up, and we shortened sail in good time, and were able to keep our course. Our chief anxiety, however, was for the gallant Henry Vernon ; for should the flag-ship drive on shore, he would to a certainty lose his life.

'We must hope for the best,' observed Nettleship ; 'the *Guerrero* was less damaged than many of the other ships, and may be able to ride it out at anchor, or claw off shore.'

As we could never manage to get more than four knots an hour out of the brig, we were a considerable time reaching Gibraltar. To our satisfaction we found the *Jason* was still there. We were warmly congratulated on our return on board, as from our non-appearance for so long a time it was supposed that we had either been lost in a squall, or that the brig had been taken by another pirate. We were much disappointed to find that the brig had to be delivered up to the authorities at Gibraltar, as we fully expected that Nettleship would have been ordered to take her home. Though she was an especially detestable craft, yet he and Tom Pim and I were very happy together, and we had enjoyed an independence which was not to be obtained on board the frigate. When Lord Robert got tired of Gibraltar, we sailed to the eastward, and again brought up in the Bay of Naples. We here heard of the failure of the expedition against the Algerines. Nearly half the troops had been cut to pieces in the repeated and resolute sallies made by the Moors. During the gale we had encountered, the ships narrowly escaped being wrecked. Several smaller vessels sank, and all were severely damaged. The troops were finally embarked, and the ships got back to the ports from which they had sailed, with neither honour nor glory to boast of. Their ill success encouraged the pirates in their warfare against civilised nations. The people of Tripoli, Tunis, and other places imitated their example, so that the voyage up the Straits became one of considerable danger in those days. After leaving Naples we stood up the Mediterranean to Alexandria, where we saw Pompey's Pillar and Cleopatra's Needle, and other wonderful things in the neighbourhood, of which I will not bother my readers with a description. On our way we kept a sharp look-out for Tunisian or Algerine rovers; but as we were known to be in those seas, they took good care that we should not get a sight of them, and our cruise was bootless as far as prizes were concerned. Lord Robert managed to eke out a few more weeks at Naples, the pleasantest place, he observed, at which he could bring up. Thence we sailed to Gibraltar, where we found orders awaiting us to return to England.

'I have managed it very cleverly,' said Lord Robert to Mr. Saunders. 'When I was last here, I wrote to some private friends in the Admiralty, telling them I was getting heartily tired of the Mediterranean, and requesting that we might be sent home; and you see how readily their Lordships have complied with my wishes. Their willingness arose from the fact that I'm going to stand for one of our family boroughs, and have promised the Ministry my support.'

'It would be a good job for Dick Saunders if he had a friend at court to look after his interests,' said the first lieutenant; 'but as he knows not a soul who would lift a finger to help him, he must be content to remain at the foot of the rattlins, till a lucky chance gives him a lift up them.'

'Don't be down-hearted, my dear fellow,' said Lord Robert in a patronizing tone. 'When once I'm in Parliament I'll look after your interests. The First Lord is sure to ask me to name some deserving officers for promotion, and I'll not forget you.'

We had contrary winds, and then we were hove to for two or three days, during a heavy gale in the Bay of Biscay. After that we were kept knocking about in the Chops of the Channel for a week, when, the wind shifting, we ran for Plymouth Sound, and came to an anchor in Hamoaze.

Lord Robert immediately went on shore, and we all wondered what would next happen to us.

We had no reason to complain. We got plenty of leave. Tom and I accompanied Nettleship to pay a visit to his family. I won't describe it just now, except to say that we were received in as kind a way as before.

We guessed that if Lord Robert was returned to Parliament we should have no further chance of seeing any foreign service while the ship remained in commission. Nettleship, indeed, was of opinion that before long she would be paid off.

I wrote home to say where we were, and in the course of a fortnight received a letter from the major, telling me to come to Ballinahone if I wished to see my father alive. I with difficulty obtained leave on urgent family affairs, and next day, going to the Catwater, I found a small hooker belonging to Cork, just about to return there. Although she was not the sort of craft aboard which I should have chosen to take a passage, yet as she was likely to afford the most speedy way of getting to my destination, I forthwith engaged berths for myself and Larry, for whom I also got leave.

Nettleship and Tom went on board with me. There was a little cabin aft, about eight feet square, with a sleeping place on either side, one of which was occupied by the skipper, while I was to enjoy the comforts of the other. The crew, consisting of three men and a boy, were berthed forward, in a place of still smaller dimensions, and only just affording room for Larry.

'I would rather you had gone to sea in a stouter craft,' said Nettleship; 'but as the skipper tells me he has made the passage a dozen times a year for the last twenty years, I hope he'll carry you across in safety.'

The wind was light, and my messmates remained on board, while the hooker towed their boat some way down the Sound.

Wishing me farewell, they then pulled back to Hamoaze, and we stood on, fully expecting to be well on our voyage by the next morning. During the night, however, a strong south-westerly breeze sprang up, and the skipper considered it prudent to put back to Cawsand Bay, at the entrance to the Sound.

Here, greatly to my disgust, we lay the best part of a week, with a number of other weather-bound vessels. I dared not go on shore lest the wind should change, and had nothing to do but to take a fisherman's walk on deck,—three steps and overboard.

Larry had, of course, brought his fiddle, with which he entertained the crew, who were as happy as princes, it being a matter of indifference to them where they were, provided they had the privilege of being idle.

The skipper, who had remained on board all the time, at last one day went ashore, saying that he must go and buy some provisions, as our stock was running short. We had hitherto been supplied by bumboats with vegetables and poultry, so that I had not supposed we were in want of any.

I had fortunately brought two or three books with me, and had been sitting reading by the light of the swinging lamp in the small cabin, when, feeling sleepy, I went to bed. I was awakened by hearing some one entering the cabin, and, looking out of my berth, I observed that it was the skipper, who, after making a lurch to one side, then to another, turned in, as far as I could see, all standing. This, however, did not surprise me, as I thought he might be intending to sail early in the morning.

Soon after daylight I awoke, and, having dressed, went on deck, when what was my surprise to find that all the other vessels had got under weigh, and were standing out of the bay.

I tried to rouse up the skipper, but for some time could not succeed. When he opened his eyes, by the stupid way he stared at me, it was very evident that he had been drunk, and had scarcely yet recovered. I told him that a northerly breeze had sprung up, and that we had already lost some hours of it. At last, getting up, he came on deck, and ordered his crew to heave up the anchor and make sail; but this they could not have done without Larry's and my assistance.

As I hoped that the skipper would soon recover, I did not trouble myself much about the matter. He had brought the stores he had procured in a couple of hampers, which I found on deck. They contained, as I afterwards discovered, not only provisions, but sundry bottles of whisky.

There being a fresh breeze, the little hooker ran swiftly along over the blue ocean; the Eddystone being soon left astern, and the Lizard sighted. The skipper told me he intended to run through the passage between the Scilly Islands and the main.

'If the wind holds as it does now,' he said, 'we'll be in Cork harbour in a jiffy. Shure the little hooker would find her way there if we were all to turn in and go to sleep till she gets up to Passage.'

'As I'm not so confident of that same, captain, I must

beg you to keep your wits about you till you put me ashore,' I observed.

He gave me a wink in reply, but said nothing.

During the day I walked the deck, going into the cabin only for meals. The skipper spent most of his time there, only putting up his head now and then to see how the wind was, and to give directions to the man at the helm. From the way the crew talked, I began to suspect that they had obtained some liquor from the shore, probably by the boat which brought the skipper off. Not being altogether satisfied with the state of things, I offered to keep watch. The skipper at once agreed to this, and suggested that I should keep the middle watch, while he kept the first.

Before I went below the wind veered round almost ahead. The night, I observed, was very dark; and as there was no moon in the sky, while a thick mist came rolling across the water, had I not supposed that the skipper was tolerably sober I should have remained on deck; but, feeling very sleepy, I went below, though thinking it prudent not to take off my clothes. I lay down in the berth just as I was. I could hear the skipper talking to the man at the helm, and it appeared to me that the vessel was moving faster through the water than before. Then I fell off to sleep.

How long I had slept I could not tell, when I was awakened by a loud crash. I sprang out of my berth, and instinctively rushed up the companion ladder. Just then I dimly saw a spar over me, and, clutching it, was the next moment carried along away from the deck of the vessel. which disappeared beneath my feet. I heard voices shouting, and cries apparently from the hooker. The night was so dark that I could scarcely see a foot above me. I scrambled up what I found must be the dolphin striker of a vessel, and thence on to her bowsprit.

'Here's one of them,' I heard some one sing out, as I made my way on to the forecastle of what I supposed was a ship of war.

My first thought was for Larry.

'What has become of the hooker?' I exclaimed. 'Has any one else been saved?'

The question was repeated by the officer of the watch, who now came hurrying forward.

No answer was returned.

'I fear the vessel must have gone down. We shouted to her to keep her luff, but no attention was paid, and she ran right under our bows,' said the officer.

'I'm not certain that she sank,' I answered. 'She appeared to me to be capsizing, and I hope may be still afloat.'

'We will look for her, at all events,' said the officer; and he gave the necessary orders to bring the ship to the wind, and then to go about.

So dark was the night, however, that we might have passed close to a vessel without seeing her, though eager eyes were looking out on either side.

Having stood on a little way we again tacked, and for three hours kept beating backwards and forwards; but our search was in vain.

The vessel which had run down the hooker was, I found, H.M. brig of war *Osprey*, commander Hartland, on her passage home from the North American station.

'You have had a narrow escape of it,' observed the commander, who came on deck immediately on being informed of what had occurred. 'I am truly glad that you have been saved, and wish that we had been able to pick up the crew. I have done all I can,' he said at length, 'and I feel sure that if the hooker had remained afloat, we must have passed close to her.'

'I am afraid that you are right, sir,' I said, and I gave vent to a groan, if I did not actually burst into tears, as I thought of the cheery spirits of my faithful follower Larry being quenched in death.

CHAPTER XXVII.

A VISIT TO FRANCE.

'WHAT is the matter?' asked the commander in a kind tone.

'I had a man on board who had been with me ever since I went to sea,' I answered. 'We had been through dangers of all sorts together, and he would have given his life to save mine.'

'Very sorry, very sorry to hear it,' he said in a kind tone. 'Come into my cabin; I'll give you a shake-down, and you must try to go to sleep till the morning.'

I gladly accepted his offer. The steward soon made up a bed for me; but after the dreadful event of the night, I found it more difficult than I had ever done before to close my eyes. I kept thinking of poor Larry, and considering if I could have done anything to save him. I blamed myself for turning in, when I saw the half-drunken condition of the skipper. His crew probably were in the same state, and had neglected to keep a look-out. I at last, however, went to sleep, and didn't awake till the steward called me, to say that breakfast would be on the table presently.

I jumped up, and, having had a wash, went on deck. The officers of the brig received me very kindly, and congratulated me on my escape. Presently a master's mate came from below, and looked hard at me for a moment, and then, stretching out his hand, exclaimed, 'Why,

Paddy, my boy! is it yourself? I'm delighted to see you.'

I recognised Sinnet, my old messmate on board the *Liffy*.

'Why, I thought you were a lieutenant long ago,' he said, after we had had a little conversation. 'For my part I have given up all hopes of promotion, unless we get another war with the French, or Dutch, or Spaniards; but there's no use in sighing, so I take things as they come.'

'That's much as I must do, and as we all must if we would lead happy lives,' I answered.

It cheered me up to meet Sinnet, and we had plenty of talk about old times. A strong north-westerly breeze was blowing, and the brig, under plain sail, was slashing along at a great rate up Channel. I hoped that she would put into Plymouth, but somewhat to my disappointment I found that she was bound for Portsmouth. I was now summoned by the captain's steward to breakfast, and a very good one I enjoyed. When I told the commander where I was going when the hooker was run down, he said that he thought it very likely he should be sent round to the Irish coast, and that if I liked to remain on board he would land me at the first port we might touch at near my home. Next day we ran through the Needles' passage, and brought up at Spithead, where the *Osprey* had to wait for orders from the Admiralty. As we might sail at any moment, we were unable to go on shore. Though I was the commander's guest, I several times dined with the midshipmen, or spent the evening in the berth.

Our berth in the *Liffy* was not very large, but this was of much smaller dimensions, and had in it the assistant-surgeon, two master's mates, the master's assistant, all grown men, besides two clerks and four midshipmen. It was pretty close stowing, when all hands except those on watch were below, and the atmosphere, redolent of tobacco-smoke and rum, was occasionally somewhat oppressive. As the

25

brig had been some time in commission, the greater part of the glass and crockery had disappeared. There were a few plates of different patterns, which were eked out with platters, saucers, and two or three wooden bowls. The bottoms of bottles, two or three tea-cups without handles, and the same number of pewter mugs, served for glasses. Three tallow dips stuck in bottles gave an uncertain light in the berth. Salt beef and pork with pease-pudding, cheese with weevily biscuits, constituted our fare till we got to Spithead, when we obtained a supply of vegetables, fresh meat, and soft tack, as loaves are called at sea. The ship's rum, with water of a yellowish hue, formed our chief beverage; but the fare being what all hands were accustomed to have, no one, except the assistant-surgeon, a Welshman, who had lately come to sea, grumbled at it.

I wrote to my uncle to tell him I was safe; for, having said I was coming by the hooker, as she would not arrive, my family, I conjectured, might be alarmed at my non-appearance. I also mentioned the loss of poor Larry, and begged the major to break the news to his family. Their great grief, I knew, would be that they would not have the opportunity of waking him. I also wrote to Nettleship to tell him of my adventure, and enclosed a letter to the captain, begging that in consequence my leave might be prolonged.

After we had been three days at anchor, the commander, who had been on shore, told me on his return that he had received orders to proceed at once to Cork, and that he would land me there. We had a quick passage, and as soon as we had dropped our anchor in the beautiful bay, Captain Hartland very kindly sent me up, in a boat under charge of Sinnet, to Cork.

Having fortunately my money in my pocket when the hooker went down, I was able to hire a horse through the help of the landlord of the 'Shamrock' hotel, and as I knew the road thoroughly I had no fear about finding my way. Having parted from my old messmate Sinnet,

I started at dawn the next morning, intending to push on as fast as my steed would carry me. I had somewhat got over the loss of Larry, but it made me very sad when I had to answer the questions put to me about him by the people of the inns where we had before stopped.

'And to think that him and his fiddle are gone to the bottom of the say! Och ahone! och ahone!' cried Biddy Casey, the fair daughter of the landlord of the inn, the scene of our encounter with the irate sow.

It was late in the evening when I reached Ballinahone, and as I rode up the avenue I saw a tall figure pacing slowly in front of the house. It was my uncle. I threw myself from the saddle, and led my knocked-up steed towards him. He started as he turned and saw me.

'What, Terence, is it you yourself?' he exclaimed, stretching out his hands. 'You have been a long time coming, and I fancied your ship must have sailed, and that you could not obtain leave.'

I told him that I had twice written, but he said that he had not received either of my letters.

'You come to a house of mourning, my boy,' he continued, 'though I doubt not you'll have been prepared for what I have to tell you.'

'My father!' I exclaimed.

'Yes, he's gone; and really from the condition into which he had fallen, it was a happy release, at all events to the rest of the family, who could not watch him without pain.'

'And my mother?' I answered anxiously.

'She is slowly recovering, and I think that your arrival will do her good,' he said. 'Maurice and his young wife have come to live at the castle, and they get on very well with your sisters and their husbands. But what has become of Larry?' he asked, looking down the avenue, expecting to see him following me.

When I told him, and had to mention how I had been so nearly lost, he was greatly grieved.

'I am thankful we did not get your letter saying you were coming, or we should have been very anxious about you,' he said. 'Now take your horse round to the stables, while I go in and prepare your mother for your arrival. It's better not to give her a sudden surprise.'

I did as my uncle told me. As soon as I had entered the courtyard I met Tim Daley, who gave a loud shout as he saw me, and at once, as I knew he would do, inquired for Larry.

'Don't be asking questions,' I said, fearing that there would be a wild hullaballoo set up in the kitchen, which might reach my mother's ears before my uncle had time to tell her of my arrival.

'But isn't Larry come with your honour?' asked Tim.

'Seamen can't always get leave from their ships,' I answered, wishing to put him off. 'I'll tell you all about it by and by. And now just take that poor brute into the stable. Rub him down well, and give him some oats, for he's scarcely a leg left to stand on.'

'Ah! shure your honour knows how to ride a horse smartly,' said Tim, as he led off the animal, while I hurried round to the front door. One of my sisters let me in, and I had the opportunity of talking to her before I was summoned to my mother. She appeared sad and much broken, but the sight of me cheered her up, and as I talked on with her I was inclined to hope that she would recover her usual health and spirit. As soon as I could I mentioned my own narrow escape, and Larry's loss, for I knew that, should my uncle tell any one, there would soon be an uproar of wild wailing in the kitchen, which might alarm her if she did not know the cause. I was right, for, as the major had thought it best to mention what had happened, the news soon spread throughout the house. As I went down-stairs a chorus of shrieks and cries reached my ears, expressive of the domestics' grief at Larry's loss. It was some time before I ventured down among them to give an account of what had happened; and as I narrated the circumstances, between each sentence there arose a chorus of cries and sighs.

'Och ahone! och ahone! and we'll never be after seeing Larry Harrigan again,' cried Biddy and Molly together.

Similar exclamations burst from the lips of the other domestics, and I confess that my feelings were sufficiently sensitive to make me thankful to get away to the parlour. The supper was more cheerful than I expected it would be. Maurice and his young wife did the honours of the house with becoming grace. Of course I had plenty of accounts to give of my adventures in the Mediterranean. They were highly amused at my account of Lord Robert; and Fitzgerald exclaimed that he wished he could get him to Ballinahone, and they would soon knock his dignity out of him. As Maurice had sheathed his sword, Denis had determined to take his place as one of the defenders of his country. My uncle told me that he hoped soon to get a commission for him in the same regiment.

'Maurice stood well among his brother officers, and that will give Denis a good footing as soon as he joins,' he observed to me. 'He is a steady, sensible boy, and with his Irish dash and pluck he is sure to get on in the army. We have plenty of fellows with the latter qualities, but too few with the former, for they fancy if they're tolerably brave they may be as harum-scarum, rollicking, and careless as they like. I wish that Denis had seen something of the world before he joins his regiment, for he's as green as a bunch of shamrock. If it could be managed, I should like him to take a cruise with you, Terence, and to run up to Dublin for a few weeks, but funds are wanting for the purpose, though, as you observe, we have managed to get the house into better order than it has been of late years.'

'I have some prize-money, though not much pay, due to me,' I answered, 'and I shall be very glad to hand it over to Denis for the purpose you name.'

'No! no! I could not allow that. It's little enough

you'll get out of the estate, and you mustn't deprive yourself of funds, my boy,' answered the major. 'We will think
of some other plan.'

I observed the next day a great improvement in the
general state of things about the house. The furniture
had been repaired and furbished up. There were clean
covers to the sofas and chairs in the drawing-room, and
a new carpet in my mother's chamber, while the servants
had a less dingy and untidy look than formerly, showing
that they had received their wages.

I had spent a few pleasant days with my relations, when
I received a letter from old Rough-and-Ready, peremptorily
ordering me to return. I concluded that the letter I wrote
from Portsmouth had not reached Nettleship, and consequently that my request for prolonged leave of absence
had not been received.

As there was no time if I wrote to receive an answer,
which very probably would not reach its destination, my
uncle advised me to set off at once. I must pass over
my parting with my mother and other members of my
family. My mother had greatly recovered, and I had no
reason to be apprehensive about her health. The major
announced his intention of accompanying me, with Denis,
as far as Cork.

'I wish that we could make the journey with you to
Plymouth; but to say the truth, I find it prudent not to
be longer away from Ballinahone than can be helped,' he
observed. 'My superintendence is wanted there as much
as ever.'

We accordingly the following morning set out, Denis in
high spirits at having to make the journey, for hitherto
his travels had not extended farther than Limerick. The
major rode ahead, and he and I followed, talking together,
though occasionally we rode up when we thought that our
uncle wanted company. A journey in those days was seldom
to be made without some adventures. None, however,
occurred that I think worth mentioning. On our arrival

at Cork, I found a vessel sailing direct for Bristol. My
uncle advised me to go by her as the surest means of
reaching Plymouth quickly.

Wishing him and Denis, therefore, good-bye, I hurried
on board, and two days afterwards was on my journey
from the great mart of commerce to Plymouth.

Part of the distance I performed by coach, part by post-
chaise, the rest on horseback.

I felt somewhat anxious lest my ship should have sailed,
and I might have to kick my heels about Plymouth until
she came back, or have to make another journey to get
aboard her. Great was my satisfaction, therefore, when I
saw her at anchor in Hamoaze. I at once went aboard.
Old Rough-and-Ready received me with a somewhat frown-
ing brow when I reported myself. On my explaining,
however, what had happened, he said that he would make
things all right with Lord Robert, who was expected on
board every hour. As soon as his lordship appeared, we
went out of harbour. We found that Parliament being
prorogued, we were to take a short summer cruise. It
was shorter than we expected.

After knocking about for a couple of weeks, we put back
again into the Sound, where we received a packet of letters,
which had been waiting for us at the post office. I got
one from my uncle, stating that all things were going on
well at Ballinahone, and enclosing another in an unknown
hand, and bearing a foreign post-mark. On opening it
I found that it was from La Touche, reminding me of my
promise to pay him a visit when peace was restored, and
inviting me over to his château in the neighbourhood of
Vernon. It appeared to me that I had but little chance
of being able to accept his invitation. I at once wrote
him a letter, stating that I was still on board, but that,
should I be at liberty, I would without fail endeavour to
go over and see him; that though we had been fighting
with his nation, I had met so many brave men among
them, nothing would give me greater pleasure than to become

acquainted with La Belle France, and to see him again. I at once sent the letter on shore to be posted. The same mail brought despatches to the captain. Their tenor was soon announced. It was that the ship was to sail immediately for Portsmouth, where she had been fitted out, to be paid off.

As his lordship was never addicted to doing anything in a hurry, he waited, before obeying the order he had received, till he could get a supply of fresh butter and eggs and other comestibles on board. We therefore did not sail till the next day. We had a fair breeze going out of the Sound, but the wind headed us when we got into the Channel, and we made a tack towards the French coast. The wind continued light and baffling, and we were three days before, having gone round by St. Helen's, we came to an anchor at Spithead. Here we had to wait until the wind again shifted, when we ran into Portsmouth harbour.

I have already given a description of the scenes which occurred when I was last paid off, so I need not repeat it. Lord Robert made us a speech, promising to attend to the interests of all the officers who had served with him, and especially to bear in mind the strong claims of his first lieutenant to promotion. He took down all our addresses, saying we should hear from him before long.

'I'll buy a golden frame to put his letter in, if I receive one,' growled old Rough-and-Ready.

'I doubt whether he'll put pen to paper for my sake,' said Nettleship.

Most of the rest of us made similar remarks. We were not wrong in our conjectures, and, as far as I could learn, his lordship forgot all about us and his promises from the moment he started for London; and we were cast adrift to shift for ourselves.

Nettleship intended to go down to Plymouth, and wanted Tom Pim and me to accompany him; but Tom's family were expecting him at home, and I hoped to get round direct from Portsmouth to Cork by sea.

The *Osprey*, which had returned to Portsmouth, was paid off at the time we were, and as there was no vessel sailing for Cork, I accepted an invitation from Sinnet to go over to Cowes, where his family were staying. We ran across in a wherry he had engaged.

As we were entering the harbour, we saw a fine-looking lugger at anchor, and while passing I inquired where she was bound to.

'Over to France, to the port of Grisnez or thereabouts,' answered a man who was walking the forecastle with his hands in his pockets.

'When do you sail?' I asked.

'May be to-morrow, may be next day,' was the answer.

'I say, Sinnet, I've a great mind, if the lugger remains here long enough, to take a passage in her, and go and pay my promised visit to La Touche. I wish you could come too; I am sure he will be glad to see you.'

'I wish I could, for I'm certain we should have good fun; but you see I have not been with my family for a long time, and they would look upon me as destitute of natural feeling if I went away so soon. If you, however, have a wish to go, don't stand on ceremony. Should the lugger, however, remain long enough, I'll take advantage of your proposal,' he said, as I accompanied him up to his house.

I was introduced to his father and mother and sisters, who were all such nice people that I was half inclined to give up my idea. Sinnet, however, mentioned the matter to the old gentleman, who at once told me not to stand on ceremony.

'You could not have a better opportunity of seeing France; and perhaps before long we shall be at loggerheads again, when no Englishman will be able to set foot in the country except as a prisoner; therefore go, and come back to us when you have got tired of frogs' legs and *soup maigre*.'

In the evening I went down with Sinnet to the quay, where a man was pointed out to us as skipper of the lugger

We at once went up to him, and I told him that I wished
to get across to France.

'I have no objection to take you, young gentleman, though
we do not generally like having king's officers on board
our craft,' he answered.

'But I'm not on service now,' I observed, guessing the
meaning of his allusion. 'What sum do you expect for
passage money?'

'Five guineas,' he answered. 'I do not care to take
less.'

'Five guineas you shall have, if you land me where I
wish to go,' I said. 'Now, when shall I be on board?'

'To-morrow morning at six o'clock. The tide will serve
to carry us out at the Needles; and I don't intend to
wait a moment longer.'

'At six o'clock I will be on board, then; and, by the by,
what is your name, captain?'

'Jack Long, though some call me little Jack,' answered
the skipper, with a laugh.

'And your vessel, that there may be no mistake?'

'The *Saucy Bet*,' he said; 'and now you know all you
need know about her.'

'Then, Captain Long, I'll be aboard the *Saucy Bet* at
the hour you name,' I said, as I took Sinnet's arm.

We strolled back to his house, and a very pleasant
evening I spent with my messmate's family. We had music
and singing. Two or three girls and some young men came
in, and we got up a dance. Altogether, I began to regret
that I had not arranged to remain longer.

My old messmate turned out at an early hour to accompany me down to the quay. As soon as I got on board
the lugger, the anchor was hove up, and we made sail.
I found a roughish looking crew, several of them being
Jerseymen or Frenchmen. We soon got a fresh breeze
from the northward, when the *Saucy Bet* walked along at
a great rate, with large square topsails set above her lower
lugs. She had a small cabin aft, neatly fitted up, and a

large hold, but now perfectly clear. She could mount eight guns, all of which were now below. Soon after we got outside the Needles, however, they were hoisted up and placed on their carriages.

'What sort of a cargo do you generally carry, Captain Long?' I asked.

'That depends on what we stow away in the hold,' he answered, with a knowing wink. 'Silks, satins, and ribbons, sometimes; and at others tobacco and brandy, a few cases of gloves or lace, and such articles as English ladies are fond of, and are glad to get without paying duty.'

'Then you acknowledge yourself to be a smuggler, captain?'

'I intend to be as long as I can make an honest living by it,' he answered, laughing. 'I'm not ashamed of it. It is fair play, you see. If I'm caught I lose my goods and vessel, and am sent to prison, or serve His Majesty on board a man-of-war. If I land my cargo, as I generally contrive to do, I make a good profit.'

As he was thus open I argued the point, trying to show that the Government must have a revenue to pay their expenses, and that his proceedings were lawless.

'That's their business, not mine,' he answered, not in the least degree moved by my observations. 'The Government could not think very ill of us,' he remarked; 'for if they want information about what is going on in France, or have to send over anybody secretly, they are ready enough to apply to me, and pay well too. Why, in the war time, if it hadn't been for us smugglers, they couldn't have managed to send a messenger across Channel. Bless you! I've carried over a queer lot of characters now and then. But you must be getting hungry, young gentleman, and it's time for dinner. Come below.'

I found a plentiful repast, which, though somewhat roughly cooked, I did ample justice to. The skipper produced a bottle of claret and another of cognac, and pressed me to drink, but he himself, I observed, was very moderate in his potations.

'If I did not keep a cool head on my shoulders, the *Saucy Bet* would soon get into trouble,' he remarked; 'still, that need not stop you from making yourself happy if you like.'

He seemed very much surprised when I told him that I had no fancy for making myself happy in that fashion.

In the afternoon the wind fell, and we lay becalmed, floating down Channel with the ebb. The smugglers swore terribly at the delay, as they were in a hurry to get over to the French coast.

In the evening I walked the deck some time with the skipper, who was full of anecdotes. In the war time he had commanded a privateer, which had been tolerably successful, but his vessel had been captured at last, and he had spent some months a prisoner in France. He had on that occasion picked up a fair knowledge of French, which much assisted him, he said, in his present vocation. He was always on good terms with the mounseers, he told me, though he amused himself sometimes at their expense.

'Some of my chaps and I were ashore one night, not long ago, taking a glass at a wine shop near the harbour, when a frigate came in, and a beauty she was, no doubt about that.' He continued: 'The Frenchmen began to praise her, and says one of them to me,—

' "There, you haven't got a craft like that in the whole of your navy."

' " I don't know what we've got," says I ; "but if there comes a war we should precious soon have one, for we should nave she."

'You should have seen the rage the Frenchmen were in when I said that, and heard how they *sacréd* and swore. But I calmed them down by reminding them that they had taken some of our frigates, and that it was only to be expected that we should take some of theirs in return.'

The captain gave me a side-berth in the little cabin, occupied generally, I found, by one of the mates. It was somewhat close, but I was soon asleep, and slept soundly until daylight the next morning.

By noon a breeze sprang up from the eastward, and under all sail we stood away to the southward. By nightfall we were well in with the French coast, but farther to the west than I expected.

'The tide will soon make in shore, and we must beat back to the eastward,' observed the skipper. 'You mustn't hope, howsomdever, young gentleman, to get ashore till to-morrow morning.'

This mattered little to me, as I had no great objection to spend a few hours more on board.

During the night I awoke, and found the vessel perfectly motionless.

'Can another calm have come on?' I thought.

I was going off to sleep again, when I heard a footstep in the cabin, and, looking out of my bunk, by the light from the swinging lamp I saw the skipper examining some papers at the table.

'Has the wind dropped again?' I inquired.

'No, we are at anchor; we have been chased by a *chasse-marée*, and so, to escape her, we slipped in here; and here we shall remain perhaps for some days, till the coast is clear,' he answered.

'In that case, captain, I shall prefer going on shore, and making my way overland to my friend's house. I shall find conveyances of some sort, I suppose?' I said.

'As to that I can't say. It isn't much of a place, but you may get along in a country cart, or hire a nag.'

As I had no objection to seeing something of the country, I did not complain of this, and as soon as it was daylight I turned out.

Being anxious not to lose time, I got Captain Long to send me ashore with my valise. A small cabaret being open, I intended to take up my quarters there until I could obtain some means of conveyance to the Château La Touche. A cup of coffee, which was at once offered me, enabled me to wait until a more substantial breakfast was prepared.

In the meantime I took a stroll through the village. It was a small place, and, as far as I could judge, primitive in the extreme. It was the first time I had been in France, yet, as I spoke the language pretty well, I felt myself perfectly at home. Indeed, the people I addressed took me for a Frenchman, and were extremely civil.

On getting back to the inn, the landlady asked me if I had been to see the wonderful animal which had been landed some time before by a fisherman, who had found him, she said, on board a vessel, navigating her all by himself.

'What sort of an animal?' I inquired.

'Ah, monsieur, they say it is a bear. It certainly looks like one, for it has a bear's head and claws, and a tail; but it does all sort of things that no other bear that I have heard of can do; and what is more strange, it can talk, though no one can understand what it says.'

'I must go and have a look at this bear after breakfast,' I said.

'Certainly monsieur would not leave our village without seeing so great a wonder,' she replied. 'My boy Pierre can show you the way. Jacques Chacot, who is the fortunate possessor of the bear, lives not more than a quarter of a league away to the west. He charges half a franc to each person to whom he shows his wonder, and the people come from far and near. He talks of taking his bear to Paris to exhibit it, and if he does he will surely make a fortune.'

Though I was somewhat incredulous as to whether the bear could really speak, and had also a doubt as to the way the woman said the animal had been found, I felt curious to see it; and as soon as I had breakfasted, conducted by Pierre, I set out for the cottage of Jacques Chacot. On the way the boy amused me by giving further accounts of the strange animal we were to see.

We found a number of other people going in the same

direction, for my landlady had given no exaggerated account of the curiosity which it had excited. Jacques Chacot evidently possessed the talent of a showman He had enlarged the front of his cottage so as to form a sort of theatre, the inner part serving as a stage. We found him standing at the door with a couple of stout young fellows, his sons, ready to receive visitors, for he allowed no one to go in until he had obtained payment. A strong bar was run across in front of the stage, which Jacques Chacot explained was to prevent the spectators from approaching too close to the bear, who, he observed, was sometimes seized with sudden fits of ferocity, and might, he was afraid, do some injury. The room was already half full when Pierre and I entered, and a considerable number of people came in afterwards. They were all country people, decently dressed, who behaved with the usual politeness the French exhibit when not excited by any special cause.

CHAPTER XXVIII.

T last Jacques Chacot, looking round the room, gave notice that his bear would at once commence his performance. In a short time a door opened, and he appeared, leading out what looked like a large brown bear, followed by one of his sons, carrying a couple of chairs. Jacques Chacot, who had in his hand a long pole with a sharp point to it, took his seat on one chair, and made signs to the bear to sit down on the other, which it immediately did. The lad then handed a glass of wine to the bear, which, making a bow to the audience, it drank off, putting the glass, it seemed to me, almost down its throat, in a very curious fashion.

Its keeper then ordered it to stand on its head, which it did with seeming unwillingness, kicking its hind legs up in the air.

'Now show mesdames and messieurs how you can dance,' cried Chacot. 'Strike up, Jean,' he added to his son, who, getting down a fiddle from the wall, commenced scraping away, and producing a merry tune. Up got the bear, and began shuffling and leaping about, in a fashion which strangely resembled an Irish jig, at the same time singing in a voice which sounded remarkably like that of a human being. The audience applauded; but the bear at length, getting tired from its exertions, took a chair and sat itself down in a corner. On this Chacot shouted to it to go on;

but the bear, being seized with sulkiness, refused, till the fellow, giving it a poke with his pole, the bear sprang up and recommenced its performance, Jean fiddling away as before.

'Now address the company, and give them an account of your adventures,' said Chacot.

The bear on this got up, and, making another bow, uttered some words which certainly no one present could have understood. Listening attentively, I caught several words which sounded remarkably like Irish.

'Who are you, and where in the world do you come from?' I exclaimed in my native tongue.

No sooner had I uttered the words, than the bear made a spring right off the stage, and rushed towards me, exclaiming, 'Arrah! I'm Larry Harrigan, Mr. Terence dear! and shure you've found me at last!'

At the first movement the bear made the audience rushed from all parts of the room, trying to effect their escape through the door, while Jacques Chacot endeavoured to seize it, and to drag it back on the stage. Larry, however, was not to be hindered, and, grasping my hand, he held it in his shaggy paws, his voice alone assuring me who he was.

'Hands off from him, Chacot!' I cried out. 'He is an honest Irishman whom I know well. If you injure him it will be at your peril. Stop, friends, stop!' I shouted to the people as they were escaping. 'The bear will do you no harm; come and assist me.' Jacques Chacot, however, fearing that the chance of making further gains by his prisoner would be lost, dragged him back by main force, while poor Larry, closely encased as he was in a skin, and padded out with pillows, was unable to help himself. At the same time, one of the sons, seizing his pike, threatened to run me through if I interfered.

I in vain called to the people to help me; they seemed to think that I was as mad as the bear, or that I was a mere bearish Englishman, who had lived so long amongst animals of that description that I very naturally took it for an old friend. Larry continued to shout out to me for help, until

26

Jacques Chacot seized his jaws, and, closing them, prevented his voice from coming out, while the young Frenchmen dragged him away.

'Keep up your spirits, Larry,' I cried. 'If there's justice in the country, I'll obtain it for you.' As I found it would be impossible at that moment to set Larry free, I followed the people out of the show, and endeavoured to explain to them that the bear was no bear at all, but a human being, whom I had known all my life. This, however, I found they were by no means inclined to believe. It was a very strange bear, they acknowledged, but they had no reason to doubt that bears could speak; and the words he had uttered were just such as might be expected to proceed from a bear.

Young Pierre had bravely stuck by me all the time, and was more inclined to believe me than any one else.

'I have heard say that Jacques Chacot is a great rascal, and if monsieur will take my advice he will go to M. Jules Pontet, the mayor, who will compel him to allow the bear to be properly examined, and if it proves to be a man have him set at liberty,' he observed.

'You are a sensible little fellow,' I answered; 'and if you will show me the way to the mayor's house, we will go to him at once. But don't let any one know, or Chacot will take means to hide the bear, or carry him off, or perhaps throw him into the sea and drown him, so that there may be no evidence of his knavery.'

'That's just what I was thinking, monsieur,' said Pierre, as he led the way. We hurried on, for I was very anxious about Larry's safety, fearful that Chacot would play him some trick. In about twenty minutes we reached the most respectable-looking house in the village.

'Monsieur the mayor lives here,' said Pierre. 'He is at home, I know, for he never leaves so early in the day.'

I knocked at the door, and, being admitted by a neat-looking woman in a high cap, was ushered into a room, where I found M. Jules Pontet, the mayor, seated, with a number of papers before him. I explained that, having been induced to go and see a strange animal said to be a bear, I had discovered a countryman, an old acquaintance of my own, who had been compelled by some means or other to play the part, that he was being cruelly treated, and desired to be set free.

The mayor listened politely.

'I have heard of this strange animal, and suspected that there was some trick,' he observed; 'I will accompany you forthwith, and if you are right in your conjectures, we will have the man set free.'

'They are more than conjectures, they are certainties, monsieur,' I answered.

I then thanked him for his courtesy, when, getting his hat and cane, he immediately set out with me, followed by Pierre, who was eager to see the end.

We found a number of people collected round Chacot's cottage, which made me hope that during my absence he had not been able, had he contemplated violence, to carry his intention into effect.

'I wish to see this strange animal I have heard of,' said the mayor in an authoritative tone. 'Go, some of you, and tell Chacot that I desire him to bring the creature out on the stage, and let him perform his tricks before me. Come, my friends, come in, you shall see the sight without payment this time.'

Whether Chacot was aware or not that I had brought the mayor, I could not tell, as he might not have observed me among the crowd.

In a short time the door of the stage opened, and Chacot appeared, dragging in the bear, who came very reluctantly, urged on by one of the young fellows from behind with a pike.

Larry was going through his performances, when the mayor said, turning to me,—

'Speak to him, and tell him to come down quickly. I see the whole trick; no bear would walk as that creature does.'

No sooner did Larry hear my voice than he sprang off the stage, before Chacot or his sons could stop him, and I rushed forward to meet him, followed by M. Pontet.

'Have any of you a knife?' asked the worthy magistrate. 'Hand it to me at once.'

A knife was given him, and he began forthwith to cut away at the bear-skin, Larry standing patiently while the operation was going forward.

He soon got the head off, when Larry's honest countenance was displayed beneath it.

Loud shouts of laughter burst from the people, mingled with no small amount of abuse hurled at Chacot for the trick he had played them.

As the mayor proceeded, a quantity of hay tumbled out, which had served to stuff out poor Larry to the required proportions.

'Faith, Mr. Terence dear, you'd better not take it off altogether before so many decent people; for, to say the truth, I've got nothing under it but my bare skin,' said Larry to me in a subdued voice.

Such, indeed, I perceived to be the case, as did the mayor.

'Bring the man's clothes at once, and let him have a room in which he may dress himself properly,' he exclaimed to Chacot, who had, by the mayor's orders, remained on the stage, and had been watching our proceedings.

Chacot, with no very good grace, obeyed, and I, fearing that some violence might be offered, accompanied him into the room.

Chacot soon appeared with a seaman's dress, which Larry, jumping out of his bear-skin, quickly put on.

As yet he had had no time to tell me how he had come into the power of the French fisherman; and as I also did not wish to keep the mayor waiting, as soon as Larry was ready, we hurried out to join him.

'I'll have my revenge on you one of these days,' I heard Chacot exclaim, but I thought it as well to take no notice of his remark.

'Come with me to my house,' said M. Jules Pontet. 'I want to hear how that fellow Jacques Chacot got hold of the English seaman. He must have been a stupid fellow to have allowed himself to be so ill-treated.'

'I have not yet had time to make inquiries, monsieur,' I said, 'but I will, if you wish it, at once ask him how it happened.'

'By all means,' replied the mayor; so I desired Larry to tell me how he had escaped from the hooker, and been turned into a bear.

'It is a long yarn, Mr. Terence, but I'll cut it short to plase the gintleman. You'll remember the night we were aboard the hooker. I was asleep forward, just dreaming of Ballinahone, an' thinking I was leading off a dance with Molly Maguire, when down came the whole castle tumbling about our heads. Opening my eyes, I jumped out of my bunk, and sprang up the fore hatchway, just in time to see that the masts had been carried away, and that the hooker was going to the bottom. How it all happened I couldn't for the life of me tell. I sang out at the top of my voice for you, Mr. Terence, and rushed aft to the cabin, where I expected to find you asleep. But though I shouted loud enough to waken the dead, you didn't answer, and not a soul was aboard but myself. For a moment I caught sight of the stern of a vessel steering away from us, which made me guess that we had been run down. The water was rushing into the little craft, and I knew that she must go to the bottom. Her masts and spars were still hanging to her side, an' so, thinks I to meself, I'll have a struggle for life. I had seen an axe in the companion hatch, and, getting hold of it, I cut away the rigging, and had time to get hold of a cold ham and some bread and a bottle of water, which I stowed in a basket. Thinks I, I'll make a raft, and so I hove overboard some planks, with part of the main hatch and a grating, and, getting on them, lashed them together in a rough fashion, keeping my eye all the time on the hooker, to see that she didn't go down, and catch me unawares. I was so mighty busy with this work, that if the vessel which had run the hooker down had come back to look for us I shouldn't have seen her. I had just got my raft together, when I saw that the hooker was settling down, so I gave it a shove off from her side; and faith I was only just in time, for it made a rush forward, and I thought was going down with the vessel, but up it came again, and there I was, floating all alone on the water.

'During the night a light breeze from the northward sprang up, and I began to fear that I might be drifted out into the Atlantic. However, I couldn't help myself, and was not going to cry die. I was mighty thankful that the sea was smooth, and so I sat on my raft, trying to be as happy as I could; but the thinking of you, Mr. Terence, and not knowing if you had escaped, often made me sad. I wished, too, that I had had my fiddle, when I would have played myself a tune to keep up my spirits. I can't say how many days I spent on the raft, sleeping when I could not keep my eyes open, till all the provisions and the water I had brought were gone. Then I got very bad, and thought I was going to die. The weather, too, was changing, and the sea getting up. I was just lying down on the raft, not long before the bright sun sank into the ocean, and not expecting to see it rise again, when I heard a shout, and, opening my eyes, I saw a small craft, which I guessed was a French fishing-boat from her look, coming towards me. She having hove to, presently a boat was lowered from her deck, and I was taken on board, more dead than alive. The Frenchmen gave me some food, and, taking me down into the cabin, put me to bed.

'It came on to blow very hard that night. For some days we were knocking about, not able to get back to port. From the heavy seas which broke over the little vessel, and from the way I heard the Frenchmen speaking, I thought that after all we should be lost, but I was too weak to care much about the matter just then.

'However, at last the weather moderated, and after several days I found that we were at anchor in smooth water. I was still very bad, so the French skipper carried me ashore to his cottage. He fed me pretty well, and I at last got strong enough to walk about. By this time I had managed somehow to make him understand me, and I asked him to tell me how I could cross over to Ireland, as I wanted to get home and learn if you had escaped. He laughed at me, however, and said that I owed him a hundred francs for taking care of me, and that I must pay him. I answered that I would be glad enough to pay him, like an honest man, as soon as I could get any prize-money, and that I would send it over to him. To this, however, he would not agree, but said that if I would help him in a trick he wanted to play off on the people, he would be satisfied. He then explained that I must dress up like a bear, and that he would show me off as a wonder. As I had no help for it, I consented. He at once made me get into the bear-skin which you, Mr. Terence, cut me out of, and showed me how I was to behave myself. After I had had some days' practice, he sent round to let it be known that he had picked up a bear at sea, which could talk and play all sorts of tricks; and in a short time people came to look at me. At first I thought it a good joke, but at last he treated me so like a real bear, for he chained me up at night and never let me get out of my skin, that I began to grow heartily tired of the fun; and it's my belief, if you hadn't found me out, he'd have been after making away with me, lest the people should discover the trick he had played them.'

I translated Larry's story to the mayor, who, being a humane man, was very indignant, but said that he had no power to punish Chacot, as Larry confessed that he had consented to be dressed up.

When I told this to Larry, he said that he should be very sorry to have Chacot suffer, as, whatever his motive, he had certainly saved his life.

In a couple of days Larry was fit to set out. With the aid of M. Pontet, I purchased two horses. They were sorry steeds to look at, but had more go in them than I expected from their appearance. Larry carried my valise, and I had my sword and a brace of pistols, though M. Pontet assured me I should have no necessity for their use. I had become intimate with him, and he kindly gave me a letter of introduction to a friend of his at Vernon, a Monsieur Planterre, who, he said, would dispose of my horses for me, and afford me any other assistance I might require, in case La Touche should be absent from home.

Bidding farewell to M. Pontet, I started on my journey at an early hour in the morning, fully expecting to enjoy the trip, as all was new and strange to me. The people I met with were primitive in their habits, and invariably treated me with civility. The inns I stopped at were small, and not over comfortable, but as they afforded sufficient accommodation for man and beast, I did not complain.

I must pass over the incidents of the journey. It was towards evening when the towers of Vernon, situated on the banks of the Seine, appeared in sight, and, passing across the boulevards which surrounded the town, I entered the narrow, crooked streets, with timber-framed houses on either side, and kept clean by running streams. On my way I inquired for the house of M. Planterre, which I found situated at the entrance of an avenue which leads to the Château de Bizy, belonging to the Duc de Penthièvre.

The house, though of a primitive style of architecture, was better than most of those I had passed. Being admitted, Larry having taken charge of my horse, M. Planterre received me with much courtesy, and, telling me that I could not possibly reach the Château La Touche that evening, invited me to take up my quarters at his house. I of course was glad to accept his invitation, and Larry was at once sent round to the stables with the horses. I took no further concern for him, being well aware that he could make himself at home wherever he was.

M. Planterre told me that he was acquainted with my friend La Touche, and should be happy to accompany me to the château the next day. I learned from him more of the state of things in France than I had before known. He told me that republican principles were gaining ground in all directions, and that the people were everywhere complaining of the taxes imposed on them by the Government.

'Discontent indeed prevails everywhere, and unless reforms take place, I know not what will be the result,' he said, with a deep sigh. 'Even in this place the people are in an unsatisfactory state of mind.'

I was introduced to Madame Planterre and her daughters, bright, pretty young ladies, who seemed much attached to their parents. They gave me a very pleasant idea of a French family of the upper middle class.

Next morning M. Planterre asked me to defer starting for a couple of hours, as he had to attend a meeting at the Town Hall, where he hoped to propose some measure for the benefit of the poorer inhabitants. He suggested that I should pass the intermediate time in taking a turn through the town, and visiting an ancient tower and hospital founded by St. Louis, and other objects of interest.

Giving Larry directions to have the horses ready, I set out. Having spent nearly two hours in visiting different parts of the town, I ascended to the top of the ancient tower I have mentioned, from which I obtained a fine view, not only of the picturesque old town, but along the Seine for a considerable distance up and down, and also of the Château de Bizy, with the fine avenue leading to it. I was about to descend, when I saw a vast number of people emerging from the various streets into a broad space called the Place, a short distance below me. From their movements they appeared highly excited, for loud cries and shouts reached my ears. The greater number were armed, either with muskets, pikes, scythes, swords, or other weapons. As I was curious to know what they were about, I hastened down, and made my way along the street leading to the Place. I had no fear of going among the people, for I did not suppose that they would interfere with me. Many of those I passed were of respectable appearance, and as I got into the Place I inquired of one of them what they were about to do.

'They have just tried and condemned to death one of our principal citizens, M. Planterre, who has always proved himself one of their best friends,' was the reply.

'M. Planterre!' I exclaimed. 'Where is he?'

My friend was pointed out to me, in the midst of a band of ruffians, who were dragging him forward, shouting, ' *A la lanterne! à la lanterne!*'

Seized with an impulse I could not control, to preserve, if I could, the life of my kind host, I dashed forward through the crowd. The people made way for me, until I reached his side.

'Good people of Vernon, what are you about to do?' I exclaimed. 'I hear every one speaking in favour of M. Planterre, and yet you threaten him with instant death.'

My friend, whilst I was speaking, stood pale and trembling; the rope was round his neck, and the ruffians had hold of the end, as if eager to strangle him.

'What has he done to outweigh his kind deeds?' I asked.

No answer was vouchsafed, the mob only shouting the louder, '*A la lanterne! à la lanterne!*'

'Who are you, young stranger? Be off with you, or you shall share his fate,' cried out a big ruffian; and many of them pressing on, shoved me aside, endeavouring to separate me from their intended victim.

I saw that it was a moment for action,—that should I exhibit the slightest hesitation the life of a worthy man would be sacrificed; and, regardless of the danger I myself ran from the fury of the excited crowd, again dashing forward, I succeeded in reaching M. Planterre, round whom I threw my arms, and held him fast.

'You shall not injure him. Back, all of you!' I shouted. 'I will not allow you to destroy an honest man. There must be some mistake. You are not executioners, you are

assassins, and are about to commit a deed of which you
will repent.'

Notwithstanding what I said, the ruffians still pressed upon
us, and attempted to drag M. Planterre away, shouting, '*A
la lanterne!*' but I held him fast.

'My friends,' I cried,—'for I will not call you enemies,—if
you hang this man you must hang me, for alive I will not be
separated from him, and you will be guilty of the murder
of two honest men instead of one.'

As I spoke a reaction suddenly took place; my words
had even more effect than I expected on the volatile crowd.
One of them rushed forward and removed the rope from
M. Planterre's neck.

'You have saved his life!' cried another.

'You are a brave fellow!' shouted a third. 'Long live
the noble Englishman! he is worthy of our regard.'

These and similar cries burst from the throats of numbers
standing round, and were echoed by the would-be executioners. Before I knew what was about to happen, a number
of them, rushing forward, lifted me on their shoulders, and
carried me along in triumph, shouting and singing, while M.
Planterre's friends, who had been watching the opportunity,
pressing forward, hurried him away in another direction.
To my infinite satisfaction, I saw him carried off, while I
was borne along by the crowd, who shouted and sang in
my praise until their voices were hoarse.

I thought it wise to submit to the honours paid me; at
the same time I could not tell at what moment the feelings
of the fickle mob might change, and perhaps they might
carry me to the *lanterne* instead of the man I had rescued.
I made the best of my position, and kept bowing to the
mob right and left, expressing my admiration for France and
Frenchmen in the most glowing terms I could command.

This seemed to please them mightily; but I was curious
to know what they were going to do with me. They appeared highly delighted at having an object on which to
bestow their admiration. First they carried me round and

round the Place, shouting and cheering, while they told all who came up what I had done. Perhaps they found it quite as amusing as hanging their townsman.

At last some one proposed that they should carry me to the Hôtel de Ville. The proposal was received with acclamations by the crowd, and my bearers set off, several of them going before cheering and gesticulating, while, as we passed through the narrow, crooked streets, the people looked out from the windows, waving coloured handkerchiefs and shawls, for by this time the whole town had heard, with perhaps a few exaggerations, of the act I had performed. On arriving at the Town Hall, I saw a number of gentlemen in full dress, with various insignia, whom I suspected to be the civic authorities, standing on the steps, drawn up to welcome me. My bearers halted when a small gentleman, in a powdered wig and cocked hat, who was, I found, the mayor, stepping in front of the rest, made me a long oration, at which the mob cheered and cheered again. I then found, from all eyes being turned towards me, that it was expected I should say something in return. I accordingly expressed, in the best French I could command, my sense of the honour done me, and my satisfaction at having been the means of saving the life of one who, from his many virtues, was esteemed by his fellow-citizens; and I added I felt sure that those who had intended to put him to death were under an erroneous impression, as was shown by the generous way in which they treated me. I now begged to thank my bearers for having carried me so long on their shoulders, and, unwilling though I was to descend from so honourable a position, I requested that they would have the goodness to put me down on my feet that I might see their faces, so that I might be able at any future time to recognize them, which I owned I should at present be unable to do.

After some demur, they at last acceded to my request, letting me down on my feet. When I did see their countenances, it struck me that they were as hideous a set of ruffians as any of those I had before seen.

Concealing my feelings, however, I shook each of them by the hand, calling them my dear brothers, and assuring them that I should never forget the honour done me. After they had shaken themselves and stretched their brawny limbs, they appeared inclined to get hold of me again and carry me off on another round of the Place. Feeling especially unwilling, for the reason I have before given, to undergo another ovation, I stepped back among the civic authorities, and got inside the Town Hall, conducted by a gentleman, who whispered that he was a friend of M. Planterre's, and that he had been sent by him to escort me back to his house.

'M. Planterre is anxious to get out of the town as soon as possible, and advises you to do the same, for we cannot tell at what moment the mob may change their minds, and perhaps take it into their heads to hang you and him together,' he said, as, leading me through the Town Hall, he conducted me out by a back door.

'We are going by a somewhat circuitous route to the house of M. Planterre, where he himself is waiting for us,' he continued, as we walked on together. 'Your horses are in readiness, and he has had one prepared for himself, so that you may start as soon as you arrive.'

As we passed through the streets we could hear the shouts of the people in the distance, but what they were about we could not tell. My guide appeared to be in a somewhat agitated state, as if he feared that they would commit some other deed of violence, to recompense them-selves for losing the pleasure of hanging M. Planterre.

On arriving before the house I found Larry holding three horses. Presently a serving-man came out and took hold of the rein of one of the animals. On looking at him, to my surprise I recognised M. Planterre himself.

'I think it wise to leave the town in this disguise, lest the mob should suddenly regret having allowed me to escape, and, seeing me go, pursue me,' he said.

I immediately mounted, and M. Planterre, pointing out the road I was to take, I moved forward, followed by him and Larry, they appearing in the characters of my two lackeys. They kept close behind me, in order that M. Planterre might tell me when to turn to the right or left. He evidently expected that we should be pursued, but though I looked round occasionally, I could see no one following us.

Upon the road M. Planterre rode up to my side, and gave me a good deal of information, both about my friend's family and that of other families in the neighbourhood.

'I am grateful to you,' he continued, 'for the service you have rendered me, and I am anxious for your safety. I would advise you, therefore, to make no long stay in France. The whole country is, I can assure you, like a volcano, ready to burst forth at any moment. The people are generally imbued with republican principles, and they have lost all respect for the priests; they complain of the heavy taxes which go to support a profligate court; and are weary of the tyranny under which they have so long groaned.'

'But has not the king a powerful army to keep them in order?' I inquired.

'The army cannot be depended on,' answered my friend. 'It is thoroughly disorganized, and at any moment may side with the people. The only reliable troops are the Swiss, and other foreigners. We are coming upon troublous times, of that I am confident.'

Until now I had known nothing of France, and had fancied that Frenchmen were a light-hearted race, thoroughly contented with themselves and their country; indeed, I even now scarcely believed what M. Planterre told me.

In less than a couple of hours we caught sight of an ancient mansion, with a high roof, and towers at the corners, standing up amid the trees.

'There is the Château la Touche,' said my companion. 'I will not present myself in this disguise at the front gate, but when you descend will accompany your servant, who has not discovered who I am, and takes me for one of his fellows.'

On arriving at the gate, M. Planterre, having given his horse to Larry, went up the steps and rang the bell, and then came down and held my steed whilst I dismounted. As soon as the door opened he led my horse off.

La Touche, who had been advised of my arrival, hurried out to meet me, and embraced me affectionately according to the French fashion.

'Overjoyed to see you, my dear friend,' he exclaimed. 'I have been long looking for you, and am delighted that you have been induced to come. I have been preparing various entertainments, as I wish to show you how we Frenchmen enjoy life.'

I said everything that was proper in return, when, after he had made many inquiries as to how I had come to France, and the adventures I had met with on my journey, he added,—

'Now I must introduce you to madame *ma mère* and my young sister. They are prepared to receive you as a friend, and are delighted to find that you possess the accomplishment of speaking French.'

He forthwith led me into a handsome *salon*, or drawing-room, in which I saw two ladies seated, engaged in embroidery work. They both rose as we entered. The eldest was a stately and handsome dame, but my eyes were naturally attracted by the younger. It was fortunate, perhaps, that M. Planterre had described her, or I do not know how I should have behaved myself. She was in truth the most lovely little damsel I had ever seen, fair, and of exquisite figure, with blue, laughing eyes. They received me without any form, as if I had been an old friend, and I at once felt myself perfectly at home. Without speaking of my adventures at Vernon, I told them of my landing, and highly amused them with the description of the way in which I had found my follower Larry compelled to act the part of a bear. I said how grateful I felt to the worthy mayor for the assistance he had given me, as also for his introduction to M. Planterre. While I was speaking, La Touche was summoned out of the room by a servant. He in a short time returned, and then, to my surprise, gave his mother and sister a full account of the way I had rescued M. Planterre from the hands of the mob.

Mademoiselle Sophie appeared to be highly interested, and kept looking at me while her brother was speaking, and, although she did not join in the praises her mother lavished upon me for what she called my gallant conduct, evidently regarded me as a hero.

'You have come into our country in what I fear will prove troublous times,' observed La Touche, as we were seated at the supper table. 'The people are inclined to take the law into their own hands in other places besides Vernon, and are specially ill-disposed towards the *noblesse*, who, they declare, have been living on the fat of the land, while they have been starving. Our friend M. Planterre, after what has occurred, not considering his life safe in the town, has come out here, but thought it wiser not to appear as a guest, lest it should be reported that I have entertained him. My people suppose him to be a lackey, as he acts the part to admiration; and he will take his departure to-morrow morning, without, I hope, being discovered, so that they will all be ready to declare that M. Planterre has not come to the château.'

'Yes, there is a sad time coming for France, from what I hear is taking place in Paris,' said Madame La Touche. 'The people have already got the upper hand, and the king himself is, I fear, in hourly peril of his life.'

'Ah! we must not think or talk about such things too much,' said La Touche. 'My object at present is to make our guest's stay in France pleasant, and not to speak of disagreeable subjects. Sophie will, I am sure, aid me in that object.'

Sophie smiled, and said that such an occupation would afford her much pleasure.

CHAPTER XXIX.

CONCLUSION.

S the supper was at a comparatively early hour, we retired to the drawing-room, where the young lady played and sang, with much spirit, several lively airs, which her brother selected. She then chose one for herself of a more plaintive character, which had, as she intended it should have, a strange effect upon me. I listened in raptures, for her voice was sweet and melodious.

'I am indeed glad that you understand French so well,' she said. 'When I heard that an Englishman was coming some day, I thought that we should have had to carry on a conversation by signs, and that would have been very stupid.'

'I fear that I do not speak it very correctly, but I must try to improve myself,' I remarked.

'You do make a few mistakes now and then, but I shall be delighted to instruct you, and to correct your errors, if you will allow me to do so.'

That night, although somewhat tired from the exertions I had gone through in the morning, it was some time before I felt inclined to turn in; and when I did at length go to bed, I remained awake far longer than usual, thinking of the beautiful Sophie, her sweet voice still sounding in my ears.

27

I was awakened next morning by Larry, who accompanied one of the servants to my room.

'I did not see you last night, Mr. Terence, and I couldn't tell what had become of your honour,' he exclaimed. 'Faith, I tried to tell the people of the house that I wanted to find you, but not a word of my best French did they understand.'

I told Larry how well I had been treated, and that he need not have any apprehensions about me. The servant had brought a cup of coffee, which I found was the custom of the French to take in the morning, and he told me that breakfast would not be ready for an hour or more. As soon, therefore, as I had dressed I descended to the garden, which was of considerable extent, with lawns, fish-ponds, fountains, statues, and labyrinths. I had not gone far, when I saw a small figure tripping on lightly before me. I was tempted to hasten my steps. She turned—it was Sophie.

'I will show you the garden,' she said, 'and my favourite spots. You might lose yourself without my guidance, and perhaps you will accept it.'

I of course had but one answer to give. We walked on in the fresh morning air. I thought her lovely in the evening, but she appeared still more so now, looking as fresh and bright as the gay flowers which adorned the parterres. I felt that I had entered into a new existence; it was no wonder, for we were both young, and she had lived a secluded life, she told me, since her father's death. We very naturally forgot all about breakfast, and when we arrived at the house Madame La Touche chided her for her thoughtlessness in allowing me to starve.

Such was the commencement of my stay. My friend insisted that I should go out with him to shoot, believing that such was the only amusement I was likely to care for; but the preserves were full of game, and we had to do little more than stand still and shoot the birds as they were put up by the dogs. We returned to dinner, and as La Touche gave me the choice, I preferred a stroll in the garden with him and his sister to a more extended excursion.

The following days were spent in the same delightful manner. Every hour I became more and more attached to Sophie. I could not but feel a desire that she should return my affection. I forgot my poverty, and that until I could obtain my promotion, I should have nothing on which to support a wife, as the Ballinahone property had been entailed on my brother. I ought, I knew, to have assumed an indifference to the young lady, and speedily taken my departure, and I was in consequence much to blame. Still La Touche should not have invited me to the château; but in throwing me into the society of so charming a being as his sister, he did no perhaps think of the consequences, or, if he did, fancied that I was possessed of wealth, or at least a competency.

We were living all the time a peaceful secluded life, for we never went beyond the walled grounds of the château, and few visitors came to the house. We heard occasionally, however, what was going forward both in Paris and other parts of the country. Matters were growing more and more serious. Risings had occurred in various places, and lives had been lost. An army of fishwives, and other women of the lowest orders, had marched to Versailles, and threatened the King and Marie Antoinette, if food was not given them.

We were one evening seated at supper when a servant rushed into the room, with terror depicted in his countenance.

'Oh, monsieur! oh, madame!' he exclaimed, 'I have just received notice that a vast array of people are marching this way, threatening to destroy all the châteaux in the neighbourhood, and the Château La Touche in particular. They declare that you are an aristocrat.'

'Are you certain that this is true?' exclaimed La Touche, starting from his seat.

'If monsieur will come to the northern tower, he will

hear the voices of the people in the distance,' replied the servant.

'Do not be alarmed, my mother and sister,' said La Touche. 'The report may be exaggerated, but it is as well to be prepared. We will close all the lower doors and windows, and set the ruffians at defiance if they come. Will you accompany me, Finnahan, and as we go give me your advice as to the best way of defending the house?'

I would willingly have stopped to try and tranquillize the alarm of Madame La Touche and Sophie, but I could not refuse my friend's request. I set off with him, and we soon reached the tower. We looked out from a narrow window towards the north, but at first could see no one approaching, though on listening attentively we fancied that we could distinguish the murmur of voices far off.

Presently a bright light appeared on the left, rising, it seemed, out of the midst of a forest at some distance from the banks of the Seine. The light rapidly increased in size, and flames began to ascend, while clouds of smoke darkened the sky.

'Ah! that must come from the Château l'Estrange!' exclaimed La Touche. 'The rabble have attacked the house, and set it on fire. Fortunately, none of the family are at home except the old domestics, and they, poor people, will too probably be sacrificed. The villains would like to treat my château in the same way, and will before long make the attempt.'

'But we will defend it, and drive them back,' I exclaimed. 'Have you a sufficient supply of arms and ammunition for its defence? We must barricade all the doors and windows; and, unless they have cannon, they will not succeed in getting in, I trust.'

'We have plenty of arms, and I obtained a supply of ammunition a short time since,' said La Touche. 'I doubt, however, the courage of some of my domestics; they would rather yield to the rabble than risk their lives in the defence of my property.'

'Larry and I will try to make up, as far as we can, for their want of bravery,' I said.

'Thank you, my friends; you will be a host in yourselves. Now let us see about preparing to give the insurgents a warm reception should they attack the château.'

On descending from the tower, La Touche entered the supper room singing and laughing.

'There is not much to be afraid of, so you need not be anxious, *ma chère mère*, or you either, Sophie,' he said in a cheerful tone of voice. 'We are going to shut the doors and windows in case any of the rabble may try to creep in at them. You can retire to your rooms or stay here, as you think best. You will oblige me, however, by keeping the women quiet, or they may be running about and interfering with our proceedings.'

'We will do more than keep them quiet,' exclaimed Sophie; 'we will make them useful by setting them an example; only tell us what you want us to do.'

'The best thing you can do is to close all the shutters and windows looking to the front in the upper storey, and to place chests of drawers and bedding against them, so that if bullets are fired they will do no harm.'

'That we will do, my son,' said Madame La Touche, rising from her seat; and she hurried off, accompanied by Sophie.

La Touche at once summoned his *maître d'hôtel* and the other servants.

'My friends,' he said, 'I have no intention of letting the insurgents destroy my château, as they have done those of other persons, and I will trust to you to defend it to the last.'

A party of Englishmen would have cheered. They, however, merely said, '*Oui, oui, monsieur;* we are ready to do what you tell us.'

Among the servants came Larry. I told him what we expected would happen, and what he was to do.

'Shure we'll be after driving the "spalpeens" back again,

he answered. 'I was little thinking that we should have this sort of fun to amuse us when we came to France.'

We lost no more time in talking, but immediately set to work to shut all the doors on the ground floor, and to nail pieces of timber and strong planks against them. The windows were closed with such materials as could be obtained. There were more forthcoming than I expected; and La Touche acknowledged that he had laid in a store some time before.

He then summoned the *maître d'hôtel* and two other servants, and led the way—accompanied by Larry and me—down a steep flight of stone steps to a vault beneath the house. Opening the door of what was supposed to be a wine cellar, he showed us a stand of twenty muskets, with pistols and pikes, several casks of powder and cases of bullets. Larry, at once fastening a belt round his waist, and tucking a couple of muskets under each arm, hurried off, the servants following his example. La Touche and I each took as many more, and returned to the hall.

His first care was to place his men two and two at each of the parts of the building likely to be attacked.

'These countrymen of mine fight better together than singly,' he observed. 'And now let us go round and examine our defences, to ascertain that no part is left insecure.'

Some time was spent in making these various arrangements. Every now and then La Touche ran in to see his mother and sister, and to assure them that they need not be alarmed.

'I have no fears,' said Sophie, on one of these occasions, when I accompanied him. 'With the help of this brave Englishman and his follower, I am sure that you will drive back the insurgents.'

'*Ma foi!* I hope so,' said La Touche to me, as we left the room. 'But they are the same sort of ruffians as those who destroyed the Bastile.'

The news of that event had a short time before reached us.

'Now let us return to the watch-tower, and try to make out what the *canaille* are about.'

The mob, as far as we could observe, were not as yet approaching. They were probably dancing and singing round the burning château, the flames from which were ascending in all directions, its towers forming four pyramids of fire.

'They are waiting to see the result of their handiwork,' said La Touche. 'When the roof has fallen in and the towers come to the ground, they will be satisfied, and will probably make their way in this direction. Ah! what are those lights there?' he suddenly exclaimed.

I looked towards the spot he pointed at, when I saw advancing along the road a number of men bearing torches.

'They are coming, as I expected, fully believing that they will destroy this château as they have the Château l'Estrange,' said La Touche. 'Now, my friend, it is possible that they may succeed, notwithstanding all our preparations. I will therefore have a carriage prepared, and the horses put to, with two others for riding. I know, should I be unable to go, that you will protect my mother and sister, and endeavour to conduct them to a place of safety, either to the coast or to the house of a friend whom they will name to you.'

'You may trust me indeed, although I hope for your sake that there will be no necessity for such a proceeding,' I answered, my heart beating strangely at the thought of having Sophie and her mother committed to my charge. I resolved, of course, to protect them to the last, and I hoped that in my character as a foreigner I might be able to do this more effectually than La Touche himself. Madame should pass as my mother, and Sophie for my sister, and I hoped that we might thus pass through the fiercest mob, whose rage, being turned against the aristocrats, would not interfere with an Englishman, whom they would imagine was merely travelling through the country for the

sake of seeing it, as many had been doing for some time
past. We had very little longer time to wait, when some
hundreds of persons appeared coming along the road
directly for the château. We could see them from the
tower, where we had remained. A large number were
carrying torches. The entrance gate was locked and barred,
and the château itself, all lights being concealed, must
have appeared shrouded in darkness.

'Let them exhaust their strength in breaking down the
gate,' said La Touche.

Scarcely a moment after, the mob reached the gate,
waving their torches, and shrieking and shouting out,—

'Down with the aristocrats! Down with the tyrants!
Down with those who pillage us, and live upon the
product of our toil!'

'Let them shout themselves hoarse,' remarked La Touche.
'They will not find it a very easy matter to break down that
stout old gate, or to climb over the wall.'

On discovering the impediment in their way, their shouts
and threats increased in fury. A number of them, rushing
against the bar of the gate, endeavoured to force it from its
hinges.

Not a word all this time was uttered by any of our
garrison. The insurgents, finding that the gate would not
yield, shouted for some one in the château to open it.
No one replied. Again and again they shook it. At last
we heard the sound of loud blows, as if it were being
struck by a sledge hammer, while several figures appeared
on the top of the wall, ladders having been procured to
assist them up.

'Why do you come here, my friends?' demanded La
Touche abruptly. 'The gate is locked as a sign that I
wished to be in private.'

'It is the residence of an aristocrat, and all such we
have resolved to level to the ground,' shouted one of the
mob.

'I warn you that you will pay dearly if you make the

attempt,' cried La Touche. 'We are well armed, and are resolved to defend the place.'

'We are not to be stopped by threats. On, comrades, on!' exclaimed another voice among those who were clambering over the wall. 'If one of our number falls, remember that every one of those inside the house will be destroyed.'

'You have been warned,—the consequence will be on your own heads if you attack us,' said La Touche.

By this time a considerable number of persons had got into the yard by clambering over the wall, but the stout iron gate had hitherto resisted all attempts to force it open.

'We might kill or wound all the fellows in front of the house,' said La Touche to me, 'but I am unwilling to shed the blood of my countrymen if it can be avoided; I will give them another chance. You are in our power, friends,' he shouted out ; 'if we fire, not one of you will escape. Go back to where you came from, and your lives will be spared.'

Derisive shouts were the only answers given to what La Touche had said. More people were all the time clambering over the wall, while continued blows on the gate showed that the mob had not given up the idea of forcing an entrance. Presently there was a loud crash, the gate was thrown open, and in rushed a number of savage-looking fellows, all armed with some weapon or other, many of them carrying torches, which they waved wildly above their heads, shouting all the time, 'Down with the aristocrats! Revenge! revenge for the wrongs they have done us!'

'They are in earnest, of that there can be no doubt,' said La Touche. 'We must drive them back before they become more daring. It is useless to hold further parley with them ;' and he gave orders to our small garrison to open fire.

Loud shrieks and cries rent the air, several people were

seen to fall, but this only increased the rage of the rest, who, running up to the front door with axes and other weapons, began hacking away at it, probably expecting quickly to force it open.

More and more people followed, until the whole yard was full of men surging here and there, some firing, others waving their torches, apparently to distract our attention, while the more determined assailed the doors and windows.

'Are there no troops likely to come to our assistance?' I asked, seeing that matters were growing serious.

'No; we must defend ourselves, and I fear that if these ruffians persevere, they will succeed at last,' whispered La Touche to me. 'We must endeavour to save my mother and sister, for the mob, if they once get in, will sacrifice them as well as the rest of us. I am resolved to stop and defend my house to the last, but I must provide for their safety by committing them to your charge. The carriage is in readiness, and there are two faithful servants to whom I have given orders how to act. Go, I beseech you, at once, and request my mother and Sophie to enter the carriage and set out without a moment's delay. Two saddle-horses are in readiness for you and your servant. You will go as their escort. Tell them I will retreat in time to follow them. Take the road towards Paris, and wait for me. Should any one attempt to interfere with you, say that you are an English officer, and that the ladies are under your charge. I do not apprehend that you will be molested; go, therefore, lose no time.'

He wrung my hand as if he would take no denial. I of course, although unwilling to leave him, was ready to carry out his wishes. I hastened to the room where I had left Madame La Touche and Sophie, and explained to them what La Touche wished them to do.

'But will he follow us?' asked Madame La Touche in an agitated tone.

'He has promised to do so, madame,' I answered; 'but

let us not delay, lest the mob should get round to the other side of the house and cut off our retreat.'

Madame La Touche hesitated no longer, but allowed me to lead her and her daughter down to the yard at the back of the house, where we found the horses already put to, and I handed the ladies into the carriage. The coachman mounted the box; another servant was holding the two riding horses; and I was preparing to mount, when Larry, sent by La Touche, came springing down the steps and was in his saddle in a moment. The French servant mounted behind the carriage; and the coach drove off down an avenue which led along the banks of a stream running through the pleasure-grounds. I was in hopes that La Touche would have followed at once, for I saw that there was very little probability of his being able successfully to defend the house against the savage mob who had resolved to destroy it. I could hear the wild shrieks and shouts and cries of the assailants, the rattle of musketry, and the loud thundering against the doors and windows; but, anxious as I felt about my friend, my duty was to push on with my charges, and with all possible speed to convey them out of danger. The coachman was equally desirous to preserve his mistress, and lashed on his horses at their utmost speed. Fortunately he knew the road, which was an unusually good one.

We were soon outside the grounds belonging to the château. Proceeding along a road which ran parallel with the river, we soon got beyond the sounds of the strife; but on looking round I saw a bright light suddenly appear in the direction of the château. It increased in size. Another and another appeared; and I could distinguish the flames bursting out from several windows. Could the mob so soon have broken into the château, and set it on fire? I feared the worst, and that my gallant friend and his servants had been overwhelmed, and too probably massacred. I felt thankful, however, that Madame La Touche and Sophie had escaped in time. Had they remained a few minutes longer, they might have been too late. Had I been alone, I should have been unable to restrain myself from galloping back to ascertain what had occurred; but to protect them was now my great object. I kept as close as possible to the carriage, not knowing what might at any moment occur. I was afraid that they might look out of the window and see the flames; but they were too much overcome with grief and terror to do that, and sat back in the carriage, clasped in each other's arms. When the road would allow, I rode up and spoke a few words to try and comfort them, although it was no easy matter to do that.

'When will Henri come?' exclaimed Madame La Touche. 'He ought to have overtaken us by this time.'

'You forget, madame, we have been travelling at a rapid rate,' I observed. 'He promised to retreat in time, should he find it necessary to abandon the château. He will probably overtake us when we stop for the night. There is no fear that the mob will follow him to any distance.'

The coachman said he knew of an inn about six leagues on the Paris road, where madame and Sophie might rest securely, as the mob could not get so far that night. It was where Monsieur La Touche had ordered him to remain. I bade him therefore go on as his master told him, although he proceeded at a slower rate than at first, for fear of knocking up his horses.

I was very thankful when the little inn was reached. It was kept by a buxom dame, who received Madame La Touche and Sophie politely, and offered the best accommodation her house would afford. I handed the ladies from the carriage. Madame entered the house at once, but Sophie lingered for a moment.

'Oh, tell me, M. Finnahan, has Henri come yet? I dread lest he should have done anything rash, and lost his life. It would break mamma's heart if he were to be killed; and she will not rest, I am convinced, until she knows he is safe. I cannot ask you to go back to look for him, but will you send your servant to gain intelligence, and bring it to us?'

'I would go back myself, but my duty is to remain and guard you,' I said. 'What do you wish?—tell me.'

'We shall be perfectly safe here, and I desire for my mother's sake to know what has happened to Henri,' she answered.

I thought that Sophie was right, and my own anxiety made me desire to ride back.

I accordingly mounted my horse, leading Larry's. I left my faithful retainer with instructions that in the event of the mob approaching, he was to drive off with the ladies. I galloped on at full speed, anxious without loss of time to reach the château. If La Touche had escaped, he would probably require my assistance. I had no expectation of finding he had beaten back the insurgents; indeed, I was not free from the fearful apprehension that he and his people had been surprised by them, and massacred before they could make good their retreat; still, as the insurgents, when I left the château, appeared to have no intention of making their way round to the back of the building, I hoped that he would have contrived to escape in time. That they would have murdered him if caught I had not the shadow of a doubt.

I had marked the road as I came along, and had no fear as to finding my way. The moon, too, had risen, which enabled me to do this with less difficulty. As I galloped on, I looked carefully about on either side, for I knew that the clatter of my horses' hoofs would attract the attention of any one coming along the road. But I met no one along the whole length of my ride. At last I could distinguish the tall towers with the flames bursting out from their summits, and I knew that the château was doomed to destruction. Suddenly both horses started, and I heard a voice say,—

'Who goes there?

It was La Touche. He was wounded badly, and unable to proceed farther. Had I not gone to look for him, he would most probably have perished.

'The château will be burned to the ground,' he observed. 'But I care not for that, now that I know, thanks to you, Finnahan, that my mother and Sophie have escaped.'

Having bound up his wounds, I assisted him to mount the spare horse, and we set out for the inn where I had left Madame La Touche and her daughter.

We met with many adventures and hair-breadth escapes before I ultimately succeeded in escorting them on board the *Saucy Bet*, and seeing them safely landed in England. I shortly afterwards obtained my promotion. And though I have much more to narrate which my readers may like to hear, I was now lieutenant, and my adventures as a midshipman therefore come to a conclusion at this period of my life.

THE END.